Mindscape

Elleni Xa Celest crouched at the Barrier, head bowed, eyes squeezed shut, thighs clenched—trying to sculpt-sing a corridor from Sagan City, Paradigma, to Angel City, Los Santos, for the eager diplomatic vehicles thrumming at her back. Seasonal corridors would not open for several weeks. Paradigma's Treaty convoy hoped to reach Los Santos and shore up interzonal alliances before tourists, spies, mercenaries, and Entertainment crews muddied the waters...

Yellow tears dribbled down Elleni's hissing hair and broke her concentration. Exchange with the Barrier required a phaseshift from one sensibility to another, like switching from visible light to magnetism or modulating spacetime. She drew in great quantities of hot, dry air and slowed her heart's drumbeat. She unclenched aching muscles and stacked her weight on carefully aligned bones. Pulling a bass note from her pelvic floor, she slid up her range, vibrating bones and organs until ultrasounds resonated in her nasal passages and shot out her skull. Her fingers danced in and out of the Barrier's domain. As she hit her highest notes, an archway crystallized just beyond her fingertips, and she almost lost the song. Struggling back onto the melody, she shaped a wider opening.

MINDSCAPE

a novel by

Andrea Hairston

Seattle

Aqueduct Press, PO Box 95787
Seattle, WA 98145-2787
www.aqueductpress.com

Library of Congress Control Number: 2005937809

ISBN 978-1-933500-03-4
ISBN 1-933500-03-4

COVER ACKNOWLEDGMENTS
Cover Illustration by Pam Sanders (www.pamsandersart.com)
Based on earth image courtesy NASA
http://nssdc.gsfc.nasa.gov/photo_gallery/photogallery-earth.html
Mask by Pan Morigan (www.panmorigan.com), photographed by
Micala Sidore (www.HawleyStreet.com)
Cover Design by Lynne Jensen Lampe
Book Design by Kathryn Wilham

Printed in the USA by Thomson-Shore, Inc, Dexter, MI
10 9 8 7 6 5 4 3 2 1

First Edition, First Printing, March 2006

This book was set in a digital version of Monotype Walbaum, available through AGFA Monotype. The original typeface was designed by Justus Erich Walbaum.

Dedicated to my mother,
Ruth T. Hairston (1923-2005),
who believed in me before I began.

Acknowledgments

Thanks to L. Timmel Duchamp and Kathryn Wilham for editorial insight and magic.

Blessings on the people who helped me survive writing this book—Brenda Allen, Len Berkman, Pearl Cleage, Kiki Gounaridou, Jessica Jacobs, Bill Oram, Micala Sidore, Marjorie Senechal and the Kahn Institute of Smith College, Ruth Simmons, Andrea Somberg, and Joel Tansey.

The Clarion West 1999 Writer's Workshop—instructors: Greg Bear, Octavia Butler, Gwyneth Jones, Nancy Kress, Gordon Van Gelder, and Howard Waldrop; workshoppers: Sarah Brendel, Christine Castigliano, Duncan Clark, Sandy Clark, Monte Cook, Dan Dick, Jay Joslin, Leah Kaufman, Joe Sutliff Sanders, Tom Sweeney, Trent Walters, and Steve Woodworth—helped turn a drama queen into a novelist.

The Beyond 'Dusa Wild Sapelonians: Ama Patterson, Sheree R. Thomas, and Liz Roberts are the best writing group any Wild Woman could ask for. Wolfgang and Beate Schmidhuber (and the whole Schmidhuber clan) offered me home and inspiration in a foreign land.

Pan Morigan read every draft and along with James Emery stopped me whenever I thought of burning the manuscript or trashing my computer. Pan and James made the writing possible.

Contents

BOOK 1

When it comes time to die, be not like those whose hearts are filled with the fear of death, so when their time comes they weep and pray for a little more time to live their lives over again in a different way. Sing your death song, and die like a hero going home.

Tecumseh

The Barrier Age
New Years Day, Barrier Year 50

We set our calendars by the Barrier, counting the hours, days, and years from the moment it engulfed our planet in its mystery. On this day of days half a century ago, astronauts returning from beyond the Asteroid Belt and the wonders of Mars reported a blood red cloud of unknown material overwhelming Earth. As the captain and crew encountered instrument malfunction, disappearing probes, and a chunk of spacetime wiped from the sky, the signal died. These last astronauts and their marvelous ships vanished from the radar screen. On the surface eyewitnesses all across the planet said the Barrier erupted out of nothing, out of nowhere. Some said it boiled up from the bowels of the Earth. Fire rainbows, tentacles of diamond dust…spreading faster than thoughts or radio signals, breaking apart land and sea, night and day, yesterday and every other tomorrow.

Younger generations take the Barrier invasion, the Earth sliced into isolated, warring Zones, for granted. A mundane, boring "given," yet the Barrier irrevocably altered our histories and identities. Who remembers the taste of wheat, the view from the moon, jetting to Nairobi, Los Angeles, Beijing, or anywhere? The twenty-first century is a distant dream, an object of nostalgic worship. Paradise Lost. Many people insist the Barrier humbled humanity, made us detainees where once we were masters. The inhabited Zones—New Ouagadougou, Los Santos, Paradigma—are mere refugee camps, the Barrier a prison wall. Others believe that the gods of our ancestors sent the Barrier as a blessing to the chosen and a curse for the damned. All agree that it cleaved reality with an impenetrable spume of lethal substance—as yet uncategorized. Those who venture too close to the Barrier wall are swallowed up, never to be heard of again, like the last astronauts. Travel between Zones is limited to a handful of corridors spontaneously generated at seasonal intervals. The Barrier offers no corridors to the stars or to the uninhabited Wilderness lands.

Every attempt to probe, codify, or measure the Barrier yields contradictory data. It resists our senses and instruments. The outcome of an experiment depends most on who the experimenters are and what they desire. Although we perceive the Barrier, it doesn't always seem to be there. Continually coming and going—from our dimension to another? No one has isolated a sample of this epi-dimensional, phaseshifting singularity for controlled study. Yet.

The Barrier has proven to be more than physics and chemistry. It does not act like a field of forces, a well-behaved crystal, or even a cagey virus infecting us with its packet of instructions. The Barrier is a self-generating network of enormous complexity and unprecedented creativity. It regenerates and evolves, sustaining itself, yet changing. A life form? Life is by nature creative, drawn to novelty, driven by challenge, grounded in history. Learning as it evolves, life calls to life. Is Earth to be consumed, rearranged, and forgotten in the pattern of some other being? Incorporated in a new web of life? Has the Barrier come to us as parasite or partner? Perhaps these are the wrong questions, grounded in Earth's natural history. Perhaps this phenomenon will defy humanity to create a new language, a new syntax of life. What consciousness might emerge from an epi-dimensional body? And who will be the *Vermittler,* the go-betweens, shepherding us into the future?

If I have risked the world but lost, as Femi Xa Olunde argues, and these are indeed the *Final Lessons,* forgive me. Remember, however, *Ijala'gun Molu*... If we risk nothing, we gain nothing.

—Vera Xa Lalafia, *Healer Cosmology, The Final Lessons*

1:   Tombouctou Observatory and Galactic Library
Outskirts of Sagan City, Paradigma
(March 20, New Years Day, Barrier Year 111)

Old age ain't for sissies.

Celestina couldn't remember who used to say that, all the time. *I'm telling you, it's stand-up tragedy, so don't laugh. You'll see.*

Was it Vera Xa Lalafia, her first teacher? Why couldn't she remember? Didn't she remember several lifetimes? A very old woman, Celestina remembered before the Barrier even, before the world had been chopped into petty little Zones. When humanity covered the planet, lush and vibrant, coming and going as they pleased, wrecking havoc in global style, racing out to the stars...

How could she remember before the Barrier, she was just a baby, not even born. It was Vera who'd lived in the other time. And Vera had gone on to dance with the ancestors, leaving Celestina to sort out this Interzonal Treaty fiasco with no clear vision. If it were Vera's Treaty about to be ratified, she wouldn't hide from the festivities in an empty planetarium watching ancient Entertainment all night. She wouldn't cringe at random adulation, run from power trips, or miss a second of pomp and ceremony. And Vera would never have said *old age ain't for sissies.* Yes, Robin said it to Thandiwe.

Stand-up tragedy. A gaggle of voices in Celestina's head screamed at her like achy joints every time she tried to make a move. She stuffed popcorn in her mouth and focused on the planetarium's giant Electrosoft screen. Nothing like old-time movies to distract you from personal crises or global insanity. Even orthodox shamen would concede that. Celestina refused to fight herself over *Do The Right Thing, Shawshank Redemption, Mississippi Masala, A Beautiful Mind,* or Chaplin's *Great Dictator...* But sooner or later the credits rolled, they called your name, bellowed praisesongs, and reality smacked you in the face.

"We apologize for the delay, ladies and gentlemen." A priority broadcast ghosted across the planetarium screen, interrupting *The Fugitive* upload.

"*Schade.*" Celestina cursed in old German. She scanned the vast auditorium for invaders. Not much longer to hide; they'd be coming for her soon.

A blurry image came into focus: Ray Valero, freedom fighter, Entertainment superstar, tall, dark, and handsome devil, beloved by all. "The architect of the Interzonal Peace Accord, Celestina Xa Irawo, will be the final delegate today to sign the Treaty into law. Rumor buster: the great Lady ditched the party scene last night to conjure a few spirits and check in with eternity. In deep trance, shamen get fuzzy on time."

"Time's not my problem." Celestina stumbled out of her back row seat, feet in one body, pounding heart in another, and fell against darkened fiberplastic windows.

"Humanity's staging a comeback!" Ray continued in close-up. Perfect teeth flashed. Celestina could see a direct line from Cary Grant and Denzel Washington to Ray Valero. *And* he had the voice of James Earl Jones! "We're a reunited world, about to inaugurate peace. Can't rush this gig. History in the making." Applause and cheers, the crowd was in his hip pocket. "Before signing, Madame Xa Irawo will follow New Ouagadougou custom and pour libation to the brave souls who died to make today a reality. Give us reformed thugs a little style."

Celestina laughed out of both sides of her mouth.

The Barrier flared outside the window, amplifying the voices in her head. Celestina swallowed her laughter and squinted. The Barrier looked as it did when she was a child—a storm of diamond dust stretching across the horizon, blotting out half the sky. Barrier wisps caught fading sunlight and turned it silver, occasionally twisting out a rainbow sign. The Barrier hadn't put on this particular show in eighty, ninety years. Was it in honor of the Treaty?

"Do you think the Barrier cares what we do?" She covered her mouth.

How had she come to this? In none of her incarnations had Celestina ever wanted an ordinary life: meet a hunk, drop some babies, fight over pennies, struggle to raise the kids up right, weep when they dashed off into *their* future, rock on the porch in sunset smog, tell big fat lies, serve sausage and *Kuchen* to the grandkids, and flirt with the young things who happened by. Truth be told, she had contempt for normal life. She'd always wanted to do something grand and glorious!

"Madame Xa Irawo will sign away a hundred years of war," Ray said. "No more Extras dying in snuff takes. No more corridor coups or organ markets. This is the glorious day we fought and died for."

What did Ray know about it?

Today was the worst day of Celestina's hundred-plus adventure years. Worse than Femi slashing her skull, driving her to insanity; worse than betraying and poisoning herself; worse than holy war, hunting down innocence to save the race. Celestina had driven away all the daughters of her spirit. She had no one to sing her song, carry her story into forever.

Could she trust Ray or any of them with the future?

A stampede of footsteps echoed in the hallways around the planetarium. They'd found her hiding place. She sank down in the comfort chair. Twenty doors into the planetarium rattled and shook but did not open.

The week of celebration leading up to the Treaty signing had been a horror show. She couldn't stand the naïve, trusting looks, feigned or sincere, from politicos and Zone glitterati who had committed almost as many crimes against humanity as she had. Last night, in desperation, Celestina had begged a cameraman for sanctuary—Aaron Dunkelbrot, a former Extra, now a bio-corder expert, what the Treaty was all about.

"Don't sweat this bullshit." He stashed her in the planetarium with his ancient Entertainment stockpile. "A million and half hours of escape," he bragged, honored to accommodate her. "I feel you."

How could this Aaron "feel" her, know what she'd done, know who she really was? Aaron, Ray, and everybody gathered at

Tombouctou for history-in-the-making expected her to glide like an angel through thunderous applause, to pass through hypocrisy like a *Vermittler*, sculpting a corridor through the Barrier unscathed. She was their hero, personal savior, God's next of kin. Her smile was a benediction; her words sacred texts; Saint Celestina, she'd put an end to war.

Not one of them suspected her of betrayal or genocide.

Lights flooded the planetarium and Aaron Dunkelbrot stuck his dimpled cheeks, chiseled chin, and blue-green-algae eyes through the emergency exit. He had the same shadow of beard as yesterday on baby-faced, flawless skin. Gene art, high-end—a renegade scientist had played around with genetic code to give him killer looks.

How can you make a treaty with these people?

"You ready?" Aaron shook her shoulder. "Gotta move." His flat, tense English marked him as a Los Santos native.

"Of course I'm not ready." Celestina grabbed her medicine bag, heavy with several lifetimes of wisdom.

"Shall I carry that for you?" Aaron asked with old-movie charm.

"No!" She clutched it to her chest.

Aaron slipped an arm around her waist and guided her out the emergency exit, through the backstage labyrinth to the Great Hall of Images, where humanity had once communed with the stars. She froze in the entranceway.

"Breathe," he commanded.

"I have a story for you." She took a breath. "When you become a director."

Aaron laughed. "In your dreams."

"Nobody's been able to tell my story yet."

"Outlaw Entertainment? Maybe after tonight, after the Treaty, they won't be banning stories, and I'll be able to shoot whatever Entertainment I…"

"Don't count on it." She gripped his arm to the bone. "I can't go out there."

"Bringing all the Zones together, that was the hard part. The grandstanding and signing is a piece of cake. "

"Promise me to tell the whole story."

Aaron opened his mouth but did not speak.

"I don't want to be a spirit without a future." Celestina pressed her fingers into Aaron's skull and brought his face close to hers. "You must promise."

Aaron struggled a moment then rasped, "It's a deal."

He thrust Celestina into the Hall. She forced a smile for the ring of bio-corders that transmitted her quicksilver eyes and craggy brown cheekbones to viewers in every Zone of the inhabited world. The synth-marble floor sent shivers from her bare toes to teeth. Ants in her pockets stung her thighs, spreading itchy heat.

"Ladies and Gentlemen," Ray shouted. "The First Lady of Peace!" He dropped to one knee and kissed her hand.

Celestina had no time to chastise Ray's silliness. VIPs from Los Santos, Paradigma, and New Ouagadougou cried, laughed, and sung her name. They crushed the guards against the stage, stretching out hands stained with blood and tears. Celestina pulled a flask from her medicine bag and poured libation. The wine stained her robes and feet and pooled like blood on the non-porous surface.

"To all who died for this peace," she said. "Bless them, bless us."

"Bless you!" someone shouted from the back.

Ten feet in front of Celestina on a transparent fiberplastic table, a paper document generated especially for the ceremony curled in the moist air. Delegates from every Zone had signed in ink as well as electrons. An aide thrust a fountain pen and a glass stylus into Celestina's twitching fingers. Her feet cramped; her hands knotted up. She couldn't move. The glass stylus slipped from her fingers and rolled across the stage.

Elleni Xa Celest, her *Geistestochter*, snatched the device before it crashed into the monitors. Her braids and skin glistened in the shadows. "Almost home," she murmured and pressed the stylus into Celestina's gnarled hands. They had not spoken to each other in six years.

"You came," Celestina whispered, tears blurring her vision.

"Last night," Elleni said.

She clutched her spirit daughter. "You came." One of Elleni's braids snaked around Celestina's wrist, spitting yellow discharge. Celestina buried her face in her daughter's hissing hair.

Sidi Xa Aiyé stood beside them, pressing palms together in a gesture of respect.

"You too?" Celestina kissed Sidi's feathery fingers.

"How could we miss your day of days?" Sidi said, a delicious smile on her full lips.

Of her daughters only Mahalia Selasie was absent.

"Will you hold this?" Celestina offered them her medicine bag.

Elleni and Sidi exchanged electric glances. Celestina felt her soul wilt.

"While you sign?" Elleni spoke first. "I'd be honored." She clasped the bag to her heart.

Perhaps Celestina wasn't a spirit without a future after all.

"Are we ready yet?" Aaron beckoned to them from behind a bio-corder.

Celestina allowed Elleni and Sidi to walk her out of the shadows and up to the Treaty table. She glanced at the paper beneath her hands. In a few thousand words, they had written down their best selves. Her story was coming to an end. The hard work of the Treaty would be done by Elleni, Sidi, Aaron, Ray, and people in every Zone.

"*Aboru, Aboye, Aboṣiṣe*. May what we offer carry, be accepted, may what we offer bring about change." The old Yoruba words relaxed her knotted hands. Celestina leaned forward and with sweeping gestures, signed the Treaty. "Our time is no worse or no better than other times. We are not inevitable. We didn't have to happen this way. There are many threads, many Earths." She waved the Treaty up to the stars then down to the ground. "We live just one of the stories, one fine line in a universe of possibilities. It is up to us to make our story beautiful."

The live audience exploded with applause, which Celestina tasted more than heard, spicy, ginger-beer applause, spraying her sinuses clear and sweet, bubbling down her throat, boiling in her belly, hot and potent. "Thank you, I am nothing..." The blight on her soul faded in her daughters' burning eyes and the crowd's stomping feet. She felt like another self—the one they imagined her to be. "You are the future. I see tomorrow in your faces."

"Bless you!" Someone yelled from the front now.

She recognized his torn face and battered hands: Piotr Osama, an Extra she'd brought back from the edge of death. His skin was silver, and he wore the white robes and moss headdress of the Ghost Dancer cult. These born-again Sioux were treaty-shy. They refused to sign away their sovereignty and were boycotting the convention. Piotr aimed a sham bio-corder at Entertainment royalty or perhaps at Paradigma's Prime Minister. Or maybe at the gestapo security.

Celestina closed her eyes, wishing to see no more, eager to die herself—*Ebo Eje*, a blood sacrifice for peace and redemption. She was, however, not eager for more killing. Still clutching the Treaty, she walked into the line of fire.

"*Aṣe...*" So be it...

Piotr's spray of bullets ripped through the paper and slammed into Celestina's chest. Her blood gushed onto the Treaty.

BOOK II

Time and space are modes by which we think,
and not conditions in which we live.

Albert Einstein

2:   Archive Transmission/Personal
(September 6, Barrier Year 115)

From: Lawanda Kitt on diplomatic mission to Angel City,
Los Santos

To: Herself, waitin' at the Barrier outsida Sagan City, Paradigma,
goin' nowhere fast

I do not believe this.

Treaty convoy s'posed to be goin' down a corridor thru the
Barrier hours ago. Why we still hangin' 'round some ole dusty
wasteland, fartin' funky exhaust? Bad air, bad dirt, and everywhere
you look shit done shriveled up and croaked. My butt's way too
big for this tight-ass enviro-suit. Miracle fibers ain't wickin' nothin'
away. Sweat poolin' at the crotch like I peed my pants. One big itch.
I can't take much more.

What's up with Miss Freaky Thang Elleni Xa Celest?!? She a
Vermittler ain't she? A go-between, Barrier griot, mutant witch,
Celestina's anointed one, WHATEVER—all her big talk 'bout not
waitin' for no seasonal corridor to travel from Paradigma to Los
Santos or Los Santos to New Ouagadougou. Yeah, she goin' make a
eight-lane super highway for the whole diplomatic convoy! She out
there in the dust, nose in the Barrier, and her evil funky hair crawlin' and spittin' like snakes in heat, so why don't she just hoodoo the
damn thang open and get it over with?

All us so-called diplomats lookin' ready to riot. Nobody's Zen enuf
to be patient no more. Well, I ain't Zen enuf, that's for damn sure.

How come I say yes? Me, Vice-Ambassador to Los Santos?
Celestina must be squirmin' in her grave. Lawanda Kitt, ethnic
throwback, in the executive suite, steada just workin' the crew? I
don't mind buildin' some houses or throwin' down a few roads. I'd
do farm labor too and beat back the desert, or hospital duty, or even
school work, save a mind. I'm down for Celestina's people-to-people
diplomacy, gettin' these Los Santos folk back on they feet. What I

know how to do. But VICE-AMBASSADOR, scopin' Treaty implementation and infractions?!? Yeah, like just bump me up to the big
house and won't nobody notice you fuckin' up the Treaty.

The Major play me like an ad-opera jingle.

So at six AM, ain't nobody been asleep all night, the whole convoy's hot to trot. Sun's comin' up over the wasteland, a picture-
perfect day for the bio-corder crews. They goin' get some trippy
Elleni footage. My vehicle be first in line cuz I don't wanna miss
the show and *Vermittler* don't make me no way nervous. Elleni and
me been around the block a coupla times. She my girl. I just wish
she'd fix herself up. Who let her out the house with that nasty hair
runnin' wild on her head?

At five after six, the Major slide by my transport, like he doin'
a publicity run. Secret Services ace checkin' on us regulars not just
the big shots, but really he wanna see me, his main squeeze. I'm
thinkin' that's too sweet and gettin' all mushy inside. Ain't me
and the Major fight for Celestina's Treaty together in Paradigma?
Didn't I rescue his cocky ass when he was 'bout to be "expendable
personnel"? Ain't I the woman who show him his heart? Now we
'bout to turn the mess all the way 'round and...

"I'm not going," the Major say.

"You not goin' where?" I ask. Clueless.

"Armando Jenassi has been appointed Ambassador in my place,"
the Major say, *sotto voce* like he really don't want me to hear.

"You lyin'." I sound like plantains sizzlin' in oil. "You gotta be
lyin'. Jenassi can't ambassador diddly in your place. What about
our plan?"

"We're promoting you to Vice Ambassador." He up in my face
tryin' to smile but can't get his mouth to do it.

"Vice-Ambassador? What the hell is that?"

"The Prime Minister's idea, but we can make it work."

"*I* got your back, not her." I sound jealous, but it's more than a
catfight. "Prime Minister Jocelyn ain't part of *our* plan."

"Unforeseen circumstances..." the Major be usin' his voice of
authority now.

"How far ahead you gotta see for straight-up truth?" I can't look at him no more. "Vice Ambassador? Y'all just make that up."

"It's good PR."

"Prime Minister Jocelyn and her posse be tryin' to kill the Treaty, and you..."

"Listen to me." He always interrupt me when he be bullshittin'. "The situation here at home is critical. Several rogue scientists have defected—"

"Mahalia Selasie leadin' more nerds astray? Naw. Snatchin' you offa our team ain't about diva scientists goin' AWOL. They been runnin' outa here since forever." I wanna run too, but ain't nowhere to go 'cept up against a transport wall. I lean my head into the viewscreen and close my eyes. Why I gotta be in love with this sucker?

"I'm needed at home. The Prime Minister is worried about security. She can't afford to loan me to the diplomatic corps. A genetic conspiracy could be brewing."

"And what is that exactly?"

"Bio-terrorists. Classified."

"Bullshit." I suck my teeth, almost too disgusted for words. "Can't you see, they playin' you?"

"Where's your proof?" He walk in close to me, his hot breath be all down my neck.

"They ain't stupid enuf to drop proof when they play a guy like you."

"So it's just speculation." He got his hands on my waist, tuggin' at me. "Intuition."

"What? You don't speculate?" I start squirmin'. I don't want him touchin' me.

"Stop it, Lawanda." He turn me 'round and squeeze me close. I feel his heart poundin'. Then he get hisself under control and I don't feel nothin'. "Calm down," he say, like a threat. "Stay frosty."

"Why? So you can sweet-talk me outa my mind? Who am I? What can I do in Los Santos?"

"You can adjust your attitude and appreciate the historic opportunity that's falling into your lap! Don't let anybody play you out of being all you can be."

"You almost have a point, 'cept sendin' me 'cross the Barrier to gangsta heaven with Armando Jenassi ain't historic, it's messed up. Man, this ain't nothin'!"

"Ahh," his voice be like a caress, hot hands on my back make me shiver, "but you're just the person to make something out of nothing. I know from personal experience. We need you in Los Santos, *especially* if they're playing us. We can't just leave the Treaty mission up to Jenassi, can we?" I feel his heart again, a different beat tho.

"Well, no, but..." My heart's beatin' just like his.

"You've got to make sure we don't let Celestina down, let the world down."

"I ain't lettin' Celestina down."

"We knew turning the tides of history wasn't going to be easy. *I need you* in Los Santos."

"So I gotta hold up the sky by myself..."

"Make Celestina proud of you."

Celestina go off like fireworks in my heart, in everybody's heart. She a saint, walkin' on water, boxin' with God, dyin' for our sins, and shit like that. We fall all over ourselves tryin' to...I don't even know what. Live up to a legend? How can I say no to that? Then the Major fill my mouth up with his chocolate kisses, talkin' 'bout he believe in me. And ain't that just what I wanna hear? So I'm moanin' and groanin' 'steada thinkin' straight or tellin' him he's full of shit.

Weak in the knees, pussy-brain pathetic.

The bio-terrorist BS is a smoke screen. Prime Minister Jocelyn be tryin' to kill the Treaty, I know it. Without somebody fierce like the Major headin' this Treaty convoy, them gangstas in Los Santos just goin' laugh at us heart-on-our-sleeves diplomats. I oughta call the shit on the world screen, speak truth to power with all the bio-corders runnin'! The Major think my attitude was set on stun before, wait! Course, who'd believe me? Everybody would just think I was whinin' to cover my own incompetence.

Maybe the Major really be offerin' me a historic opportunity, maybe not, but I let him make love to me then walk outa here like he ain't just worked me over. Any way I turn, feel like somebody else be callin' the shots and when it get nasty, tellin' me to chill.

Chill out yourself, motherfucker, that's all I got to say.

Elleni and her booty-ugly *Vermittler* self need to open up the Barrier and get this show on the road.

3:   Wasteland outside of Sagan City, Paradigma
(September 6, Barrier Year 115)

> The universe is permeable, continuous beyond comprehension. All Barriers are the magic of Mind.
> —Vera Xa Lalafia, *Healer Cosmology, The Final Lessons*

Elleni Xa Celest crouched at the Barrier, head bowed, eyes squeezed shut, thighs clenched—trying to sculpt-sing a corridor from Sagan City, Paradigma, to Angel City, Los Santos, for the eager diplomatic vehicles thrumming at her back. Seasonal corridors would not open for several weeks. Paradigma's Treaty convoy hoped to reach Los Santos and shore up interzonal alliances before tourists, spies, mercenaries, and Entertainment crews muddied the waters. Or that was the lie Paradigma's Prime Minister told. Elleni hadn't challenged her. She had seized the opportunity to offer safe passage through a corridor of her own making. Now was the time to stand and deliver.

Her fingers burned; her voice throbbed; but the Barrier refused to open. She squinted up at the frustrating enigma, seeking a sign. The Barrier didn't look like much: no roiling fireworks display, no jewel mountains reaching to the sun, just geysers of smoke and shadows, milky undulations stretching across the horizon and up beyond the sky. A traveler from the twenty-first century might have mistaken it for a harmless fogbank, rolling in from the northwest.

Behind her in the wasteland, cordoned off by Paradigma's security forces, a mob of physicists, tech grunts, biologists, Los Santos Entertainment crews, politicians, and unaffiliated gawkers sucked in a collective breath and shuffled their skeptical feet. Eddies of gray dust swirled across the featureless landscape. Ordinary Paradigmites had come to watch Elleni make a fool of herself on the world screen. Sagan City scientists, however, were desperate for hard data on *Vermittler*, desperate to unmask the mechanism of her "magic." Entertainment crews from Los Santos just hoped for a good show. Gelatinous bio-corders whirred furiously, yet these organic smart-machines weren't able to capture Elleni, a visual, acoustic blur as she sang impossibly high arpeggios and clawed at the Barrier to no avail.

Yellow tears dribbled down Elleni's hissing hair and broke her concentration. Exchange with the Barrier required a phaseshift from one sensibility to another, like switching from visible light to magnetism or modulating spacetime. She drew in great quantities of hot, dry air and slowed her heart's drumbeat. She unclenched aching muscles and stacked her weight on carefully aligned bones. Pulling a bass note from her pelvic floor, she slid up her range, vibrating bones and organs until ultrasounds resonated in her nasal passages and shot out her skull. Her fingers danced in and out of the Barrier's domain. As she hit her highest notes, an archway crystallized just beyond her fingertips, and she almost lost the song. Struggling back onto the melody, she shaped a wider opening.

Femi Xa Olunde, his lean form hidden by bulky mudcloth robes, his dark hands and feet dusted with ashes, blocked Elleni from moving into the corridor. The cloud of white hair framing his face glowed. Elleni managed one more note in the sound beyond sound.

"*Vermittler* traitor, drunk on power, Barrier whore!" Femi said, his beard and bushy eyebrows flecked with the cinders that burst from his mouth as he spoke. "Playing on the enemy battlefield, you are the enemy!"

Elleni vomited blood. The old shaman was dead. Gunned down by an assassin.

Celestina Xa Irawo was also dead, yet she fussed and fumed at Femi. Iridescent starfish clung to her hennaed braids. Her hands glowed red. "Who are our enemies but our other selves?"

Femi flicked bony fingers at Celestina, dismissing her question, and the corridor around the ghost shamen started to break up.

"Wait." Elleni reached for them.

"No time. The world has been thrown off its course." His mud-cloth robes danced in a hot breeze. "And who are you but the enemy?" His words caught fire.

"Who indeed?" Celestina nudged Femi aside. Opalescent eels circled her belly. She pressed a clay funeral pot against her cheek, then hurled the pot at Elleni's feet. "Fire and water, mingle the ashes." The clay shattered, and the archway dissolved.

The Barrier was once again a foggy veil. *Drunk on power, Barrier whore!* Elleni's hair crawled across the damp skin of her exposed back. The dead shouldn't be coming down the Barrier to invade her mindscape and dissolve corridors. Not even legendary Healer shamen like Celestina and Femi could do that. Barrier corridors connected one Earth Zone to another, perhaps tunneled through spacetime to other star systems or universes, but corridors couldn't connect the living to some mythical afterlife. The phantoms blocking her entry with old West African proverbs must be interference, amplified distractions from her own mindscape, or a message from the Barrier to be decoded. Nothing more.

She tried to sing again, but after ten milliseconds, her throat was on fire and the notes were blood. Behind her in the wasteland, Elleni felt a bone snap. She shifted to human standard time, careful not to skid down to tree or mountain time. Techies from Paradigma and grips from Los Santos exchanged blows over incompetent biocorders. Two men were bleeding from their ears and broken noses. The audience had been standing in the wasteland since dawn; they had a touch of Barrier fever. Elleni felt a knife pierce dangerously close to a heaving lung. Paradigma's security whisked the culprits away before blood touched the ground, but a trace of pain lingered. Her great moment on the world screen wasn't going as she'd imagined it. A frantic braid slithered across her cheeks. She pushed it away from her eyes and, since swallowing hurt too much, spit bloody saliva on the ground.

She wouldn't be able to sing another note for days.

"Elleni?" Ray Valero's bass voice rumbled in her ears. He stepped from a swirl of dust. "What's wrong?" She leaned into her Entertainment Hero. His Barrier dawn eyes sparkled, and he smelled like a storm brewing. "Talk to me, babe." He ran his fingers through the tangle of bangs, beads, and dreads that fussed on her forehead. She felt a shiver of desire, but her hair settled down under his touch. "You milking this for high drama or what?" He smiled a camera-ready, Entertainment grin.

The diplomatic vehicles inched closer, their motors whining at her. Elleni ran burnt fingers across Ray's cheeks, then waved at a shadowy Barrier. A consummate actor, tall, muscular, Los Santos handsome, Ray had played most of his life on the world screen for a fickle public, and after twenty top screen years, they still loved him. What on earth did he see in her?

He slid his hand around her waist, as if he were playing a love scene. "What's up?"

Drawing on Barrier energy, Elleni modulated spacetime for both of them.

"Whoa," Ray groaned at the still life of angry diplomats, biocorder techies, and scowling spectators behind them. "Hyper-slow motion is rough on my brain." He squinted at staccato bursts of light snagged in the Barrier's murky tendrils. "I really hate you mucking around with—"

"Sorry." She put her fingers on his lips. "I don't know about you or anybody going to Los Santos today." English consonant clusters hurt her throat. She wished Ray spoke Spanish or Yoruba, but those languages were dead to him. "We'll have to wait for seasonal corridors."

"Come on." Ray flashed her a thousand-watt grin, playing the audience even in private. "Don't let this hostile crowd throw you." He nibbled her burnt fingers.

She winced and pulled her hands away. "I don't need an actor's pep talk." She turned her back to him.

"What do you want, a kick in the butt?"

Elleni bit her lip. Several of her braids snaked around his neck.

"Oh, you want to strangle me," he said.

"I can't explain this to you."

"I know what's going on with you and the Barrier."

Elleni's hair stiffened around his throat.

"You're not the enemy. You're opening the Barrier for peace." He stroked her shoulder. She turned to face him, pulling her dreads from around his neck. "They're dead wrong about you."

She moved close again, sucking him into her. "What do I taste behind your words?"

Elleni watched Ray with unblinking eyes. Time was practically at a standstill. Waiting was easy.

"The Healers Council sent a warning."

"It was Sidi, wasn't it? *Geistesschwester* watching out for my soul."

Ray shook his head. "Some sister."

"How? Healers don't transmit across the Barrier."

"A state 'gift' you brought for Prime Minister Jocelyn Williams."

"And you have a copy. Show me."

"Later."

"Now," she said softly.

Ray sighed and thrust his Electro mini-pad at her. Elleni steeled herself for Sidi Xa Aiyé's midnight eyes, velvet skin, ochre braids, and plum lips. But instead of a warning speech to the Prime

Minister, Sidi'd sent animated calligraphy, text that morphed into music and images and then back to words:

> The Earth broke from its orbit and smashed through the asteroid belt, dragging the Moon in its wake. A bloody Elleni, carrying ancient weapons, staggered through crumbling forests and fallen cities to an ocean on fire. As the Earth raced past Saturn, the Moon collided with the ringed giant. Shock waves ripped apart the fabric of spacetime. Elleni was dragged into a black tornado that sucked up the Sun.

> Nobody despises fire and wraps it up in a cloth.

> Barrier junkie, drunk on power, while the world has been thrown off its course.

> Playing on the enemy battlefield, you are the enemy!

> Sidi Xa Aiyé and Duma Xa Babalawo
> for the Healer Council Majority.

Sidi and the ghost shamen in the Barrier used the same words to attack her.

"You can't let them shake you," Ray said, "you know what's what." He shouted something more at her, but she didn't hear him. Blood roared in her ears. Her heart was a Tama drum, beating so fast she could barely breathe.

The Barrier was on the side of her enemies.

The ground fell from under her. She let the Electro screen slip from her fingers. Ray caught the mini-pad before it smashed on the ground. Perhaps he caught her too, like a good hero. But what did that matter? Elleni was *Murahachibu*, outcast from the Barrier.

4:   On Location outside Nuevo Nada, Los Santos
(September 6, Barrier Year 115)

> Conflict and diversity are the crucible of change
> and the axis of survival.
> —Celestina Xa Irawo, "Preamble to the Interzonal Peace Treaty"

"Mr. D, I hate to, to…" Moses Johnson, the assistant director, mumbled over the Electro, priority screen one. He was handsome enough to be an actor, with curly blue hair, prominent cheekbones, deep-set violet eyes; but his squeaky stammer broke the gene-art illusion. A tight close-up distorted his face and made him seem edgier than usual, like an Extra who'd run out of borrowed time, who'd be dead in the next shot.

"Ghost Dancers slip through the south gate again?" asked Aaron Dunkelbrot, the producer-director.

"No. I have a hot situation at Rock Center with…Mahalia Selasie."

"It's 4:30 AM. I don't give a shit about your woman problems, I'm storyboarding the climax." Residual Barrier burn in Aaron's left foot was jacking him up. Celestina's remedies were hard to come by on location. "I'm working, I'm a demon." Twenty-five screens spit images at him; he was OD'ing on story visuals—his brain couldn't handle unedited human contact. "Deal with it and piss off!"

Jewel-surfaced Electros covered the walls of Aaron's otherwise austere location trailer. He scanned gems from cinema's golden age—*Seven Samurai, It's a Wonderful Life, Daughters of the Dust, Dances With Wolves, Schindler's List*—plus rushes and prelims for his current project. Public Relations transmitted versions of Mifune Enterprises' publicity bomb on screens nine through thirteen. The launch date for the studio's PR blitz was next Monday. Aaron had to stop procrastinating and pick a clip. As the ad-operas came to a close, shots and editing converged. A lean figure with strategic dimples and a golden haze of beard ambled through Extras and stars into a close-up. Aaron slid from his comfort chair. The chilly synth-marble floor soothed the burn in his foot. He touched the thin lips on screen then jerked his hand away as the Electro phantom broke into a smile.

"Wow!" Aaron compared his reflection in the trailer window to the on-screen figure. The PR golden boy pushed sandy hair out of light eyes, grabbed a battered, dusky Extra, and grinned for the bio-corders, for the whole world. The startled Extra smiled shyly at the epitome of Los Santos's *new world* image: a rugged man of the people, familiar, reassuring, no Piotr Osama assassin, in fact not a hint of bad boy violence. Celestina's confidante—strong jaw line, eyes like sparkling water—someone you could trust with your babies, with your mind. Several years now and it still took Aaron effort to recognize himself. Mifune Enterprises' top gun, when would he get used to the skin he was in?

"Boss." Moses cleared his throat.

Aaron turned back to the assistant director's violet eyes, pinched nose, and sweaty upper lip on screen one. "You still there? What're you looking at?"

The gene-art rosebud on Moses's right cheek pulsed, as if it would burst into bloom—Mahalia's handiwork. She was the best gene artist around. "Nothing, boss, I…"

"Dump the boss bit, and do I have to break this connection myself…"

"An emergency." Moses transmitted on a priority channel. "I'm out of my league."

Aaron was disgusted. Who would he have to kill, just to work in peace? "Mahalia Selasie's a mind fucker. That's part of her genius charm."

"I got a squad of goons breathing down our asses at Rock Center."

"Random thugs or from another studio?"

"Swat team, and they're not leaving without Mahalia."

"Just waste the scumbags!"

"I thought everything'd be different with Celestina's Treaty."

"In your dreams. Treaty's just a piece of paper, Mose."

"But I didn't think we'd have to..." He shook sweaty blue curls out of his eyes.

"Defend ourselves? What Zone are you in, man?"

"Mahalia called us her sanctuary," Moses said.

Screens six to eight burst into battle orgies. Dead samurai, dead cavalry, and dead Nazis plummeted down trailer walls. The last evil samurai was a shower of blood. A bell rang and an angel got his wings. Aaron tried to shuffle his brain together. "What?"

"I can't just hand her over, *not to this crew.* "

"Break it down, into plain English."

"Suicide squad—do the mission or die kinda crew—demanding you and Dr. Mahalia, live, in fifteen minutes or else. Check this." Moses transmitted images from security bio-corders watchdogging the set. Screen two filled with colored snow.

"I can't see shit. Too much Barrier distortion."

Moses adjusted the transmission. Scattered across a re-creation of Rockefeller Center was a battalion of thugs looking ready to riot. Heat lightning turned the dawn sky golden, and more thugs swarmed into the skating rink. Gargoyle Electrosoft masks, blood-colored enviro-suits, and weapon-appendages reminded Aaron of giant fire ants. One thug aimed a pulse rifle at a sea mammal fountain. Mifune security surrounded the enemy troops, had a balcony advantage and three times the firepower. If it came to a showdown, the home team would win, but the plaza would be trashed.

"What the hell were you pussyfooting around for?" Aaron shouted.

"You think I should've just handed Mahalia over?"

"No! But..."

Aaron couldn't afford to build another twenty-first-century metropolis what with health benefits, Electrosoft fees, and Extra salaries. Los Santos Entertainment "taxes" took a hefty bite out of the budget. Plus Aaron held to Celestina's Treaty, even worked a secret contract with rebel unions. No shoving half-dead terminals into the Barrier or selling body parts on the organ market for quick cash.

That meant not a dime in the production budget for impromptu heroism.

Aaron blew a shot of Rapture to clear mental static and get his brain up to attack speed. Ray Valero was due in with the Treaty convoy from Sagan City. Any minute now, he'd come riding down a Barrier corridor carved by his freaky ladylove. Who could ask for better PR?

"I can't be dicking around with wildcard gangsters over a renegade scientist and her underground choir of geeks."

"Mahalia's not just minor league," Moses said. "And you owe her."

Mahalia got Aaron his big break at Mifune Enterprises. True, he owed her the skin he was in, but not his whole damn future. Shooting so close to the Barrier, his crews logged three foul-ups and two breakdowns for every half-ass success. The idiot production designer backed the city's slum sets into the Barrier and almost got fried himself. Moses, however, was topping all previous fuck-ups with this fiasco.

"Why couldn't you hold 'em at the gate?" Aaron clenched his teeth. This felt like a bad movie. "How'd goons crash the power nets and get on the lot?"

"Boss Samanski's people were tracking disappeared scientists, so I...well... I authorized entry."

"Samanski?" Aaron shoved hair out of his eyes.

"Blow these thugs away, a hundred times as many would come gunning for us, and like that—" Moses snapped his fingers—"it'd be a gang war."

"I pay beaucoup bucks to keep Samanski out of my hair." With a legendary stockpile of high-tech weapons and endless storm troopers, Carl Samanski dominated the loose federation of syndicates that constituted Los Santos's so-called government.

"Should've called me to the gate." Something didn't sync up. "How can Mahalia pitch sanctuary at us?"

"Yeah, we're not good guys ready to ride in for the rescue."

"What's she done?"

"Why don't you ask Boss Samanski?"

Aaron tried Carl Samanski's public and private Electro channels and got static. Samanski never responded to middle-of-the-night panic. Aaron didn't leave a message, just a signature pulse. Before he said anything, he needed a plan, and his mind was still like scrambled eggs. A burst of singing startled him. "What's that? Blues or some ethnic throwback music?"

On screen one, Moses shifted the framing so Aaron could see Mahalia Selasie, lethal eyes, bronze skin, raven black hair to her waist. Her mouth tilted to one side and slid into a lone dimple. Despite ancestors from old Africa and India, she didn't tone herself down. Not a genuine throwback, but her clothes were a polyrhythm of bright patterns, beads, mirrors, and bells. A middle-aged lady, unadulterated—no gene artistry, yet she cut through Aaron like an icy scalpel. Not how genius should look. She walked the Barrier's edge, thrusting her hips about, singing her heart out. A premier Sagan City scientist on the verge of going native, she and her underground choir of geeks had done well in Los Santos. What Entertainment junkie could resist jazz-singing wild genius? She finished the blues wail and squeezed Moses's arm.

"What's this about, Mahalia?" Aaron used his most severe director frown.

"To make outlaw Entertainment, you got to be ruthless," Mahalia said in a gravelly gin-and-tonic voice.

Did she know about Celestina's story? Had she gotten wind of his outlaw footage?

"If you want to betray yourself, I always say don't half step, go all the way."

"Outlaw Entertainment's just a PR scam to hype the public," Aaron said mildly.

"I know you, an outlaw among outlaws. Scamming squared."

"A lot of disappeared scientists. How come they're after you all of a sudden, Dr. Selasie?"

"You can't help me, can you?"

"That depends," Aaron said. He wasn't going down for anybody, not even his personal savior.

"What do you do with flops and traitors in this Zone?" Her jazzy tones shifted from chest to nose resonators. "Back home, we don't do chase scenes or action-packed poetry, nothing entertaining. We just dump people on the street to die."

"We used to dump losers in the Barrier, when the organ market was glutted. We'll have to come up with something less colorful. A firing squad?" Mahalia laughed too hard at Aaron's bad joke and almost fell over. "Are you high?"

"Very. Gene artists suffer from a god complex. " She grabbed Moses and lurched into an unfocused close-up. "I couldn't do a suicide mission."

"It's looking bad, babe, but maybe we can think of something."

"Fight Samanski, boss?" Moses said.

"Patch the enemy's head honcho to this channel."

"He said it's gotta be in-the-flesh, boss. For security."

"You can snoop live just like you can snoop Electro transmission." Aaron rubbed his perpetual shadow of a beard. "It's a scam, Moses. Live, I'm a hostage."

"No." Mahalia stood up straight and smiled at Aaron. Her gums were a soft violet, dark-skinned inside and out. "They only want me."

"And what the fuck have you done?"

"I hear Ray Valero's coming in for a star turn." Mahalia's voice was deep in her chest again. "Your new Entertainment will storm the Zones. Hit the top ten of all time. What's it called?"

"Who cares about that now?" Aaron said.

"I just want to know." Mahalia shrugged. "If you don't want to tell me…"

"*The Transformers.*" A half-ass attempt at telling Celestina's story.

A distant burst of weapons fire and shattering glass made Moses and Mahalia jump. Aaron ran to screen two, wincing at the burn in his foot.

"That was live, Mose, show me."

On screen two, shards of the crystal sea mammal decapitated trees and flagpoles in the Rockefeller Center set. Shattered plate-glass windows looked like spilt sugar. A geyser of gray water from the ruined sculpture disappeared out of the frame.

"That was a warning shot," Moses said.

"I've seen Rock Center on a history-Electro," Mahalia said. "Radio City, Alphabet News, no sea mammals—Prometheus floating over water, not stealing fire, not pushing a rock uphill, but flying, like he was free at last, Lord, free at last."

"You're scrambling up mythology," Aaron said. That wasn't like her. "Sisyphus and Martin Luther King..."

"You're the one who can't keep his stories straight."

Moses broke away from Mahalia. Mifune security surrounded her.

"If we do Mahalia ourselves," Moses whispered, "quick bullet in the brain—no torture and we don't worry who she talks to."

"We'll hand her over to Samanski's squad but leak it to the Ghost Dancers." Aaron was finally feeling the Rapture; his mind was back online. "Dancers will do a rescue ambush in the wasteland and take all the heat."

"Come on, boss! You only got eight minutes. We need a real plan." Moses picked at dry mucous in his nose.

"That's the plan. Get your fingers out your nose and meet me at Rock Center with Mahalia."

Screens one and two went dead. Aaron wrapped his foot in ice bandages and donned an enviro-suit. Goddamned kamikaze death squads were rigged with chemical implants—do the mission or die and take everybody with them. Aaron wasn't getting caught with his pants down. The A-Team rushed to his side as he jumped from his trailer into the dust. Turkey feathers on the bottom step had everyone sweeping the area for Ghost Dancers.

"Clean," tense voices reported over the Electro. One guy sucked feathers up with a vacuum nozzle, and his hands shook.

Aaron pocketed a feather. "Ghost Dancers like saving lives." He spoke from experience. "Carl's goons are another story."

Piling into a mini-tank with the A-Team, he wondered how long his elite fighting force would stay loyal if his credit reserve dried up or if Carl Samanski burned him. Syndicates always needed extra firepower in Los Santos's gun democracy. Other bosses would snap up his A-Team so fast, and then it would be open season on Mifune Enterprises.

Rock Center was seconds away. Contacting Dancers and inventing a satisfying Mahalia story-line for all involved would be a feat of narrative genius, especially with a convoy of do-gooders and snoops about to bust through the Barrier. Aaron needed to solve this mini-drama before Armando Jenassi and Lawanda Kitt were looking over his shoulder.

Aaron glanced at the chronometer on the mini-tank instrument panel. It was already morning in Sagan City. Elleni Xa Celest must be blazing her way through the Barrier. That spectacle would be the perfect wrinkle-in-spacetime image for *The Transformers*. Aaron hadn't gotten anywhere on the crisis storyboards, but real life always answered his story questions. This Mahalia intrigue was probably just the distraction he needed to jump-start his sluggish imagination.

5: Wasteland outside of Sagan City, Paradigma
(September 6, Barrier Year 115)

An obsession with realism can gut the imagination.
Like the man say, dreams are maps.
—Geraldine Kitt, *Junk Bonds of the Mind*

Elleni felt betrayed by a lover whose faithfulness she had taken for granted, whose passion 'til now had been unconditional and without limit. No matter what worms crawled in her belly, no matter how freaky she seemed, the Barrier welcomed her song; a monster lover opened itself to her touch and danced her from one world to another.

Ray doused her face with lukewarm juice and water. "What did you expect?"

"Sidi is not my enemy. She is…a part of myself."

"That's news."

Elleni pulled away from Ray. "The Barrier shouldn't take Sidi's part against me." She sat down in the dust.

"The images are changing." Ray displayed his Electro.

A blue-violet Barrier morphed into a maze of corridors, reaching out in every direction.

"Evolving." Elleni clutched her throat and wheezed.

Ray jacked his Electro into the bio-computer and loaded another program. "We could mimic your music and open a corridor." He had worked up this techno-wizardry with a renegade scientist to use in emergencies.

"With all these people watching? It's too risky."

"Just go super fast. What's anybody going to see?" Ray sat down next to her. "I need to get the hell out of this wasteland." He hugged her. "Figure it out when we get somewhere."

She stood up slowly. "All right."

As Ray cued up the corridor chant, Elleni modulated back to human standard time. His prickly relief at this shift flooded her a delicious instant, then a lean figure jumped from a transport vehicle and strode through the dust toward them. Ray went on alert.

"Danny Ford, one of Carl Samanski's bad-boy diplomats," he muttered.

"I know him. He signed the Treaty." Elleni gazed into Danny's sweet face. With his shock of multicolored hair, gentle brown eyes, and impish grin, Danny was like a hummingbird moving in for the kill.

"What's up, man?" Ray headed Danny off before he reached Elleni.

"Is there a problem? Can I help?" Danny scanned the scene for clues.

Elleni licked blood from the corners of her mouth. "We were just saying goodbye."

"You know how love is," Ray said. "Goodbye takes time."

"Ah." Danny glanced from Ray to Elleni and shuddered. She pretended not to notice. "Standing still, I feel like a target," Danny said. "In Los Santos we like to keep moving." He'd been in Sagan City discussing trade and disappeared scientists with the Prime Minister.

"Less than a minute," she said and dismissed him.

Danny shrugged and jogged back to his transport. He almost collided with Lawanda, who stormed out of her vehicle. The Captain of her security followed close behind. Lawanda had a bag slung over her back, a visor pulled down over her eyes, and the look of someone trying to make a getaway.

"Where are you going?" Elleni's voice was exhausted, but Lawanda heard her and halted. "We're just about to get started."

"I had to get me some air." Lawanda did not turn around.

"The air will be better when we get out of the wasteland into Angel City."

"That's right," Ray said. "The air here makes you crazy."

Lawanda danced in place. The Captain stood off to the side, eyeing her like she was prey about to bolt. Elleni put her hands on Lawanda's hunched shoulder. Tense muscles softened under her touch.

"When exactly are we outa here?" Lawanda asked.

"As soon as you're back in your transport," Elleni said.

Lawanda swiveled on one heel and headed for her vehicle. "If I suffocate over there in gangsta heaven, I'ma hold you two responsible!" The Captain shadowed her without comment.

"This better work," Ray said, engaging the bio-computer.

Elleni raced in so close to the Barrier, her breath caused it to dimple with color. Lavender and rose curlicues danced away from her lips. Ray played the corridor chant as Elleni mimed sculpt-singing. "Celestina, I promise to mingle your ashes with Femi's." She stroked the Barrier. Her monster lover shivered under her touch.

A corridor blossomed and disappeared into the horizon. No ghost shamen blocked the way. Elleni didn't move. It was too easy.

"It's beautiful." Ray started his engines.

"*Aṣe.*"

Elleni scampered onto the battered power nets of Ray's mini-tank and sculpted a corridor four lanes wide. The walls were slow-motion fireworks, a Chinese New Year all the way to Los Santos. In short order the Treaty convoy was rumbling through the gateway. Traversing the Barrier without a communion of spirits, Elleni felt queasy. Her blood was like sludge. She wanted to scratch at jangly nerves. Despite their charade, she still felt *Murahachibu* from the Barrier.

The ashes of Femi Xa Olunde, beloved wise shaman and former Council Center, were kept in a sacred shrine at the Library of the Dead. Nobody knew what had happened to Celestina's remains. Femi and Celestina had been bitter opponents in life. Mingle their ashes indeed! How would Elleni ever keep her promise? A roar from the crowd behind the convoy interrupted her anxiety. Enemies or not, the mob was on her side...for a microsecond.

6:   Cross-Barrier Transmission/Personal
(September 20, Barrier Year 115)

From: Lawanda Kitt on diplomatic mission in Angel City,

Los Santos

To: Sweet, Sweet Major in Sagan City, Paradigma

Two weeks, damn! How can you not be on the other end of this signal?!? I don't want your ole stank Electro static. I want you! I know you got an open channel. My sister, Geraldine, hooked you up with one of them fancy bio-computer models that transmit thru the Barrier anytime, just like mine. You ain't gotta wait for no seasonal corridor like everybody else, so you don't wanna talk to me, is that it? Too bad, cuz I gotta talk to somebody 'fore I lose my mind over here in Entertainment Lala Land!

Scope this: thirty minutes ago, me and the Captain leave a interzonal summit and is stumblin' thru pot-hole canyons in the sidewalk to our fancy diplomat quarter. Hard goin'. Gangstas braggin' 'bout hardly no power-outs in Los Santos, but Angel City ain't got streetlight the first and the sun's sneakin' behind skyscraper ruins. Twilight's when Ghost Dancers fall out, lookin' for converts. Ghost Dancers ain't no Los Santos urban legend, but a buncha renegade *Vermittler* and born-again Sioux snatchin' souls and gettin' ready for the end of time. Captain don't want a spiritual confrontation and be tryin' to hurry my butt up. I'm too busy runnin' my mouth for any kinda speed—complainin' about another long-ass eco-meetin'— Rasta-fructarian macro-neurotics from New Ouagadougou piss me off with they sacred bunny shit. Ain't nobody talkin' 'bout Mahalia Selasie, disappeared scientists, food riots, fire-virus breakouts, or anythin' real.

And then snap! Captain tackle me so I don't be tippin' into the friggin' Barrier.

Another millimeter and I'da been crispy crunchies. Damn Barrier look goofy, like somebody up in the sky be blowin' trillions of red, yellow, violet, and green soap bubbles 'cross the horizon, and if I stick my finger in, the whole psychedelic mess would chain-reaction pop and rain down on us in swirls of colored goo.

'Fore I do somethin' foolish, Captain grab my hand and drag me up outa the dust—away from the Barrier. I shake my head. For half a second, feel like somebody's in there with me, like a boogey crawled under my skin and now they escapin' out my eyes back into the Barrier. I hold onto the Captain and blink and bat my eyes 'til I'm dead sure it's just me in my head, in my skin. I look around. We alluva sudden in the Cripple Creek wasteland, three or four kilometers from Angel City. Mystery shit like that mess up my mind, but Captain look more outa it than me.

"How we walk all this way the wrong damn direction, *without noticin*?" I ask. Captain ain't studyin' a word I say, cuz a hundred fifty meters away, a buncha thugs is chasin' this woman thru tumbleweed and cactus. She ain't wearin' helmet, suit, no kinda enviroprotection, just a cloud of fuzzy red hair and pale skin glowin' in the twilight.

"Ain't no Ghost Dancer, but a Extra, I bet, with a location crew on her tail for raw Entertainment, like in the good ole days before the Treaty."

Captain power up a long-range weapon and say, "Maybe, maybe not. Extras don't usually wear underground choir robes."

Captain's right. In Los Santos, folk ain't gotta go underground or throwback to do art like they do back home. So what is up with the robes? Thugs back mystery lady up against the Barrier, snatch at her syn-silk sash, almost catch her. Then I swear spacetime kinda dilate. Lady lock eyes with me from a hundred fifty meters. No lie. Captain take aim—at the thugs—but the lady nod at me, then run right into the Barrier, singin' ole-timey blues from way before we was born, like Mahalia Selasie be singin' all the time. Spacetime's all twisted up now. Captain never pull the trigger. Thugs break outa there so fast. The funkadelic bubbles in the Barrier erupt, sound like firecrackers and monster gongs, and I gotta hold my ears. I ain't never *heard* the Barrier before. Course back home in Paradigma we ain't got people gettin' run into it. Not in Ellington, anyway. A river of piss yellow and vomit green roll along the horizon and up into the sky. Wispy lookin' nothin' smell like engine exhaust, make me dizzy. Then snap, the Barrier drop back to half-hearted colored ripples in a curtain of dingy white.

That mystery lady didn't even break the beat with a holler. What a way to go. (I'm checkin' the image bank on her while transmittin' to you.)

Rape, snuff Entertainment with Extras—that's the sorta ugly we s'posedly come to Los Santos to stop. Been hearin' wild tales all my life 'bout thugs roundin' up terminals and politicos and usin' 'em as Extras in Entertainments, marchin' 'em into the Barrier, sellin' they organs. I know we got the unrest and riots back home too. Folk do freaky shit every time there's a power jam. But damn— you ever see the Barrier zap somebody live? It's nothin' like what be on the Electro. Los Santos gangstas act like the Barrier's some kinda lethal work of art, like everythin' be Entertainment. Well, after "the show," I'm so messed up, Captain have to just 'bout carry me the three kilometers back to our quarters. Only thang stoppin' me from comin' home to Paradigma right away is havin' to go back thru that freaky Barrier. Seasonal corridors don't open for a few days and Elleni's gotta go to New Ouagadougou City. Said she had to "mingle the ashes." Yeah. So I'm stuck here on stupid.

Bad idea, Major, sendin' me cross the Barrier to ambassador to these big-time illusion junkies. Course *you* can make anythin' sound noble. You got that dark rumbly voice, say somethin' soft, chocolate sweet, and I can't help myself. Show me pictures of Los Santos Extras dyin' nasty deaths, then get sexy 'bout what *we* goin' do to change all that. And dumb-ass me, I feel this erotic thrill thinkin' *we can save folks*, thinkin' *we* ain't just a waste of good spacetime. Too many ethnic throwbacks be lost in the past, leadin' a museum life, but not me! Hookin' up with you, doin' this Treaty gig, mean I am somebody who matter in this scary universe, now and in the future. Cuz *we goin' feed starvin' babies, stop the wars and extinctions, turn the tides of history...*

Then you ditch me at the Barrier.

Talkin' 'bout Madame Prime Minister won't let you head the Treaty delegation no more cuz you gotta take care of intrigue at home—all them scientists goin' AWOL and shit, but she think Armando Jenassi goin' do just fine ambassadorin' in Los Santos. Right. She don't trust nobody from the entire Sagan City Political Ministry 'cept this sleazy hustler? Armando tell me to my face, most folks ain't worth savin'; social work be bad ecology: everybody survivin', not just the fittest, and where's that goin' get us but a genetic wasteland? I mean the man voted against Celestina, called her a disaster! Now he the boss of Treaty implementation and I gotta take orders from his reactionary butt?!? Why you wait 'til the last microsecond to drop this shit on me?

You and me was s'posed to be a dream team, Major.

Elleni breakin' the Barrier open for peace and I go from dip-dip angel of mercy to Vice Ambassador! I breeze into this Los Santos gangsta Zone feelin' like ten kindsa fool. These thug bosses be expectin' a ruthless technocrat holdin' the reins of world power in one data glove. All they get is two-faced Armando Jenassi and a raggedy butt novice who ain't negotiated rain down the drain or shit thru a pipe. (And Major, you and I both know, diplomacy ain't never been my strong suit.)

Armando Jenassi could give a crap 'bout rehabilitatin' Extras or rescuin' disappeared scientists, he just cuttin' back room deals and turnin' his eye the other way. So it's all on me, AND WHAT IF I JUST CAN'T CUT IT? I got six piddly months to turn the tides and whip these suckers into shape, or both Paradigma and New Ouagadougou will suspend trade with Los Santos. Then all hell will break loose. We'll slip back to corridor coups and interzonal war so fast, like the Treaty never happened. I don't understand Ms. Jocelyn Williams, she a political genius, the Prime Minister, but this Treaty trip is a total setup. A fuckin' suicide mission. Man, y'all play me like Electro-synth. Well, you useta torture people, break and enter they minds like it was nothin', so what do I expect? Truth?

Sorry. Talkin' to wavy gravy lines on the Electro steaduva live human bein' bring out my road rage. I don't mean to hit and run. I know you got your hands full with the big J. And Reunification is a bitch. Sidi Xa Aiyé and the retro Healer BS make everybody wonder 'bout "One World Now." But that ain't no kinda excuse for you not once openin' a live channel to me *in two weeks*! I'm dyin' over here. Los Santos don't sound right—ain't no good rhythm and rhyme. It don't smell right neither. And it is hard not to turn into a stranger when ain't nobody comin' back at you with you.

I'm s'posed to be some big Treaty diplomat from Sagan City but these thugs ain't no way impressed. They don't hardly show to the lame public hearin's Armando be sendin' me off to. I'm a joke and Celestina's Treaty might as well be toilet wipes. You think Paradigma folk be jacked up, wait! These Los Santos fools strip-search every impulse, every inspiration, and then wonder why creativity done gone AWOL. And talk about rigid! These gangstas make New Ouagadougou Healers seem like Jello.

I'm freaked. My hands be shakin', droppin' shit all the time, and I can't keep no food down. That recon-slop be tastin' worse every day. My right eye just wanderin' round my face, I swear. That make it hard to look at thangs, you know what I'm sayin'—when they kinda split apart and dance 'round. I got half the Captain chasin' the other half up a wall, one ugly butt gun be four guns shootin' each other, and fragments of Electro-screens steady slicin' up Armando Jenassi.

Scope this: image bank give me three matches for mystery lady who dash into death. (Sister Geraldine's bio-corder ain't no way fuzzy near the Barrier, give me real sharp images, put Electrosoft Corp to shame. Geraldine got all the genius genes in our family. Make her Vice-Ambassador and she'd tear it up.) Twenty-five percent chance that mystery lady be one of Sis's colleagues from Sagan Institute, ten percent that she on Mahalia Selasie's disappeared research team, one of her underground choir folk, and seventy-five percent that she be a Extra. What do that tell you?

Oh, shit, that was an explosion. Close by, in the diplomatic quarter. Folks here ain't exactly welcomin' us with open arms. Gettin' blown up, dyin' for the cause, I'd scream, piss myself, be a nasty mess, but I think I could handle that in my soul. But dyin' for bullshit, for nothin', a set up!—that's what I'm scared of—all the time, in my sleep even.

I gotta go check out this bomb mess. Talk to you later.

Lawanda

7:   Studio City, Los Santos
(September 26, Barrier Year 115)

> Loving yourself when you're down and dirty is hard, but loving yourself into the next transformation, that's the real trick.
> —Tadeshi Mifune, *Surviving the Future, Last Minute Notes*

The distant explosion was not a special effect—the natives were restless—but that didn't really register. Lights dimmed in the main screening hall of Mifune Enterprises. The giant Electro-screen went fuzzy. Armed guards paced the aisles—for an in-house showing of a rough-cut! The security on *The Transformers* was absurd. Ray Valero squirmed in his comfort chair, the best Studio City, the best Los Santos, had to offer. He stowed his medicine bag under the fake fur seat cushion. Elleni had given him his own bag, a piece of herself to fortify him. Twenty years of stardom and still he hated watching himself act, especially in public. At least the audience wouldn't get up in the story with him. Hardly anybody could afford the gear for that bandwidth—mass market steered clear of virtual Entertainments.

Ray pulled off his boots and sank bare feet into the plush purple carpet. A guard aimed a weapon at his head that could have blown a building away. "Give me a fuckin' break!" Ray shoved his boots at the guard. "No bombs, see."

"You don't need to stalk talent!" The first assistant director pulled the man away.

Ray couldn't remember his name. Moses? Jesus? He used to remember everybody's name. "Keep these bozos on a better leash."

The AD flared his nostrils, then covered his irritation with a sullen nod. An ectomorph who haunted the gym and popped bodybuilders and bio-enhancers, he had a bland, handsome face to go with the muscle job. A cosmetic scar on his left cheek, a flower bud, irritated Ray for no reason. Blue hair, violet eyes, just the kind of gene-art wonder they were casting as heroes these days. Audiences loved people who risked death to look cool.

Ray blew tension out of his lips but refrained from grabbing his chin and shaking out his tight jaw. Not in this crowd of up-tight sharks. They might think he was a retard and pull him from the project; or some idiot guard might shoot him. Danny Ford was in the back row, snooping for Carl Samanski. His feathery, multicolored hair was hard to miss. Sweet Danny was a fan, a Treaty booster—they didn't need to act tough for him.

Keeping Mifune Enterprises on the far side of disaster was no mean feat. Aaron Dunkelbrot gambled on *The Transformers*, an epic-adventure series on the Barrier from its first appearance right up to Celestina and "One World Now." A mass-market dream, M. Enterprises's salvation, if PR could pitch it around the Treaty controversy or if some other studio didn't scoop the idea. Ray chuckled to himself: nobody else would have the balls. He longed to work with a director like Tadeshi Mifune again, someone with vision and crazy ambition, someone he admired. Fat chance of *that* anytime soon.

According to PR, Dunkelbrot's *Transformers* was going to be an outlaw blockbuster, but Ray wasn't buying the ad copy. Dunkelbrot didn't have the juice. Gangs of armed security haunting the production felt like much ado over nothing.

The screening was twenty minutes late.

Ray had the lead in one hundred years of history playing a different hero each episode—yet he wanted to dash out of the hall before the rough-cut of the first episode was screened. He reached for his boots. Aaron Dunkelbrot sat down in the aisle seat and blocked his getaway.

"Not thinking of skipping out on me, are you?" Aaron said. "Wouldn't look too good."

Ray slumped in the chair. "Who are you impressing with the trigger happy yahoos?"

"Everybody. Never let the pressure down!" Aaron turned to stare in the faces of his select audience of producers, studio execs, and gangster luminaries. "I need them," he whispered. Sometimes Aaron acted like he and Ray were friends.

"It's what's on screen that counts," Ray said.

"You really believe that? That's why you're an actor, huh?" Aaron waved at a man being escorted to his seat by the AD. The bulky frame, gleaming bald head, and ornate Healer walking stick were unmistakable. The latecomer was Achbar Ali, character actor turned script doctor and production guru. Guards weren't in *his* face with powered-up weapons. He sat across the aisle from them.

"Hauling out the big guns. I didn't realize you were worried about the script." Ray nodded at the caped figure, who raised his walking stick in reply. "Achbar" was the name of a Mogul emperor of India and meant "greatest." The formidable Mr. Ali was known to friends and foes alike as *The Achbar*. "How'd you woo the Achbar?"

"You don't get where I am on looks," Aaron said.

You get pretty far, Ray thought, looking around at all the beautiful people.

"I'm an ambitious SOB. I want the best. I get the best," Aaron said.

A commotion at the back of the house had the audience craning their necks, except for Achbar Ali, who sat on the edge of his seat and hummed *The Transformers*' opening music. A man and a woman in white robes and moss headdresses were silhouetted in the back door, their silvered faces sparkling. Ghost Dancers.

The AD dashed down the aisle.

A dark-skinned woman leaned against the two Dancers. Ray had seen her before, somewhere, but his memory was getting worse by the second. Her mane of black hair and colorful beaded clothing were spattered with mud or blood. Ray didn't want to know which. The Ghost Dancers argued at the guards, insisting they be let in. The woman wanted to see *The Transformers*. One of the guards raised his weapon and fired. Ray looked down at the carpet, at his pale toes squirming. He winced at two more bursts of rapid fire. Acting wasn't worth all this. He should leave the screening hall, walk off the shoot even, jump in his mini-tank, and exit this jacked-up Zone. Better yet, he should walk down the aisle and see about those Dancers. Play the hero in real life. But he couldn't make himself move. He just kept watching his toes. When he finally looked up, the back doors were sealed. The audience was quiet except for Achbar's humming. Ray was ice cold and sweating.

"Did the guards shoot them?"

"Probably not, but how should I know? I'm sitting beside you." Aaron scanned the audience. "It'll make everybody think twice. I'm playing for keeps."

"You can't just gun people down anymore." Ray couldn't put up with gangster tactics the whole shoot. "Look, Aaron, you know I won't act if—"

"Self-defense is the only time the home team shoots to kill— goons from another studio is another story, can never tell when they might shoot," Aaron said as a starry nebula filled the screen. "You've done worse, Valero, worked some killer projects."

Ray blinked away a storm of violent images. "But that was before…"

"Your great transformation? Ha!" Aaron shook his head. "Don't you start on the Treaty. I've had enough righteousness for one day."

The AD appeared out of the darkness. "Ghost Dancers snatched Mahalia Selasie in the wasteland. Samanski's thugs are dust. Not a trace or trail. Dancer Voodoo." He spoke in a melodramatic stage whisper.

"That's between Boss Samanski and the Dancers," Aaron said a little too emphatically. This scene, Ray thought, was being played for Danny Ford and whoever else was snooping for Carl. "Not our fight."

The AD faded back into the darkness. Achbar's mustache drooped, as he banged his walking staff against an aisle light. The protective covering popped, and a lamp exploded. Tension rippled through the audience. The giant Electro screen froze on the Milky Way, but guards didn't converge on Achbar. He wiped his bald head with a red handkerchief and met Ray's eyes. The Entertainment started up again, and Achbar turned back to the screen, before Ray knew what to make of his expression.

"I won't put up with gangster tactics," Ray said. But he already had.

The Achbar was laughing, a deep, lion-roar laugh.

"Don't worry." Aaron's mood had inexplicably softened. He shook Ray's shoulder. "Get your back down. Try to lose yourself in the images."

Ray snorted. "Right. That's what I came here to do." He focused on the screen.

8:   New Ouagadougou City, New Ouagadougou
(September 27, Barrier Year 115)

"Nobody despises the snake and wraps it around her waist for a belt," Celestina Xa Irawo was fond of saying.

Seasonal corridors were about to open and everyone—common Ouagadougian citizens, acolytes, healers, and shamen argued in the

Council Hall over what to do about the diplomats and tourists who would be coming in from the warrior Zones. So many secrets to hide, so much truth to twist with a public face. Lurid Entertainments were already terrible pollution, but what rituals would protect the people from live interactions?

Elleni didn't care if foreigners got access to the Herbarium, the Insect Pavilion, *and* the Library of the Dead. She hadn't communed with the Barrier in three weeks. Crossing from Los Santos to New Ouagadougou, she had had to use Ray's bio-corder, and the humiliation still stung. Her hair gnawed at thread-metal barrettes; her eyes kept phaseshifting beyond the visible spectrum; and she couldn't tell which language, what dangerous metaphors dropped off her tongue.

As the sun plunged behind the western mountains and faces morphed into electromagnetic gibberish, Elleni excused herself from the tourist deliberations. Council didn't need her to weave the subtleties and protect the integrity of New Ouagadougou. Elleni had to mingle the ashes and find a corridor back into the Barrier or she would go crazy.

Maybe she'd already gone crazy.

Elleni stumbled over a thinking-stool and fell against the pink adobe wall of the Library of the Dead. A glass-covered sand mandala slipped from its mount and slid toward the floor. Elleni broke the fall of the mandala with her thighs. Her medicine bag banged her kidneys, and she fell into the wall again. A purple bruise blossomed on her forehead. A few dreadlocks escaped her syn-silk bandana and hissed. Elleni scanned the long arcade where the wisest men and women came to meditate. The vision corridor and shrine room were deserted.

The sand painting she'd knocked off its mount depicted a stocky, snake-haired woman with midnight eyes and yellowish brown skin racing through an ocean of fire, blood dripping from her serpent locks; the ruins of New Ouagadougou City smoldered in the background. Elleni hoisted Sidi Xa Aiyé's mandala above her head. Her muscles strained against the weight. Femi's words echoed in her ears. *Playing on the enemy battlefield, you are the enemy*. With trembling hands, Elleni placed Sidi's sand painting back into its niche.

Nobody despises the snake and wraps it around her waist for a belt. The people chose Elleni to center them. Yet if they caught her stealing Femi's ashes she would never again be welcome in any city or village in New Ouagadougou; no *Vermittler* would be trusted with the *Final Lessons*; Council would empty Elleni's medicine bag into the Barrier and many lifetimes of wisdom—Femi's, Celestina's, and her own—would be lost; and Council would surely break the Treaty with Paradigma and Los Santos, plunging the world once again into famine and war. A bloody Elleni would run through the smoldering ruins of New Ouagadougou City, just as Sidi had envisioned.

Elleni averted her eyes from the wall of mandalas and scurried over meditation mats and thinking-stools to the inner sanctum. She easily located Femi Xa Olunde's shrine. Two large spiders chased each other across a fifty-stringed Kora, which rested between an ebony thinking-stool and a transparent image-board. Elleni didn't see a funeral urn.

More braids and dreads broke free of the bandana, spitting at Femi's totem spiders. This unruly motion triggered a hologram loop in a dark niche above the Kora. A red-violet Barrier girdled a blue planet and pulled it out of its orbit. The planet wobbled and exploded, setting off a cascade of fireworks inside the Barrier. Standing on her toes, Elleni reached through the repeating laser show and searched the recesses of the shrine with her fingers. She felt several live insects caught in a sticky web, waiting to be sucked dead. As the planet exploded for the fourth time, her thumb found a furry spider and a curled handle. Elleni dodged the poisoned fangs and pulled the clay urn through the cascade of fireworks. It was no bigger than her hand. Elleni brushed away the spider's web, stuffed Femi's remains into her medicine bag, and hurried from the shrine room. The hologram faded behind her.

Racing down the vision corridor, she looked neither right nor left. The Library of the Dead rose only two stories, but it sprawled a mile and a half around the lake. The distant doorway to the outside looked like a deep blue eye in a brown marble face. Elleni longed to drink in the twilight, to taste air that wasn't heavy with the spirits of the ancestors. She ran full-out the last half mile, quiet as a whisper, barely breathing. Three steps before she reached the opening, the door slammed shut. Elleni twisted to the side and somersaulted across the earthen floor, having no desire to bang her head a third time.

"No one treads so softly through the chambers of death unless she has a heavy heart." Awa, the oldest Council member, spoke English with Yoruba formality. She sat perched in the window frame above the door. Silky white braids fluttered in the breeze around her tough, weathered face. She narrowed ice blue eyes to slits. "Awa Xa Ijala, daughter of heroes, greets the Center of the Healers Council, Elleni Xa Celest, granddaughter of the stars."

A formal exchange of honorifics was a bad sign. Elleni clutched her medicine bag to her belly.

"Why did you hurry away from Council tonight?" Awa jumped down from her perch like a snow leopard pouncing on prey. Elleni stood her ground, smelling Awa's cold breath, tasting her sweat, desperately trying to read the signs. "The others were ready with a nasty story, but I would hear what you say."

"I only center the vision. Everyone makes the future." Elleni matched Awa's formal tone. "Celestina says I must mingle the ashes."

Awa's eyes widened. The folds in her face fell away for a moment. "Celestina speaks to you still? Celestina asks for this ritual?"

Elleni nodded. The truth or part of it was always her best alibi.

Awa paced in front of the door, her thoughts so quiet, Elleni could have been alone. "And how will you mingle the ashes?"

Elleni shrugged. "What brings Awa Xa Ijala, daughter of heroes, to the Library of the Dead while Council deliberates?"

Awa scratched at her neck. "I am an old woman and I appreciate my ignorance. One who seeks answers is always welcome here." She tapped her bony fingers against the door. "You should hurry, the night is short. Stay ahead of suspicion." The door began to open. *"Was für ein Wunder ist das Leben!"* Awa brushed icy lips against Elleni's bruised forehead, then pushed her out into the gathering darkness. "Don't let the miracles catch you off guard."

Elleni turned back to hug Awa, but chilly eyes dismissed her. Awa tapped the door, and it slammed shut. Elleni hurried off, away from Council and into the woods.   ·

9:   Cross-Barrier Transmission/Personal
(September 26, Barrier Year 115)

From: Lawanda Kitt on diplomatic mission in Angel City,
Los Santos
To: Sweet, Sweet Major in Sagan City, Paradigma

Not a blip from you yet, Major. You ain't even accessed my first message. I could be dead meat for all you know. Thangs be blowin' up all over the place.

Last week, some hype-meister promise Armando Jenassi a gene-art makeover. Jenassi let down his guard, and this kamikaze terrorist waltz right past our power nets with funky chemicals and suspect apparati, then blow hisself up, takin' two transports and a buncha security with him. Captain don't let me near the dead zone, cuz I take everythin' to heart. Ain't nothin' of those people left to bury anyhow.

Jenassi be poppin' Scud and blowin' Rapture 'til he too tight to talk or piss straight, but they suit him up in a museum tuxedo and point him at the bio-corders. When the hot-babe interviewer say he still alive after a real close call, he grin on cue. Unreal.

Scope this: since gangstas almost blow up Jenassi's designer ass five times, his security jack-offs figure maybe WE oughta take better precautions. And since I'm so hot to do good, they ship me off to a forum on famine, steada riskin' the man hisself. Like I can do jack shit at a "public forum"—slap a few wrists, tell 'em they bad boys, and meanwhile I'm target practice. Jenassi and his posse think I'm a retard.

I don't argue. Me and my squad hit the road like good girls and boys. But I'm speculatin', we ain't gotta drive to no chump-change forum. Why risk booty for this foolishness? We can park the transport somewhere nice, chill 'til the seasonal corridors open, then high-tail it outa this friggin' funnyhouse. Course, I don't get 'round to mentionin' this plan to nobody. It's like I'm two people and the wild child's in charge.

On our way outa town, I have the Captain liberate one of Armando's black market soybean transports. His security's too messed up to notice. Then we bust thru the wasteland a hundred eighty kilometers a hour. How they goin' catch us? Dreamin' and schemin'—maybe I can turn this stand-in-for-the-man routine into somethin' good.

Forum be in Sol, a big town near where Las Vegas got swallowed by a Barrier quake. Sol so ugly, it hurt your eyes. Blocks of dingy, blood-and-piss-stained concrete crumblin' in the glare of the sun. Los Santos Treaty Commission stick us up in a broke-down Entertainment hall to "accommodate the crowds." Look like a bunker from old Beirut after a few bombin's. Inside, the ground stick to your feet and make a sucky noise when you walk. Half the lights is busted, pink scale be growin' on the funky chairs, and I could swim in my sweat cuz they way too cheap for climate control. Captain load in, do the security thang: power net shieldin', detectors, and a auto-bomb squad. Little electronic spies look like a buncha silver fish crawlin' all over everythin', flyin' too, make me itch, but the little buggers is keepin' us safe so what can I say? I load the giant

Electro. It be so warped, picture goin' interfere with itself. Ain't settin' my butt down on those nasty chairs so I wait around on stage in
a grimy pool of light that turn the yellow in my skin green. (Don't
tell me Entertainment thugs still don't know how to light colored
folks—these suckers tryin' to make me look sick on purpose.)

Forty minutes after we s'posed to get goin', big shots still be trick-
lin' in. They don't wanna hand they guns in at the door, even when
the Captain promise 'em two for every one that get lost. Talkin'
'bout this ain't no police state like Paradigma, it's every man for
hisself. One gun, one vote at a public event. Compromise: Captain
take ammunition and leave big shots holdin' they empty pieces and
lookin' bad.

It's gettin' later and later. The idiot "general secretary" of this
Sol region grin at me and shrug. Hitchcock, I think his name is.
Green flakes dribble down his stubbly chin to a dried-up splotch
on his shirt, like the man don't never wash. After two hours of
this waitin' BS and Hitchcock's bad-breath grins, I'm 'bout to walk.
Then I say, blast that, folk be starvin', I can't be stuck up in my ego.
Prime Minister Jocelyn, Armando, and maybe even you, Major, set
me up, but I don't have to fall down.

I start the meetin' by askin' straight up where the grain ship-
ments from New Ouagadougou be disappearin' to. A bad-boy
Entertainment director jump up on stage and tell me there are
only seven stories in the world—no, seven stories in the whole universe! Not just Entertainments, he mean in real life, in everythin'!
I look at him like he a stone fool. One of them tall, handsome boy-
wonders with a dimple in his chin and a dustin' of beard on his
cheeks. The Captain say his name be Aaron D-somethin'. Hands
on my hips, suckin' my teeth, rollin' my eyes, I say, who you think
you are, tryin' to derail this forum—get on the agenda. He start
laughin', say the whole "ethnic throwback" talkin' bad English bit
is cute but passé; it's even illegal, far as he know, which ain't far, cuz
Paradigma outlaw other languages, not "bad English."

"Why the hell send us a throwback ambassador who can't even
talk straight?"

All the thugs is laughin' at me, but I don't go off, I take a deep breath, work calm in my center, like Ray Valero do to act. Ethnic throwbacks be like the ole Israelis bringin' back Hebrew after two thousand years, after so many words was fightin' against 'em. Why anybody wanna speak the truth, raise they children, know themselves with gas-chamber language? Survival be havin' words to call home, havin' idioms and syntax to heal the Diaspora. In your cultural rhythm and rhyme, that's where the soul keep time. But I'm not goin' go there with these no-mind gangsta folk. They tryin' to distract me. Laughter die out when it don't make a dent in my spirit. Wonder-boy director tell everybody to shut up and let me finish, but they already quiet.

I say we here to deal with syndicates dissin' the Treaty, not to talk 'bout the poetics of my life or how many stories fit on the headuva pin. I say we a reunited, one-world people now with common law, so gang bosses gotta bag the post-apocalyptic anarchy and get with the program. I mean, who the fuck care how I talk? Ain't hardly nobody got jobs in Los Santos, education sucks, and folk be starvin'! Gun democracy's a bust.

Bad-boy director put his arm around my shoulder and give me a pale, blotchy smile. He smell all innocent, like cotton candy and cherry pop—I almost gag. Captain go on alert, weapons powered up, but Mr. Director ain't fazed. All silk and sleaze, he say don't you see, same seven stories over and over, like history repeatin' itself, like universal laws of motion. He actually expect me to be impressed with this slop cuz I'm from Sagan City, a "Science Zoner" and all. I'm 'bout to say his unified field theory for story is lame when he admit he just love to hear hisself talk. He love squeezin' every life, that was and goin' be, into his seven-story formula. He a director, creatin' a universe in seven days like God, so no way *he* got time to chase after Ouagadougian grain or worry 'bout Extras dyin' from hunger or the germ of the week. Then he quote the Bible—the poor will always be with us. I ask, what about snuff art, what about gettin' smoked in the Barrier? He say, it's just survival of the fittest.

"Damn, boy, physics, Jesus, and Darwin be on your side," I'm yellin' now. Mr. 7-Stories scowl and mess up his dimples. Crowd cheer and hoot. "I ain't playin' with y'all. No more bio-tech wizardry from Sagan City, no more grain or medical from New Ouagadougou 'til y'all get behind the Treaty!"

"Sure, babe!" they holler.

"Can't stuff the Treaty down people's throats," 7-Stories whisper. "That's not how things work here." He pat his empty weapon. "We're kinda loose."

Man must think I'm stupid. "I'm here to help y'all tighten up," I whisper back.

Center stage, the Captain crack open a crate of soybeans. They don't roll far on the sticky synth-wood floor. I hold up a buncha official-lookin' Electro outprint. I'm a throwback. I like shit on paper. Thugs stop hootin' for half a second.

"Don't let 'Black Marketeers' be direct-depositin' to your accounts when they workin' stolen Treaty goods with you!" I have they undivided attention now. Captain open a raggedy backstage curtain on a mountain of soybean crates. "Cuz we will confiscate the stolen booty and your whole damn wad!"

A big boss shoot out his front row seat, makin' a loud fart noise with his mouth. Look like heart attack material. Armando probably tole him the Lawanda chick's a dip-shit who won't cause no kinda trouble. Man turn purple then dash down the sticky aisle, his guards scramblin' and scurryin' behind him.

"That's Jesus Perez," the Captain whisper, "the soybean king."

I shout at his back. "Mr. Perez, if I'm holdin' your beans and all your money, how you goin' keep yourself supplied with weapons, drugs, and essential thug paraphernalia?" Suddenly folks' butts be hurtin' in the hard seats. Everybody shift, grunt, pick in they noses. "Any questions?" I'm smug now.

A skinny guy with two mini-canons slung low on his hips stand up. I see his trigger fingers twitchin', but this cowboy take one look at the Captain's automatic long-range pieces and change his mind 'bout gettin' violent with empty guns. He spit at me and miss. "You can't just take all of somebody's money. That's against the Treaty."

"Oh, so now you talkin' Treaty." Actually I hacked they system and data-chilled Perez' assets, but who gotta know that? "Well, wanna watch me do it again?" Nasty crowd laughter make cowboy sink down. The hall smell really rank now. "Scope this." On the giant Electro, I throw up projections of local traffic in illegal goods. Look like a morph program gnoshed my data. Captain mess with the resolution and scale 'til it ain't so twisted. "Y'all at the center of a bodacious rip-off pattern. Since Celestina's Treaty freed the Extras, outlawed the organ market, and mandated democracy, y'all think you can't make no big money—'cept with porno-trash Entertainments, drugs, and rippin' off the Reunification. Yeah, we trackin' the whole scheme." I bust they "secret" operations wide open with 3D graphics cuz I know gangstas be some no-readin' folk. "Surprise! I'ma help you diversify." Folk jump up on the seats, snarl, shove. Ain't nobody listenin' to a word I say—too busy flashin' useless weapons.

"Where are your manners?" 7-Stories director got a voice amp for his deep baritone. "Get down off those chairs and shut up! Quiet on the set!"

And snap, these rude crooks do just like he say! Like 7-Stories director be a ganglord or somethin'. I thought he was just a artist. Captain say he a maverick into outlaw Entertainment, useta to hang with Mahalia Selasie 'fore she disappeared. I got my eye on him now.

"This dropped out of your papers." 7-Stories hand me a big purple and green feather (how'd it get in my stuff?!?), then turn toward the audience. "Seems we'll have to comply with the lady's wishes." He grin back at me. "An unexpected twist to your first episode."

He make a show of studyin' my projections. The crowd scope my data too, eyes buggin' out, lower lips hangin' down, like it's a shock that a ethnic throwback know anythin' at all, let alone top-secret dirt. Just cuz we choose to reach back thru two hundred years and snatch wisdom offa the tongues of our ancestors, that don't mean we stuck on stupid!

A power jam cut short the graphic show-and-tell. Blackout shit can happen anytime in Los Santos, ain't orderly like at home. We ain't in the dark but a second, then a nice rosy color shine on everybody. This ole movie hall don't have emergency nothin', but wherever we go, Captain always riggin' somethin' up, just in case.

"You were saying?" 7-Stories give me the cue, like it's his script now.

He piss me off, but I wave Electro outprint at Jesus Perez' empty seat and calm myself right down. "Mr. Perez' money and ten thousand kilos of soybeans is goin' for Extra rehabilitation." If I can swing it! "No capital—no power, right? How long y'all goin' last as big bosses if you busted?"

7-Stories and the resta these thugs laugh like this the biggest joke, but the next mornin', missin' recon-food shipments miraculously appear outa nowhere. Entertainment crew bosses be furiously signin' Extras for jobs on location shoots. Three castin' directors find a "misplaced" med-shipment while they shoppin' for talent at Extra camps in the Nada wasteland. Now how you "misplace" a thirty meter med-transport but find it alluva sudden when my Captain be filmin' a report on Extra rehabilitation?

I try to feel good for a minute, like I done somethin', then Jenassi tear into me, say I ain't have the right to threaten these gangstas or use the digital divide against 'em. Due process, not hackin' and data-chillin' assets be the way to a lastin' peace. Can't resort to terror tactics, gotta find a way to change they spirits. (Since when did he get religion?) He goin' try to undo the damage I did in Sol 'fore it backfire on us. He don't mention black-market soybeans.

On Friday Captain defuse a letter bomb addressed to me from my "fans." They probably wanna off me with paper cuz I'm a throwback. Entertainers like to kill you with metaphors, but Jenassi coulda sent it too. This evening I get a invite from Ghost Dancers, IN MY TRANSPORT, parchment wrapped in purple-eyed feathers, layin' on a pillow. "If you liked Sol, you'll love Paradise Healthway." The

Captain pitch a fit. How the hell Ghost Dancers break our codes, get insida my bedroom and ain't leave a trace or a trail?

Jenassi be right about one thang. 7-Stories too. Who the hell am I to meet these illusion junkies on they channel, Major, and get to deep change? I ain't foolin' nobody, so come clean, why'd y'all send me to ambassador on the frontline? I mean, I wanna turn the tides of history, but that sure ain't one of the seven universal stories. And what about you? You in with the good guys or the bad guys? Or playin' both sides against the middle?

Let me hear from you.

Lawanda

10: Studio City, Los Santos
(September 26, Barrier Year 115)

> I'm mad-dog ambitious. Not about money or fame, but about being able to say what I mean, about every frame carrying people into my vision. Nothing else matters.
> —Tadeshi Mifune, *Surviving the Future, Last Minute Notes*

The Wovoka, born-again Sioux spiritual leader, and his Ghost Dancers were a guilt-mongering, retro death cult not even recognized by the Treaty. What did Dancers expect—crashing a screening in full regalia? Of course they'd get shot at. The Wovoka's voodoo only worked on viruses—Dancers weren't immune to bullets. And no matter what Achbar Ali or any baldheaded, mystic weirdo thought, nobody wanted to see Ray Valero play hero except on screen. Ray sank into his comfort chair and let the screening room blur out of focus.

On screen, a crescent moon hung in a navy blue sky. The music swelled: ancient violins and drums, ethnic throwback music—a Celtic ballad. Below the moon, the Great Wall of China vibrated. A woman in furry pelts and high-tech boots scaled the Andes. Libraries in twenty-first century Abidjan glittered. Two kangaroos hopped away from an old woman playing a didjeridoo. A crowned nineteenth century colossus reached up from the Atlantic with a torch. A radar technician, played by Ray Valero, glanced beyond a woman he was seducing to a blaring computer and groaned. Impossibly, it was a moonlit night all over the world, over a hundred years ago.

"What the hell?" The radar technician talked at his computer. "That thing's off the charts." A blond blur of a woman shrugged and pulled up her lingerie strap.

The computer went dead, along with the lights and an old-style video box in the corner. Everywhere blinked out: just the black bowl of heaven remained. Violins and drums cut abruptly. Silver shards of energy ripped apart the night sky. The Barrier exploded into the frame, a shower of colored bubbles caught in jagged sheets of light. In its wake, the Great Wall was a thin ribbon of dust on crumbling mountains; skyscrapers toppled and disappeared as Abidjan slid into the sea, as the entire Côte d'Ivoire boiled away. In deafening chaos people scrambled across the screen, trampling each other. Again jagged shards of Barrier energy broke apart the image. Sudden quiet, except for the didjeridoo, as the Barrier sliced through the Earth's crust and soared into the atmosphere like a fluffy cloud-mountain, blotting out the moon. A blond blur ran into the milky Barrier mist and set off a rainbow explosion. The radar technician, olive skin, square jaw, curly dark hair falling in eyes the color of a Barrier dawn reached for the blond, but halted at the Barrier's edge. A tremble in his full lips slowly built into a total body convulsion.

The jaded audience in the screening hall gasped. Even Ray had to snatch a breath. The sequence looked as good as it felt when he was shooting it. Maybe this Entertainment wasn't just epic slop.

Ray glanced at Aaron. The director watched with a stony face; he ate popcorn from the dispenser in his armrest, crunching one kernel at a time.

On screen, missiles and fighter planes blasted off from land and sea toward the now crystalline surface of the Barrier. Earthquakes and tidal waves assaulted cities and forests, and rearranged the face of the Earth. The sun came up; the Barrier Wars had begun. The deafening chaos of mob violence rushed in and out of view. A child whimpered. The camera wound through miles of debris. It paused at the gigantic spiked crown and monster torch in a shattered fist, then moved out to sea. An ocean liner, caught in a whirlpool, slammed into the Barrier, and winked out of existence. Colored jewels of light sparkled on calm waves. Overhead, the Barrier loomed like a frosted glass veil. Missiles and fighter planes flew into the dazzling surface and disappeared. A line of Canadian geese drifted across the sun. Nuclear explosions mushroomed, at first in the distance, but the camera zoomed too close and the screen went white.

The radar technician dashed out of gray smog. Bloody and ragged, he zigzagged through a bombed-out lab. A corpse tripped him up, and he almost dropped a small computer and a large weapon. Clutching these high-tech scraps to his chest, he screamed into a cell phone that had gone dead, then hurled it. A dirty, hairy hand snatched the phone from the air. A gang of men jumped into the frame, pouncing on the radar technician. He crashed onto the concrete floor, and his computer was totaled; maybe his jaw was broken. Anti-science terrorists pounded him. In the confusion of bodies, the radar technician cocked the large weapon. Just as he would have blown his assailants away—

A kangaroo hopped up to the Barrier, stared at jagged sparks in the misty veil of energy, then hopped across a jackknifed bridge to a freeway littered with abandoned cars. The Barrier Wars were spiraling out of control. Tattered refugees streamed across a bloody river. In a field of rubble, an upside-down bicycle wheel spun furiously next to a half-naked man perched on a toilet bowl. The man wept as mobs broke into the frame from every direction and clashed over devastated land. Combatants slid from view, and the camera plunged into fiery pits of burning bodies. In the aftermath of bullets and bombs, bacteria and viruses raged; infected people exploded from within, their organs, bones, and muscles bursting. The camera revolved around flames and melting flesh as it hurried through the megademic.

In the audience, Ray closed his eyes and let his head fall back; the fire virus had almost killed him. This first *Transformers* episode didn't mangle history too badly. Ray just should have brought food. The Ghost Dancers and their dark-haired companion had put a hole in his stomach; yet he could never bring himself to eat stale dispenser-popcorn.

Hot breath tickled Ray's neck. "You all right?" A guard nudged him with the butt of a weapon.

Ray sat up with a jolt of adrenaline. "I'm fine."

"So watch," Aaron said. "Look lively or else."

"You gonna shoot me if I don't?"

On screen it was night. The climber in furry pelts vaulted out of her tent, which clung to the cliffs of a glacial mountain in Patagonia. An avalanche thundered behind her; the Barrier loomed in front. Panic filled her eyes, and then the Barrier unfurled like a crystal flower, revealing an opening. An instant before the collapsing snow mountain swept her off the cliffs, the climber lunged through the portal. The deafening blast of the avalanche was muffled. The climber raced down the Barrier corridor toward a green opening. Electric rainbows sparked and chimed around her. Humid heat made her strip down to camisole and panties. She emerged from the Barrier under cathedral trees in a coastal rain forest. The camera rushed through hanging vines, past the bulging cheeks of the old woman playing didjeridoo, to a family of sea mammals leaping above choppy gray waves. Beyond them in the Barrier, a crystal archway led to azure water. The sea mammals swam off into the Wilderness, and the ocean corridor dissolved.

People in the audience snickered, and Ray cringed. The avalanche-sea mammal bit was too cliché—the sort of mythic image that embarrassed desperados. He looked over at Achbar, who stared back at him, mumbling to himself, jabbing his finger in the air. Ray grabbed his chin and shook the tension out of his lower jaw.

"Why do actors flap their jaws around like that?" Aaron said as Ray accidentally chomped down on his tongue.

"We can't shoot people when we're nervous or pissed off!" Ray said, wondering why Ghost Dancers would risk their lives to watch this Entertainment.

Aaron whispered into his personal Electro then leaned over to Ray. "A few warning shots, nobody dead. Feel better?"

"Should I believe you?"

"Of course." Aaron turned back to the Entertainment. "I don't lie to you."

On screen, the Barrier Wars petered out. Gangs captured Los Santos. Europeans gone native shepherded by African gurus over-ran the rain forest settlements of New Ouagadougou. In Paradigma ragtag nerds and battle-scarred warriors hunkered down in the ruins of big cities, defiantly declaring democracy. Everywhere unwanted refugees were turned away or shot down. Bodies hurled at the Barrier exploded into points of color. A boy with tousled blond hair and tear-streaked face whimpered in a close shot. The wounded radar technician raced away from a mob and grabbed the child. He ran with him to the edge of the Barrier then turned to face metal pipes, guns, and twisted faces. Sucking in a deep breath, the technician ran into a corridor. The Barrier irised shut and halted the mob.

The radar technician, hand in hand with the child, limped over mounds of rubble. In between their jerky steps, the technician spit blood on shattered stained glass. A rifle, slung over his bandaged shoulder, shifted onto a wound. He grimaced as they shuffled past a blasted sign advertising holiday trips to Mars in English, German, and Japanese. The camera pulled back to a long shot of a wasteland and two human specks. The Barrier loomed before them, a dazzling rainbow mountain with corridors branching in three directions.

The technician sank into rubble and sand.

"We can't stay here. Everything is dead," the child said.

The technician dropped the rifle, scooped up the boy, and limped down a corridor. They disappeared into hazy light as the old woman played didjeridoo under cathedral trees. Stick players and dancers joined her. The Healer from the Andes rocked with the music, the colored beads and bones at her neck banging against each other.

"We can't stay here," Ray said to himself as the scene blurred out of focus.

11:   Cross-Barrier Transmission/Personal
(September 26, Barrier Year 115)

From: Lawanda Kitt on diplomatic mission to Los Santos

To: Elleni Xa Celest in New Ouagadougou, New Ouagadougou

What up? How you doin'? They treatin' you right? Armando don't share official communiqués, and the facticity of Los Santos news channels definitely be a negative number. Course ain't nobody gotta tell me you kickin' butt in the New O, cuz I know that already. When Prime Minister Jocelyn fast-track me to Vice Ambassador, you say, buzz you if it get rough. Well, it be rough to the third power. All I can do not to come out my face at these fools.

So, yesterday, I'm inspectin' a seasonal corridor and a lady drive in from Paradigma. Got some mickey-mouse scrambler and wanna scam mass destruction weapons thru the Barrier, like she can hide shit behind static. Barrier let her get all the way 'cross, then blow when she exit. Ain't ice just her, but every last soul in the corridor, durin' a crush hour too. Never hearda that before. Corridor turn to a storm of crystal, slicin' up transports and people, then spacetime like bust apart. I blink twice and the Barrier be smoky undulations rollin' 'cross the horizon again. No sign of a corridor, nothin'. Ain't that some stuff? I lose it right in the VIP lounge over the real food buffet, howlin' and shit at the lobster and zucchini, very undiplomatic. If it wasn't for the Captain...

Folk say you safe in a seasonal, long as you don't show your ass. The Barrier only zap big-bomb-runners and smugglers, then business as usual for everybody else. This time, the whole damn corridor collapse and nobody, comin' or goin', can get thru. Still.

You the Barrier queen: do that make sense to you?

So us VIPs be all jacked up, ain't nobody talkin'. Customs is chasin' down records on the dead and the idiot that put the woman up to this suicide run swagger in to claim his booty. Clueless motherfucker be advertizin' how he can transport anythin' to anybody anywhere. Thinkin' he's all that, up to when Boss Samanski's squad nail his ass. They get the whole story outa him in less than ten. I don't ask how. (Captain snoop the interrogation, not me.) Turn out, the sucker be in with renegade Paradigma scientists—they got some kinda gene-art bio-scrambler that he claim scam contraband thru the Barrier once before.

"Why are you here?" 7-Stories, fancy-butt director, be in the VIP lounge too, stuffin' his face with dirt vegetables at the buffet. "Expecting a shipment? Too bad, huh?"

Just 'tween you and me—this gangsta Zone be workin' my last nerve. I'm at the seasonal, kinda scopin' the joint for a getaway, just in case. Barrier nip that.

"Downtown Angel City's booty-ugly and funky too," I tell 7-Stories. "Can't go nowhere 'less you all suited up. Toxic. I needed me some fresh air, countryside." Captain smirk at this lie. We hangin' in a wasteland.

"You want crystal palaces, you should go to New Ouagadougou," 7-Stories say.

"Maybe." I puff up, try to look important. "When I finish ambassadorin' here."

"Talk about gene art, witchdoctors can bring a whole species back from the dead."

"I believe it when I see it." I exchange looks with the Captain, who shrug.

"This corridor coming apart, quite a spectacle," 7-Stories say, like he been watchin' a show. He guzzle a liter of Jolt, and the pink drain out his chizzled cheeks. Man lean way too close to me and burp a nasty aftertaste all up in my face. "I bet you know where I could get my hands on one of Tadeshi Mifune's genius bio-corders..."

"Damn, is that all you can think of?" I say.

"Tadeshi was a fierce director, could get anything on film." He still whisperin' just at me. "She was tight with you Paradigma nerds. I could make it worth your while."

My eyes is achin', scramblin' up the view, and butterflies be partyin' in my stomach. "We just witness a massacre—a thousand folk never goin' home again, and you dealin'?"

"Didn't know 'em." He shrug. "My whole family went for organs. I got a reprieve because Paradigma middlemen didn't want to glut the market and have prices drop."

I ain't goin' let him guilt me. Throwbacks never could afford the organ market no how. "You lucky," I say.

"LUCKY? I was an Extra five years. I've seen everybody die, every kind of way."

"So you should be pissed at these lyin', murderin' smugglers and do somethin'..."

"What? Join the rebel Extras? No way, lying and cheating gives you a survival edge."

"And the sermon today is from Machiavelli." I have lost my cool.

"Seriously, ethics and altruism are overrated. I'm talking from experience. What can you expect from a bunch of selfish genes?"

"I've seen folk with a whole lot less do much better than this," I say.

"Settlement girl, getting homesick for the 'hood, huh?" 7-Stories kiss my hand. "Come visit me on location. I got sets you'd love:

Rockefeller Center, Neuschwanstein, Abidjan." He struttin' off to a squad of thugs in the outer lobby and yell over his shoulder at me, "Or maybe that's not ghetto enough for you."

This gangsta sure know how to toggle somebody's switch.

Ellington, where I'm from, ain't no trophy suburb, just a poor settlement. Buildings barely holdin' themselves up, ain't tryin' to look good too. Not much better than Angel City. That's what we get bein' throwbacks. But I love how Ellington taste, real food every Monday mornin', no recon-slop—grease sizzlin', hickory smoke ri-din' the breeze, candied yams, cornbread and greens, refried beans and cilantro salsa. Even after mad chickens and terminal wheat, nobody turn a empty stomach away. Ellington all the time soundin' good too—and just the faces of my friends, how they step and strut, swing they hips. Saturday night in candlelight, boogeyin' they brains out, rhymin' on anythin'. Power-outs can't cramp real style, words is all the electricity we need. The poet posse track down the truth, make it sound sweet and on the beat, star catchers and dream rappers, gettin' down, getttin' funky, folk who can talk the ugly outa anythin', hip hoppin', astral poppin' into your heart. Throwbacks all the time choosin' who we wanna be, no matter what be comin' down on us.

7-Stories don't know shit about it.

Captain drag me outa that VIP lounge and say a good diplo-mat wouldn't let this gangsta get to her, but 7-Stories sure get to me. I figure you understand, puttin' up with Sidi and that uptight Council majority. Don't you just wanna strangle 'em?

Contraband explosion cool my jets 'bout escapin' down a sea-sonal. (Don't believe the spin Boss Samanski put on this disaster. Everybody in that corridor was not frontin' contraband.) I'd appre-ciate any tips you got on sloggin' thru BS. Geraldine would know what to do. Sis probably make sense of the collapsed corridor too. I been livin' in the shadow of her genius too long. I guess I ain't used to thinkin' thangs thru. Barrier's gettin' funky tho. Captain say when it's time to go home, we goin' hook up with you, Elleni. That's a relief.

Is 7-Stories talkin' out the side of his mouth or can y'all shamen really bring a species back from the dead? Let me hear from you, when you get a minute.

Lawanda

12:   Studio City, Los Santos
(September 26, Barrier Year 115)

> The stories we tell, tell us.
> —Geraldine Kitt, *Junk Bonds of the Mind*

The Transformers' theme music petered out. The giant Electro-screen went blank and soft lights powered up in the auditorium. The audience sat dazed in their comfort chairs. Danny Ford choked back tears as he squeezed Ray's shoulder.

"What is this!" Ray tousled Danny's rainbow hair.

"New kidneys too." Danny grinned.

"Oh." Ray checked the snap judgment. The kidneys didn't have to have come from the organ market. "Done well for yourself."

"Not as good as you." Danny pointed at the screen.

"Old-fashioned potboiler."

"The witch girlfriend—that's a freaky wrinkle."

"Jealous?"

"Not my cut of meat. Never pegged you for a politico, though."

"Look who's talking, Carl Samanski's right hand!"

Danny sighed. "Carl's too smart for his own good. No room for A-listers."

"He's got you." Ray smiled.

"He could do better; our whole way of life is on the line." Danny noticed Aaron and Achbar approaching. "I'll catch up with you, later."

"If something better doesn't catch you first," Ray said.

"I mean it, for old times' sake." Eyes glistening, Danny brushed his lips across Ray's brow and exited through the sniffling crowd. Danny was a serious fan, but Ray hadn't expected a weepy response from studio sharks or thug guards, hadn't expected to be so moved himself. Watching *The Transformers* made him long for a home he'd never had. Aaron knew how to hit people where they lived.

"It needs juice." Aaron offered Ray a flask of Jolt. "More drama."

Ray swatted the drink away. "I don't touch that slop."

Achbar rested his chin on the walking stick. "Just because it's a story doesn't mean you can tell it." Everyone leaned in to hear what else the production guru had to say. Achbar took several deep breaths but said nothing more. The audience shuffled away.

"It was Healers in the rain forest, not throwbacks," Ray said.

"We gotta cut that ethnic throwback doo-doo-die thing any-how," Aaron said.

"Didjeridoo. I don't think Aboriginal women played it back then—"

"Never let the facts get in the way of a good story."

"Is that the deal?"

"The shaman Frau walking from glacier to rain forest... too much."

"Not one of your seven stories, huh?" Ray slid cold feet into his boots.

"You should save a couple cute babes." Aaron opened anoth-er Jolt flask. "That daredevil stuff you do with Greta Allen or Bella Lee."

"Greta died last week. Some quack gene artist put up a shingle on the Interweb and—"

"Are we in a bad mood? You didn't even like Greta." The ceiling went dark, and the emergency aisle lights glowed a sickly green. "What's with the power, guys?"

Ray looked around for Achbar. He had disappeared. Footsteps scurried about them. A duster or cape fluttered against Ray's cheek. He gripped the armrest, his breath suddenly shallow.

"It's just people leaving, Valero." Aaron picked at popcorn stuck in his teeth. "We need a flashy scene with a *Vermittler* like Elleni, sticking her hand right in the Barrier, making her own corridor, for real. We'd get a lot of hits to see that."

"You want Elleni?" Ray's throat burned.

"Elleni could be good." Achbar's voice boomed from behind them somewhere. "If you work the technology."

"Elleni would never do it," Ray said.

"What if *you* ask her to do a corridor—not a fucking eight-lane highway, something simple?"

"Did you cast me thinking that could get you Elleni too?" Ray asked.

"I try to optimize every investment," Aaron said.

Ray stood up. "Elleni couldn't put up with—"

"Sidi's on her ass too. Retro New-Ager battles *Vermittler*—that's a final episode. Sidi's not hard on the eyes either." Aaron started shooting this Entertainment in his head. He furiously tapped notes on his magic pad.

"Sidi Xa Aiyé, daughter of Earth, would just as soon see you swallowed up by the sea or blown out into space before she'd set foot—"

Unedited images flashed on the screen: a full-moon night at the Barrier cove in the Ecuadorian Wilderness. Sea mammals swam with an old woman at the edge of death. Celestina, at her crossover ceremony—that's where Aaron was going with the sea mammal/goddess bit, cashing in on retro-nostalgia. A silver polyhedron glided out of the Barrier and soared through the sky. Golden spits of energy surged around the almost spherical ET ship as it dropped to the surface of the water. A porthole in the vessel opened at sea level. Celestina and the grinning sea mammal were scooped up, and the ship took off again. A Barrier tendril surged off screen, splashed Ray's face, and burnt his cheek. He swallowed a scream.

"Whoa!" Aaron focused on a screen outside his mind. "Cut that now!" He vaulted to his feet. "And lock it up."

The Electro-screen went dead, and lights popped on. Ray clenched a couple hundred muscles and shut his eyes. Behind his lids, the dark-haired woman and Ghost Dancers floated by in a river of blood. It was as if Elleni or the Barrier touched his mindscape with visions. Or maybe he didn't have the stomach to work in Los Santos anymore. He opened his eyes and shook his head, trying to break up the image and get back to the here-and-now.

"Somebody leak your surprise ending, Aaron?" Achbar said from the open back door. Ray noted no bodies in the street beyond, but what did that prove?

"Stick to fantasy, boss." The AD ran for the booth. "Nobody gives a shit about that." The bottom of his jumpsuit was stained with mud or...blood.

"I don't think you know who to trust." Achbar lifted his walking stick in salute. Guards aimed weapons at him from the last rows. One shot off a round, and projectiles smashed into the sound-absorbent ceiling. Achbar barely flinched. "Come talk to me, Aaron, when you get the time. I like to play with fire too. Bring Valero." As Achbar vanished, the AD pounced on the loose-trigger guard.

"Somebody's going to get killed." Ray sealed his boots with shaking hands.

"You-all clear out. I gotta think!" Aaron herded his A-team to the exit. "You too, Mose."

Moses didn't budge. "I say, only deal with trouble once. Do a fast, lethal strike and—"

"OUT!" Aaron shoved Moses through the door, then walked down the aisle favoring his right foot. "Not you, Valero. I want to talk to you."

Ray's stomach somersaulted.

"What do you know about this?" Aaron limped toward him.

"Nothing." Ray replied evenly. "What're you asking me?"

"You saw the ET ship come out of the Barrier at Celestina's crossover ceremony."

"Official Los Santos policy says there was no extraterrestrial ship." Ray sneered. "No visitors from the great beyond. Mass hallucination."

Aaron was in his face. "You were at the ceremony, acting like a devout Healer, doing the rituals and the rites for Celestina."

"Who's to say those rushes aren't computer generated?" Ray wanted to back up but didn't.

"I shot some of the footage," Aaron said. "Don't bullshit me."

"If you were there…" Ray didn't remember Aaron being there.

"Computers can't fake the Barrier. Most bio-corders can't even record it. When your girlfriend did that special-order corridor, our crew got nada, just wiggly slop."

"Oh yeah?" Ray hated Elleni mucking around with spacetime, but it had its advantages.

"Tadeshi's bio-corders got an actual piece of the damn Barrier, not just images." He grabbed Ray's burnt cheek. "Nobody else can do that. How'd she do it?"

"Why don't you ask her?" Ray pulled Aaron's fingers off his face.

"Don't fuck with me! You and Tadeshi were tight. She confided in you." As Aaron spoke flecks of saliva spattered in Ray's eyes. "Maybe this sneak preview was your idea?"

Ray backed away. "I don't have access to Tadeshi's private Entertainment stock. Or her genius bio-corders. Only you've got that."

"Somebody's trying to sabotage my project. We've got a traitor on the team."

"Man, you're all over the place. Accuse me of one thing at a time." Ray was yelling now. Aaron worried constantly about treacherous crews or gangster bosses bumping him off. They'd let him finish the Entertainment first, though, since gangsters preferred stealing finished products. "You're paranoid."

"Me? You believe extraterrestrials scooped up a dying shaman and kidnapped Earthers to who-knows-where."

"Nobody was kidnapped! They all wanted to go."

"How do you know? Did she tell you that? Your, your..."

"Witch girlfriend." Ray slumped down in his seat. "Sure you want Elleni for *The Transformers*?"

Aaron stood over him. "No other studio will risk working with you, Valero."

"They wouldn't risk that ending either. But casting me and showing ET ships will guarantee it's a mega-hit! Of course if Samanski catches you doing outlaw shit before it's a hit, you can kiss Mifune Enterprises good-bye." Ray felt lightheaded. "I'm an actor. I couldn't film the Barrier to save my soul, and I'm not conspiring against you." He put his head between his thighs.

"Who is?"

"If I knew—" Ray kept his head down— "I'd tell you." His breath caught in his throat.

Aaron reached out to slap his back. "It just doesn't sync up."

Ray grabbed Aaron's hand before he hit him. "Does it have to sync up?" His cough sounded liked a brush fire.

"That ship coming out of the Barrier, snatching Celestina, Tadeshi, and company—that's dangerous footage." Aaron squeezed Ray's hand before letting it go. "Danger's bankable. With Lawanda and Jenassi putting the screws on, Entertainment's the only game in town." Aaron limped up and down a dark aisle.

Ray reached under the seat for his medicine bag. His hands brushed over squishy popcorn and dust.

"Nobody's gonna take *me* out," Aaron said.

"Good, because I want to act." Ray groped under the seat.

"You're a real-life hero, risked your life fighting for the Treaty, but..."

Ray got down on his hands and knees and peered under the chairs.

"Good thing Danny Ford didn't see Celestina flying off to— What're you doing?"

"I lost my bag." Ray choked down another brush-fire cough.

"What bag? You didn't have a bag in here." Aaron got down on the floor with him. "There's nothing here."

"Maybe I just thought I had it with me." Ray stood up and headed for the door.

Aaron got there first. "You're just going through the motions on camera, Valero, and that's not good for the product. We want audiences hitting back for the sequels."

"Yeah." Ray ran his fingers through his hair. "I can do better." He couldn't blame editing or a bad epic script for lousy acting.

"I've changed the production schedule. We're going on location, near Nuevo Nada."

Sweat beaded on Ray's forehead. His jaw felt like a vise, and his voice was stuck in the back of his throat. "You knew that before the screening. Why didn't you tell me?"

"Security measures. Don't get worked up. A location shoot won't take forever."

"I hate going on location."

"Look, we won't go crazy, gangbanging and killing Extras or whatever you're imagining. You saw for yourself. We didn't mistreat a single Extra shooting the first episodes." Aaron put his arm around Ray. "You need to work with more actors instead of opticals. You're better at playing opposite flesh."

"Opposite women, you mean."

"Yes, and skin is cheaper..."

Ray barely listened as Aaron, apparently now in a jovial mood, rattled off notes and anecdotes like he'd forgotten the Ghost Dancers and the security breach. Aaron couldn't sustain terror like Ray could; that's why he was a director. Ray tried to breathe deeply. A coughing jag blurred his thoughts.

Aaron jumped away from him. "Are you coming down with something?"

Ray shook his head. "Dust," he lied and stumbled over nothing. "Allergies."

Aaron grunted and got back on track. "Celestina, that dead Healer witch, I did her a favor once, now she's handing us the keys to the kingdom. Don't you love irony?"

"Irony's okay." Ray had definitely brought his medicine bag with him. He had several treatments to go before he'd be rid of the fire virus. And someone had stolen the bag right from under his feet. He'd come to Los Santos to make art, for his health.

Some cure this turned out to be.

13: *Seelenwald,* New Ouagadougou
(September 27, Barrier Year 115)

"Memory is the master of death and the host who welcomes a bright future!" Elleni smashed Femi's funeral urn against a calabash filled with seawater. Splinters from both vessels sliced into her flesh. Cold seawater soaked through thin rayon pants to her skin. Femi's ashes clumped into gray clots at her toes as tiny cuts oozed blood. Elleni stood at Celestina's ceremonial grave in a grove of cathedral trees and prepared to "conjure the spirits." The trunks of the trees groaned as dark bushy crowns swept across the stars. Elleni shivered and stifled a moan. Only for the Barrier, for Celestina would she come out on a chilly, moonless night to *Seelenwald*, the forest of souls, and perform a nuptial ceremony for the dead. Unruly braids demolished her syn-silk bandana and wriggled into her mouth. She spit out the bittersweet hair. "Mingle the ashes" had sounded so easy—until she was faced with old-time ritual and mythology. Recently, nothing that she attempted proved easy.

"Celestina, Femi, you live on in the changes you made and in the stories we tell." The two shamen had bitterly opposed one another for more than fifty years. Now after their deaths, Elleni's task was to bring them together—if she read the signs right. *No enemies.*

Dancing a tight circle, Elleni held the cracked urn and broken calabash up to the stars. Light from New Ouagadougou City turned the western sky salmon-pink and washed out all but the most potent cosmic lights. She placed the funeral vessels in the tree roots. She had planted this grove herself, including the wispy alora vines—Celestina's favorite. The iridescent blossoms opened only at night. The leaves were poisonous unless consumed with the flowers; combined, they sharpened the senses, opened the mind to "healing" spirits, even brought a person back from madness. Elleni chewed leaves and blossoms, savoring their sweet, oily taste. She gathered up the cracked funeral vessels and stood stone still, wondering what "spirits" would come.

In minutes, hundreds of weaver ants slid down alora vines into Elleni's hair. She made herself smell like home, like the queen, a shaman trick she'd learned from Celestina. A tapestry of motion covered her head. Diligent workers braided her into their nest. With a practiced shake of her hair, she dispatched most of the spindly bronze insects into the breeze. Ants rained down to the ground and ran in spirals across Celestina's shallow grave.

"Mother of my mind and spirit, I've kept my promise. I have stolen Femi's ashes and mixed them with the ocean that claimed your soul. With this ceremony I recall the love that bound you two together in life." She scooped up salty ashes and dribbled them on the grave. "The dead don't remember the living, Celestina, and you *chose* death. Femi also. So why do you haunt me? Why has the Barrier closed its heart to me? I feel the danger but cannot read its face. I am an ignorant, unworthy initiate, fumbling through life. Tell me how I can set the world back on its course. Grant me wisdom and vision."

She lifted the broken vessels again to the stars. Water and ash sloshed into her eyes. She couldn't blink the sting away. "*Was für ein Wunder ist das Leben*! Yet today it is difficult to rejoice. Tomorrow…" So much prayer, even in old German, made her tongue crawl. Elleni hated long-winded ceremonies, especially those to recall the dead. She skipped the endless praisesongs and jumped to the end. "*Igi kan ki s'igbo*," she said in Yoruba. "One tree does not make a forest."

Elleni poured the final libation of ashes and ocean on a grave where no flesh rotted and no bones decayed. Her sister Phoolan with Celestina, Tadeshi, the scientist Geraldine, and the other lucky ones had gone off-world in an ET ship on a grand adventure, while *she* was stuck on Earth making sense of Barrier gibberish and realizing somebody else's impossible dreams.

"*Igi kan ki s'igbo*," she said again, trying not to feel sorry for herself. How many trees were in her forest? She felt Awa's cool lips on her forehead, Ray's arms around her waist, Lawanda's words sizzling in her ears, and the dance of the Barrier in her head. Were they enough?

"*Aṣe*," Elleni whispered and deposited Femi's funeral urn, the broken calabash, and a small telescope, talisman of Celestina's great passion, under the arching cathedral tree roots. Femi's ashes had yet to mingle with the dirt. It took every micron of her discipline not to scoop up the gray sludge and scatter it from a distant mountaintop.

A wave of Barrier fever made Elleni's lips burn. The Barrier called her once again! Elleni hugged the cathedral sapling she'd planted at Celestina's death. Its glassy black trunk was already three times her height and too thick for a single embrace. A chain of weaver ants braided nests in its bushy crown.

"I miss you, Celestina," Elleni murmured. "We parted badly, so much we never got to say to one another." She pressed her cheek against cool ebony, dug fingernails into marble-hard bark, then glanced around the grove for spies on her grief. A weaver ant soldier slid down an unruly braid and pitched itself at distant ground. Otherwise, she was alone. "Celestina, I try to honor your vision. *You* would know what to do! *You* would know how to reach Sidi and the Healers Council, how to turn their minds and spirits to peace."

The cracked urn sliced into Elleni's toe, and blood dripped on a wayward ant. Other ants quickly surrounded it, eagerly sucking up the droplets. The Barrier's burning call spread across Elleni's back and buttocks, down her arms and legs. Her eyes steamed up. She'd never felt the call so intensely.

"The Barrier is changing. The great shamen are dead…Who am I but a faint shadow?" She crushed the urn and calabash and scattered the pieces in the grove. As she slung her medicine bag over her back, yellow tears fell from her hair onto dark earth. The ants avoided this acidic brew. "I am not you, Celestina."

Heading for the Barrier, Elleni danced off through the underbrush without disturbing the rodents or birds who nested in the dense tangle of branches, roots, dirt, and decaying leaves. Her feet beat a hypnotic rhythm against the earth; the Barrier's call was a sharp ache in her chest, a buzzing on her skin. Her hair sparked green static. Elleni felt a twinge of reluctance. Her trust in the Barrier had frayed.

Someone purred at the edge of her awareness. Elleni danced in place. She sensed a large mammal stalking her in the dark. Dipping into its mindscape, she felt its attraction for her fleshy scent and ample muscles, for the promise of succulent organs. Elleni whirled to face the predator. Her startled adversary halted and sniffed the damp air. Spacetime dilated as they considered one another across a puddle of scum. The creature was foreign to her, a great cat from the Wilderness, marking new territory. Panic coursed through Elleni's veins. What was this species doing in New Ouagadougou? Trying to ward off the rush of emotion that flowed into its mental landscape from Elleni, the she-cat reared up on powerful hind legs, boxing and snarling at empty air.

Elleni growled. Her hair hissed and spit violet venom like a hundred black snakes poised for attack. The cat trotted off into the shadows, deciding to hunt an easier meal. Elleni phaseshifted to track the animal as it loped into the hills around New Ouagadougou City. She finally lost its singular magnetic thread among a jumble of similar patterns. Too many hungry predators and disoriented prey wandered down strange new corridors from the Ecuadorian Wilderness into New Ouagadougou. For one hundred years no seasonal corridors had connected the inhabited Zones to the Wilderness. The rules were in flux, the Barrier was changing, and she didn't know what to expect.

How could she have ever thought that a puny *Vermittler* commanded the Barrier?

Elleni vomited until her wretched stomach was empty. Her heart and lungs ached. Phaseshifting was murder on internal organs. She pushed back a wave of exhaustion, stretched achy leg muscles, then continued her journey-dance. Squabbling spider monkeys chased each other around cathedral trees. One hung by its tail and pelted her with nutshells as she danced by. Council robes billowed to the beat of her furious feet; her hands signed spirited images in the shadows. The monkey tossed ripe walnut flesh at her face. She caught it with her teeth and chewed quickly.

"What a miracle is life!" she said. "*Ein Wunder.*"

Signing in two-part harmony, she danced on, forcing all anxiety into her hair.

14:   Cross-Barrier Transmission/Personal
(September 28, Barrier Year 115)

From:	The Major, Head of Sagan City Secret Services
To:	Lawanda Kitt on diplomatic mission in Angel City, Los Santos
<u>Re:</u>	<u>Barrier As Lethal Work Of Art</u>
Question:	Can you be more specific about walking toward diplomat housing in Angel City and ending up at the Barrier in the Cripple Creek wasteland?
Assumption:	You don't mean you got lost; you believe forces disrupted spacetime and infected your will, resulting in an unintended Barrier confrontation.
Observation:	You should consider stress and your mental state as well as fantastic possibilities. Memory lapses aren't as uncommon as you might think.
Notes:	No such Barrier behavior has been reported in a hundred years of scientific observation. Not even in anecdotal, Barrier mythology. *Vermittler* are reported to commune with the Barrier, "read minds," alter spacetime perception, and influence behavior, but not over great distances. I have heard of "Barrier fever" but have no adequate definition. Rumors abound that Celestina, Femi, and other dead ancestors are interfering with *Vermittler* corridors, but I can't comment.
	Don't assume you know motives of "thugs" chasing woman into Barrier. Perhaps they use "snuff art" to camouflage other agenda. Also consider actions of mystery red head that might have prompted chase. Extras, rebel or otherwise, although members of an oppressed population in Los Santos, are not by virtue of oppression beyond suspicion.

Paradigma's underground choirs have inflated reputations (as if singing throwback music necessarily frees the mind). Mythic status and alleged radical creativity do not exempt these "singing nerds" from criminal intent.

Recommend: Don't get involved with disappeared scientists or other renegades. Keep focused on legitimate Extra issues and Treaty implementation. Monitor your mental states with bio-computer and do not jump to conclusions. Never willingly suspend your disbelief no matter how compelling the images.

Re: <u>Diplomatic Mission To Los Santos For Interzonal Treaty Compliance</u>

Assumption: *They* will all underestimate you. *I* know I can count on you.

Observation: You have the resources if not the official training. Do not underestimate yourself. Paradigma's energy crisis and natural resource disaster has brought Jocelyn, a relatively new Prime Minister and first woman to hold the highest office, under the gun. Despite her backing by Electrosoft Corp, she is wary of aligning with Elleni, a supposedly unscientific Healer. Yet Elleni, as a Barrier "griot"—translator, praise-singer, diplomat—isn't bound by a seasonal corridor schedule and can sculpt Barrier passageways anytime to go anywhere she pleases. She can also transport prohibited cargo—mass-destruction weapons or Wilderness animals and plant material (chickens, cows, wheat) extinct in inhabited Zones—through her corridors without fear of Barrier reprisal. Jocelyn would like unlimited access to the natural resources and wealth of the Wilderness. Who can blame her? Madame Prime

Minister juggles many contradictions. I am not un-sympathetic to her predicament.

Question: Why appoint a "passé" ethnic throwback "talkin' bad English" Vice Ambassador to Los Santos? Consider that language, despite science fantasy projections, is essentially conservative, hence our ability to communicate across generations. Even the hippest multi-channeling gearhead uses two-thousand-year-old metaphors, slang (such as "hip") from 1900 that's now standard, as well as jazzy, take-no-prisoners inspeak that leaves the rest of us down a corridor as the portal collapses. The battle over language, over naming and experienc-ing the universe, over what constitutes reality is always fierce. Ethnic throwbacks are ideal warriors in these gory cultural skirmishes. Sending you with Armando Jenassi to "ambassador at the front-line" is an exquisite tactic.

Notes: I am not part of a "setup." True, my waiting until the last microsecond to inform you gave you no chance to refuse your promotion to Vice Ambassador, but Jocelyn expected the Los Santos mission to fold without me. What happens now is anybody's guess. We have the advantage of surprise. (See attachments, not included in earlier info dumps, on diplomacy, Los Santos politics, re-cent history, and economics.)

Regarding "7-Stories"—artists in Los Santos be-come gangsters to control the production process. (Consider the paucity of women directors. In a de-cidedly macho, violent landscape, Tadeshi Mifune is the exception that proves the rule and even she has a man's name and a gangster persona.)

Turkey feathers are Ghost Dance paraphernalia—
a peace offering or invitation.

Recommend: To quote Celestina, "although the snake cannot
fly, it catches the hornbill whose home is in the
clouds." It is your time to script truth. Just take
care not to get yourself blown up.

Re: Of Course I Want To Talk To You

Observation: I have left Sagan City, crossed the Barrier through
a seasonal corridor, and am en route to New
Ouagadougou City via village hinterland. (See
attachment on ecosystem diversity.) The Treaty
Conference keeps me very occupied. I'm not one
for stories, and most of my activities are classified. That doesn't leave much to tell. Live, I would
discuss my recent analysis of Celestina's assassination and of events that transpired at her funeral.
Even after four years, Celestina is very much alive
in the imaginations of the people I encounter in
New Ouagadougou. Many claim the great shaman
is not actually dead. She allegedly communicates
in dreams, but also with non-sleepers during a full
moon when the incidence of "Barrier fever" sky-
rockets. Given her mysterious disappearance, ghost
stories abound, about Femi as well. I catalogue the
most outrageous and the mundane. But I'm breaking all my rules. When you are with me, it is more
difficult, but much easier. Contradiction is an aspect of complexity, yet I have never found its challenges invigorating.

Note: You were silent two weeks as well.

Recommend: Keep an open channel.

15:   Ghost Story

> Only the universe knows its every flash of light, its infinite
> whirling mysteries and countless elegant permutations. Initial
> conditions slip through even the finest sieve of perceptions.
> Uncertainty is a function of our ignorance, not of electrons,
> quanta, or other enigmatic bundles of spacetime. If the universe
> spoke the whole truth to us, our minds would explode.
> —Vera Xa Lalafia, *Healer Cosmology, The Final Lessons*

They say, *Death is afraid of Celestina.*

Villagers from New Ouagadougou even murmured this as a prayer to ward off disease. Yet after a century of scaring death, Celestina floated off the coast of the Ecuadorian Wilderness at her crossover ceremony, dying. A bird with no name glided over black sand and squawked at the moon. Southerly winds gusted through cathedral trees, cutting the surface of the water into inky froth. Celestina savored the ocean's buoyant warmth, its ripe seaweed smell, and prickly undercurrents. The synthetic skin covering her wounds dissolved, and blood drizzled out in hot eddies. Celestina had kept all her promises and would live on in the changes she'd made. Why should death be afraid of her anymore?

A family of dolphins swam a tight circle around her. The old matriarch Aieee!-Aieee! held Celestina's head above water, as if the shaman were a dying dolphin. Although Celestina could not speak with sea mammals in the sound beyond sound like a *Vermittler*, Aieee!-Aieee! always understood her. She would attend Celestina until the spirit passed. Just beyond the dolphins, close enough for her to witness tears, trembling lips, and clenched hands, a funeral entourage of Sagan City seavans hovered above choppy waves on a thin layer of air. Friends from every Zone had come to touch the water at the passing of Celestina's spirit. Once enemies, they were now her family, her country, the new world she had created. A hundred years of wounds and war, and she had signed the Treaty with her blood, *Ebo Eje*, a sacrifice to heal them. With such a final triumph to paint her mindscape, who would not rejoice in crossing over?

On an almond-shaped seavan, Tadeshi Mifune's camera crew rubbed their eyes and squelched yawns. They'd been waiting hours for the final moment. Celestina wanted to smile into their biocorders. This was, after all, not a sad passing, but her face muscles were sluggish. Or she couldn't remember how to smile. Elleni stomped in front of the cameras, her hair snarling at the cinematographer. Celestina managed a lopsided grin before Ray and Phoolan, Elleni's sister, pulled Elleni aft. Many reasons for Elleni to be angry, but the daughter of her mind and spirit should rejoice…

Lawanda Kitt hurried around the slippery deck of the neighboring seavan. She lit white candles in wooden bowls and handed them out to everyone. Arms reached across the water to pass lights from seavan to seavan. Lawanda gave the last candle to the Major who stood motionless in front of the seavan control panel. Celestina's eyes welled up as flames flickered around her on all five seavans. At a signal from Lawanda or perhaps the Major, the seavans settled down into the water, and everyone launched the bowls of light on the waves. Instead of offering a candle, Elleni tossed a roll of parchment, then she hugged Phoolan, and the *Vermittler* sisters sang in the sound beyond sound with the dolphins. Lawanda also sang—an astral lament. To Celestina's waterlogged ears, they sounded like distant angels. A hundred candlelights twinkled in the black water. Celestina floated against Aieee!-Aieee!'s belly in a warm water galaxy, yet her legs were cold and numb. Her arms seemed not to matter anymore.

Aieee!-Aieee! nosed a sputtering candle and Elleni's rolled parchment into the funeral circle. As Celestina lifted her head and reached for the soggy paper with her lips, she caught the Major looking away. His swarthy face and green-flecked angular eyes were blank. He gazed at the Barrier, which hung like a frosted glass veil under the moon. Didn't he hear the angel beside him? Or perhaps the Barrier called to him with urgent images.

Just hours ago, when Piotr Osama had taken aim and fired, the Major would have taken Celestina's place in the line of fire but arrived an instant too late. He caught her as she spiraled to the ground.

Her limp fingers slipped across his face; her blood splashed his pristine uniform. The Major held Celestina's wounds together. He could have chased down Piotr; instead he stopped her from bleeding to death with the clamps and sutures he carried in a weapons belt. He pressed his lips to her mouth and sucked death from her lungs. They raced in screaming vehicles from Tombouctou Observatory to Sagan Institute so he could hook her up to a breathing/heart machine. She pleaded with him to turn around, to take her to the Barrier, to let Elleni sculpt-sing a corridor to the Wilderness so she might die in the ocean surrounded by her new world. He wouldn't think of such a thing, he told her. Don't think, Celestina whispered before her voice gave out and consciousness slipped away. Though a torturer, a murderer, the Major brought her down to the water to die. *Was für ein Wunder ist das Leben.* He turned from the Barrier to face her again. Celestina strained to see if his thin mustache twitched, but the details of his face blurred. Did he have second thoughts, she wondered? Did she?

The Major took off his data glove and ran naked fingers through the fuzzy hair at Lawanda's neck. Everyone else watched Celestina. For her last breath, for the money shot, she heard the cameraman say. He sounded like Aaron D., but she couldn't make out his face. Lawanda leaned into the Major's touch and cried. So many crying angels...

Don't worry, rejoice in the new world we've made—my suffering is almost over and I welcome death, Celestina thought as Elleni reached across the waves to touch her. Aieee!-Aieee! blasted air and sea from her blow hole and doused the candle in Elleni's hands, but Celestina saw the flood of yellow tears and felt Elleni's shudder in her bones.

Today, it was hard to rejoice.

Celestina wanted to shout that one passing dreamer is not the end of dreams. But she couldn't remember how to shout or what she just thought or how she'd lost her feet her hands her back her breasts her mouth...

A smooth, silver polyhedron with so many facets it looked like a sphere dropped from a Barrier corridor in the sky and scattered the seavans and dolphins. Only Aieee!-Aieee! did not desert her. With no time for shock, Celestina and the dolphin were sucked through a cold, salty vortex into the alien ship. Celestina choked on rubbery seaweed and tiny fish with spiky fins. Just before losing consciousness, she thought *Death is afraid of Celestina.* Or was that Elleni touching her mind as she floated, weightless, at the edge of time, thinking funeral thoughts again and again?

"Elleni," Celestina said. "Mingle the ashes. Femi and me. No enemies."

The sweet song of dolphins chased away the last traces of her pain and...

Celestina floated in a magenta sea the temperature of her puckered skin, very much alive. The upturned bowl over her head was too shallow for sky. She looked down at her body. Mortal wounds had healed without scarring. How long had she floated here thinking in circles? Days, years? She clutched a roll of soggy parchment against her wrinkled, sagging chest. Elleni's funeral offering. She glanced around. No dolphins frolicked in the placid sea. She was alone. Blank translucent walls contained her and beyond the walls she saw darkness, broken by occasional smears of light. She felt the unmistakable presence of the Barrier and the faintest hint of Elleni. A chill slithered across her spirit.

"What's going on? Where am I?" She gagged. Panic threatened to overtake her. She slowed her breathing and chanted silently from Vera Xa Lalafia's *Final Lessons*: *If the Universe spoke the whole truth to us, our minds would explode...* She tried talking aloud again. "I am a shaman on a death journey! Who are you to kidnap my last moments?" She churned up the viscous, magenta fluid. Globules floated up in all directions—like magic or the weightlessness of space. "I've kept all my promises!" She flailed in the strange sea, her dark limbs and hennaed braids sending a shower of tiny magenta orbs in every direction. A string theorist, gene artist, a *Vodun* and Chi Gong master who had survived Double Consciousness, her mind was a fortress—yet she didn't want to face her conclusions. The Barrier carried her out to the stars.

Death was still afraid of Celestina.

BOOK III

*The spirit of acting is the travel
from the self to the other.*

Anna Deavere Smith

16:   On Location outside Nuevo Nada, Los Santos
(October 4, Barrier Year 115)

Something didn't sync up.

That was Aaron Dunkelbrot's last thought before falling asleep and his first thought as the shock alarm tore him from dreams to consciousness. Aaron surfaced in the back compartment of his location trailer, crumpled in a comfort chair, fire in his foot and a hammer in his head. He squinted through crusty eyelids at the disable button on his desk. It seemed miles away. Did he set the alarm or had it been triggered? According to the desk chronometer he'd been asleep four hours after working *The Transformers* for seven straight days.

Who would he have to kill for eight hours of peace?

A bundle of feathers in his chest pocket tickled his chin. Recognizing the blue-green eyespots and iridescent purple shimmer of wild turkey feathers, he flailed and drooled. The Wovoka, born-again Sioux spiritual leader and royal pain in the ass, summoned him to a Wounded Knee dance. Mahalia Selasie was probably driving them crazy. Aaron couldn't afford more Mahalia intrigue or a thousand-mile hike in the wasteland. But Dancers didn't take no for an answer. They would hound you to death and beyond.

The shock alarm screeched again. Aaron bolted from the comfort chair onto the cold synth-marble floor. The impact sent thrills of pain from his burning foot into his lower back. His sleeping quarters blurred, shapes breaking apart, colors slipping to gray then black, but the alarm's intermittent shriek wouldn't let him pass out. He fell against the wall and scoped the surveillance Electro for danger. Bugs slithered across a three-day old dinner; otherwise he was alone and had been alone *all night.*

Even fleas left a footprint, but Dancers got tail feathers up his nose without getting snooped. Why not just wake him up and tell him what the hell was going on?

He lurched toward the desk. Decaying salmon and rancid Gorgonzola made his gorge rise. For years he'd eaten recon-slop, eyeing rich stiffs in real-food delis, ready to murder for crumbs; now that he could afford sea fish and vegetables grown in dirt, he worked himself out of an appetite. Irony, he was drowning in irony. Aaron stuffed the feathers in a vase on his desk. Unzipping his rumpled jumpsuit, he staggered into the john. Sleep deprivation was punching holes in his mind. Sitting on the toilet, he blew a hit of Rapture.

"Damn," he cursed out loud as the toilet sucked away his jumpsuit and sprayed his ass with disinfectant. He'd been wearing the same clothes so long that his personal flora and fauna had gone wild. "Get a grip."

He stared at his naked form in the mirror: a perfect specimen. Before the Treaty, anybody poor with a runny nose or rich with a big mouth and the wrong attitude could get listed and end up "Extra." Most died on location, but Aaron had beaten the infections, the gang rape, the snuff takes, and stayed alive, barely. When Ghost Dancers found him, he was totaled. They patched him up and slipped him into Dr. Mahalia's operation. Sanctuary, she called it, a Promised Land.

"*Ein Wunder,*" said a voice in his head. The same voice had talked in his dreams.

Freaking out never made demons shut up or go away. "Celestina Xa Irawo, if you are well, I am well."

"Barrier burns flaring up *überall,*" Celestina said. He could just make out her sad eyes and hennaed braids at the periphery of his vision.

"What's up?" he said.

"Termites colonize your mind. They eat you from the inside out."

"Termites?" Aaron squeezed into a silver spandex jumpsuit so tight you could tell his religion. "What kind of retro-metaphor is that? Something for hunter/gatherers?" He donned a sparkling blue duster to match the jumpsuit. "How 'bout something useful?"

"You almost lost Ray."

"It's rough trying to tell your whole story. Throw me a bone!"

"Who are our enemies but our other selves?" Celestina said and vanished.

"Wait." Aaron glanced around the compartment, embarrassed.

No food, no sleep, and a gun at his head at every turn—that would make anybody crazy. Aaron stuffed his foot in an ice bucket, pressed a cold pack to his temples, and stumbled into the main compartment. He looked like a disabled superhero.

All twenty-five Electro wall screens ran in mute mode: classics, flashy ad-operas, studio updates, *Transformer* rushes, M. Enterprises hits. On the furthest wall screen, Carl Samanski tapped his lips in close up. Aaron stumbled over the ice bucket. The big boss was no demon, floating through his sleep-deprived mind. He was coming down a priority channel onto screen one, live. His cloud of white hair, droopy gray mustache, and puppy-dog eyes called to mind Albert Einstein. Aaron enabled his transmitters just as Samanski looked ready to break the connection.

"Carl," he said warmly.

"Aaron." Samanski scrutinized him. "You're a mess, Mr. D."

"Working too hard." He tossed the ice pack.

"Get some sleep. You entertainers don't know when to stop."

"And you do?"

Samanski laughed. "Yeah, but, I never sent a suicide squad your way to collect Mahalia Selasie." He shook his head. "Talk is cheaper, especially with a cooperative fellow like yourself."

Aaron barely held on to his balance. "Yeah?"

"Some hotshot's fronting my name, strutting down the wrong corridor, scamming you." Samanski looked sympathetic. "Rumor has it you're working hot property, with an outlaw edge. Controversy's good for business, but art ain't worth dying for, right?"

"Right."

Samanski leaned into the shot, eyes blazing like a mad scientist about to pass on the deadly secrets of the universe. "Want some advice?"

"Sure. I'm dying to hear what you got to say," Aaron said.

"There's a shitload of product out there. Competition is savage. What story hasn't been told a billion times? We don't have unlimited thrills and spills to offer. Probably boil it down to six or seven plots. The ancients had virgin territory to mark with genius—they didn't face an audience glutted on spectacle and addicted to hype. Fart and it was a great insight back then." Samanski quoted Aaron's thoughts, stuff he'd barely mentioned to anybody. "Life's a bitch, but what's the point whining? Somebody's going to make a megahit, why shouldn't it be you. Are you with me?"

"Of course."

"Some stories can't be told. People die trying, then nobody believes 'em anyhow."

Aaron stepped back from the screen. "Are you threatening me?"

"You're sharp, Dunkelbrot. I haven't met anyone sharper in a long time. I like you. But your problem is, you don't know who to trust."

"Is there anybody I can trust?"

"Rebel Extras are gaining ground." Samanski leaned back. "Too spicy for your taste? Check out our guests from Sagan City. Armando Jenassi wants us to believe he's harmless, a greedy hedonist—the man's a bad actor. But Lawanda Kitt's the genuine article, an old soul. You're both pro-Treaty—don't bother to deny it. I suspect you have a lot in common. Keep me posted." He broke the connection, and Moses's curly blue hair filled screen one. He was transmitting down the priority channel too.

"What is it, Mose?" Aaron's voice was scratchy.

Moses's head bobbed up, revealing puffy eyes in a streaked face. "Boss, I hate to…"

"I know." Aaron stuffed his numb foot into a boot. Moses always acted like the world was coming to an end in the very next frame. "Just spit it out."

"I'll show you." Moses adjusted his Electro field to a wide angle and walked through the ruin of the sea mammal sculpture at the Rock Center set. "Dancers blew it up. They're in with rebel Extras." He fished soggy gray feathers out of the fountain.

Aaron was about to explain those were pigeon feathers, not turkey feathers, but Moses stepped over a body in a moss headdress and bloody white robes.

"We plugged one of 'em, but the damage was already done." Moses did a close up on the battered silver face.

"Is he dead?" Aaron said.

"She's dead all right. Bullet through the brain."

"Did she say anything before you...plugged her?"

"She laughed, said we played for the wrong team, said Mahalia was on the loose."

Aaron groaned.

"I told you not to trust spirit warriors getting ready for the end of time. Just 'cause they helped you once, they can do no wrong? What kind of cracked logic is that?"

"Yeah, yeah. I'm on my way." Aaron broke the connection.

Samanski was right. Aaron didn't know who to trust.

17: Cross-Barrier Transmission/Personal
(October 5, Barrier Year 115)

From: Lawanda

To: Sweet, Sweet Major

You are some cold dark matter! Your personal transmission be about as close to absolute zero as a human can get. Why am I all surprised? We been together a coupla years, been all insida each other, and I don't even know your name. Is that top secret too? Or one of the rules you don't be breakin'? Captain won't tell neither. So, what, all y'all just a rank in the secret service of the Prime

Minister and nothin' else? Well damn, why ain't you a colonel or a general by now?

I do appreciate the diplomat info & instruc you sent and your up-front concern for my mental health. Haven't gone insane yet, but gettin' close. I had a coupla Celestina "visions" too, but it ain't nothin' some human contact wouldn't cure. I'd settle for live Electro exchange—my private channel be wide open 24-7, you just ain't tunin' in. What's the deal?

Los Santos folk got some funky personal Electros (the few who can afford it). Steada minipads & headphones, alotta of 'em wear monster half-masks. Look like bugs or aliens, and you never know what channel they be on. It's rude and they ain't got enough attention span to be spreadin' it 'cross ten Electro channels plus real life. I know you do split-channel too, Major, but there's alotta you to go around. I mean, I always know you're there, somewhere.

Never thought I'd be achin' for your face on a damn Electro-screen.

Armando got me four weeks "on location"—jitterbuggin' thru Sol, Angel City, Paramount Way, Nuevo Nada, plus a day trip to the Vegas-suck-down-site. Studios gonna wine and dine me, show me the sights, a few Entertainment adventures 'fore I hit Studio City and real negotiations. Armando and Hitchcock, the general secretary of this region who wear his lunch steada eat it, cook up this bullshit runaround to keep me outa they business. But Captain say I got these goons by the balls. Maybe the Captain's more objective...cuz I feel like I dashed offa cliff and I'm runnin' on air.

Sorry. I'm procrastinatin'.

Ghost Dancers send me a second invite—over the Electro this time—to check out healthcare for Extras. Word is Ghost Dancers ain't just religious fanatics committin' ritual suicide to bring back a dead past. They hooked up with rebel Extras and fought Los Santos' ganglords even though they didn't sign the Treaty. Some gangstas is still gunnin' for the Wovoka and other born-again Sioux leaders, so Indians be under real deep cover. You can't just search 'em out on the Interweb. But they sure know how to get to me.

Anyhow, yesterday on this born-again tip, Captain and me is unof-ficially walkin' 'round Paradise Healthway, a Extra "hospital" in the wasteland halfway between Angel City and Sol. Our visit be so unofficial, we have to leave the resta the squad and the bio-corder at the transport fifty meters from the entrance (which I know is risky and stupid, but...)

Paradise Healthway useta be a holdin' station for the organ market, where folk waited 'round to get chopped up. Ain't nothin' but nasty shacks and a big red circus tent surrounded by a steel mesh quarantine wall with half-ass power net shieldin' to keep folk in and out. Under the raggedy big top, patients be stacked on triple-decker shelves like aboard a slave ship, lyin' in they own (and every-body else's) puke, pus, and shit. We gotta shuffle down the slimy aisles sideways, single file, and we be bumpin' into patients' heads and feet all the way. Space-age drug-proof viruses and bacteria be havin' a field day. Folk rottin' away in front of my eyes. That make it hard to tell what landed 'em here in the first place. (I'ma send touch-up drawin's with the official report tomorrow. Hard to mind-doodle in my enviro-suit.) Why'n't they just do these suckers quick and get it over with?

Old folks say God don't like ugly. Which God is that I wonder?

Los Santos be so corrupt, anti-Treaty folk don't even bother to front. We talkin' bodacious scammin'. Gangbangers highjack ship-ments of herbs and supplies. Doctors, nurses, orderlies be collectin' hefty paychecks, don't never show for they shifts. I scoped the log-in records—just a few guards at the gate for lockdown. Healthway's Ouagadougian medical envoy, Zumbi, is a sorry-ass novice who couldn't make it thru *Healer First Aid*, forget the *Final Lessons*, and he gotta cover ten of these wasteland quarantine camps. That's ten thousand square kilometers and over twenty thousand sick peo-ple. Why'd the Healer Council send him? New O's settin' people up big time. I mean, Zumbi's heart be in the right place. He claim me and the Captain is tourist thrill-seekers and walk us past the guards. He even guide us thru the Electro-maze of records, highlightin' in-visible corruption. Ready to do whatever he can, but there ain't no tiger in his tank. Yellow skin gone gray, stringy hair in knots, hands shakin', one eye hangin' down slack—he look real sick hisself. Not much better than the patient he standin' over.

"Gene art backfiring," Zumbi say. "A lot of that recently. Not a pretty sight." A orderly, one of the healthier lookin' patients, dump the body in a waste bin 'fore I get a good look. "All I do is bury the dead," Zumbi complain. That's a metaphor, he mean throw the dead at the Barrier. I think sometimes he be tossin' live ones too. We walk by a little boy, look like he eat a bomb and explode. I'm starin' at him and can't move. "Fire virus," Zumbi say, steady mumblin' to hisself in old German or Swahili. You know how Healers be with metaphors and dead languages. He don't stop to check the kid out, just signal for somebody to dump him.

"This can't be happenin'. Elleni found a cure for fire virus: ants and that nasty tropical fruit, malangi?" I say, but Zumbi don't hear me. My Electro be on a private channel to the Captain.

"Malanga." The Captain push me to move on. "It doesn't seem that they have the fire virus cure here, does it?"

I'm 'bout to jump bad 'bout Healer shipments and greenhouses in the wasteland when the little boy open his big brown eyes and blink long dark lashes twice. He reach his hand out to me. I jerk back cuz I don't want him touchin' even my enviro-suit. His sallow cheeks flush a moment with color. "They said you were coming." Kid talk so quiet I gotta amplify the sound to the max. "I didn't believe them." He try to hand me a scrap of outprint. "I made you a picture." I have to force myself to snatch the slimy thang and shove it in my enviro-suit pocket. "Nothing ever happens like they say." Kid's voice ain't nothin' but air. "You're not a dream, are you?"

"I'm real, I'm here," I say, but only the Captain hear me.

Boy look down at hisself, insides splattered all over yellow underwear and naked knees. His face twist up, like he tryin' to cry or scream. Then the spirit leave his eyes, and his face go hard. The patient-orderly stumble up, draggin' a long, thin cart behind her. She roll the kid and his beddin' up in the lime green plastic they use for Barrier bio-waste.

"Said he wanted to be buried in the Promised Land," Zumbi say. I look at him funny, so he explain—"Dancer name for the Barrier. I try to grant last wishes. Everybody wants the Promised Land now."

Kid don't weigh nothin'. Orderly toss him on top the cart and stumble off.

I got on my high-tech suit & helmet with the vacuum seal; ventilator runnin' at max s'posed to keep me cool, collected, and germ-free, and still I'm gettin' sick all over myself. Everybody moanin', groanin', and gaggin'. Me too. How can people do each other like this? I gotta get outa this funky hellhole posthaste.

Captain grab my arm and say, "Nothing we could have done for him."

I switch my Electro to public speaker and make up a big lie for slack-eyed Zumbi, like I'ma meet up with hotshots and talk Treaty talk, try to do somethin' 'bout this health crisis mess. I break bad for a second, almost chokin' up with tears. "No way am I goin' just grin, shuffle alotta Electro outprint, and let folk croak in they own shit, when we got cures! No fuckin' way!" Now why I say alla that?

These terminally sick people hear me BSin' and think I'm a acupuncture ace workin' Chi "vital essence" like Elleni, come to replace the dip-dip, slack-eyed novice who be one step from the grave hisself. These terminals *believe* I'ma channel Chi and make 'em well with my bare hands. If they can just get me to touch they naked skin, spit down they throats, or stick acupuncture needles in they skulls, they won't have to suffer and die. Maybe they even live forever. Gangstas believe any ole no-sense crap. Proof ain't a issue at all. Plus they can't tell a ethnic throwback from a shaman/ *Vermittler*. False hope wash over 'em like a flash flood. Alluva sudden I got this horde of half-dead, crippled-up folk chasin' me down narrow aisles in a circus tent. Woulduv been funny 'cept we slippin' and slidin' thru bodily fluids and stumblin' 'round patients that ain't exactly mobile. Zumbi try to restrain 'em, but the mob beat him back and keep on comin'. You'd think sick folk'd be kinda slow too, but that ain't necessarily so. Runnin' as fast as we can, we knock over the pitiful medical equipment Zumbi done scrounged up and step on folk who don't even scream.

Finally we bust out the tent into the open and head for the gate. A coupla gangsta guards watch the show from a catwalk along the quarantine wall and crack up. Like we antique slapstick Entertainment, Whetstone Cops or somethin'. Please. Captain turn and shoot a volley over the sick folk's heads. Mob don't stop but a second or two, then they get a surge of adrenaline and pick up speed. Crutches, splints, and filthy, ole-timey bandages flappin' in the wind—I ain't seen no recon-skin. It's a ghastly sight: me and the Captain chargin' thru the wasteland in frontuva Day of the Dead parade. Gangsta at the quarantine gate think this the funniest joke he done ever seen. We ten meters away, and he crackin' up, closin' the gate on us, and chargin' up the power nets. I keep on runnin' cuz I don't believe any of this shit really be happenin'. Captain runnin' right beside me, but with a plan. Gangstas be underestimatin' your dream team, Major. Captain deploy one of your fancy scramblers and fuck up gate man's electromagnetism. He don't know what hit him. Power net shieldin' fizzle, gate swing open, automatic weapons drop offline. We run by the creep and don't explain shit.

"Can't be a power-out!" He mumblin' and fumblin' all over hisself, talkin' 'bout goddamned witchdoctors, like we zapped his retarded ass with magic! He don't notice the horde of livin' dead comin' right at him. Captain get our transport up and runnin' with the remote and be whisperin' commands to the home squad when we hear weapons explode behind us. Captain shove me toward the transport and swing 'round, weapons armed, ready to fight and die for me. That trip me right out.

But ain't nobody comin' at us! The crazy sick folk who breached the quarantine perimeter be trashin' the gatehouse. Three gangsta guards is up on the catwalk usin' personal weapons to shoot 'em down. A fourth guard be wavin' his weapon and screechin' at 'em to go back. I'm hangin' at our transport power nets, paralyzed. I scope the fourth guard jump down into the mob. He have to shoot a few but then they snap to and start listenin' to him. Folk stagger and fall back toward the gate. Gangstas on the catwalk steady, shootin' 'em down like it's Electro-spiel *even after the Extras be inside the quarantine wall!* Fourth guard curse out his trigger-happy cohorts while he herdin' Extras into the big tent and shacks, bullets zingin' by his helmet, folk droppin' all 'round him. Compu-grid come back online and gate swing shut. Three gangstas on the wall still shootin'. Now they got lasers too, and Extras bust out in flames. I wonder if the fourth guard on the ground goin' make it. Mob startin' to trample itself.

More ugly, and God don't do nothin'.

Captain hustle me inside the transport, say it's not good to watch atrocity, 'specially when you can't do nothin'. I'm beyond worthless at this point, fallin' all over myself. My mind's on the run. I don't wanna think or feel anythin'. Somehow the Captain get us both sterilized and outa that wasteland in less than three minutes.

"I'm getting too old for this crap." She shiver. "Way too old."

I stare at her, grateful for somethin' to do sides relive the freak show. In all this time, don't know that I ever *really* look at her before. Just kinda takin' her for granted, like a invisible force at my back. Who look at the wind? You just watch what it do. So I stare at her good now. Captain got a short cap of silky white hair, dark velvet skin, not one wrinkle, and muscles that look industrial strength like yours, Major. Her ancestors been 'round the world to make that face or at least all over the Pacific. She the kinda lady you draw walkin' on water and boxin' with God. I gotta smile cuz for a second I feel like me and her can turn this mess around. "Too old? For what?" I ask.

"Ghost Dancers, anybody could have set us up back there."

"Naw, Ghost Dancers be hookin' us up with the truth, tryin' to open our eyes."

"That's politics. I'm security. I don't trust anybody. I know better than to just walk into a situation like that."

I try to get her to say more, but she don't talk the whole trip back to Angel City. She already say enuf for me to know the Day of the Dead parade really mess her up—comin' face to face with the Evil Empire, you know what I'm sayin'?

Nobody back home would believe this, like a refugee camp in hell. Before the Treaty, Los Santos thugs be workin' terminal Extras to death on action-adventure and snuff Entertainment, or be marchin' 'em into the Barrier. Now they marchin' 'em into Paradise Healthway, which definitely ain't my idea of the promised land, more like middle passage to the grave. The Treaty is a bust! What the hell good is all that cyber-static declarin' no more Death Percent or gang rapes? All the Treaty really mean is unrestricted junk trade and alotta thrill seekers on the loose. Celestina must be squirmin' in her grave.

I ain't tell Jenassi diddly squat 'bout Paradise. He'd wanna get a payoff, not do a shake down. Him and most thug leaders in Los Santos be livin' very high drama. It's like I'm stuck in a bad Entertainment. Nothin' seem real. Cartoon characters, Electro-spiel victims, surreal shit. I keep wonderin' where are the real people at? Guess I'm worryin' 'bout the kinda character I'm playin' too. I'm so over my head it ain't funny.

What am I s'posed to do with alla this, Major?

Some big shot's throwin' a gala for us tonight, to make out like he ain't anti-Treaty. Fireworks got me jumpin' out my skin already. Jenassi be the guest of honor. He want me to dress up and slink in there on his arm. Afterward everybody goin' party back at Jenassi's place. He don't never wanna be seen in public with me, so what's up with *that*? Captain got me mad-dog suspicious. And I'm still pissed at you, but mostly just missin' your chocolate kisses and whirlwind hugs. I wanna curl up insida you, like in the eye of a storm and let the resta the world rush on by. Ain't that pathetic? I just wish I knew how this story was goin' go down. Course, maybe it's better not to know. The ole folks say—a coward, he die a million times, a brave man only once.

Love you, Lawanda

18:   New Ouagadougou City
(October 5, Barrier Year 115)

Vermittler are Barrier griots—musicians, oral historians, praisesingers, and diplomats. Like their old West African counterparts, they force us to feel beyond our time, to understand the past and appreciate the future. Barrier griots negotiate community but always seem like monsters at the table.
—Vera Xa Lalafia, *Healer Cosmology, The Final Lessons*

Elleni raced down the old highway. She'd lost her way in *Seelenwald,* running in circles for days, craving a fix... Her hair chewed remnants of a syn-silk bandana; her tattered robe dragged prickly pears and twigs; blood and Femi's ashes stained the hem of her pants. Villagers on the outskirts of New Ouagadougou City scurried away from her. No one wanted to cross paths with a *Vermittler* on a dark night at the Barrier's edge.

Queen of the night, riding electric rainbows to hell and back. Barrier spawn.

Loud thoughts echoed in the ruins of a twenty-first century mall.

Elleni shifted her medicine bag off skin it had rubbed raw and slowed to a walk. Monkeys pelted her with dung. Anxious weaver ants climbed her braids and dreads, stinging exposed flesh. She had no energy to calm them. Across the Canyon Bridge, she glimpsed the Insect Pavilion and Council Hall. Too far.

She crouched down a short distance from where the road ended and the Barrier cut off New Ouagadougou from Los Santos to the northwest and the Ecuadorian Wilderness to the south. Magnetic fluctuations spread across her body, and a Barrier thread smacked her cheek. Bitter blood oozed across her lips. She licked it away and dropped into a Barrier trance.

In the vision, a Barrier portal opened like the petals of a flower. Inside this opaque blossom, countless Barrier corridors converged. Naked and singing not a note in the sound beyond sound, Elleni moved through the Barrier blossom.

"No enemies." Celestina greeted her at the corridor crossroads, whispering with her fingers. "Heal us." Blood spurted from bullet wounds in her chest.

Seaweed robes dissolved as Celestina morphed from one wounded body to two. Gelatinous gargoyles the size of mountains tumbled down at Elleni's feet, and the two Celestinas vanished. Green fluorescence leaked from the gargoyles' bruises and burned Elleni's toes. Magnetic squiggles, monstrous sponges, and spiky foam rolled across her flesh. She wanted to scream, but she had no voice. She wanted to run from alien beings she didn't see but could taste and feel. They swarmed onto the crossroads and crept into her naked spirit. Elleni merged again and again with grotesque, wondrous beings until finally she no longer made sense to herself.

Elleni broke trance. Her toes were gripping pebbles, and her skin was cool and dry. White foam drizzled out of her hair and soothed her. She stuffed alora leaves and blossoms into her mouth and chewed slowly. On innumerable occasions she had *sung* a corridor through the lethal energy field, but a *silent* journey could be suicidal, even for her. She swallowed the alora, took a deep breath, and crawled close enough to touch the Barrier's milky "skin."

"Do I have to actually go? Why can't you just paint an image on my mindscape?"

For every experience a thousand visions. For every vision a thousand poems. Celestina's voice or Sidi's: Elleni couldn't tell which the Barrier used to offer wisdom from the *First Lessons*.

"Do you take Sidi's part against me?" Elleni flushed with shame. She reached toward the Barrier. Just beyond her fingertips, the petals of an opaque flower began to open. No roiling fireworks, the rest of the Barrier flared a dead purple. Bruised blood streamed across the bowl of heaven, blotting out stars and galaxies, until the night sky was like a raw, aching wound. "Who am I to heal you?" she asked, jerking her hand back.

The flower opening was the size of a cathedral tree sapling and growing. Leaning in, she glimpsed no crossroads, ghosts, or demons. Light simply vanished. Elleni was agitated and excited, yet felt no compulsion to step through. A wounded Barrier invited her to attend its suffering. She was a *Vermittler*, a Healer. How could she refuse?

Elleni drew back from the portal and shook tenacious weaver ants from her hair. She undid the Electro twined in a braid and stripped off medicine belt, feather jewelry, and Council robes. The ants scrambled into the folds of her familiar scents.

"*Aboru, Aboye, Aboşişe.* May what we offer carry, be accepted, may what we offer bring about change. *Aşe.*"

She danced naked and silent into an alien universe.

19:   On Location outside Nuevo Nada, Los Santos
(October 6, Barrier Year 115)

The explosion aggravated the dull headache Ray had been trying to ignore. A distant firestorm rolled across fields and trees, vaporized a swath of muddy water at Cripple Creek, and finally roared itself to nothing over the Nuevo Nada wasteland. Camera crews in copters and tanks chased down devastation for what seemed like miles. Ray's legs shook even after the shock waves had dissipated. He upped the ventilator settings of his enviro-suit and wiped the moisture on his visor.

"Is trashing good farmland really necessary?" Ray queried Aaron with a private Electro transmission.

"The audience wants action authenticity." Aaron replied over a public channel.

Ray swallowed a cough. "We could do this in cyber-space. They wouldn't know."

"I'm on a tight budget and real life is dirt cheap. Nobody has an FX budget like in the glory days."

Ray squinted into the ravaged landscape but couldn't locate the director's perch. Aaron was a disembodied voice barking at him from nowhere. "Define dirt cheap," Ray said.

"What are you doing out there, Valero? We're not ready for you yet."

"What are you-all hiding from me?"

"Some evil shit must have happened to you on location. What was it?"

"You do not want to know."

Nearby, Extras ran from fiery geysers and flying debris. A woman's clothes burst into flames, and her raven black hair turned bright red. As she flailed against the blaze, her screams were gut-wrenchingly real.

"She's burning alive!" Ray shouted over the Electro. "Get the med-team over here!"

Ray couldn't look away or pretend it wasn't happening. He wasn't that much of a coward. He bolted into the shoot perimeter toward the burning woman. A guard jumped him before he got ten feet. Ray slammed the guard against a wind machine. The man crumpled to the ground, unconscious. Ray vaulted over his body. A cloud of soot obscured his view, but he ran toward a red shimmer.

"Check the overactive imagination, Ray. This is Entertainment! No real-life heroics, please." Aaron's voice was hard to read over the Electro. Was this an execution Ray wasn't supposed to see?

He stumbled up to a pile of smoldering rags. Through swirls of soot, he scanned a bombed-out slum street in a twenty-first century metropolis. Just beyond dilapidated tenements the ramparts of the rich rose above the smog.

"Where is she?" A gust from the wind machine almost toppled him. He grabbed a shattered old-age street light. "Where the hell is she?"

"Where is who?" Aaron asked. "I hope somebody's getting Ray's improvisation."

"The deal was no gangbanging or killing Extras, Aaron!"

"You're seeing things, Ray. Are you getting enough sleep?"

"Don't bullshit me, Aaron."

"Then get a grip, man. You can't fall apart before we do your sequence."

The wind subsided. Ray heard muffled cries from a nearby shack. He kicked down the door and raced inside. Four burly guards rushed through cutaway walls and tackled him. He hit the ground so hard, he thought his lungs had collapsed. The guards hauled him to his feet and dragged him back beyond the shoot perimeter.

"You can't do snuff takes anymore, Aaron!" He struggled against the guards.

"I've never done snuff takes." Aaron's voice crackled with static. "Never."

"That's what everybody says now. It was always the other guy."

"How clean is your slate, Valero? Were you a hero, a man of the people in the good old days? No gangbang parties? No stand-in Extras died for you on camera?"

Ray quit struggling. "I'm talking about a woman burning up right this minute."

"You're acting like that Lawanda harpy." The assistant director joined the Electro-chat. "Seeing Treaty violations everywhere."

"Shut up," Aaron said.

"Dark-ages bitch. Somebody oughta take her out," the AD said.

"Back off Lawanda, Moses," Aaron said.

"Easy on the merchandise," Ray said to the slash-faced bruiser who jammed his arm behind his back, almost popping it out of the socket.

"Let him go." A melodious tenor pierced the static. Achbar Ali emerged from a swirl of golden dust, pounding a Healer staff against broken concrete. A flock of pigeons took flight. The guards released Ray but held powered-up weapons on them both. Achbar opened his satin-lined burnoose. "We're unarmed. Not even an enviro-suit, just a copy of the holy Koran and a script of *The Transformers*." The guards lowered their weapons.

"That's the best acting I've seen you do, Valero," Aaron said.

"Yes, quite the hero." Achbar's live voice was a sharp contrast to the Electro-chat.

"Spare me." Ray fought a wave of nausea and dropped his head to his knees.

"No one to save, huh?" Achbar pounded the concrete. Pigeons cooed above him.

"What are you doing about anything, Achbar?"

"Script doctor, production guru, here to serve our fearless leader."

"What do you need, Ray?" Aaron said. "More backstory, better motivation? Talk to me."

"I don't need to see Extras burning up." Ray stood up straight, a little too fast.

Achbar broke his fall. "Look around. Who's burning up?"

Pyrotechnicians with long black wigs suited up for the next explosive shots. Crew dashed about, dressing the set. Ray recognized the rigs. They were prepping for the long take he and Aaron had rehearsed all week. No cuts, it would just be continuous daredevil action. A blind bird with a flaming wing flew into the back of his helmet. Crew scooped up the half-dead creature before Ray could tell what it was.

"Under such surreal circumstances it's hard to know what you're seeing, harder to know what good you can do." Achbar wiped dust from his face with a red syn-silk handkerchief.

"So, you're on my side now?" Ray reluctantly leaned against him.

"That's where I've always been," Achbar stroked his droopy mustache.

"You gotta concentrate that wild imagination on your scenes," Aaron said. "The next sequence is right down your corridor—meaning and whatnot, all right?"

A pyrotechnician, glossy black hair swinging around his waist, howled like a banshee. Achbar thumped him on the back with his

Healer walking stick, and the pyrotechnician choked down a final scream. Ray felt like a fool.

"She sounded so real, not... Sorry everybody. Been cranky since I lost my bag..."

"You've been looking a little flushed too," Achbar said.

"Are you up for this today? I know I've been pushing everybody," Aaron said.

"I'm fine." Ray moved away from Achbar. His last treatment should have held another week. His muscles ached and his lungs burned, like he'd snorted lightning. The fire virus was jacking him up 'til he couldn't scope the difference between special effects and reality, between courage and hysteria. The medicine bag wasn't just a good luck gift from his lady; he kept the disease at bay with Elleni's remedies. Some creep was on to him for god knows why. He wasn't fine at all.

"Check with the transport captain. I think he found a bag like yours," Achbar said.

Ray switched off his Electro and whispered, "thanks." Achbar touched the Healer walking staff to Ray's chest, then disappeared behind a tangle of techies.

If transport didn't have his bag, Ray wouldn't wait for Elleni to pop in for a visit. He'd drive to the wasteland and find a greenhouse with fire ants and malanga tonight. Meanwhile he had to hit acting focus. Closing his eyes, he imaged Elleni's music, her griot's Kora, fifty strings stretched across a mountainous calabash gourd, plucked at the speed of light, resonating against her belly and breasts in the glow of the moon. Her dreads danced a slow drag around his agitated brain while her song captured his heart and lungs. Pain got suspended in the upbeats.

20: Cross-Barrier Transmission/Personal
(October 6, Barrier Year 115)

From: Lawanda

To: Sweet, Sweet Major

It's goin' be two for one with you and me, and I shouldn't take it personal, right?

Somebody try to poison Armando last night at his party. I left early, before a chem-attack in the transport ventilation system knock out him and everybody on his team. Captain say they is very lucky puppies. Course, she be programmin' our flyin' auto-bomb squad to stay on the lookout for chem-weapons. She just ain't deployed the slimy silver fish thangs in Jenassi's digs cuz his bugs might fight our bugs as intruders, and we s'posed to be safe there anyhow. How can his security be so lame?

Jenassi be puke sick, ain't up for the big-dog summit meetin' he call. He wanna bag on everythin', talkin' 'bout it even be too dangerous for me to go in his place, but I ain't one to cancel. How can we disappoint all these ganglords, studio hotshots, and politicos that be comin' on location 'tween Sol and Nuevo Nada, where nobody got the upper hand, to talk the future with us! Gettin' iced at a real summit meetin' sure as shit beat jitterbuggin' thru the wasteland to jaw with backwater nobodies.

Captain and squad get me over to location central early so I can psych myself and they can do a security drill. Another circus tent like Paradise Healthway, but this one ain't no ways raggedy: gold fiberplastic surrounded by state-of-the-art power nettin'. Diameter's gotta be a hundred meters—what do that much fiberplastic cost? I glide 'cross a portable synth-marble floor to the inner conference square. Production design musta hauled out authentic lookin' old-age carpets and hangin' lanterns to go with the big fat comfort chairs crowdin' each other for space. Synth-wood table is laid out with real food, no recon-slop, old-Asian cuisine to match the carpets. General Secretary Hitchcock tell me action-adventure ganglords don't believe in roughin' it. I scope a fortune in burnt flesh, broiled sea fish, and dirt vegetables, stir-fried. Not a Jolt flask in sight, just fruit juice and bubbly designer drugs. My belly always got a hole in it for food that ain't been squeezed from no damn tube, but after Paradise Healthway, the whole luxury scene make me wanna shoot somebody.

"Stay cool," Captain say softly, like she see me boilin' under my skin. "Stay frosty and you'll get through this."

7-Stories (he tell me his name but I forget, Jesus, Aaron, Moses?) scope me pacin' the conference square, workin' myself up, and he pounce, say he got big Treaty business to discuss. "I thought you was a busy artiste, creatin' universes, no time for social services," I say, hopin' he can distract me from loopin' thru Healthway images. Ain't even twenty-four hours and the whole hospital episode's seemin' like a exaggeration.

You ever feel like you can't believe your own self, Major?

7-Stories sit me down in a double comfort chair and stick a tray of sushi, chop hoo-ee, and sweet and sour tempura under my nose. He plop next to me, so close I can smell the dim sum he been eatin'. His guards and the Captain and her squad face off. I hand over my feast and tell 'em all to share. 7-Stories crack up. It's a minute 'fore he quit laughin' and get on track. He want Ray Valero to play his murderin' gangsta uncle, Mort Valero, in a biographic segment of *The Transformers* that goin' be worth trillions. 7-Stories see Mort as kinduva reverse Robin Hood who steal from the poor, give to the rich, and whip alotta ass in between. Long-winded sucker go on 'bout how whack Ray's behavin' and since I'm tight with him and Elleni, maybe I could talk sense to the boy, do my diplomacy thang, maybe convince him *and* Elleni to jump into this once-in-a-lifetime-platinum opportunity.

I finally get a word in. "Why would I wanna do that?"

"You scratch my back I scratch yours," 7-Stories say.

Captain bristle, but I give her the eye. I'ma play this scene to the hilt. "How's that goin' work?"

"With a Mort Valero episode, we can't lose. Nobody knows where Mort's hiding out, the rogue-titillation factor alone." 7-Stories be burnin' with enthusiasm. "Ray won't even let me pitch it to him, but you..."

"Uncle Mort shot Ray's sister, Chris, down like a dog when she tried to stop him from gangbanging an Extra. Rumor has it, Mort also offed Femi Xa Olunde. Why would Ray play the murdering bastard in your Entertainment?" the Captain ask.

I ain't never hear the Captain curse before. 7-Stories look at her like *she don't count, so what she talkin' for?* Danger Quotient's low, so his guards be stuffin' they faces with chop hoo-ee and tempura, spacin' out on they monster Electro masks, waitin' for the next command or confrontation, but they ain't participatin', barely payin' attention— 'cept for one guy with blue hair and a funky lookin' scar on his cheek. I guess 7-Stories think the Captain's just my slave firepower too. Or maybe it's the woman thang, who the fuck knows?

"You don't understand actors," 7 Stories say to me. "Ray just needs the right person asking him to play Mort—for the Treaty."

"And you don't understand me." Like I be so sure of myself.

"Don't underestimate me." 7-Stories wiggle his finger at me and glance around.

Tent's startin' to fill up—alotta tall men with ashen faces, ridiculous muscles, skin-tight power suits, and floor length, color-coordinated dusters—blue, black, and silver. Thermoplastic polymers be easier to come by since the Treaty. Guards got Electro-gargoyles for heads—some multi-channelin' rude suckers. With all the bio-corders, extra weapon appendages, and monster masks, I swear we on a Entertainment set. Me, the Captain, and the two ladies in our squad are the only women at this big-dog summit, far as I can tell, and all wearin' red. Tadeshi Mifune was the one female director in Los Santos and she be long gone. Least the Captain be tall with alotta muscles too.

"You got principles, Madame Ambassador, I know that. Your soul is not for sale." 7-Stories smile. He got perfect teeth and pink gums.

"Meeting's about to start." Captain haul me out the comfort chair away from him.

7-Stories grab my hand. He have cool, sleek fingers and baby-soft skin. I wonder if all of him feel like that. My squad and his greasy-mouthed guards go on alert. "You get me Ray and Elleni, and I'll get you real hospitals for the Extras. I'll get you real changes in this Zone." Me and the Captain exchange looks, and she stop pullin' me away. Do 7-Stories know 'bout the Paradise Healthway visit, or is he bluffin' us out?

"How I know you ain't talkin' out the side of your mouth?" I ask.

7-Stories laugh at me again. "Why'd they send you?" With his arm pushin' against my waist, he draw me away from the comfort chairs. Our entourage follow close behind. The Captain don't like it one bit, but I motion her to stay back. I wanna go as far as I can with this sucker.

"What you mean, why send me?" I ask. "You don't think I got the brains to…"

"It's not that." He walkin' me away from all the hotshots stuffin' they faces. "The way you talk, act, in public, nobody's going to take you seriously. Obviously somebody in Sagan City wants this mission to fail. Believing in your ethnic throwback self guarantees Los Santos resistance—and your failure." He pause, drop his jaw, and poke his tongue in his cheek, like I can read this face. "I do appreciate the irony and pathos, but I think we should rewrite this script." Is he a mind fuck or what? (I know you don't like me swearin' so much, Major, but I can't help myself. This Zone give you a foul mouth.)

The Captain look embarrassed for me, but don't say nothin'. "Damn," is all I can manage.

"You're the past we left behind, my dear." 7-Stories pat my hand.

"And you the future that was always goin' happen, right? Why should I trust you?"

7-Stories look over to the Captain like he know somethin' 'bout her I don't. "Why should you trust anybody? Especially when they're setting you up to take a fall!" He signal his guards and pull me into a storage space behind a stack of conference tables. The Captain is rip-shit, but I gotta hear him out.

"Ain't enough room for three in here," I whisper to her. "Stay frosty and watch my back. I got this." Captain look like she goin' shoot me herself, but then she just disappear in the shadows at the storage entrance...

Ah shit, Jenassi's squad done surrounded my transport. It don't look like a party.

I'll finish later.

Lawanda

21: On Location outside Nuevo Nada, Los Santos
(October 6, Barrier Year 115)

"Did you hear what I said? Ray, RAY! Are you all right? Are you ready to work?" Aaron Dunkelbrot's voice echoed through slum canyons and then got blown into the wasteland by wind machines.

"We're ready for you, Mr. Valero."

Ray forced his eyes open. An aide gingerly tapped his arm and pointed toward the smoldering slum set. A pyrotechnician with silky black hair hung from an elevated transport trellis. Ray glanced at his chronometer. An hour and a half of deep meditation had passed like a few seconds. He switched on his Electro. "I'm ready. Get me out of this enviro-suit!"

Camera crew began with short takes of a half-naked Ray hanging by a thread as the world exploded and history came to an end. Aaron had promised Ray human beings to act with, but he simply exploited Ray's rugged good looks and gymnastic prowess for impossible hero shots, like a Jolt ad-opera. Tadeshi, Ray mused, would have made *The Transformers* a people story. Even the ruptured landscape would have had personality, character. Ray sighed. A bit of Tadeshi's spirit had somehow survived Aaron's script revisions. If Ray held out through murder and mayhem, he'd get a crack at a few promising moments. He could even work the close-up hero shots for meaning. Tadeshi always said an actor's eyes screened in on the soul, and Ray still followed her direction.

The oblique light at sunset made catastrophe sparkle with romance and mystery. In a single take, Ray back-flipped over a mountain of flame, ran up the wall of a collapsing financial fortress, and pranced along a swaying high wire to humanity's final outpost. He snatched spears of exploding debris from the air nanoseconds before the last beautiful survivors would have been impaled. With a lady on his back and another in his arms, he raced along the crumbling edge of a postmodern world. Twice he lost his balance, and he and the ladies almost plummeted to a grisly demise. With a last spurt of superhuman energy, Ray vaulted over imploding slum bars and cyber cafés. The beauties clinging to his blood- and sweat-streaked body burst into tears as he shoved them toward a Barrier corridor. Inside the crystal archway, they melted into his powerful embrace. Ray's choreography was flawless, his muscles rippled on cue, and by some miracle he let his soul act. As he gazed one last time on the devastated metropolis, the anguished backstory of humanity's exploded possibilities was etched across his body. The rage and pain of lost generations poured out of his eyes. Gathering himself and the two beauties up from despair, he dashed down the crystal corridor toward an uncertain future.

A hush fell over the set. Even jaded techno-weenies were taken in by the tenderness and fury of his inspired artistry. "Impossibility specialist," Elleni called him, "dream technician."

Aaron's voice boomed down from the clouds. "We got to do that take again."

"What?" Ray almost collapsed. No way in hell he could do *that* again.

"Just kidding." The director's perch materialized out of gray smog. Its skinny wheels, high-riding body, and long telescoped neck called to mind an alien giraffe. Aaron looked almost beefy, sitting in the captain's seat, his lean and mean assistant director hovering behind him. The director's thin line of a mouth broke into a smile. "A miracle. When you focus, Ray, you're not some second-rate stud muffin! You trip into a whole different spacetime, way beyond us puny mortals. I'm not just yanking your chain. Keep the heat up, and *The Transformers* will bust the Zones wide open!"

The AD cheered. "Ray's the man! Let's say it again!"

Cheering with the AD, Extras and crew stormed out of exploded storefront, subway, and cyber café facades. Lust, delight, jealousy, and awe crashed into Ray. The roar of hungry voices, the force of so many voracious hands straining to touch him brought tears to his eyes. His skin barely contained the intoxicating rush that ripped through his body. Heart pounding, nerves tingling, he abandoned himself to an adoring public. His feet left the ground, and he surfed across hands, arms, shoulders, and backs. Nails and teeth tore at his costume and clawed into his flesh. Finally the crowd deposited him on Aaron's perch, which had descended almost to ground level.

Aaron winked at Ray, who wiped away tears. "Nothing like a dose of spontaneous love. You're a god!" He bear-hugged his star and disappeared into a mobile lab. Aaron's departure signaled business as usual. The cinematographer cursed tomorrow's clouds; they would ruin continuity. The AD barked commands on every Electro channel. Ray tried to get his bearings as the reality around him was dismantled for the next sequence. A guard, the man he'd knocked cold playing hero, helped him suit up.

"Thanks. Danger Quotient's kinda high today. Pollution, radiation…" Ray didn't know what else to say to the guy. He couldn't get "sorry" to drop out of his mouth. Most guard/assistants were studio spooks trying to hack his mind for the big bosses. Why should he feel sorry for punching one of them out?

Ray staggered the quarter mile from the designer slum to vehicle lockdown. Twice he almost blacked out from the virus's renewed assault. He vented painkillers and tranqs but knew he'd be in no condition for playback or performance notes anytime soon. Finding the medicine bag was imperative. He wandered rows of vehicles until he fainted against his red mini-tank, which luckily recognized him. The side entrance was rigged with a lift that dumped him into the driver's seat. Half-conscious, he activated the power nets and sank into fake fur upholstery.

Potted alora plants hung above the passenger seats, blooming in dim light. He stuffed flowers and leaves in his mouth, savoring the Healer remedy. Elleni's animal tapestries were mounted on the instrument panel. He stared at the woven menagerie of extinct mammals until he found the giraffes. The drugs he had inhaled finally numbed the pain, and the alora cleared his head a bit. When he drove off through scorched apple orchards toward location central, he was high as a satellite.

The portable studio of lab tents, inflatable crew warehouses, security tanks, recon-food service stations, and location Entertainment shacks always bummed him out. Bumpy, haphazard roads that one afternoon led nowhere were major thoroughfares the next morning. Ray made a wrong turn and ended up driving through elaborate mobile sets where outrageously costumed Extras rehearsed the glory of the twenty-first century. Traffic slowed to a standstill. Ray was stranded in Aaron's fantastic visions of before the whole world was like the Third World, but he was too high for aggravation.

The digerati were hip-hopping the Interweb in cyber cafés. Impossible robotic architectural structures served up opulent meals and designer drugs. Hook-ups accessed the known sentient Universe—a thousand satellites downloaded images from beyond the solar system. Hero-Doctors in pale blue medical togs and fluffy green masks covering half their faces labored with baroque twenty-first century instruments on a screaming patient in an emergency room setting. Bug-eyed microscopic glasses extended their vision. Blood and other bodily fluids artistically discolored their uniforms.

Ray didn't remember an emergency room bit in the revised script he got off the Electro. He peered out the side viewscreen. Camera crew with fancy bio-corders, courtesy of Paradigma, hung from a scaffolding web around the set. They swooped down on synthetic silk threads for elaborate tracking shots and close-ups like spiders coming in for the kill. The performer/patient looked like the burning woman. Ray blinked. This was an actor wrapped in synthetic skin. There was no burning woman. He had to stop obsessing and guilt-tripping himself. That wouldn't make him a real hero. He was just an entertainer. Traffic started to move again.

Transport always located itself at the location "frontier." *The Transformers'* camp sprawled to the edge of a rocky canyon. Transport perched on the cliffs. Ray put his vehicle in lockdown at a bluff overlooking a river once named for Indians, but he couldn't remember which: Navajo, Missouri, Cheyenne, Lakota, Kickapoo… The attendant eyed him and his tank suspiciously. Hardly anyone but bad-boy gangsters and corrupt politicians had personal transport. Who could afford gas, let alone a vehicle? Directors, stars, and crew bosses traveled in studio trailers.

"A gift from a fan," Ray said. "Liked my acting, my eyes."

"Wow." The attendant leaned into him. "You want to clean up? You're safe under the tent." He had Ray out of the enviro-suit in a flash. "We got a shower back here, real private, no Electro-snoops."

"I could use a little tender loving care." Ray savored the heat from the young man's body. "First some business. Where's your captain?"

"Work that charm, and fans'll give you anything." He indicated a man lumbering into a recon-food station. "I got everything you've ever done in my Electro memory."

"Not everything." Ray brushed the attendant's neck with breath and fingers, lingering long enough to feel him shiver. Shameless, he thought so loud that the attendant must have heard him, and blushed. "How 'bout a private showing?" Ray strode away before the

answer. Drugs, daredevil acting, and adoring crowds made him all
appetite and no brain. On the way back, he'd avoid the attendant.

"That Arab fellow, used to be a hit man, scary hombre," transport captain said.

"The Achbar?" Ray said.

"Yeah, he was talking to me—yesterday? this afternoon? when
I found that bag or turned it in to security. I don't know. I talk to a
thousand people a day and forget nine hundred."

How do you talk to a thousand people a day?

Security always hung tight to transport, so the star lost-and-
found tent was next to shipping. Low-priority services didn't rate
bio-computers with voice recognition, and no staff was on site. Ray
wasn't illiterate and could type in his inquiry. He described Elleni's
painted Barrier-scapes—a storm of hexagonal shapes sliding across
fractals of saturated color. When he mentioned ants, the bag tumbled out of a soft chute. He buried his face in the cool fabric and
caught a cinnamon whiff of Elleni. What he wouldn't give for all of
her right now. A spicy, bitter-coffee, snake brew—nothing on Earth
tasted quite like she did. He hadn't heard from her for several weeks.
Of anybody, she could certainly handle whatever came down on her.
Still, he liked hearing her voice, knowing she was all right. Not that
she would tell him if she wasn't. Not that he'd tell her about Ghost
Dancers, the burning woman, or his stolen bag. What could they do
but worry about each other?

Audio-Electro screeched at him as he walked by: "Complaints
about missing contents after you've left the premises will be
invalid."

"Roger that." Ray knew port studio was crawling with snoops,
so he waited for the privacy of his mini-tank to check out the medicine bag. It was practically empty: no fire ant colony, malanga fruit,
or herb packets, just a wad of synthetic skin and a few tapestry-aids.
Whoever cleaned him out put twenty hits of Rapture in the main
compartment. Half a fire ant twitched in the specimen sleeve. Big
useless eyes and powerful jaws spit potent chemicals at him. He
placed one of Elleni's soothing tapestry strips over the wounded

ant, closed the sleeve, then vomited out the side viewscreen into the canyon. Real-life intrigue always made him sick to his stomach.

His Electro buzzed with invitations. Ray finished throwing up then politely (with visual & audio) turned down an offer from Jesus Perez, local bad boy, to wine and dine Vice Ambassador Lawanda Kitt at his canyon floor villa. Lawanda would be disappointed, but the party sounded like a horror show. He deleted Danny Ford's cryptic lust sonnet without reply. Their thing had fizzled a while ago so what was the point? Sweet Danny had an outlaw edge that was thrilling for a minute, but he lacked the vision and crazy ambition that made danger delicious. Or maybe Danny and Ray were too much alike, fancy packaging around hollow products... Ray sent form rejects to the other invites. Aaron didn't like reclusive stars, but tough shit.

Ray leaned his head against the steering frame, coughing up spits of blood. His guts were on fire. The virus was on a rampage. Med-unit on his bio-computer said he wasn't contagious yet, but at this rate he might be dead in a few days. He had to score fire ants and malanga fruit fast. He thought of buzzing Elleni, but she was into something deep or she would have contacted him. Why go running to the great lady for help when he could handle this little emergency himself?

He queried the regional maps in his bio-computer for a Healer greenhouse. The organic smart-machine gurgled and whimpered. "What's the matter—hungry?" He pumped it full of a super-charged protein drink, and the effort made him sweat. The bio-computer gurgled and farted several minutes before locating the nearest greenhouses in the Nuevo Nada wasteland. Auto-drive plotted a four-hour round trip. Lightheaded, Ray sped off down a dilapidated Canyon Road to find a cure.

22: New Ouagadougou City, New Ouagadougou
(October 7, Barrier Year 115)

> If everybody is the same, nobody is anything.
> —Vera Xa Lalafia, *Healer Cosmology, The Final Lessons*

"Elleni Xa Celest! What obscene spectacle do you perform sprawled naked before the Barrier?"

Words played on a Tama drum pounded Elleni's skull. Her hair crawled in the dirt, chasing away beetles and spiders. Tiny pebbles irritated raw skin on her belly. Weaver ants scurried over brush-burned skin to suck droplets of blood. She couldn't recall what had happened once she'd stepped into the Barrier beyond light. A nasty magnetic pulse throbbed between her thighs, and static lingered in her mouth. Her mindscape was a wasteland. Had she failed so miserably that her monster lover stole her memories and spit her out like a bad taste?

"Those who shit on the road will meet flies on their return." The drum voice continued.

Elleni opened her eyes to electromagnetic chaos. Her brain refused to order visible light into recognizable patterns. Instead, she "saw" ghostly magnetic motifs—signs of earthly life forms— dominated by the brilliant lattice emanating from the Barrier.

"If you fight on the enemy battlefield, you are the enemy!" A human voice chastised her in a modern Healer dialect. "Speak!" It was a woman's voice, sharp and sweet—a voice she loved. "Or have you forgotten how to be human?"

Elleni blinked the visible world clear. Someone pounded a teak and ebony corridor staff by her head. Ancient warriors raced around the staff's dark wood, disappearing into the fiery crystals of a Barrier corridor, leaving a smooth space for a hand. It was Femi's staff, but not his hand—Femi was dead. She had stolen his ashes for a nuptial ceremony, and...

"You're a disgrace!" A lithe man with angular features, sad gray eyes, and a mane of once-blond silver hair, challenged her in drum language. He punctuated each rhythm by painting the night air with momentary color. It was Sidi's consort, Duma, showing off. "Villagers said we'd find you here groveling at the Barrier. Explain yourself."

"Duma Xa Babalawo—father of mysteries, one who greets all with open hands," Elleni said.

"I know who I am, do you know yourself?" Duma towered over her. He towered over almost everyone. At Council only Sidi stood eye to eye with him.

"*Keine Feinde*," Elleni said in old German.

Sidi repeated Elleni's words—"No enemies?" Light from the Barrier flashed in her almond eyes. Dark plum lips frowned at Elleni from a golden face framed by wispy ochre braids. Tiny amethyst disks revolved above Sidi's head as ornaments of personal power. Elleni could taste her vivid colors. A shiver of lust made Elleni cover naked breasts with her arms.

"We host the world, dignitaries invited here at your insistence, and for days you, Council Center, are nowhere." Duma said.

"Nowhere, so long?" Elleni tried to organize a chaotic tumult of sensations. "No time...lost in a cut glass flower...beyond light, in a black hole, hosting the universe." If she could remember the plot, meaning would come.

"Even liars have more honor, weaving bold tales to show respect. You offer nothing." Duma's drummed assault resonated through the cathedral-tree forest all the way to the Insect Pavilion and Council Hall. He wanted everyone to hear his righteous tirade.

Femi had bequeathed his ebony corridor staff to Duma, and Duma relentlessly championed his martyred idol's legacy, risking his life to protect the sanctity of New Ouagadougou. Yet Duma lacked vision. For although power was his drug of choice, he was a follower, not a leader. Sidi, on the other hand, honored Femi but followed her own vision. Elleni's hair wriggled as the image-swamp covering her mindscape cleared. Sidi was the one the Barrier desired. Elleni must reach her, persuade her to...

"*Mo so awon enia mi po*," Elleni whispered in Yoruba and scrambled to her feet.

"You haven't brought your people together. You break us apart!" Sidi spit in the dust.

Healer Councilors in ceremonial regalia, carrying green-fire torches and gold-flecked rayon banners, marched out from the shadows of the cathedral trees and lit up the night behind Sidi and Duma.

"No enemies," Elleni said as yellow tears dribbled from her shriveled dreads. Sidi considered the Barrier a demon invader— an abomination grudgingly tolerated because it protected New Ouagadougou from the warrior Zones. The Barrier was nothing to take into your body, nowhere to lose your soul. Elleni leaned against Femi's corridor staff to steady her twitching limbs.

Duma recoiled. "You will enlighten us to the ways of the world, na?"

"We must be as one." Saliva flew out of Elleni's mouth.

"Spare me Celestina's Treaty propaganda!" The air around Duma was mud-colored.

"Please." Elleni's hair reached out toward the Councilor's sputtering torches.

Duma and the Councilors retreated. They waved green fire in her face and spit in the dirt.

"Cover yourself." Sidi held her ground. She was a head taller and half as wide as Elleni. Close-up, her flying amethyst disks resembled spiral galaxies and smelled like lightning burning holes in the night. Elleni savored the delicious ozone scent. How could she be jealous of her spirit sister? Sidi pulled plum lips tight against straight white teeth and gestured at Elleni's ample breasts and thighs crisscrossed with Barrier burns. She whispered, "You've never been an attractive woman..."

"I can't help what I am—"

"Yes, but, running naked through the night, sputtering and convulsing? You shun your honored guests, and for what? A lewd rendezvous with an unholy fissure in reality? Of course they're disgusted." She motioned toward Council. "They think you're crazy."

"You and I, as one to avert a terrible disaster." Elleni grabbed Sidi and staggered with her toward the Barrier, toward memory. Sidi did not resist.

"I saw our world, our Earth..." Elleni crumpled in pain.

"What is it?" Sidi held Elleni up, but her voice sounded far away.

"I am the Barrier's griot, singing praisesongs to..." Images from the corridor beyond light inundated Elleni's mindscape. The old highway disappeared. She was nowhere and everywhere, no body at all. Just blackness, a universe giving birth to itself. The jagged signatures of distant stars and galaxies warped into impossible patterns then burst into clear constellations. Overwhelmed by beauty on a galactic scale, Elleni cried a comet tear. Her sigh was a solar wind. What had she become?

Blinking away more comet tears, she scanned a blue planet swathed in wispy clouds, close enough to touch. Voluptuous brown landmasses framed blue-green oceans. Pungent magnetic gyrations, hot and cold passions, and thunderous voices—the full spectrum of life cascaded across Elleni's senses. Earth, a delicious bio-mosaic, was girdled by a roiling red-violet monster, pulsing as if it were Elleni's breath and blood. Vast tentacles sliced through sky, oceans, and continents, disappearing into... another dimension? another universe? The Barrier—had she merged with the Barrier?

A massive eruption shattered the watery face of the planet, burst a kidney-shaped continent, and hurled clouds of matter out into space. Elleni shuddered at the impact. It seemed as if her bones had exploded and pulverized her organs. She was Earth and Barrier, assassin and victim, all inside-out and outside-in, a Möbius strip of desire and pain. In no time the riot of Earth's life became a dull whimper within her. Instinctively, she reached out to break the Barrier's stranglehold on this fragile spit of stardust with bare hands. But she had no hands, and her flailing Barrier gestures exploded the planet's core. Elleni screamed, and her voice was a scorching red wound in the black sky. Spacetime unraveled, and a shattered Earth was sucked down a black-hole corridor. Comet tears raced away in every direction, trailing a million miles of icy dust. Gravely wounded, Elleni's mindscape blazed white.

23: Cross-Barrier Transmission/Personal
(October 6, Barrier Year 115)

From: Lawanda

To: Sweet, Sweet Major

Sorry 'bout the interruption. Jenassi s'posedly puke sick but still itchin' to debrief me 'bout the big-dog summit. He gotta send out the cavalry cuz I ain't get 'round to him fast enuf. See what I'm dealin' with? What he got spies for? He can intimidate me all he want, but I sure ain't goin' tell him what he can't snoop for hisself. Now you, Major, get the whole summit story, despite my better judgment. That's love.

So under the big top with gangsta hotshots skulkin' 'round, actin' like they ain't impressed with nobody but themselves, and the Captain standin' guard, 7-Stories drag me into this cramped storage space and power-up a communication scrambler—ain't goin' be no electronic eavesdroppin' on our tête-à-tête. We stand in the shadows, too close, smellin' each other, breathin' each other's breath for a long minute or two. I lean against the fiberplastic tent wall. It take all my weight, and I be very grateful. My heart's thumpin' and my legs is pretty shaky. I wonder how long I been a nervous wreck. 7-Stories look a little funky 'round the edges too. Sweat is drizzlin' thru his scraggly beard. He lick at it with his tongue.

"So what you got for me, Mr. Man?" I figure he's waitin' on me and I wanna get this over with. "Who's settin' me up? What's the scoop?"

He say, "People are still talking about back before the whole world was like the Third World and how those glory days will come again. Nostalgia sells, big time."

"Tell me somethin' I don't know." For a second, it's like his skin open up and his insides be fallin' out. I reach over and catch him. "You all right?"

"I'm a post-op transracial," he confess, not one bit surprised that I'm scoopin' him up in my arms.

"No shit?" I scan his straight sandy hair, pale skin, and crystal blue eyes. Man ain't got no mouth, just a slash where his lips s'posed to be. I wonder how he look before. "Why you advertizin' to me?"

"I believe...I can trust you. I want you to know you can trust me."

He sound so desperate. I give him a squeeze, set him up straight against the tent wall, and take a step back. My sister Geraldine warn me 'bout this gangsta gene-art fetish. "Look, ethnic throwbacks do culture not identity politics. We don't put stock in color. Race is how the world see you, ethnicity is how you see yourself."

He shake his head and kinda chuckle too hisself. "Yeah, no, you're right, but..."

"My sister Geraldine's paler than you, got a head of blond hair too, but she choose how to be on the inside, for her deep self. That's how we do where I come from." I don't tell him she have the high-power, Sagan Institute job while dark me be languishin' back in a impoverished settlement, 'til I hook up with you, Major. "Who care what color you was once or what skin you in now?"

"You misunderstand." 7-Stories put his arm around my waist, his mouth against my ears. I feel his hot, moist breath, like feelin' his words. "I offer you my dark secret, not my past color, as a sign of trust. No one else *knows* what you know." He look into my eyes, like he in a close-up and the next shot's a kiss.

"That don't mean I gotta fuck you."

He grin, like we on the same page of his script. "Top-flight gene artists tuck your butt, sharpen your nose, give you any skin color you want." He stroke my face with pale fingers. My skin feel rough under his baby touch. Take all my will power not to smack him. My hug wasn't no come-on and he know it. "Everybody wants white. Not many transracials go black. A lot of the Death Percent was on the dark side."

"So you trans-raced yourself to white. I ain't holdin' survival against you."

But, Major, your info dump say ANYBODY could end up a Extra. Not a hereditary color thang—just on top the world one day, catch a virus or piss off a thug boss, and the next day you be dyin' in a snuff take and cut up for the organ market.

"Celestina's Treaty changed all that—no more marching dusky Extras into the Barrier to postpone famine," 7-Stories say, like he sleep talkin' from a dream.

"Postpone famine?" My lips pout out and I got my hands on my hips. Ain't none of this in the factastic attachments you be sendin' me 'bout Santosian history and economy, Major. Course 7-Stories could be scammin' me.

"You thought we were just uncivilized monsters who sold babies to butchers and killed Extras for fun." I don't answer, but he read my mind. "You Paradigmites like thought experiments, here's one: if you have a limited food supply, would you let healthy people starve to feed terminally ill people, to feed losers, criminals, enemies? Who'd be Extra?" I'm 'bout to argue this sick logic, but he got his hands in my hair. Bein' diplomatic don't go that far so I shove him away. He look smug and satisfied, like he get off on women who do it rough. "There's a lot you're in the dark about, Lawanda." He lickin' his lips like he know just how I'm goin' taste.

"You goin' enlighten me?" I gotta do somethin' with my hands 'fore I strangle this dick wad, so I take out my sketchpad and start drawin'—mind-doodlin', you know—gettin' my head straight.

"Dark-skinned pop's down by sixty percent in Los Santos. People are literally dying to be white. Now, I worked with a real genius, but any quack can put up a rogue shingle on the Electro and say he's a gene artist, a miracle worker who can do you a whole new skin. Ninety-nine percent are hustlers and head jobs. Only one or two can do a whole new skin. Still, dumb fucks pay frauds all their money to lighten up and most of them kick off!"

"That's rough, but what's your point?"

"People in Los Santos want to go back to when the whole world wasn't like the Third World, even so-called "rebel Extras." They're dying not to be like you. So why would they let you lead them into a brand new day?" He pause, lift his eyebrows, and poke his head at me. It's like an elephant stomp my chest. Images on my sketchpad blur. "They're on to you, honey. Emptying bank accounts, liquidating assets. You won't data-chill another boss's resources. Armando Jenassi's definitely not playing on your team. You want Celestina's Treaty to work, you want deep changes, you need me. Illusions rule." He is up in my face again. "We need each other."

Cool as ice, I say, "All right, it's a deal. I'll get you Ray and Elleni for the Mort Valero biographic and you..."

He point at my sketchpad, "What are you doing?" He sound real insulted.

"Takin' notes." I show him the doodle, a sensuous tongue with alotta teeth. Furry words chase each other all over the page then morph to castles in the sky or maybe spaceships flyin' by two ladies tangled up in the stars. Ladies look kinda like Celestina, but 7-Stories grab my sketchpad 'fore the image finish flowin' out my hand.

"What is this shit?" He flip the pages, casually invadin' my deep thoughts, undressin' my mind like I ain't nothin'. "I don't believe I'm risking everything on a fucking throwback!" He toss the pad back at me and it fall on the ground. "Do you actually expect to get anywhere doing this kind of retro-crap?" I tole you these folk is jacked up! I think we doin' just fine and then *snap!* 7-Stories be shakin' my shoulders and goin' off on a high-horse rant, like I'm togglin' some major switch of his. "Live art bit it with electricity. Computer graphics iced drawing. Now Electrosoft's SV is about to do the movies. Don't you get it? We can't survive clinging to a dead past."

He gotta dog me like that cuz I'm mind doodlin'? Like he never hearda thinkin' with your hands. "What the hell is SV?" I ask, tryin' to divert him from the BS.

"Carl's crazy. What's trusting you get me? You're from the dark ages."

"Naw, Dark Ages be when Europe kicked they glorious past to the curb. I'm like a Renaissance woman—they was throwbacks too—to Greeks and Arabs." Man look like he 'bout to puke. "Whyn't you just answer my question. What is SV?"

"SV is virtual reality, bitch: Sim-Vue!"

"Who the hell can afford the rig for that? You need a lot more prosperity 'fore virtual is a mass-market joint."

He snarl at me. That's how guys be over here. Short fuse—one minute ready to bone you, the next explodin' over nothin'. He be explodin' over less than nothin'. I can't understand a word he sayin'. Smooth as syn-silk, Captain pop out the shadows and haul me back toward the conference square, but I ain't done with 7-Stories.

"I don't take that 'dark ages bitch' mess 'less I'm in a Treaty meetin'. Then I ain't me, I'm the whole reunification thang. So keep bitchin' at me and you can kiss trillions of Entertainment revenue good-bye."

7-Stories stumble into a stack of tables and start a avalanche. My squad and his tired-lookin' bodyguards alluva sudden drippin' funky sweat. Man with flower-bud scar on his face got a weapon out. Everybody's nerved up. 7-Stories bite his pink slash lips. "Sorry." He grab me again, his mouth on my ear.

"Don't keep puttin' your hands on me, like I'm your latest hunka meat…"

The Captain got a weapon at his temples. "Release her!"
He don't.

Everybody flashin' weapons now. "You forgot this." He jam the sketchpad into my ribs and whisper. "Mention Paradise at this meeting and those very sick people you care so much about will be very dead people by this evening with no evidence, nothing. Trust me." He give me a look like a missile blast, then let me go.

"We have to start the meeting," Captain say and pull me away.

"If you want more, bitch, catch me on location," 7-Stories snarl at my back, like he a jilted lover or somethin'. He always playin' the audience.

Me and my team stagger 'cross the synth-marble floor, and I almost burn myself on a hangin' lantern. Production design got the nerve to use real candles. We push thru broad backs and sculpted chests to the podium. I scan silver-caped white men with blue/green dagger eyes, blood in they faces—hardly a nap to be seen, 'cept beefy black muscle bodyguardin' from the shadows. These pale ganglords, studio hotshots, and politicos be at the helm of Los Santos's gun democracy. I wonder how many is "really" white, then feel stupid wonderin'. My shit be raggedy the whole summit session. Everythin' distract me. Women in whiteface, wearin' pink, see-thru kimonos, float around servin' sushi, gigglin' and shit—nipples on they titties is bright red. Shakahachi old-Asian flute music on audio-Electro be workin' my nerves. I sweat all over my sketchpad, wishin' I had me more of them genius genes my sister Geraldine got.

7-Stories grin all over nothin' and I keep thinkin', Santosians risk dyin' not to be in my skin. Dark, mystical inferiority wash over me, like a oil slick on fire. This how colored folks have felt for centuries. It's weird, like being locked up in somebody else's eyes and ears, a soul on fire. Ain't s'posed to be that way no more.

Gangstas start gettin' restless. I make a fool of myself jabberin' 'round the stage, but it don't matter what I say, ain't nobody in the audience really listenin'. My skin's so loud, blot out my voice. I can't even hear myself.

I let the wild child take over, do a freedom rant while the resta me retreat.

Thug bosses trot out lame excuses, then vow to make nice with the Treaty. One big fat lie after another. When I promise not to hold up med-shipments, 7-Stories decide the meetin's goin' end on a high note. He blast me with his missile glare, jump up on a seat, and get every last sucker to give me a standin' ovation, even the whitefaced girls in pink. Captain think we make a great comeback. I never do mention the Paradise Healthway scam. What the hell is great?

THIS SHIT'S TOO COMPLEX FOR WORDS. I been mind doodlin' since the meetin'—full-scale murals—tryin' to make sense, tryin' to draw myself sane, tryin' to figure the next step. I cover the transport walls with explodin' Extras in slave-ship bunks, deep-cover Ghost Dancers, pinstriped gangstas, geishas in pink kimonos, colored folks in whiteface. Captain watch me like I'm a danger to myself.

I hand her paper and a multicolored drawin' utensil, but Captain's as bad off as you, Major. She can't draw, dance, sing, write down her story, *nothin'*! She ain't familiar with her own thoughts, with the poetry inside her body, with the deep images of her soul. Claim she ain't got no talent. Back home in Ellington, folk barely got a pot to piss in or a window to throw it out, but everybody can mind-doodle, search-sing, rhyme the truth. Talent ain't got nothin' to do with it. It's about art! Tell you the stone truth tho, everywhere I look 'round Los Santos, seem like creativity be in the breakdown lane. Good art's just an accident in this Zone. It's enough to make you believe in the talent myth. It's enough to make you lose your mind.

Captain disinfect the slimy outprint from that kid in Paradise Healthway and I hang it on the transport wall. Kid draw his head on fire as he fall into the Barrier. Got a coupla ole ladies on a dolphin floatin' by him. (Celestina?) Underneath he write, "Barrier claims gene-art traitors at Wounded Knee." If I knew the boy's images, I could get somewhere. But I ain't gettin' no where. What you know 'bout Ghost Dancers? I can't find nothin' real on 'em. You got the Mercedes of search engines, so help me out.

7-Stories is right. Who do I think I am? What the hell am I s'posed to do, zap these fools with a magic wand and *snap!* it's a better world? 7-Stories see right thru the crap. He want somethin' and not just Ray and Elleni actin' in no shock-jock Entertainment, but can I trust his sleazy behind? I don't feel like trustin' nobody. I just wanna run.

Yeah and what you got to say for your no-name, dark-matter self?

Lawanda

24: Cross-Barrier Transmission/Personal
(October 7, Barrier Year 115)

To:	Lawanda Kitt, in response to your Cross-Barrier Transmissions
From:	The Major, Head of Sagan City Secret Services
<u>Re:</u>	<u>Being Intimate But Not Knowing My Name</u>
Question:	Will a name cross our barriers like a *Vermittler* (old German for go-between, negotiator, griot) and bring us closer together? Will a name shield you from doubt?
Assumption:	Your anger and suspicion at me are exacerbated by absurd circumstances.
Observation:	You confuse the name of a thing with the thing itself. You know me.
Note:	Given my scientific inclinations, I don't usually engage in poetry, yet I do believe in adopting whatever form(s) necessary to prevent adversaries from directly perceiving or accurately assessing the extent of my power. Being "dark matter" so to speak is thus excellent cover.

Recommend: They will continue to assault your identity. You
              face a conspiracy of ideas protected by a bodyguard
              of lies. Celestina said to "name" the universe that
              supports our best selves. If I understand her, that
              means you should define your world and resist oth-
              ers who would confine you in theirs. You know and
              practice this already. Don't let them push you off
              center.

Re: <u>The Day of the Dead & Ghost Dancers</u>

Assumption: Your urgency to solve problems in Los Santos will
              increase exponentially with the extremity, with the
              horror, of those problems.

Observation: An impossible task always seems like a setup.

Notes: I possess scant info on Ghost Dancers/born-again
              Sioux (Ojibwa name for Lakota, et al.), mostly ur-
              ban legends. In Paradigma as well as Los Santos,
              Dancers and shamen have been conflated with
              ethnic throwbacks, given these groups' intense re-
              lationship to history, to embodying past wisdom.
              The Wovoka, Dancer spiritual leader, is named
              for a Paiute medicine man who at a solar eclipse
              (circa 1888) allegedly met the Great Spirit in a
              trance and heard from him of "a return of the
              dead" and a restitution of the "old ways." In our
              time, born-again Sioux believe people who died
              in the Barrier will be returned to us. The Wovoka
              offers immunity to what you call "space-age,
              drug-proof viruses and bacteria" and immortality
              through secret Barrier rituals. No Dancers died in
              the fire-virus megademic, which lends credibility
              to his mythology. Dancers resisted Los Santos gang-
              lords for twenty-five years, providing sanctuary to
              Extras on gangster hit Lists, eventually function-
              ing as the religious wing of the Union of Rebel
              Extras. However, the Wovoka refused to ally with

Celestina—more than irrational treaty-angst operating here.

As Spirit Warriors, Dancers eschew the use of violence. Wounded Knee, site of failed white promises and Indian massacres, is sacred ground. Anomalous Barrier behavior in the region has precluded regular human habitation, however Dancers supposedly gather at Wounded Knee for mystical ceremonies during the fall and winter months.

The child artist at Paradise Healthway who offered you his mind-doodle may not be native to Los Santos. Paper drawings are only common in Paradigma's ethnic settlements among throwbacks and in New Ouagadougou among Healer acolytes. You will recall that 89% of the Los Santos population is illiterate.

Recommend: You and I should challenge the Healer Council to keep Treaty promises. (Example: one subcompetent Zumbi Xa Dojude does not constitute true medical aid. Xa Dojude means child of darkness. All Ouagadougian names are meaningful.) You should continue to follow good leads and sound advice. An alliance with born-again Sioux leaders would be worthwhile, an invitation to a Wounded Knee ceremony, invaluable.

Re: 7-Stories

Questions: Does he use sexuality to humiliate and manipulate you (or me), or has he been stricken by your considerable charms? Are you a challenge to his ego, an exotic titillation for a starved erotic imagination? Does he think jealousy will make me reckless? Or does he seek a pure soul he can trust?

Observation: You threaten 7-Stories' identity delusion. Few people understand ethnic throwbacks' devotion to

performative knowledge. Mind-doodling, search-
singing, embodying the language/wisdom of the
ancestors, etc. will strike most as trivial distraction
or misguided posturing. They won't see parallels to
the European Renaissance or Twentieth-Century
Israel. As you point out, the Captain and I, fellow
Paradigmites, are untutored in what you consider
common expressive arts. Technology is generally
perceived as superior to biology, as an improvement
on our senses and capacities. Working through
forms of embodied knowledge to access the vast
resources of the whole body, of the non-conscious
mind, can seem like "voodoo." I, myself, even
knowing the efficacy of your methods, am still
somewhat skeptical.

Notes: We possess no hard data on Santosian population prior to Treaty enactment, no stats on Death
Percent Extras who died in snuff takes, for the
organ market, or were simply marched into the
Barrier, and nothing reliable on current Los Santos
demographics. Daniel Ford (Samanski's right hand
thug) promised Prime Minister Jocelyn he would
fill in the statistical gaps but so far has not delivered. He seems more like a hustler than a demog-
rapher. Jocelyn is infatuated with his flamboyance.
At any rate it would be impossible to analyze the
relationship of an individual's "color" to frequency
on Death Percent List. I'd certainly have provided
you with such information. I remain skeptical of
anecdotal analysis, however plausible—even Los
Santos should be beyond petty racial politics. Your
informant could indeed be "scamming" you, trying to play the old race card. Yet, we should never
underestimate "the persistence of the old regime."
Human culture is fundamentally conservative

and operates primarily beyond conscious control, despite our illusions to the contrary. We may no longer believe in "race" as a significant human category, nevertheless we continue our racist practices. (The distribution of wealth and power in Paradigma is still mildly correlated with color.)

7-Stories is Aaron Dunkelbrot (old German for dark bread). Four years ago during the unrest—before the Treaty was signed—he and Moses Johnson, the assistant director with rosebud scar, burst on the Entertainment scene—literally out of nowhere. They helped produce Mifune Enterprises' outlaw exposé on Extras and *Vermittler*. I believe they also got footage of Celestina's funeral ride—Mr. Dunkelbrot had a curiously intimate connection to the great shaman. When Tadeshi Mifune disappeared into the great unknown, she left Mr. Dunkelbrot in charge of the studio. A mass-market wizard, he has made several unremarkable ad-operas for Jolt and Electrosoft in her absence, all mega-hits. Aaron and Moses are also "dark matter." Ruthless gangster sensibility is insufficient to explain their meteoric rise in M. Enterprises.

I don't need to tell you that it will be difficult to convince Ray or Elleni to work on a Mort Valero project. A *Transformers* episode glorifying the assassin who shot down Femi Xa Olunde, the Healers' greatest shaman and beloved leader, starring Ray and Elleni, would be so repugnant that I suspect that Sidi Xa Aiyé would have the necessary emotional ammunition to depose Elleni and secure New Ouagadougou's withdrawal from One World Now.

Recommend: You must judge how far you are willing to go (on all levels) with the unscrupulous Mr. Dunkelbrot.

(Don't forget who-all he's in bed with.) Stay frosty
as the Captain says.

Afterthought: I don't know what to say for myself. I quote you:
this shit's too complex for words.

25: New Ouagadougou City, New Ouagadougou
(October 7, Barrier Year 115)

At the crossroads, we cannot walk backwards. Celestina's hushed
tones echoed through unbearable brightness. Two voices—talking
as one—soothed Elleni's wounded mindscape, called her back from
chaos to herself. Still, in the throes of Barrier fever, she pressed
Sidi toward a black crystal archway that opened to a corridor beyond light.

"I'm no Barrier junkie," Sidi shouted. "Let me go!" Her whirling disks broke into Elleni's trance and they stumbled back.

You and Sidi, save the universe in yourself. Heal us, Celestina's
voices said.

Elleni looked from the Barrier to New Ouagadougou City glowing mauve in the distance. "You ask too much."

Duma and the Councilors edged toward the scraggly cathedral
trees that bordered the dead mall. Sidi stomped the old highway,
spraying Elleni's eyes with dust.

"Too much Barrier surfing," Sidi said. "Your mindscape's in
shambles."

"Celestina was in there, somewhere." Elleni's hair danced in
the breeze, still heartened by the image of her *Geistesmutter.* She
clutched Sidi. "Alive."

"You saw Celestina?" Sidi's voice trembled. A disk swooped toward Elleni. "In the Barrier?" The black crystal archway dissolved as she spoke. "In that?" Sidi closed her eyes and whispered, "Heal us." A faint connection rippled between Sidi and Elleni.

"The mother of our mind and spirits doesn't haunt us. She's alive," Elleni said.

Duma pulled flax robes tighter around his muscular body. "What do you mean 'alive,' Elleni?"

"I loved Celestina as you did, Elleni, but how can she be alive?" Sidi's disks hovered in a circle just above her eyes.

Duma waved his corridor staff at Sidi. "Celestina was murdered. We attended her crossover ceremony!"

"A starway ship came to...*Zwei Leute, hautnah, unter einer Decke*," Elleni said.

"Two people, skin-close under one blanket?" Duma said, "Do you mean in cahoots? A conspiracy?"

"And Celestina flying on the back of Aieee!-Aieee!," Elleni said.

"A flying sea mammal?" Sidi arched her eyebrow.

Duma bristled. "We are not pathetic Ghost Dancers silvering our faces, disco trance-dancing, and waiting for the dead to return the old ways, na? This Celestina apparition is a Barrier mirage."

"Or something conjured from your own mind, Elleni," Sidi said. "Are you so colonized, so polluted that you believe what they say of us? That we're superstitious witchdoctors, technophobes lost in a primitive past, ruled by dead ancestors and animal spirits?"

Elleni felt their fragile connection unravel. "No, I—"

Duma stepped between Sidi and Elleni. "Open trade and travel, cultural exchange, foreign aid—all sound benign, enlightened. However, I saw Mort Valero, your consort's uncle, machine-gun Femi Xa Olunde in the head! I saw Celestina blasted in the chest by Piotr Osama, an Extra she herself called back from death—one of the people you want us now to save, na?"

"Somebody ambushed Piotr's mind—" Elleni said. "We don't know whose hand pulled the trigger."

"Indeed, these crimes still go unpunished," Duma said, "but there is no mystery. In the warrior Zones, violence is glamorous, sexy, profitable—Mort Valero is a hero! Are gangsters and technocrats people we should trust with our future?"

"Celestina…walked into the line of fire. Why did she want to die, that's the mystery," Elleni said softly. "Would you be made whole by naming enemies?"

"Femi warned us. History warns us," Sidi said. "They are our enemies."

Elleni turned back to the Barrier. Her hair hung limp. "I am not enough. Never enough."

"You would have us honor treaties with these murderers. Explain this. That would be enough," Sidi said.

"Celestina is…alive in two bodies." Elleni blurted this out when she meant to say nothing at all. A Councilor's sharp intake of breath encouraged her. "In a corridor between the stars. Everywhere, nowhere, now and then. Beautiful. The Barrier needs *Vermittler* to make sense, griots to negotiate meaning…weave stories. Paradigma, Los Santos—no enemies—amazing grace." She lost language and gestured gibberish.

Sidi's disks scattered in the air above her head. "Barrier griot, you sing a praisesong to monsters and murderers." Sidi turned away from her to the other Councilors. A strong wind off the Barrier tore at their rayon banners. As the green-fire torches burned low, they shivered and pulled their robes tight. But perhaps they too caught the regret in Sidi's voice. "How can I listen to that?"

"Wait." Awa Xa Ijala, the oldest Council member, finally spoke. The wind made a blizzard of her silky white braids. "Before judging, let's hear all she has to say. I feel the *Egun* are with her."

"Ancestral spirits would not grace such an undisciplined mind," Duma said.

"Stand on the shoulders of the ancestors and you become who you are. We are all in a state of grace, messengers of mystery, carrying the past to the future," Awa replied.

The rest of Council gestured agreement.

Elleni staggered away. Who was Duma, who were any of these people to set themselves above her? She had tasted miracles and reveled in a universe they would never know. Fools. Without her their world might be annihilated, yet they were willing to throw her away like a difficult language nobody could be bothered to speak anymore.

Elleni walked so close to the Barrier, it burnt her nipples and knees. Golden ripples formed around her. "If *Vermittler* cannot knit our people together, then—disaster… The Barrier calls for… *Ebo Eje*."

She backed away from the undulating wall, frightened of the images clarifying in her mindscape. The Barrier didn't want Sidi *instead* of her! *Her monster lover wanted them both.* She and Sidi, naked and without song to protect them, must plunge through a Barrier wound bigger than the sky and journey to the crossroads where dimensions collide. Her nerves popped like firecrackers; cinnamon sweat dribbled between her breasts and down her belly. How would she ever convince Sidi? The Earth exploded in Elleni's mindscape and she fell to the ground, her hair grabbing at the air around her. "I'm not enough. *Keine Feinde* or the Barrier will destroy us."

Duma groaned. "Without the sense to recognize enemies Elleni is permeable to any influence, any dis-ease. How can we trust her, Awa?" He raised Femi's corridor staff above his head and enveloped himself in a splash of burnished gold. "She spreads propaganda disguised as vision, then threatens the end of our world, as Femi predicted. Is New Ouagadougou to be a subsidiary of Electrosoft Corp, an ad-opera vacation resort, a Warzone-of-the-Week special?"

"Don't presume to see for me, Duma," Awa said. "You carry Femi's staff, not his spirit power."

"Why should we trust these ghost stories and histrionic threats?" Duma asked.

"I hear incriminating fragments, but not the full weave of her thoughts." Awa's piercing ice eyes silenced Duma and the murmuring Council. "I hear the Barrier call Elleni to sacrifice herself for us. I hear Elleni's naïve desire to unite all the Zones, and I feel her deep doubt." Then Awa quoted the *First Lessons*. "For every vision a thousand poems. That is what we tell our children."

"This pact with the warrior Zones will destroy us," Duma said. "Let's settle this once and for all."

"No, Duma. Awa is right." Sidi raised her voice above the Councilors' rumblings. "*Vermittler* are convoluted. During the megademic Elleni risked herself to call many of us back from death. Each breath you and I draw, Duma, is her gift to us." Elleni clung to Sidi's words. "Let's not waste ourselves arguing the Treaty where Barrier fever disrupts reason. Let's leave Elleni to meditate on her vision and retire to Council." Amethyst disks settled on her eyebrows and braids. Light from the Barrier colored her skin with jewel tones.

The Councilors nodded. Sidi's voice was like mangoes and cream. It made your mouth water to do what she said. Elleni was a bitter brew. Awa reached out a hand stained blue and gold from mandala dyes and let it hover just beyond Elleni's squirming, hissing hair.

Duma grabbed Awa's outstretched hand. "I am but a flicker to Femi's roaring fire, yet he honored me with the corridor staff, na?"

"Elleni has his medicine bag, a lifetime of wisdom…"

"But tell me, Awa—and there is no jealousy or malice in my heart—great shaman or not, how is this mutant to sit on Femi's stool and center us in the face of disaster?"

Awa jerked her hand from his. "You think you could do better, Duma?"

"I'm sorry, Awa," Sidi said. "When our guests go back across the Barrier to their own homes, we'll put this question to a full Council and see where Elleni stands."

Sidi strode across Canyon Bridge toward the center of New Ouagadougou City, her amethyst disks dodging low hanging branches and vines. Duma and the other Councilors followed, leaving Awa with Elleni.

Elleni wanted to call Sidi back. But she didn't trust her mouth with another word.

26: On Location outside Nuevo Nada, Los Santos
(October 7, Barrier Year 115)

> Never leave a trail that your enemies can follow back to you.
> —Tadeshi Mifune, *Surviving the Future, Last Minute Notes*

Hovering at the edge of sleep, Aaron Dunkelbrot sat in the ruins of the sea-mammal sculpture on the Rock Center set, his achy foot dangling in frigid water.

"She's dead."

"Not yet."

"Okay, so she'll kick off in a few hours."

"Time makes all the difference."

"There's nothing we can do. She's danced her last dance. "

Achbar and Moses paced along the balcony above the fountain and skating rink, arguing over the burnt body of Mahalia Selasie. Mahalia would have burned to death at the shoot this morning, but Achbar put out the fire with his burnoose, gathered her up before Ray caught what happened, and disappeared down a side street in the slum set. Inside his personal transport, he wrapped her in recon-skin and pumped her full of Healer herbs. Yet Achbar had only postponed death. Eventually Aaron would have Mahalia's blood on his hands. She would be his first snuff take, unintentional, a goddamned conspiracy, with not even a pretense at art.

Watching her burn on playback from so many angles, Aaron was totaled. He remembered nights strung out on such intense pain he had wanted to die, but Mahalia sang him into the next day. Astral laments, old time blues, cosmic swing...

Mahalia was into some deep gene art that ticked off a lot of the wrong people, but Aaron couldn't figure who would pull this burning stunt or why. Moses had interrogated the lackey operatives who'd set her on fire, but chemical implants had wiped their memories. One guy exploded and got brains all over Needle Park. Aaron couldn't trust the usual spooks and stoolies to solve this caper. Anybody could be a double agent. Why didn't Mahalia just hideout with the Ghost Dancers? Nobody could have reached her in the Badlands. Aaron looped through these thoughts, trying to shake-down the truth. The conspiracy was probably staring him in the face, but his brain was on the blink.

He nodded off a few seconds and jerked awake again as a jagged fin in the ruined sculpture gouged the side of his head. He splashed cold water at his face and watched a cascade of red droplets scatter around his foot. The A-team claimed they couldn't secure this set against Dancers, rebel Extras, rival studios, or whoever the fuck kept blowing it up. Moses suggested Aaron stick with a Prometheus sculpture like in the old Rock Center, as if the terrorists were pissed at his choice of mythological subject or his disregard for authentic history. Aaron was disgusted. He couldn't remember why he was doing this suicide gig anymore. For Celestina or to break the top ten of all time? Nothing was worth the bullshit he had to suck down. Nothing was worth Mahalia in flames.

Celestina clicked her tongue at him from the corner of each eye. A twin attack, in stereo, something about him not being a coward and telling her story, outlaw footage and all. If the old witch was going to scold him, she should do it in plain English instead of that dead lingo Healers spouted all the time. He wasn't really thinking of quitting anyhow. He was just bone, soul weary. A Healer should understand that and leave off with the tongue action. A Healer should provide relief.

One of Achbar's pigeons flapped too close to Aaron's nose and woke him from a micro-sleep. Achbar strode across the balcony behind the fountain and roared at Moses. With such monumen-tal voice, presence, and killer focus, Achbar could have been a star. Mahalia's blood stained his white burnoose, brocade cummerbund, and pointy embroidered slippers. He looked like a bedraggled hero out of *The Arabian Nights* or *The Thief of Baghdad*. Moses was dressed for *Gangster Heaven*. This irritated the shit out of Aaron. His only friends in the world, and he didn't know if he should trust either one. They could even be in cahoots trying to topple him.

"Doctors would finish her off, you mean," Achbar shouted.

"No, I mean, they can't help her," Moses shouted back.

"Los Santos medical care is an oxymoron." Achbar dropped his voice dramatically. "Keeping you ill to hit a profit is all those incompetent bastards know how to do."

"I loved her too, but I'm facing facts: seventy-five percent of her body burned. We gotta save who we can."

"Are you that much of a coward?" Achbar said.

Moses's violet eyes blazed in the twilight, like he wanted to shoot Achbar.

"He's no way a coward," Aaron said. When they were Extras, Moses had twice risked his life to save him.

Moses scratched at the rosebud scar. "Why risk transporting contraband personnel when there's nothing to do against space-age bacteria, except—"

Achbar drew a curved sword. Moses reached for his side arm but squelched the impulse as Achbar sliced through a low-hanging pennant that obstructed his descent to the skating rink. "She'd have a chance with a shaman."

"Healer voodoo? Give me a fucking break."

"Not with voodoo, but *Vodun*, or acupuncture, drugs, trance, herbs, surgery, Chi Gong—with any healing art they know." Achbar had spent time with Healers. He went down a seasonal corridor with Mort Valero to raid New Ouagadougou, but claimed a shaman healed him of his gangster ways.

"Boss, there's that guy right at the Healthway, what's his name?" Leaning over the fountain, Moses poked Aaron in the chest with a piece of rubble.

"I'm awake, Mose, just resting my eyes." Aaron tried not to drool. "Zumbi something."

"Zumbi Xa Dojude's nothing but good intentions," Achbar said. "An apprentice, not a shaman. People get dumped in Paradise to die. Health reform's gonna take awhile." Brandishing his scimitar, he waded through icy water to Aaron and dragged him from the fountain. "Get your boots on, Mr. D."

"No, my foot's burning up." Aaron walked barefoot through the rubble. "Did Mahalia save your ass too?"

"Celestina," Achbar said, "and a drowning dolphin."

Before Aaron could digest this, Moses butted in. "We take her down a seasonal corridor to New Ouagadougou, and Carl Samanksi's thugs will have us in a flash."

"We get her to Ray, let him think she's an Extra. He'll do the rest," Achbar said.

"Security lost track of Ray after the shoot," Moses said.

"He's got better tech—Paradigma gear, Healer overlay," Achbar said.

They hurried through arty slums to reach his transport: a camouflage all-terrain job parked by the service vehicles. Aaron admired the design, definitely a silent runner, in and out before you knew you'd been raided. Security couldn't track the Achbar either.

"How do we find Ray and dump a half-dead lady in his lap without getting caught?" Moses said.

"I have a good idea where he's headed," Achbar disabled the bomb lock and opened the side door.

Aaron hesitated before climbing in. "What are you and Ray up to?"

"Ray is up to nothing. I on the other hand take my job as script doctor and production guru very seriously. All aboard, please." Achbar ushered Aaron and Moses in, then disappeared into the back. Aaron was relieved that Mahalia wasn't in the main compartment.

Moses looked equally relieved. "Risking your neck to rescue a dead person is stupid."

"That's what she did for me. I owe her," Aaron said.

He had never been in Achbar's private domain and was surprised by the simple décor—geometric patterns on the walls and upholstery, vines growing down from the ceiling, and scimitars above the viewscreens. Two Healer image-boards displayed illuminated calligraphy in Arabic script. The texts resembled copulating insects as they morphed into music and images and then back to words. Since when had Achbar become a big scholar? A flock of warbling pigeons flew into cages that opened directly to the outside world.

Next to the cages a vase fused to the wall contained wild turkey feathers. Dancers had summoned Achbar to Wounded Knee also.

He emerged from the back in clean black burnoose and pants.

"Did she say something to you?" Moses asked.

"Out of her head since I found her." Achbar dropped into the driver's seat.

Aaron slid into the seat beside him.

"I don't want her talking us into anything." Moses plopped down next to Aaron. "Stick your neck too far out, and somebody will hack off your head."

They headed off toward the Studio gate. The guard at the barricade let them through without blinking. No one would search with Aaron on board. If the guard wondered at their light security he didn't let on. Achbar picked up speed as he drove down Canyon Road.

"Where are we going?" Aaron asked.

"Ray's heading for the closest Healer greenhouses," Achbar replied.

"Why?"

"He's got a nasty problem with an empty bag." Achbar activated the power-net shielding. He looked grim navigating through potholes in the broken down road.

"If you want Mahalia dead," Aaron said, "why not just quick and dirty, a bullet through the brain? This elaborate shit, it's like somebody's making a gangster movie."

"No, a terror flick. Trying to scare us." Moses scratched at the rosebud scar.

"So I suggest an alternate ending." Achbar swerved. They plunged down into a ravine and Aaron's stomach jumped up to his throat. "Sorry about that," Achbar said.

"Someone's trying to sabotage me," Aaron said.

Achbar glanced sideways at him. "We have an indecisive terrorist. He's leaving a back door for us hero types."

"Heroes?" Aaron looked from Moses to Achbar. "That's a dangerous game."

"Way too convoluted. Occam's Razor says go for the simplest solution." Moses was obviously quoting Mahalia.

"Occam's Razor is for chemistry, physics, simple shit, not the human psyche," Aaron said.

"Indeed. Any one of us is more convoluted than lightning, photosynthesis, or a barren moon running around the solar system," Achbar said.

Chasing this thought and private terrors, they all got quiet. At least that's what Aaron did. In the middle of a sigh, he descended into black-hole deep sleep. With his last trace of consciousness, he panicked. What would ever wake him? Before angst attained a psychotic pitch, psychology stretched thin and snapped altogether. He slipped beyond the event horizon, beyond biology and photosynthesis, beyond the laws of chemistry and physics. Nothing mattered except the cold, tight blackness.

27: Nuevo Nada Wasteland, Los Santos
(October 7, Barrier Year 115)

> We have to time travel. Change the past with the actions we take
> now. Rehearse the future. Live each moment like it's forever.
> —Celestina Xa Irawo, "Preamble to the Interzonal Peace Treaty"

As soon as Ray got past location traffic he let the tank drive itself and fell into a fitful half sleep. In his dreams, fossil-encrusted canyon walls whizzed by the viewscreen. Stars vanished, the sky turned black, and a brisk wind picked up. Wily Ghost Dancers watched him from the cliffs. After exactly two hours the tank pulled into a wasteland transport lot and roused him with Kora music. Haunting melodies, close harmonies, and dense polyrhythms—Elleni's music. A twinge of guilt unsettled him. He'd been so close to seducing the transport attendant, and the man wasn't even that attractive... Healers were notoriously polyamorous, so Elleni wouldn't care, but he wasn't partying through atrocity anymore or hiding out in high-wire sexual adventures. He was living a different story.

Ray stepped out of the tank and bumped into voluptuous magenta blossoms hanging from an old-age trellis. Delicate birds the same color as the flowers buzzed by his ears. Sturdy fruiting bushes scented the air sour-sweet. Fields of grasses, an undulating mélange of purple and gold, made him gasp. A few years ago nothing lived near the Barrier. Aquifers dried up, topsoil died, and the desert encroached on farmland several inches a day. The Treaty had changed all that. Shamen and scientists worked their science/magic, what Celestina called *Wiederaufbauwunder*—reconstruction miracle in old German. Microorganisms reclaimed the soil. Ice mountains from the Wilderness, shipped and stored by the Barrier, were a fantastical water supply. Greenhouses beefed up the harvest. Extras no longer died from nightmare viruses, and they weren't marched into the Barrier to postpone famine or shipped in pieces to Paradigma's organ market.

Ray sucked a ripe blackberry until sweetness exploded in his mouth. Licking juice-stained fingers, he wished he'd grown up in New Ouagadougou or Paradigma so he'd understand all the bio-magic. Los Santos's so-called schools skimped on education. Although ignorant, his appreciation was boundless. The back of his throat clenched up and tears filled his eyes. He just didn't get Treaty opposition.

What ignorant, jacked up fools would want to fight miracles?

Ray blew his nose and stumbled across the empty transport lot to the greenhouses. Behind him the Barrier shifted from silver to iridescent purple. His back prickled with the surge of its energy. He resisted the urge to turn and walk toward it. But as in a dream, where the dreamer heads one direction yet ends up somewhere else altogether, Ray found himself standing at the Barrier's undulating surface. A pearly splinter of energy reached out to him. His stomach burned, his legs trembled, but his mind was calm. As the splinter pierced his body, fleeting images formed and dissolved at the border of consciousness. He glimpsed a raging black river. At its muddy banks, two supple bodies flowed seamlessly into each other as they made love across turbulent water. Under the lovers' archway, a sea mammal grinned and a lithe athlete, her eyes the color of a Barrier dawn, ran on water. *Chris.* Ray's throat tightened at the image of his murdered sister—a hero running into battle. He lost his balance and with it the Barrier connection. The splinter of energy danced in front of his stumbling figure then dissipated.

Months ago when the Barrier had first "talked" at him, he'd been queasy and resistant. He'd kept the encounters secret, even from Elleni, yet he valued the glimpses of Chris, looked forward to them even. The images baffled him. Why Chris?

The energy surge from Barrier fever pushed back the fire virus. It also heightened his senses and sharpened his thoughts. He looked around—the transport lots were too deserted. Where was everybody? He hurried to the main greenhouse. Desiccated plants hung across jagged glass and crumpled Electro frames. He ran the last few yards and leapt up the broken stairway. The power-net shielding had been demolished. The door hung on blasted struts.

He stepped over a pile of debris into the dim interior. The lighting didn't respond to his presence. He activated the flash beam on his Electro and scrambled through several shadowy chambers. Shattered plants, melted fiberplastic, and spent ammunition casings littered the earthen floor. The vandals had been thorough, slashing and uprooting everything. Bullet holes, laser burns, and blood told a story of struggle. No bodies, though. Ray's heart pounded and his mind raced. What happened to the people who worked here? Executed or taken hostage? He could only think of one explanation, anti-Treaty goons sabotaging Celestina's *Wiederaufbauwunder.*

A coughing jag slowed him down. He was drenched in sweat and couldn't have said if it was fever, exertion, or fear. He trained his Electro beam on the remains of a malanga bush. These plants were rare in the wild and hard to grow in captivity. Anti-Treaty thugs were courting another megademic! Malanga fruit and the ants that tended their roots were all that kept the vicious fire virus in check. Whose stupid idea was this?

Residual Barrier fever compressed spacetime and literally turned his mind inside out. It was as if a fire-virus epidemic erupted around him in hyperspeed: first children died—hair falling out, skin sloughing off, guts spewing from every orifice—then adults exploded, all more vivid than reality. Ray felt their pain in his body as fiery tumors ruptured muscles, bones, and skin. As he backed away from this virtual nightmare, a familiar voice crowded him.

Nobody makes big money on a cure, nothing like they do on people who never get well. Why vaccinate when you can medicate? Elleni gave it all away. The voice of Aaron's assistant director, Moses Johnson, echoed through the Barrier at him.

Whimpers from here-and-now startled Ray back to his own senses. Someone had survived the terrorist assault on this greenhouse. He ran toward the sounds. Barrier images chased him to the entrance. He tried to wipe interference from his mindscape, but a persistent illusion blocked the doorframe. Naked lovers formed an archway across a raging black river. Two bodies morphed into one. As Ray recognized Celestina, the image dissolved in the moonlight. In the backglow of the Barrier, he saw a woman swathed in white synthetic skin crumpled on the greenhouse steps.

He bent down to her, trembling all over, even his voice when he spoke. "What happened here?" The woman shook her head— an obviously painful gesture. "Where is everybody?" He focused the Electro beam. Her hair had burned away and recon-skin was patched across her skull. "The burning woman."

Raven black hair burst into flames again. This Barrier illusion destroyed his last shred of balance, and Ray tumbled down the broken steps. Impact with the hard ground made him unclench his jaw and gulp at breath. A cloud of dust glinted in the moonlight as it settled on the roadbed. An all-terrain transport vanished in the night. Voices from the vehicle echoed off the Barrier in his mind. *Elleni gave it all away. Who's gonna sit still for that?* The burning woman made a dry, gurgling noise. He squirmed away, not wanting to hear her, not wanting to know anything about her.

"I've lived enough real-life adventure for several reincarnations, okay? No more!"

He had charged into the shoot perimeter to rescue this woman when he thought she was an accident or a sick studio stunt. But finding her this way was like the Interzonal Wars all over again. Ray hoped she would fade like a Barrier illusion. The moon rolled in and out of storm clouds, and wind off the Barrier sent chills through his sweaty body. The burning woman smelled like war, like death approaching. She finally passed out but didn't disappear. Ray jumped to his feet and marched toward the transport lot, planning to abandon her in the dirt. Yet in less than a minute he found himself standing over her body again, confronting the unbearable.

"I'm an actor. I just play heroes. I don't want any part in this, you understand?"

She didn't.

How to pick her up? Ray swallowed his revulsion. She was like a side of half-cooked meat that still whimpered. He scooped her up and staggered back to his tank. Her labored breath was sour-sweet and made his volatile stomach flip-flop. He looked away from the greenish pus oozing out of her wasted flesh and watched the Barrier until he had laid her on cushions in the back compartment of his vehicle. Blessed be the fan who spared no expense seducing him.

A sound like machine-gun fire against the roof made him race to the steering frame to engage the power netting. He'd been too cavalier, acting as if the world was at peace. Checking the surveillance-Electro he didn't scope land or hover vehicles in normal shooting range, but the weather report looked suspicious. Balls of hail from a single cloudburst banged against the roof. He stuck his hand out the side viewscreen, caught a few icy bullets, then activated the power netting all the same.

The burning woman moaned. Should he have laid her on her side instead of propping her in a semi-reclining position? He worried about fluid in the lungs but didn't really know what he should do for her or for himself. His Barrier fever reprieve wouldn't last. The fire virus would come back with a vengeance, might even turn contagious. He buzzed Elleni's Electro, but she still wasn't available for live transmission. He left his channel open, posting a priority flag for her to buzz him as soon as she could. Without the fire ants and malanga, the virus might kill him in a month, next week, or tomorrow. And not just him.

He changed out of blood- and pus-covered clothes. Smearing slush across his feverish face, he activated the bio-computer and slumped into a passenger seat.

Megademic. It would take more than a fake action-adventure hero to deal with that. He closed his eyes. The tank drove itself from under the one-cloud storm and headed back to location central.

28: New Ouagadougou City, New Ouagadougou
(October 7, Barrier Year 115)

> Our struggle is an old one, perhaps down into our cells, our genes. *Was der Bauer nicht kennt, das frißt er nicht.* What the farmer doesn't know, he won't eat.
> —Celestina Xa Irawo, "Preamble to the Interzonal Peace Treaty"

Angry voices echoed across the Canyon Bridge as Healer Councilors returned to the city, arguing with Duma and Sidi. Was Elleni, a Barrier junkie, fit to center them? Phaseshifting, never settling on a form—did she feel the world as they did?

Elleni squirmed in the gravel at the Barrier's edge. The Councilors' words cut into her, deeper than the stones slicing her naked breasts and thighs. Only Awa had not deserted her. The old shaman pulled a flask from her medicine bag and, stroking Elleni's face, poured a sweet liquid onto her lips. Elleni swallowed and sighed. The potion soothed the fire in her belly, and Awa's touch made her sane for a moment.

"Do you believe Femi's vision, Awa? Will I destroy the world?"

Awa took a moment to speak. "All by yourself? I think not."

"I wish Celestina had left mandalas or illuminated calligraphy in the Library of the Dead."

"Celestina hid her mandalas and image-boards in a fortress on Fire Mountain."

Elleni stared at Awa, mystified.

"She bomb-locked the door. Booby-trapped the whole place." Awa massaged Elleni's neck.

"It's ten years since I've been there." Elleni drew herself up on bruised elbows. Fire Mountain made her feel anxious, inadequate.

"Celestina said her visions were nightmares, penance for several lifetimes of sin, nothing to share."

Elleni was stung by her childish naiveté. "I thought she stock-piled wisdom too beautiful, too dangerous for Femi and his followers." Without meaning to, she'd sainted Celestina long ago. "Perhaps Duma and Sidi are right and someone has colonized my soul without me knowing it."

"I don't believe that. Neither do you. You know what is gathered inside of you."

Elleni clutched Awa's hand. "In the Barrier, I felt as though I *was* truth. Now my visions seem insane. How could Celestina be alive, twice? How can she be alive at all? The Barrier is more than I can comprehend alone in my skin, more than a single mind can think."

Awa pulled away from Elleni, clenching her fists.

"Please, Awa, don't give up on me!" She would have crawled after Awa, but she couldn't coordinate locomotion. Instead her hair groped the chilly air for warm-blooded contact.

Awa stepped back within reach, and Elleni's hair gripped her ankles. "Not you, child. I am offended with myself, with the others. We have treated you...and the other *Vermittler*...abominably."

"What others? Untutored, undisciplined, they are not true *Vermittler*." Elleni didn't know how much Awa knew, how much it was safe for her to know. "A few raw ones disappeared into the warrior Zones. Those…who remain in New Ouagadougou…are not aware of themselves."

"Celestina thought it was best that way."

"She told you—about *Vermittler*?"

"Celestina and I agreed that I should not speak of this to anyone until… When she was gone, I'd know whom to tell and when…but it's so terrible a story, too terrible."

Elleni stared with unblinking eyes at the old Healer struggling to speak. With so little control, she could not touch Awa's mindscape. Instead, white foam dribbled from the tips of her dreads, floated on the breeze, and burst, scenting the air with patience.

Awa's eyes suddenly filled with tears. "Seventy-five years ago Celestina's sacrifice was Double Consciousness."

"I never completed the *Final Lessons*. I don't understand," Elleni said, ashamed of her ignorance.

"Two people in one body. Femi's doing, but the whole Council condemned her. I'm the only Councilor left from that time."

"How could anyone have thought of Femi as wise and—"

"The dangers Femi warned us of from the warrior Zones were—are—real. Celestina is proof of how easily we could betray ourselves and jeopardize the whole community, the future. In Paradigma and Los Santos, there is a ruthless disregard for what is most valuable in life. This permeates all that they do, all that they are. We in New Ouagadougou must always be vigilant if we are not to be contaminated by them, not to become them. Yet…Femi feared *Vermittler*—he thought the forming of new species by genetic recombination and co-evolution was an abomination."

"What of chlorophyll, mitochondria, and—"

Awa waved her hand. "Not enough to convince him. He waged Holy War against *Vermittler*." She sighed. "Femi swept through us like an Orisha, a bold deity riding the spirits of his acolytes, holding us hostage to his fears. What we did—we were no better than our enemies... I'm still ashamed. We can only change the past with the actions we take now." She paused. There was more to the story, yet she had come to the end of what she could bear to tell.

Celestina, *Geistesmutter* and shaman, who had initiated her to the mysteries of the universe, whose medicine bag and lifetime of wisdom Elleni now carried, this woman had been two people in one body and no one that Elleni knew at all.

"What will your sacrifice be, Elleni? What does the Barrier ask of you?"

Elleni felt the world explode from her insides out. The Barrier swallowed all of history. A bold braid snaked around Awa's blue and gold fingers and spit sparks, but Elleni could not force her Barrier experience into words despite all the languages she knew. After a long silence Awa sighed, shook free of Elleni's hair, and without another word disappeared into the cathedral-tree forest.

Elleni felt as if even shadows raced away from her, rejoining their hosts rather than sharing the darkness with her. With alien fears and unworldly thoughts multiplying, her mind slipped far from the human realm. How would she find her way home again?

29:   Cross-Barrier Transmission/Personal
(October 7, Barrier Year 115)

From: Lawanda

To: Sweet, Sweet Major

A quick hit to let you know I ain't give up the ghost, yet. Whyn't y'all send me to the New O to ambassador? Least Healers kill you with kindness. Tell you the stone truth, seasonal corridors be lookin' real good again. Last few days I keep endin' up at the Barrier's edge without knowin' how I get there. Don't laugh, but there's a boogey in my head, talkin' with Celestina's voice, and she be sendin' out like a SOS from the Barrier. Take all I got not to just hat up and tip on in. Captain ain't gettin' no sleep trailin' my ass. Don't worry, I ain't gone mental. What it is—I'm way past my expiration date as Vice Ambassador to LaLa land, you know what I'm sayin'?

I ain't gettin' shit done here, so what's the point?

After a miraculous recovery, Armando Jenassi done got back in the driver's seat, which be just fine by me. Course, when I talk to him 'bout Treaty violations or significant shit, it's like ain't nobody home. What I got to say to anybody anyhow?

Who's that triflin' chickenhead bitch from Troy talkin' 'bout the sky's fallin', let's get the fuck outa here, Cassandra? And ain't nobody listenin' cuz the sun god work his mojo on her, cuz she don't think he cute. Like he don't have enuf bitches tellin' him that nonsense all day long. Why he gotta have her too? Greedy motherfucker. So then the sky fall down, catch everybody out, mess 'em up good too, but they mad at Cassandra, not the sun god. Ain't the sky his realm? Ain't the nasty shit that twisted they lives his fuckin' fault in the first place? What the hell kinda god is he? Folk jammin' his altar with they girl children and still ain't nobody listenin' to Cassie, call her crazy and shit, wanna off her cuz she ain't 'bout to give it up to no sun god, just cuz his chariot go at the speed of light. And the sky fall down on 'em again.

That's how I feel in Los Santos, like the sun god's after my ass, so I'm layin' low. Got the Captain worried—no appetite for protein sticky. Shoot, that recon-food make me gag, look like maggots on toast.

I been gettin' tons of Ghost Dance feathers, like peacock's be shakin' booty all over my transport. Feathers in my bed, pressed in the pages of my sketchpad, in my funky drawers—no security so tight these born-again Sioux can't squeeze thru. Captain say maybe it's cuz they be renegade *Vermittler* messin' 'tween our spacetime and another dimension and they just come up static. Whatever. Feathers're some kinda code, but I can't find nobody who know what the hell it all mean. Nobody who'll talk to me, that is. I think it's somethin' big tho, so I got the Captain puttin' out feelers. I'm on this, like you said, see if I can work a Ghost Dance alliance.

7-Stories almost apologize for gettin' nasty with me 'bout mind-doodlin'. Bring me violet orchids and fizzy drugs and say he come up from the bottom, survive a stint as a Extra and make hisself over, that's why he don't know how to act all the time. When you a Extra, they try to steal your humanity, so he be all the time tryin' to steal it back.

Man sure know what to do to get my attention. Talk his way right into my transport, sayin' I shouldn't be a colonized woman livin' insida somebody else's story, need to write my own story. He make hisself at home on my sofa bed, a real smooth operator, rappin' hisself silly. Fifty minutes go by and I don't say nothin' but hmm hmmm. He talkin' bout hookin' up Paradise Healthway with Ghost Dancers and this "Union of Rebel Extras." You ever hearda them? 7-Stories say, I'd fit right in with 'em—alotta do-gooder folk that ain't happy 'less they riskin' booty for somebody else.

He drop a born-again Sioux contact on me, but warn me not to play around, promisin' shit I can't deliver. Dancers be serious as a heart attack.

I'm hangin' on 7-Stories' every word and then the sucker start talkin' shit: my eyes be like a mysterious blackout and red syn-silk pour down my curves like wine. He get halfway thru some nonsense 'bout my smile, but gag on hisself when he peep my stash of feathers. Just like he'd seen a ghost. He pretend he ain't freaked, but alluva sudden he gotta go. I see thru that. At least he set me straight first. (You know how I hate bein' ignorant.) Feathers ain't from no peacock. Wild turkeys got a tail of blue eyes too, but that's all he say for now. After he get over this production hump he promise me his undivided attention. Sounds ominous. I hang the feathers on the wall with all the other shit I can't figure out.

One thang for sure, the default settin' for humanity in this Zone is white. The resta us be aliens, freaks of nature, or invisible, like who we are don't count. That don't mean Los Santos be some whitebread Zone, they steady bitin' off colored folks' style, but conveniently wipin' us from the collective consciousness. Frontin' like *everythin'* was they idea in the first place. They even invented *gettin' down*! Freaky. Folk look right thru me or get ripped cuz I don't wanna talk they talk or walk they walk. Like 7-Stories trippin' over mind-doodlin' and virtual reality, Sim-Vue, SV mess, they all maddog pissed cuz I ain't so shamed of myself that I wanna throw me away. Look, they say, Los Santos got black popes and Asian general secretaries. What I care one way or another 'bout all that, 'less it mean I can be who I wanna be?

Hey, I ain't goin' fuck they sky god, no matter how fast his chariot go.

I don't see how colored folk put up with this funky shit for all those years. 1492, when the Indians discover there's a Europe out there or 1555, when the first slave ships come to America, just numbers the old folks make us learn. I never feel the numbers in my body 'til I come to Los Santos. Centuries and centuries, that's a long time to be under spirit assault. I'm 'bout to freak after a few weeks!

Even when I'm feelin' ambivalent, sendin' down a channel to you lift my spirits, make it so I can hold out. I know you busy, so you don't have to respond or anythin'. It's just, nothin' is like I thought it would be.

Not even me.

Lawanda

30: Nuevo Nada Wasteland, Los Santos
(October 7, Barrier Year 115)

> Ain't no statute of limitations on responsibility. Just cuz somethin'
> went wrong a thousand years ago don't mean we ain't gotta make
> it right today. I'm a optimist. I say it's never too late to change.
> —Geraldine Kitt, *Junk Bonds of the Mind*

"THE PROMISED LAND." The burning woman's scream was
like a laser-blade slicing through Ray's skull.

They were halfway to location central and she was crying out at
every curve and bump in the road. Ray dragged himself to the back
compartment wondering what he might do, short of strangulation,
that would keep her quiet. The synthetic skin on her stomach had
completely dissolved. Gummy discharge coated his cushions. Seeing
her, he wanted to vomit, but his stomach was mercifully empty.

"My greenhouse," she said. "What have they done to my greenhouse?"

"Don't worry about that." Always the good actor, he affected a
soothing tone.

Her eyes fluttered open, and she reached her hand toward him.
"Why vaccinate when you can medicate? Elleni gave it all away."

Could she hear the voices off the Barrier too? "What?" He
stepped closer.

"You'll take me to the Promised Land?"

"Sure." Anything to keep her quiet. He gently grasped oozing
fingers. "To the Promised Land." Synthetic skin and dead flesh
pulled away from her bones. Ray thought of an overdone turkey
roast and gagged. She flinched, but held on to him.

"Robin and Thandiwe were right. Femi was wrong. The Barrier's
alive, gobbles up everything. A lavish symbiotic affair." She drew
Ray's ear to her lips and whispered. "Robin and Thandiwe had
Barrier intercourse: they know. Symbiogenesis."

He furrowed his brow at the unfamiliar word.

"Symbiogenesis, new species formed by genetic recombination and co-evolution." Panic flitted across her face. "But the fire ants, we must save the ants, before it's too late, before the Barrier gobbles us up too." Her eyes were wide and clear. "I saw the Earth explode." She was suddenly agitated, twisting and kicking. "Going to the Promised Land and we'll sing truth with Robin and Thandiwe."

"Yes." Ray nodded. "Easy now. We'll sing with Robin and Thandi. Just rest."

"You know Robin and Thandi?" She sounded thrilled.

"Well…"

"They are your friends?"

"Yes," he lied. He didn't want to know them. They were obviously bad news renegades or crazy Ghost Dancers.

"Beautiful lovers like a bridge over troubled waters, brilliant gene artists, but murdered, like me! My own fault." Green fluid dribbled out of her lips. "Genesis to Revelations in a flash. Femi was wrong. Sing…" She lost consciousness again.

"Damn!" The Barrier had shown Ray lovers arched like a bridge over a black river. He hoped she would speak again and clutched her fingers several seconds before noting that the synthetic skin had dissolved. Raw bones and slippery noodles of scorched muscle revolted him. He had to stifle an impulse to fling her hand away. The bio-computer squealed at an anomaly in the road, and Ray jumped. Power nets crackled, brakes screeched, and the tank reluctantly halted.

"Don't worry. Sing," she said, straining at a melody to calm him. Her body was wrecked, yet she still had the voice of an angel…fallen angel.

Ray let go of her hand and smeared her skin and blood on the ceiling. The self-cleaning surface gobbled up the sticky proteins. He lurched over to the steering frame on wobbly knees. The road anomaly was a welcome distraction. He jacked his surveillance-Electro into the bio-computer for better analysis. On screen, a rabbit family waddled across Lazarus Road. No computer had seen that for a hundred years. Ray shut off the power netting and stuck his head out the side viewscreen to catch the spectacle live. Ordinary brown rabbits with dirty white tails scampered away from his high beams. When the last tail disappeared in the roadside gloom, the mini-tank got underway again.

Ray slid back inside the vehicle and squinted at the burning woman. "Symbiogenesis," he said out loud. She wasn't an Extra on location doing *The Transformers*, she was a gene artist working Celestina's *Wiederaufbauwunder*. One of the disappeared scientists doing reconstruction miracles for bunnies and human beings, and anti-Treaty retro-thugs had burned her up—a snuff take as a warning to others. Half dead she was perfect publicity—just like in the old days. The psychotic sons of bitches were waging image war on miracles. Burning their message on her skin...

Ray's hands shook as he pulled fresh recon-skin from his medicine bag and layered it on her burned flesh. The sleazeball who'd cleaned him out had made sure he had more than enough to dress her wounds. Ray gave her a hit of Rapture for pain and blew a hit himself for rage. He had murder on the brain. Fans storming him, missing medicine bag, synthetic skin, burning woman—Aaron and his Muscle-Beach AD played him like a chump in a sappy Entertainment melodrama.

"Damn." Gangsters masquerading as artists had no finesse. No way could he go on starring in *The Transformers* after this stunt. Killing Aaron and the boys would be easier than doing art with them.

Ray ripped into his munitions locker and pulled out a long-range weapon that the Major had given him for extreme emergencies. The black metallic plastic was cold against his fingers and feather-light, yet it could take out a city block with one shot. In the mini-tank he was almost invincible. He'd blast through their pathetic location power nets and smoke the bastards before they knew what hit 'em.

The burning woman burbled and reached in the air for him. "To the Promised Land, take me to the Promised Land—before it's too late. Let me cross over."

The weapon slid from Ray's hand. He should go to New Ouagadougou. If he couldn't find Elleni, there'd be other Healers who would help both of them. He sighed, wishing the Rapture would kick in, wishing he felt nothing real. He reprogrammed the bio-computer to drive the tank to New O City via the east Barrier. The seasonal corridors were open, but he couldn't do an official crossing with a wounded renegade. He'd fry the first guard who hassled him. That left emergency procedures: using his bio-corder to mimic Elleni and sculpt a corridor. Elleni was fierce about keeping this secret, but given the situation, he'd have to risk it. His jaw clenched. Driving a corridor was his worst nightmare—too many vivid memories of people near and dear getting smoked in the Barrier.

The tank lurched through a pothole and Ray was thrown into the driver's seat. He activated the safety belt and set an alarm to warn him at the Barrier's edge. Auto-drive didn't function with Barrier interference; he'd have to steer the tank down the corridor himself. He smashed his hand against the front viewscreen and blew two more hits of Rapture into his veins. He wasn't a low-life thug. He couldn't afford to have murder on the brain.

31: Miracles

> You see what you think you see. You find what you look for. If you
> can't imagine it, it won't happen for you. Imagine the impossible,
> imagine the spirit of your enemies, imagine miracles, imagine the
> last moment of your life, imagine eternity. Imagine what you can't
> imagine.
> —Vera Xa Lalafia, *Healer Cosmology, The Final Lessons*

They say Celestina died once, but had to come back to life.
Death didn't want her storming his domain. For citizens of New
Ouagadougou this was no quaint urban legend, but poetic truth.
They longed to know the story behind the story. Who would tell
them, now that Celestina had gone on to dance with the ancestors?
Elleni should write a suite for the fifty-stringed Kora. *Daughter of
my mind and spirit, do you hear what I say? Sing my song, Elleni.
Dance my struggle.*

The sun drifted below the hills surrounding *Seelenwald,* the forest
of souls. Celestina was two people again, Thandiwe and Robin, sixty
years ago, just moments before she betrayed herself. Alora blossoms
unfurled in the twilight, splashes of color popping open among the
shadowy cathedral trees. Enchanted by their florescent glow, Robin
leaned against a slippery tree trunk and slid to the ground.

Forty years of sun and wind, of unanswered questions and hard
living, had mapped deep lines in Robin's forehead and around her
hazel eyes and inward-turned mouth. Bad gene art had thinned
her wavy brown hair, so she'd cropped the sparse tresses to a downy
skullcap. Thandiwe ran her fingers through this elegant buzz cut
while plucking alora blossoms. Robin rarely smiled, but this evening, savoring Thandi's touch and gazing up through branches and
vines, she grinned so hard her jaw ached. Fearless weaver-ant sen-
tries spit venom at the giant intruders as their younger sisters re-
paired a storm-ravaged nest.

"Old-lady weaver ants are fierce about protecting their homeland," Thandiwe said.

Robin didn't hear her. She was on another track. "I can't believe you just sashayed into Council and snatched the Healers' top-secret holiest of holies from the shrine." Robin pointed a teak and ebony corridor staff at the flurry of life above her. Warriors worn smooth from years of handling cavorted around the wood. Femi's staff was almost as old as the Barrier. "Nobody in Paradigma has ever gotten their hands on an artifact from another dimension. Hell, people don't know these corridor staffs exist."

"It's a secret in New Ouagadougou as well. Only Council, only those initiated in the *Final Lessons*, know about opening the corridors."

"We're about to change everything! Vera Xa Lalafia's final wisdom belongs to the world. No more retro secret-society politics, no more holding truth hostage, no more barriers keeping us from one another, no— Ow!" Robin sliced her hand on the red orange crystals above the warriors. "That's sharp!"

"Can you see the new world we're making? What does it look like?"

Robin sucked a bloody finger. "I don't know, but I'd like to hurry up and get to it. When do we cut a corridor and get the hell out of Dodge?"

"They'll be watching the Barrier for miles, checking everyone. We couldn't get close enough to make a corridor. But Council won't look here. People come to *Seelenwald* to speak to the dead or die. We're safe for a few days, then we can leave." Thandiwe hovered above the renegade scientist. Spidery robes clung to her sweaty skin but concealed nothing. An ordinary middle-aged brown woman with gentle eyes, plump cheeks, and an expressive jaw, she whispered prayers in the twilight. She asked the universe to forgive them both in a language Robin did not speak.

"I thought most Healers didn't believe in God, so why are you always praying?" Robin asked.

"We believe in *prayer*, in the power of words to transform reality," Thandiwe said. "The mind feasts on metaphors." Deadly alora vines filled her arms, and she showered them down on Robin. "The alora bloom only one night."

The spicy fragrance of the blossoms and Thandiwe's earthy scent intoxicated Robin. Although she was loath to let Femi's staff slip from her grasp, she leaned it against the tree and pulled her beloved to the ground, kissing at raisin nipples through the spidery robes. "I could die right now," Robin said.

"What?" Thandiwe's body stiffened.

"Don't Healers say that in one of your multitude of languages?" Robin sat up and gazed at Thandi who was framed by black marbled roots arching out of the ground. "God, you look so serious. That's my dour face, not yours."

"We don't play with death," Thandi snapped. Her eyes filled with tears. "I never understand you."

Robin brushed the back of her hand across Thandi's cheeks and lips. "Figure of speech. Doesn't mean anything, just, I'm on the threshold of the greatest adventure of my life. You and I, my sweet, about to go down in history. I'd like to hold this moment, forever."

Thandiwe pulled Robin between her thighs. Their skin stuck together. Robin's shorts had crawled up to her crotch.

"Alora leaves sharpen the mind, chase away madness." Thandiwe broke leaves off the vines. "Chew slowly, it's like a veil lifted, like a moment of forever."

Robin hesitated. "Are they all right to eat, straight from the wild—without washing? How do they taste?"

"Sweet," Thandiwe said. "And the rain has washed them clean."

"For you, my love, anything." Robin opened her mouth and closed her eyes. Thandiwe balled up a fist of leaves, but brought it to her own lips instead. Robin, her mouth still gaping open, peeked at Thandiwe with one eye. "What are you doing?"

Thandiwe placed the lethal leaves on Robin's tongue with shaking hands.

"You're not having any?" Robin chewed slowly and swallowed. "Forever tastes pretty good. Something in this mimics neurotransmitters?" She jumped at a branch snapping in the woods. "What's that?"

"The wind, an animal, some spirit moving in the twilight." Thandiwe looked toward the sound. "Not a posse chasing us down for our crimes. Not yet."

Robin stared into the gathering darkness. "Do Healers really believe *Seelenwald* is haunted?"

"Of course not. Our imaginations are haunted, not a grove of trees." Thandiwe turned back to Robin, tears blurring her eyes. "You still can't see who we are, can you?" She fed herself leaves and wilted flowers.

"Second thoughts? Don't worry, I have you to guide me through ignorance." Robin pressed her mouth against Thandi's belly and enjoyed the quivering that radiated from her lips. At a loud gasp of passion, Robin felt triumphant. "I'm stealing you and his corridor staff, Femi will certainly be jealous, when he finds out."

"Indeed. He is *der Geistesvater,*" Thandiwe said tonelessly.

Robin's lips went dry against Thandiwe's trembling stomach. "The 'father of my mind and spirit.' You won't tell me, what does that mean, you were lovers...what?"

Thandiwe sighed. "More than lovers. Femi is my teacher, mentor. We..."

"What?" Robin asked, feeling something awful flicker across Thandi's skin.

"No. I cannot explain to the uninitiated."

"Not even to me?"

"It is a question of experience, not words. An experience that I desecrate by..."

Robin squeezed her. "It's okay. You'll initiate me to all of your secrets, in time. Going against Femi feels like betrayal, but we can't stand by and do nothing as he wages a secret war on *Vermittler.*"

"Stop," Thandiwe pleaded. "No talk of..."

"It's genocide. Rank-and-file Ouagadougians wouldn't go for it, if they knew the truth, I don't care what Femi says about evil empires threatening the future of New Ouagadougou—"

"What he does is wrong...yet, if your whole future is under assault, there's sometimes nothing else but the wrong thing to do. But let's not speak of this." Thandiwe pressed one hand on Robin's mouth and gestured in the air with the other as if to ward off bad spirits, but it was too late. They both conjured images of Femi: a bull of a man, short and stocky, reddish brown skin, bushy eyebrows that met a little off center. For an instant he took up all the room in their minds.

"It's as if he watches us now." Thandiwe squinted through trees and bushes.

"Femi's a warped genius, thinks your thoughts before you do. Kinda makes my heart race," Robin said, "but he's not right. Am I so evil, that I've ruined you?"

"Perhaps I am ruining you," Thandiwe said.

"Ha!" A wave of dizziness blurred Robin's vision and shuffled her stomach about. "This alora kicks in fast."

"Hmm." Thandiwe grunted. Her mind was very clear.

"Hmmm," Robin said. She pressed her face between Thandiwe's warm breasts and savored the musky odors. "I'm rambling. What're you so quiet about?"

"No matter what, I love you." Thandi rested her cheek in the swirl of hair on top of Robin's head. "This is a moment we will always have."

"Romantic." Robin leaned back against the tree trunk to gaze at Thandiwe. The rise and fall of breath, breast, and belly through spidery iridescence was hypnotic. The spicy aroma of their mutual arousal forecasted a night of sweet coupling. Optimism claimed her spirits. "Council's not all against us. The lady with the white blond hair...practically down to her knees...fierce."

"Awa." Thandiwe ripped dead blossoms from a vine and thrust them at Robin.

"I bet we could persuade Awa not to kill *Vermittler* too. What? They're a little wilted, honey." Noting Thandiwe's clenched jaw and scrunched eyes, Robin took the droopy flowers and stuck them behind her ears. "Think what we can learn from *Vermittler*. They're not just hunks of wood and crystal with a few set operations, albeit miraculous. *Vermittler* are a living conduit to another...dimension. Why would Femi want to exterminate a biological treasure?" Robin welled up with tears. "Symbiogenesis—a new species formed by genetic recombination and co-evolution."

"Vera Xa Lalafia was a great shaman to work with the Barrier..."

"A hell of a gene artist, a biological revolutionary..."

"Your passion carries you away, you forget the threat the Barrier poses..."

"No, what Vera did, the *Final Lessons*, it's incredible!"

"You don't know the half of it."

"So why don't you tell me about it?" Robin's tongue seemed to swell and fill her mouth. "Do I sound funny? Drunk or something?"

"No." Thandiwe gathered Robin into her arms with such a grand gesture, Robin felt weak in the knees, like a teenager at first love.

"Femi hates me." Robin's mind was clear as glass, just as Thandi promised. If she shook herself too hard, though, these moments might shatter. "But I understand."

"Do you?" Thandiwe looked directly in her eyes. "He hates us both."

"He thinks I'm stealing your precious Barrier secrets and desecrating sacred mysteries for profit, for SCIENCE, for power."

"Aren't you?"

"No, you know that." Robin laughed. "Sharing secrets, busting the Barrier open won't be the end of the world. New Ouagadougou won't get swallowed up by Paradigma."

"History argues against you."

"History didn't have us to, what is that old Yoruba saying—*Mo so awon enia mi po*—I tie all my people together?"

"I want to believe you, but..." Thandiwe looked up to the stars.

Robin tried to lift her arm, but it took too much effort. She nuzzled Thandi's neck with her nose and lips. "Yeah, okay, so at first I was coming to steal, to desecrate, whatever, but that was before

I got to know you, before I fell in love with you, your whole way of life in New Ouagadougou. What'd I know before?" Thandiwe glanced at the corridor staff she'd stolen from the shrine. "Come on, Healers don't believe in God, so how could Femi claim we're desecrating anything?"

Thandiwe pressed Robin against her. "Honoring the sacred has nothing to do with God. It's a crime, what we've done, what I've done. I am gambling my homeland on the word of a stranger who acts without clear vision."

"What do you mean? Okay, I don't throw colored sand into images, my mandalas are questions." Robin kissed Thandi's salty skin and whispered. "It's like a fairy tale, a miracle. The wicked scientist comes to paradise to seduce the fair maiden..."

Thandiwe groaned.

"All right, seduce the dark, mature Healer woman and steal her world," Robin continued, "but instead of betraying the mighty wizards of the land, the wicked scientist goes native. She and the mature Healer woman PROMISE to work together, to create a bright new world, as yet unseen, undiscovered. There they will live happily ever after."

Sparklers spit light all around *Seelenwald*. For a moment Robin thought dead souls had come to chase them from paradise and she would have to shout them back down to their subconscious realm... But she couldn't remember how to shout or what she just thought or how she'd lost her feet her hands her back her breasts her mouth...

Thandiwe rocked Robin's almost lifeless body.

"You must be careful with fairy tales. There are always many stories behind the one story." Femi's mellow bass filled Thandi's ears. Councilors in funeral regalia, carrying white rayon banners and sparklers, stepped from the shadows. Femi retrieved his corridor staff as they surrounded Thandiwe and Robin. He kicked aside wilted blossoms, his eyes blazing, fire dripping from his lips. "Thandiwe Xa Femi, alora leaves are lethal without the flowers. You know the punishment for murder."

"If you take a life, then it is yours." Awa quoted Council law. She stood beside Femi shaking her head, white blond hair glowing in the dark.

Other Councilors moved in close to hear Thandiwe's response.

"I did what you told me, Femi, to save the world from catastrophe. Our secrets are now safe." Thandiwe pressed against Robin and refused to let Femi take up all the room in her imagination. "I betrayed Council, I betrayed Robin, giving her knowledge that she could not bear. That was my crime, this is my sacrifice. I knew it would mark my spirit as I put poison in her mouth, but how could I think of saving my own soul when the world was at stake."

A few Councilors clicked their tongues and sucked in whistling breaths.

"So, this is your trap, Femi, to be rid of them both," Awa said. She doused her sparkler in the dirt and stepped away from him. "I must walk away from your circle."

Before other Councilors could break ranks, Femi whirled through them, touching uncertain shoulders, glaring into guarded eyes, pounding Awa's objection into the dust. "Those who betray us to the uninitiated condemn themselves. Only a murderer would get snared in such a trap. Thandiwe did not find another way to save the future. Playing on the enemy battlefield, you are the enemy. We must proceed before it's too late. Robin will not linger among the living. Our justice must be swift." He gave the Councilors no time to disagree. "Thandiwe Xa Femi and Robin Wolf, you stand condemned to Double Consciousness." Calling to the Barrier, he sang low notes almost beyond the range of human hearing and pounded the ground with his staff. The Earth was his drum, the stars his witnesses. Who could walk away now?

"Promise you won't leave me alone," Thandiwe whispered in Robin's ears as she laid her on the ground. "Your way would destroy us, but I promise never to betray myself or our dreams again. Don't leave me now, and I'll initiate you to all my secrets. I'll find another way."

Awa turned away from the circle and before Thandiwe could blink, Femi slashed her head with the red orange crystals on his corridor staff. The pain was so loud and dense, she slumped down against an unconscious Robin, gasping and drooling. A shaft of Barrier energy split the night sky. It arced over cathedral trees, passed through Robin, then flowed into the corridor staff. The crystals turned black, like a massive collapsed star. The last thing Thandiwe saw was Femi snorting ashes and sculpting a corridor between her and Robin. In a terrible instant, Thandiwe was engulfed by an alien presence and everything that she had been seemed lost forever.

The sweet song of dolphins chased away the lingering pain, and...

Celestina floated in a magenta sea on the Barrier starship, clutching the soggy roll of parchment that Elleni had tossed in the ocean at her funeral. Elleni was here with her. Elleni was a witness.

Sing my song, daughter.

Femi and the other Councilors never expected Robin and Thandiwe to survive more than a few moments in the same skin, never expected them to keep all their promises. How they managed life imprisonment together for seventy-five years was quite a sordid story, *ein Wunder*, but surely Thandiwe and Robin's debt to society had been paid in full. As architect of the Interzonal Treaty, Celestina had kept all her promises, brought peace to the world. Robin and Thandiwe's suffering should be over now. Why couldn't she die?

BOOK IV

Standing in a rainstorm, I believe.

Bernice Reagon

32: At The Barrier's Edge, New Ouagadougou City
(October 12, Barrier Year 115)

There is one ocean in all our veins, one breath of life to share.
—Celestina Xa Irawo, "Preamble to the Interzonal Peace Treaty"

Elleni phaseshifted.

Sharp ground tickled her belly, and her giggles bubbled through the dust. Cold sweet air slithered across her tongue, like popsicles and ice treats, like the magnetic trail of honeybees, like owls feasting on skunk or the scent of lovers in orgasm and babies being born. Pungent panic soothed by furry paws saturated her skin. The electric storms of sleep were a tonic. Elleni loved the taste of a chill fall's night, but so jumbled up, the world made no sense at all.

A demon sat on her chest and laughed. It had imprisoned her in an invisible cage, allowing only a vague horizontal sprawl. If she could just work her muscles in concert to fight against it, she could stand tall. She had conquered the demon as a babe and remembered flying across the ground and leaping up at the stars. But alas—does anyone say *alas* anymore?—she had lost herself to the Barrier and couldn't remember the simplest spells. That was the joke the demon laughed at, pressing its voluminous girth down on her 'til air escaped from her lungs in a wheeze, in mouth farts, or perhaps she laughed too, as she was of many minds about the matter. Too many minds.

Crumpled up at the Barrier's edge on the outskirts of New Ouagadougou City, her naked butt caught a chill wind that penetrated deep inside. She hadn't washed or eaten or been close to human for days. Not since Sidi and Awa abandoned her to the demon. Villagers thought she performed bizarre *Vermittler* rituals and gave her a wide berth as they scampered down the old highway to lovers' trysts and secret heists. Dead malls had been born-again. Revolution brewed in market ruins. Across the Canyon Bridge, Council rumbled with the words of dignitaries, agents of god, and genius politicians in an Interzonal extravaganza—and Elleni was missing the show. First she had to vanquish the weighty demon and find her way to people again, then she'd worry about politics, about the world lurching off its course and coming to a bad end.

She phaseshifted again.

In the frazzle of energy waves around her head, Elleni barely perceived the finger that touched her nose. Not from a human, monkey, or squirrel hand, in fact the finger was not a finger at all. She might as well have said branch or—what was that other thing? A claw? No, a wing. A wing of Barrier energy tickled her nose. That was how she had gotten into this mess in the first place. Traipsing down a Barrier black hole, beyond light to... It made no sense.

Well, some sense. After years of secret society silence, Celestina wanted Elleni to play a praisesong to her double life on the fifty-stringed Kora. Stealing Femi's ashes was bad enough. Elleni didn't dare make a public praisesong for a murderer. Sidi would never trust her then. But why would Sidi ever trust her? Elleni was too far from human. A human being would be appalled by what Celestina had done, would be too revolted to sing her praises. Elleni was fascinated. Her *Geistesmutter*, the woman who had saved, believed in, and inspired her—"Saint Celestina"—betrayed then killed herself and had to live murderer and murdered all these years in one body. How had she/they not lost their minds?

Elleni grabbed at these thoughts, but they scattered away from her. She tried phaseshifting. but sometime during the travel from one self to another she had lost the way home. The demon danced on her head with glee. Without Ray or Lawanda, without some trusted body to anchor her, every phaseshift took her to more alien ground.

A gaggle of fairies mesmerized Elleni, faceless, tinsel-skirted energy smudges undulating through the blackness beyond her, billions and billions of twinkling fairies, light in the night, reaching for infinity. Her mind was running too fast, if she could just slow herself down...

Elleni didn't want to phaseshift again without someone pointing her in the right direction. She might get so far away as to lose home all together. The demon squatted on her head and chased her thoughts apart.

Not yet, not yet, not yet.

Elleni gathered herself together to make an appeal. If she were not to be scrambled beyond all recognition, if she were ever to convince Sidi to heal the Barrier's wounds and save the universe in herself, she would need a guide to help her find the way to people again. Her monster lover must put out the call, send a message before the demon shattered her or she ran off with the fairies to the circus at infinity.

The branch-claw-wing of Barrier energy rippled with her passionate plea but offered her no sign of its intentions. She would have to trust that what the Barrier made of her request would save them both.

33: Council Hall, New Ouagadougou City
(October 14, Barrier Year 115)

A sharp sting from the earphone attached to the Major's skull signaled an urgent message coming down his priority Electro channel. The fingers in his data glove itched. Lawanda, no doubt, was transmitting from Los Santos and being excessively vigilant. Her timing was terrible. He was standing with Jocelyn and twenty interzonal dignitaries in a "tableau vivant" on the vast Council Hall stage, a prisoner to Healer protocol and Jocelyn's whimsy.

Ten thousand people had gathered in New Ouagadougou's grand opera house for the public ceremonies of the Interzonal Treaty Conference. The theatre was *nouveau Africain*: bold woodcarvings, mudcloth upholstery, and bead and raffia décor. The Conference stage set was epic and relentlessly intercultural. Giant masks, stick puppets, and pageant wagons crowded the stage. The Major gazed at the riot of colors and styles, at Siegfried being dipped in dragon's blood, Rama flying through the jungle amidst an army of monkeys, and Ogun clearing the primordial jungle with a scared machete. If elephants hadn't gone extinct they'd be up on stage trumpeting and defecating their way to glory with the rest of the shysters and showmen. Jocelyn hoped a live appearance at this Wagnerian culture clash would bolster her ailing image as Prime Minister. She desperately wanted to court the rising power in New Ouagadougou despite the Council's open hostility to progress in general and the Treaty in particular.

Security was a nightmare.

The Major couldn't bring mass-destruction weaponry down a seasonal corridor without getting zapped by the Barrier, but then nobody could. Small comfort. He scoped the exuberant ten-thousand-plus audience for suspicious behavior. His squad prowled sculpted catwalks high above the stage and brushed against plush tapestries as they burrowed into the orchestra pits. What artistic wonders greeted his patrols upstage of the midnight blue velour curtains, the Major could not imagine. Healers viewed every bit of spacetime as an opportunity for aesthetic experience. Beauty was not a luxury here, but a basic human right.

So why did he long for a scrawl of graffiti, a few cigarette butts, and the ugly glare of Electro billboards? Did he need to stand in relief to a little dirt, swill a dash of chaos for comfort?

Lawanda accessed his priority channel a second time, no doubt chastising him for not responding. But how could he? He was participating in an historic event. For the first time in a hundred years, isolationist New Ouagadougou welcomed delegates from the "warrior" Zones with live-action high art. Unlike cyber-kinetic Los Santos Entertainment, everything ran in real time. Biocorders were verboten—there'd be no official record of anything, only pirate recordings and ephemeral memories. Life here was not played for the cameras.

Downstage center a chorus of long-winded poets sang praises to each of the twenty dignitaries in several dead languages while sand painters transformed the stage floor with elaborate mandalas of densely packed humans and spirits spiraling around unknown (mythic? extinct?) fauna and flora. One image contained a tall military figure with salt and pepper curly hair, green Asian eyes, broad African nose, and thin mustache, struggling against a monkey on his back. The Major was impressed by the almost photo-realism of the portrait; still, his likeness was stripped of data glove, Electro belt, scrambler, and weapons. There was not a hint of technology in any of the sand paintings—New Ouagadougou was in the throes of serious technophobia.

After standing three long hours in the honor tableau, a thin layer of red, yellow, and blue sand coated the Major's boots and uniform. He tasted sand on his tongue and wiped it out of his nostrils. If he broke the tableau before the final Potlatch gifting ritual to check his Electro, he'd ruin ephemeral sand images and probably precipitate an international incident. His duty was to conquer contempt and fatigue while smoking out terrorists

It would be six hours at least before he could review personal messages.

Thinking about Lawanda induced an intense heat reaction in his abdominal skin cells that quickly spread to the rest of his anatomy. He experienced a rush of emotions, images, and sensations—complex desire, not the focused but empty lust he'd been accustomed to before her. He quickly clamped down on non-professional bodily responses and focused his attention on the Los Santos delegates standing nearby. A sweet-faced thug with rainbow hair and lightning reflexes nodded in his direction—Danny, or Daniel? Lawanda found that seventy-eight percent of Los Santos males had Hollywood or biblical names. In ancient mythology the Lord protected Daniel in the lion's den and let everybody else get eaten alive. A sign?

A flurry of sound and movement just beyond the stage interrupted the Major's rambling thoughts. He and Daniel reached for hidden weapons. An acrobatic musician in a hundred layers of weightless synthetic silk whirled down the aisles in an impromptu embellishment of the ceremony. She paused in front of the Major. He couldn't scope the instrument at her back or what she looked like, except for the static snapping across her pitch black eyes and whiting out her face. Her form flickered in and out of shadows, as if she weren't all there.

Without knowing why, the Major was certain that this woman wanted something from him, that the image before him was an SOS. As he scanned for meaning, his data glove and surveillance gear generated a torrent of error messages. Seconds passed before he realized that unless his equipment deceived him, the musician was suspended in the air. Her feet dangled several centimeters above the stage floor, and a gigantic Kora on her back played itself. The Major jumped back as the audience applauded her theatre magic. Swallowing a ball of static, the mystery performer turned away from the Major and careened out the rear gate without ever touching the ground. She left behind a trail of polyrhythmic harmonies and fragrant airborne filaments—the Major identified scents of cinnamon and jasmine. Where had she come from? Front door, rear gate, and aisle security hadn't alerted him.

"A person could get killed like that." Daniel made a third attempt to bond. "Back home, in Los Santos."

"I know what you mean," the Major said. He preferred concrete exchanges to magic realism.

Carl Samanski, the undisputed top gun in Los Santos had sent Ambrose, his current consort and Ray Valero's former lover along with Daniel, also one of Valero's old flames, to represent him. A sign? The Major studied the exhausted Ambrose as she leaned into Daniel. A tidal-wave blonde with glassy eyes, sans lines, sans pores, she looked airbrushed in real life, definitely Entertainment high art. From Ambrose to Daniel to Elleni, Ray Valero was a man of extremes. The Major found it hard to take Ambrose seriously, but

Lawanda believed that she, Daniel, and Carl supported the Treaty, and that upstart thugs like "7-Stories" Aaron Dunkelbrot were the real problem in Los Santos.

The Major repressed a spike of jealousy as a vivid image of Dunkelbrot, his tongue in Lawanda's mouth, flashed across his mind. Blood in his weapon hand throbbed painfully against his fingertips. He tried to shake out the tension. Lawanda was a terrible distraction. She blurred his edges and put his timing off. He thought every day about ending their liaison in some brutal way. Head of Paradigma's Secret Service, Jocelyn's security advisor, Internal Affairs ace, and right-hand hatchet man for eighteen years, and he couldn't count on himself. Jealousy was ridiculously unprofessional; murdering Dunkelbrot would be a waste of mental and physical resources. He held the throbbing hand over his head, defying gravity and pain. The entire honor tableau followed suit. Healers thought nothing of stretching achy muscles in public, and mimicking a move was a sign of honor.

The Major shuddered out a sneeze. He put eighteen years of ruthless efficiency, a brilliant career, the very security of Paradigma and the future of the world on the line, and for what? A throwback settlement woman, an exotic piece of ass? Luckily, in the pre-ceremony sweep his team uncovered no unexpected plots or weapons. The delegates were on very good behavior, and violence was still an aberration for native Ouagadougians. Even a corridor coup with Mort Valero and his sadistic thugs hadn't turned these witchdoctors around. Peace and tranquility (or actually the usual fear and repression) reigned.

Monkey puppets descended from the jungle treetop set and landed on the delegates' shoulders. The Major thrust a gun in the mouth of the little beast perched on his neck but realized the extremity of his response before blasting its head off. Stunned Healers stared at him, contempt dripping from their smiles.

"You wish to execute this puppet?"

The Major withdrew his weapon. He was very grateful that bio-corders had been banned from this ceremony and that Jocelyn hadn't appointed anybody from the opposition to the delegation.

The audience squealed as the furry creatures nuzzled and teased the guests. Everyone was a clown for a moment. Healers believed in comic relief.

A third urgent message from Lawanda made the Major's pulse spike. Perhaps her transmissions weren't just personal. He glanced at the chronometer in his thumb.

It took eighty minutes and twelve seconds before he responded professionally. He didn't have that kind of time; in twelve seconds the world could end. He might not be able to *talk* to Lawanda, but he could listen. With his data glove, he reoriented the earphone attached to his skull and commanded his Electro to decode the audio portion of the transmission for immediate access. Visual would have to wait. The griots and poets were finally done praisesinging, and Potlatch had begun. He vaguely recalled that Potlatch was an old Amer-Indian trade ritual, but what was the Healer spin? He was definitely slipping, not to have researched more thoroughly.

A slight woman with a gold-streaked face and purple disks revolving above her head beckoned the Major to walk through colored sand images to the poet's platform center stage. Sidi, rising star of the Healer Council, presided over the gifting ritual, not Elleni. A sign? Sidi, with her cascade of delicate ochre braids and voluptuous blackberry lips, was certainly a better face to turn to the world than the macabre Elleni. No detectable physical or electrical mechanism supported Sidi's swirling disks. This seemed beyond the usual bag of tricks that constituted ordinary shaman display—Femi breathing fire, Celestina covered in ants, Duma painting the air with holograms of color. The Major initiated the hyper-dig mode on his computer for a full probe of Potlatch protocol and Sidi's disk phenomenon. Kicking up green and gold sand and exuding charm he didn't feel, he sauntered downstage.

Sidi stood eye-to-eye with the Major, and he was a tall man, a centimeter beyond two meters. He glanced at her feet and to his dismay, they were bare. He was surprised that her height should unnerve him so. Her slender shoulders, full breasts, and narrow waist were reassuring, the opposite of Elleni, whose robust muscular physique made you want to wrestle her to the ground. If Sidi noted his silly discomfort, she didn't let on. Her smile was like an embrace, and her every gesture choreographed to welcome. She sang a few haunting lines in a dead language and presented him with an ancient Yoruba mask, the Orisha "Eshu."

The wooden helmet with four elaborately carved faces pointing in different directions fit the curve of his skull perfectly. The weight spread out along a padded bar across his shoulders. As he split into multiple selves, the Major felt an immediate connection to this old West African trickster god. He bowed warmly to his bewitching host, Sidi, muttered an alert to his squad, intensified the flying disk/Potlatch probe, adding Eshu to the inquiry list, then let his mind absorb the content and tone of Lawanda's messages.

34: Cross-Barrier Transmission/Personal
(October 14, Barrier Year 115)

From: Lawanda

To: Sweet, Sweet Major

You goin' talk to me live some time soon? Is the big J workin' your booty off or you done find you a hot babe? I ain't playin' over here, this shit is urgent!

I'm transmittin' from a bombed-out greenhouse. I'm here to meet a Chief Executive Ghost Dancer to discuss feathers, health care, and the Union of Rebel Extras. 7-Stories tole me not to get my hopes high. Dancers might send a envoy who can't talk or don't know nothin'. I know why they paranoid too. Los Santos is off the hook. Anti-Treaty squad get here before us. Fools be poisonin' malanga plants. Captain say, herbicide, genetically engineered. I bet the same gene-art fool let designer mites loose on fire ants. Nasty slime eat right into they little ant brains and lay eggs there. I scoped a kilometer column of dead ants and millions of mites crawlin' 'round lookin' for hosts. That's why no fire-virus cure at Paradise Healthway. When did gangstas hook up with that kinda gene artist? Nobody in Paradigma can come close, right? Or is that what all the noise over Mahalia Selasie and disappeared scientists be about? Ah shit!

While I'm transmittin', half-dead Dancer drag her naked self in the greenhouse to tell me about a Wounded Knee gatherin'—in honor of Robin Wolf and the Promised Land. A day of the dead thang. That's the deal with the feathers. You need a dozen to make it to the Knee in one piece. I got ten. Ever hearda Wolf—a Sagan City scientist? My sister, Geraldine useta talk about her. Or a Healer named Thandiwe? Fancy gene artists, high end, callin' up lost science from the twenty-first century. Naked Dancer die in my lap tryin' to give me Robin & Thandi's story. I lean down to the poor chile, face to face listenin', and I get her last breath in my mouth. You ever swallow somebody's last breath? It's deep. I feel I got her soul now and it's on me to... I don't know what.

Captain think 7-Stories mighta doublecross us and ambush her. I don't know. She his contact, but we ain't tell him—nobody— 'bout the meetin'. Dancer say creeps catch her pickin' blackberries. They take her for a Extra—no silver face—and be juiced for live Entertainment. They jump on her so fast, she ain't have time to call her spirits for protection. Random joy ridin'. After scumbags dump her in the weeds for dead, them sweet spirits carry her to me and the Captain. She all broken up inside, hands and knees look like she crawl all the way. Captain say, it truly be a miracle she live this far! This Chief Executive Dancer's several shades darker than you, Major. Just FYIin' you.

Gangbangin' Extras still be a pop sport in the countryside. Progress, liberation? Free the slaves and next thang, you got share-croppers, nightriders, and death-wish motherfuckers.

This last week since the "hospital visit" and my heart-to-heart with 7-Stories has been unreal. I wish you was here. Then we could get somethin' goin' on. I'm chill like you say, tryin' not to let nothin' touch me—but when you swallow somebody's last breath, that's kinda rough. I sure as shit don't let nothin' show, a shield over my heart powered up 24/7. I'm waitin' to feel everythin' when I get home with you, so watch out. But let's be real. I'm a waste a space-time over here. Which one of these Los Santos bad boys is ever goin' listen to dark me? I'm a insult on a hundred channels.

7-Stories be hole up in the Nada wasteland to shoot epic slop, and I almost miss him. He stay on my channel with how Dancers save his booty with the race-erase thang. He owe 'em, and now they callin' in the debt, so it's hard to be his usual charmin' self. I don't trust the man as far as I could throw him, but ain't no proof one way or the other—I'm speculatin', all right? I just don't *feel* he ambush that Dancer. He would have made sure she was dead—forget the sexcapade. So I'ma get him to introduce me to his genius gene artist and see what happen.

I mean, I gotta do *somethin'*. Without malanga fruit and the ants, folks goin' be droppin'. Fire virus don't take no prisoners. I scoped the data. That funky germ do a breakout on us, make the last mega-demic look like a block party. You got some tips? This some scary shit! I know we Paradigmites s'posed to be mentally superior, but I can't figure how to enforce a Treaty if ain't nobody listenin'. I mean if I ain't got no enforcers, I'm just fartin' in the dark.

Flyin' auto-bomb squad's on the blink, dive bombin' anybody who go near a toilet, make it hard to do your business. Dealin' with temperamental bio-junk, gangsta double talk, and all these sleazy afterhours folks be workin' my last nerve. Tell you the stone truth, I ain't holdin' together too good. How am I s'posed to go for that eighth impossible story? You do what you gotta do, but, wait— I gotta call you back!

Sorry 'bout the time out. Dodgin' the bomb squad. Captain be paranoid the bad boys mighta left a surprise behind for us. If you screenin' transmissions, I'd really appreciate a live hook-up. Come on, man, you can't just leave me out here like this!

Love you, Lawanda

35: Barrier Corridor, Los Santos to New Ouagadougou
   (October?, Barrier Year 115)

> "Survival of the fittest" be the sort of raunchy, take-no-prisoners metaphor that folk throw 'round to make the universe seem like some sorta competitive meritocracy where the best and brightest get all the props and jacked-up failures get dusted (it's they own fault too). What universe is this? Darwin oughta be hollerin' in his grave.
> —Geraldine Kitt, *Junk Bonds of the Mind*

Ray gripped the steering frame of his mini-tank so tightly the circulation in his fingers was cut off. He sat scrunched up in the driver's seat, soaked with cold sweat for no good reason. The burning woman was resting quietly. Inside the Barrier corridor, the ride was smooth and the landscape unremarkable, like he was driving through smoked glass. The Barrier walls were transparent yet so thick the outside world was shadowy distortions. Overhead, stars blazed closer than normal. A few changed their positions when he wasn't looking. The moon didn't put in an appearance, but it was probably busy on the other side of the world by now. Ray's destination, *Seelenwald*, was a dark smudge on the horizon. He was a renegade sneaking in the back door. An hour's drive or two days, he couldn't tell, there were no reliable spacetime references.

Elleni's voice, broadcast from his bio-computer and amplified by the Electro, echoed back on itself again and again until a poly-rhythmic chorus of Ellenis accompanied him. Gaps in the music as she slipped beyond the range of human hearing broke up the musical syntax. Scattered pockets of silence rattled him. Elleni after all was at home in this alien place. Ray was an interloper, and a sheer wall of death beckoned him to veer right or left into oblivion.

Glancing in the mirror, Ray noted his ghostly pale face, red-rimmed eyes, and bluish lips. Behind him the burning woman burbled and gagged. He'd done his best to clear away junk and cushion her ride. Fear sliced up his insides. He couldn't go any faster and keep control of the steering, yet he was afraid she'd die before he could locate Elleni.

A surge of alien energy slithered up Ray's spine. He slammed on the brakes and reversed the engines. Inertia carried the vehicle along the almost frictionless surface for quite a distance, but finally the tank skidded to a halt. Ray eased out of the driver's seat and stumbled down into the back compartment. His skin burned. Claws of Barrier energy broke through the viewscreens from all sides and reached out to him. He thought of horror Entertainment as he backed away from the undulating blobs and tentacles. The Barrier had never touched Ray in a corridor before. It took him a moment to find the necessary calm to relate. The Barrier waited for an invitation, then rushed into him as he closed his eyes.

Images overwhelmed his senses so thoroughly, he was transported to another time and space, twenty-six years ago.

"Clock me, but first the kiss! You promised."

Ray opened his eyes and Chris, his older sister, sank down in front of him at the starting gate of an ancient racetrack in the Sol wasteland. The track was in good shape except that the Barrier had gobbled up the finish line. Chris, sporting shiny green racer togs and her champion's badges, was about to run her final race—into the Barrier. Drug resistant bacteria were eating her from the inside out. Rather than wait for the micro-orgs to finish her off, she chose this day to die. Ray was the only person she would ever trust or love in her short life, and she wanted to know how love felt in her body. She had begged him to help her go out with style, with the romance of ancient Entertainment. Ray would have done whatever Chris asked, even made love to her, if that would have stopped her insane race into the Barrier. But besides a moment of farewell passion, all she wanted from him was a lifetime of great art and deep truth.

"I know you can do it," Chris said. She was always bossing him around.

Ray whined at her. "Truth and beauty, come on…"

"Don't be one of them," she said, sucking back snot and tears.

He had promised that already, so the only thing left was the kiss.

"Wait," Ray said. This was his sister for godsakes. He felt shy and desperate, and he didn't want her to die. "Please."

"I can't," Chris replied.

He always wondered: if he hadn't kissed her, would she have run anyway?

"Now or never, hero!" Chris grinned at him.

He had to smile at her boldness, and then he kissed her, not a brother's chaste touch of lips to cheek or forehead, but a deep lover's kiss—performed with the innocent passion of a fervent young actor and adoring brother. She was the best person he had ever known. His impending loss heightened the erotic charge, and her willing mouth dissolved his inhibitions. His hands moved across her body, muscle and soft tissue contained by the thinnest layer of athletic polymers. Feeling her respond to his touch, he would have plunged into her, but Chris slipped away from his tongue and fingers and dashed off toward the Barrier.

"Clock me!" she shouted.

Fumbling with his chronometer, Ray complied. As Chris streaked away from him, the infected gunshot wounds in her shoulder oozed black blood. Two years and Los Santos doctors couldn't push back the bacteria—they weren't Healers. Yet high on Rapture and Barrier fever, Chris broke her previous records for speed. Ray wanted to scream, but he was so aroused, so choked with tears, he could barely breathe. When she disappeared into a brilliant cascade of Barrier energy, semen, tears, and snot gushed out of him. Appalled, he scratched at the dirt to bury his shame—in vain. The ground was rock hard.

Ray groaned across all the years since that day. His Uncle Mort had murdered Chris, not the Barrier, shot her down in cold blood on a location shoot in Nuevo Nada when she wouldn't stand around and watch him and his crew rape an Extra. That final race was Chris's eulogy, her funeral parade. After the Barrier claimed her, Uncle Mort had set Ray on the road to stardom. Ray had been too much of a coward to resist. Talent alone would never have gotten him so far in the industry, and what actor could resist playing heroes and gods? He'd been fourteen with a gun at his head. What was he supposed to do, die or be a star-hero?

Chris was the real hero. She joined the rebel Extras and stood up to their gangbanging, murdering uncle. She died for what she believed, while Ray was a common gig slut, playing to the highest bidder. Whenever he lost himself in a role, he tried for the art Chris had asked for, but Mort always extracted his percentage. Deep truth was an adolescent fantasy. Chris hadn't understood the world or she would never have asked him for something so impossible.

Every day for twenty-six years, he had replayed Chris's final race. This Barrier-amplified version was devastating. Sticky semen slid down his thigh. There was no time for shame to crowd his spirit. Instead of dissolving into bright nothing, Chris charged through red alpine roses in a snowy mountain meadow. She turned to smile and wave at him. When he didn't reply, she put hands on hips and scowled. The ugly wounds in her shoulder had healed. The gray in her braids and thin lines around her eyes startled him. She had aged, but this was still his Chris, demanding a response. Sheepishly, he waved, then even managed a grin.

"Clock me, hero!" She raced up a blue white glacier. Golden Barrier energy shone through her body, and although she was dashing away from him, she seemed close enough to touch.

"Chris?"

All his life he'd heard Ghost Dancer con men claim that one fine day the ancestors would come back from the Barrier and liberate the oppressed spirits of true believers. Chris had been into it, but Ray never bought a word of their retro-trash. Yet here was his murdered sister come back from the land of the dead, close enough to hug.

"Make me a believer," Ray said and reached for her.

The Barrier fever had broken. His fingers grazed the burning woman's face, not Chris's or... He shook his head, trying to clear his vision as his fingers touched Elleni's swollen lips. She struggled to form a word on his fingertips. *Ray...* And he ached with her longing for him.

Barrier twilight suffused the back compartment, and Elleni disappeared. Ray lay on the mini-tank floor shivering and sweating. The Barrier was using Chris to guide him to Elleni.

The burning woman whimpered and writhed on sticky cushions. He brushed his fingers against her lips. "I'm on my way." He hoped Elleni could hear him. The burning woman grew still under his touch. He hurried to the driver's seat and released the brakes. All this time not being able to reach Elleni, and it had never occurred to him that she might be in danger and need him. Too many years as a sex toy or adventure fantasy had cramped his imagination.

36: Council Hall, New Ouagadougou City
(October 14, Barrier Year 115)

Fire virus don't take no prisoners. Lawanda's words hurtled through the Major's mind like torpedoes locked on target. Things she'd said were always blasting him at the core, but he could never predict what it would be. If he believed in magic or Freudian psych, he'd have said she bewitched him. Except Lawanda didn't twist him up in lies and illusions: she allowed him to feel the danger he was in, the danger they all were in.

"Nice hat," Jocelyn said, sliding her fingers across the Eshu mask. "A stupid wooden bird that's gone extinct—that's what Sidi dumped on *me*." Jocelyn thrust the ebony sculpture in his face, and for a second time this historic evening, the Major's pulse spiked. Reluctantly, he dragged his focus back from Lawanda's transmission to the Council Hall stage and his Prime Minister's irritation. "Talk about a waste of spacetime! I think five hours of griots spouting gibberish and sand men decorating the moment qualifies as torture. Who are Healers to complain about atrocities in Los Santos?"

He checked the chronometer in his thumb—another hundred-seventeen minutes lost. Potlatch was over and the tableau vivant dissolved into power caucuses. The audience departed in an orderly fashion, with no storming the rest rooms or exits. Upstage, Ogun and Rama fought over two giant monkeys. Ogun's costume gave the illusion he strutted through flames. Rama's endless sleeves were like a rainstorm. Was this part of the post-show extravaganza or everyday shaman display? The Major's earphone buzzed with squad updates. Nothing significant, or rather, nothing violent.

"I've got sand everywhere." Jocelyn fingered Eshu's back visage. Her wavy red hair hung loosely over bare shoulders dusted with a sprinkle of brown and gold freckles. The fine lines around her green eyes and chapped red lips seemed deeper than usual. The fatigue of the real-time day was showing on everyone. Jocelyn forced a smile for Healer Councilors arguing in the audience, just out of acoustic range. "What is that, old French or German?"

"One is German, too many consonant clusters for French. The other, Italian. Hear the lilt in the phrasing, the music. The third person uses sign language, dances as she talks." He squinted at the tall woman. "She's not from New Ouagadougou. The markings on her face, like illuminated calligraphy but gene art, Healers don't do that."

"What a passionate response." She smiled at the Major, then deposited her bird sculpture in a collage of trees in Ogun's realm. "New Ouagadougou's like a whole Zone of ethnic throwbacks. A thousand squabbling groups, each living in their own limited vocabulary, ready to die defending obsolete languages and petty ethnicities." She was second-generation Electrosoft Corp. Her father and uncle led the crusade for monopoly, not diversity. Electros on every belt, *don't get caught out of the loop.* "God, we outlawed all that a generation ago! That's all it takes."

He stared at the woman with the animated gene-art calligraphy on her hands as well as her face. She wasn't one of the delegates from Los Santos. "Then why is our superior Paradigma crawling with underground choirs and ethnic throwbacks?"

Jocelyn ignored his insubordinate question and wiped blue sand from between sweaty breasts. "I can't stand multi-kulti affectations. How do they get anything done?" She placed the damp hand on his arm.

He resisted the urge to flinch. "They manage, Madame Prime Minister." Physical contact reassured her, and she enjoyed asserting her dominance over him in this gentle way. Until recently the Major had never enjoyed being touched. He had tolerated it only for sexual release. His newfound pleasure extended even beyond intimate contact with Lawanda. He cursed the historic rush of events demanding his attention. He'd much rather consider the changes overtaking him. But the balance of power was shifting, and he was at command center. He set the Eshu mask on the stage floor. He'd been holding it almost two hours, and his muscles ached.

"All these dead male heroes and dead languages are giving me a headache." Jocelyn massaged her temples. "Don't flash me that hipper than thou look, Major. You're a scholar, but I don't make a fetish of diversity. Ethnic wars were very diverse!" She took every opportunity to trash Lawanda. A sign?

"Allow me." He slipped his left hand out of the data glove, letting the device dangle from straps at his wrist, and wrapped his fingers around Jocelyn's head.

"What are you doing?" She sounded frightened, as though he were about to crush her skull or twist her neck from the spine.

"Your life is always in my hands. Trust me." He paused to savor her flash of anger and fear, but found only hollow delight in his momentary dominance. Disturbed, he applied pressure to points on her neck and forehead, a shiatsu technique learned from Celestina. Jocelyn's blood rushed to his fingers, and tension dissipated—hers and his.

"This ceremony mumbo-jumbo is murder on the nerves. I'm jumping at my own shadow." She closed her eyes and relaxed into his touch.

The Major was certain something else had her agitated, but he went along with the lie. "New Ouagadougou is an acquired taste."

"What nonsense!" She pulled a communications scrambler from her green satin jacket and activated it. Although to electronic spies and casual observers, they were now hidden behind a flurry of sparks, she spoke in a whisper. "Bottom line: a credulous, ill-educated mob cannot support true democracy. Science is like a candle in the dark of our ignorance. We can't let it be extinguished by superstitious witchdoctors and throwbacks who'd like to plunge us back into the dark ages."

"Actually the Dark Ages is when Europe lost touch with the past, with the wisdom of Egypt, Greece, and Rome." He paraphrased Lawanda. "Throwbacks have a renaissance sensibility more in line with that of Leonardo and Galileo, drawing the arts and sciences together—if you want to make that sort of comparison."

"We are certainly spoiling for a fight today."

"Relax. Conflict and diversity are the crucible of change and the axis of survival," the Major said, not knowing what had come over him.

"Who said that?" Jocelyn asked—then waved her hand as if to ward off curiosity.

"Celestina Xa Irawo in the Preamble to the Interzonal Peace Treaty."

"Tell that to the Healers. The Council intends to dump something foul on us tomorrow. Let's not get caught with our pants down."

"What's the strategy?" The Major's fingers were a lattice across her face.

Jocelyn leaned into him. "We disavow alleged intelligent creatures coming down the Barrier from the great beyond to scoop up dead shamen and kidnap Earthers."

"You mean we ignore the evidence from Celestina's funeral and instead suck up to Sidi and..."

"Such language, Major, 'Suck up to...'"

As if summoned, Sidi and an entourage of drummers and dancers paraded across the stage raising a cloud of colored sand. Her disks traced exuberant pathways in the air. One flew right by the Major's head. He aimed a short-range weapon at it, but refrained from firing. The disk arced around his weapon and darted back to its enigmatic mistress. The Major's probe on disk phenomenon had dug up nothing significant. Upon becoming shamen, Healers wore illusion costumes or jewelry as proof of their power. Sidi and the acrobatic musician who'd crashed the ceremony performed tricks that defied explanation.

"Elleni's a powerful lady," Jocelyn said as the last of Sidi's praise-singers and dancers disappeared behind midnight velvet curtains. "She can quell an uprising, dance the Barrier open, hoodoo gangsters. But Sidi is the consummate politician."

"The signs are obvious," the Major said as Sidi's music continued backstage.

"I can't let Elleni take us down with her." Jocelyn sounded odd, not quite herself.

"Sidi is the woman of the hour," he said. Everyone onstage chanted these words, Daniel Ford crooning over the others. The Major was about to chime in again, but caught his tongue mid-sentence. That was not what he meant to say at all...

"Armando's doing better in Los Santos than projected," Jocelyn said.

"You mean Lawanda is."

"Whatever, but we have to cut Los Santos loose. New Ouagadougou isn't going to tolerate an alliance with those gangsters much longer."

The Major opened his mouth to speak but could formulate no counter-argument. He withdrew his hand from her forehead. Not wearing the data glove he felt blind, deaf, a naked intellect without perspective. To deal with Jocelyn during power plays, he had to operate at peak. He thrust his fingers into the electronic web and stifled a sigh.

Jocelyn took a deep breath as well. "Did Elleni really think she could hold the world to that wild Treaty of Celestina's? My head feels great, thanks."

"Free the slaves, and the next thing you got sharecroppers and nightriders." He quoted Lawanda again and picked up the Eshu mask.

"Sharecroppers? Yes, our dependence on Healer grain, natural resources, and medical supplies is intolerable." She twisted Lawanda's line to her purposes. "Recall the diplomats and fact finders from Los Santos before the seasonal corridors close."

"On what pretense? Or do you mean to openly break the Treaty?"

"Use the truth. Los Santos is too dangerous for civilized diplomacy. With all the attacks on Jenassi's life, we're lucky he's still breathing."

"My intelligence says they're self-inflicted attacks," the Major said.

"Yes, I don't think Jenassi is right for Los Santos. More reason to bring him home."

"Lawanda's in the middle of sensitive negotiations. It won't be as easy to convince her to abandon the mission as Jenassi."

"I'm sure you have your ways, Major." Jocelyn tapped the grinning Eshu head that tilted to one side. "You're such a handsome devil. Don't know how I've resisted you all these years."

"Your discipline exceeds even my own." The Major bowed his head slightly to her.

"Recall the Vice Ambassador or terminate her. Her security is under your command, correct?"

"Correct, the Captain would die for me," the Major said without flinching.

"Good. If you must, make it look like a gangster raid, but I want no loose ends convoluting our plans."

Jocelyn dispatched Lawanda to Los Santos knowing she intended to join forces with Sidi and break Celestina's Treaty—whether gangsters complied or not. Lawanda risked her life for show, for nothing. Jocelyn never divulged the complete plot to him, but appointing Jenassi as Ambassador and promoting Lawanda to Vice Ambassador was a dead giveaway. The Major was hoping to reduce terrorism and stabilize the economy in Los Santos before Jocelyn dumped Elleni. Risking Lawanda for political expediency was for the greater good. And with the Captain and his dream team, Lawanda had a fighting chance. The Major certainly never imagined that Jocelyn would call for her elimination.

"And what are your plans?" he managed to ask, not expecting much of an answer.

"I want to work this Healer power upheaval to our advantage, and I want corridor capability ASAP. We're too vulnerable without it. The technology exists. Get it for me, Major. No more playing footsy with deranged *Vermittler*..." A smile slithered across her lips. "Gangsters murdering our diplomats would be just the right touch."

"For what? That sort of caper turned Celestina into a martyr for peace," he said, a little too quickly. His pulse was erratic, his discipline in shambles.

"Those were different times. We've lost that idealistic glow."

"We have?" His face was a mask, but his abdominal skin cells crawled away from one another, squeezing the organs beneath, and he found it hard to breathe.

Jocelyn planned a more brutal end to his liaison with Lawanda than even he had imagined.

Madame Prime Minister would stage atrocities and play along with Ouagadougian witchdoctors until she didn't need Healers, *Vermittler*, or seasonal corridors to cross the Barrier to other Zones and to the vast natural resources in the Wilderness. With Barrier access she'd be invincible.

"And then what?" he asked.

Jocelyn's green eyes sparkled. The shiatsu had revitalized her. "We'll have routed the thugs and the throwbacks. We'll have won. Civilization, democracy, free market, science." She disabled the scrambler, squeezed the Major's shoulder, and walked past a vanquished dragon through Siegfried's realm.

"I thought holy war was Femi's game." Although he knew that she'd dismissed him, that she'd made up her mind and there would be no reprieve for Los Santos or Lawanda, he followed after her, searching for an argument to change her mind. He hesitated when she passed under a shower of dragon's blood.

"Don't be silly. It isn't real, just a light show," she said. "Retro-New-Ager nostalgia." A torrent of red gushed over her, staining neither skin nor green satin jacket and pants. The illusion was compelling. The Major stuck his weapon hand in to check the magic. "Always the scientist," Jocelyn said, shaking her head. She turned her back on his experiment and ambled toward the sweet-faced gangster with the shock of rainbow hair. Daniel was leaning against one of several giant rocks arranged in an awkward circle—a set designer's perversion of Stonehenge, no doubt.

The dragon's blood penetrated into his fingers, turning them red and making them burn. The Major wanted to pull his hand from the shower but couldn't. He was paralyzed—not a single muscle responded to his brain. Even the chronometer in his thumb had stopped or slowed almost to a standstill. The air around him seemed charged, and he could almost see a storm of static rushing his way. As the dragon's blood diffused into his palm, the stage floor under him quivered. He struggled for balance. Something like acid stung his face and sent a shock through his bones. He snorted a blast of ozone, and his lungs ached. A vivid image, like a waking dream, surrounded him. With the Eshu mask for a head and three hundred sixty degrees of simultaneous vision, the Major stood at a burning crossroads. As with Ogun, the flames seemed real enough, but didn't harm him. Cold revolution brewed in his body, keeping him safe. Jocelyn, dragging useless ebony wings in the dust, stumbled away from the burning crossroads toward a crumbling precipice. The last bird of a hapless species, she was about to leap to extinction rather than be burned at the crossroads and renewed. The Major shouted to her, tried to explain that the flames weren't lethal, but she wouldn't turn around, wouldn't change directions. He reached out to her.

"Anybody's expendable," she said and jumped.

The flames burned his mind and suspended thought. He couldn't argue.

37:   Archive Transmission/Personal
(October 14, Barrier Year 115)

From: Lawanda

To: Herself

Some clowns try to take out Jesus Perez, the soybean king, when he head into Nuevo Nada for Interzonal elections. They blow up four city blocks. Officials still countin' bodies, forget the vote—so much for democracy. Captain say Perez be lookin' shaky to his fellow thugs cuz I data-chill his shit to kingdom come. Rival gangstas overestimate the damage I do and move on Perez, but while two gangs race to take credit for smokin' his ass, man be on the other side of town, a model citizen, votin'. Plenty of corpses to take credit for tho. I feel sick, like those dead folk be my fault.

I try all my channels and can't get nobody live. Major, Elleni, 7-Stories, Ray, I even try to hook a vibe with my sister Geraldine out there in never-ever land. I get alotta static, but nobody tunin' in. Everybody might as well be lost in space with Sis. Well, the Captain's here, but she don't say much. I could use me a talkaholic on a jag.

Who the fuck am I to ambassador my way thru alla this and a megademic too?

I wouldn't put this psycho ice-the-fire-ants-and-malanga-conspiracy past Jocelyn, Sidi, or Carl. Maybe they all in it together! Them and the Major think I'm the biggest fool, got me babysittin' trigger-happy thugs while they trash the Treaty, screw Celestina's *Wiederaufbauwunder*, and launch a fire-virus megademic. Like 7-Stories say, I'm just another colonized woman chasin' behind a loose-dick, withholdin' motherfucker with a god complex. Ain't nobody never been that cute. Sure am sicka myself. Course, these conspirators would love nothin' better than to put a wedge 'tween me and the Major. I'm all locked up here, don't know what to think.

I wish I could Houdini my ass outa here.

Captain and me cover that murdered Dancer lady with dust, as close to the Barrier as we can stand, like she ask. I close my eyes to search-sing a few notes, not for the dead, for my own self. I'm reachin' at a high note and it feel like the air be on fire. So I clam up and sneak a peek. Hundreds of Barrier tendrils be pokin' 'round the grave. Look like veins feedin' a cancer. I freak and start squeakin' steada singin'. I hear voices hissin'—SSS OOO SSS. Captain peep this funky Barrier action too but act like she don't see or hear what I'm seein' and hearin', act like ain't nothin' unusual goin' down, talkin' 'bout it be good to grieve. She walk away from the Barrier, pretendin' she need distance to call the squad to come get us, like Barrier interference mess up her Electro transmission. She motion me to follow her. I can't. Panic spiral. Why move?

Nowhere to run, nowhere to hide.

Captain gotta drag me away from the grave.

A buncha rebel Extras recognize us and wanna talk at me 'bout all the bad shit goin' down in Nuevo Nada, random violence, gangs attackin' each other, blowin' up everybody, like I can do somethin', like I'm a Messiah come to lead righteous souls to the Promised Land. What a sick joke on Los Santos I turn out to be. Captain get rid of these folk, cuz I start goin' mental, talkin' in tongues, completely off the hook.

And don't you know, me buggin' out just cinch it for 'em. I see it in they eyes. These fools really believe I got the juice to make a difference, to help save they asses.

Couldn't even save myself if I had to.

38:   On Location outside Nuevo Nada, Los Santos
(October 14, Barrier Year 115)

"*Es ist ja noch nicht aller Tage Abend.* All our suns have not yet set. *Keine Sorge.*"

Another spirit jabbered at Aaron from the dark, not Celestina, but a voice he didn't know, talking dead languages at him, telling him not to worry. He wasn't worrying—just trying to sleep himself into oblivion.

"*Mo so awon enia mi po.* To tie people together, I need your help. Come to me."

She was more than a dream, but less than reality.

"Listen babe, I got blood on my hands. A snuff take. You don't want my help."

"But I do. *Sie haben mich vergessen.* I thought you'd recognize me."

He didn't. Pity, it was a singer's voice, hit parade quality, resplendent with overtones and resonance, a voice he'd cast in a hot second—put it with another body if he had to.

"Help me!"

"How? I can't wake up," Aaron said. "I fell down a black hole. I'm lost."

"Not yet. Watch your back." A giant ant with snake hair and lightning eyes raced down an old highway in a ruined landscape that Aaron didn't recognize.

"*Elleni gave it all away. Who's gonna sit still for that?*" Moses's voice on the drive home from the greenhouses broke into Aaron's dreams and woke him up. His eyes popped open. It was dark again, or rather dark for real. Someone had made up a bed in the back compartment of his trailer, tucked him under fake fur covers, drawn the metal blinds, and closed the partition to the front. Aaron couldn't imagine Moses getting domestic, so it must have been the Achbar. He remembered falling asleep on Achbar's shoulder as they drove off to play heroes. If Ray Valero took the challenge, maybe there was still hope for Mahalia.

The smell of cinnamon, sage, and fresh-baked bread made his stomach rumble and his mouth water. He couldn't recall the last time he'd eaten anything. How long had he slept? He almost felt rested and safe, as if all his foul-ups had gotten sucked down a black hole, while he had floated free.

A faint rasping, like breath down a dry throat, startled him out of wishful thinking. *Watch your back.* It was pitch black. Aaron hated being vulnerable, hated not seeing who or what was coming at him. He threw back the fake fur and blasted his Electro flash beam at full.

A man with silvered face and long black braids quivered a step from Aaron. Two diagonal scars crossed just above the intruder's long, hooked nose and wiggled with his agitation—fancy gene art of lizards at a crossroads. The intruder was about to shove wild turkey plumes into the breast pocket of Aaron's jumpsuit, but adrenaline catapulted Aaron into the man's chest. His fists pummeled the scarred face, even though a heartbeat after the launch he knew he wasn't in any danger. Ghost Dancers delivering feathers never got out of control. They left their messages and faded into the breeze. And if Dancers had gone psycho, Aaron would have been chopped meat a while ago.

The intruder didn't fight back, retreat, or wince, just grabbed Aaron's wrists and pressed him back into the makeshift bed. Blood leaked from one of the Dancer's nostrils, and a cheek turned purple. His eyes were empty, like he'd popped too much Scud and gone zombie.

"What's going on?" Aaron said.

The Dancer thrust the feathers in Aaron's pocket, wiped at a trickle of blood that stained moss green trousers, and turned to leave.

"Wait. Where are you going? Just like that?"

The man headed for the partition to the front room, not hurrying, but moving like he had somewhere else to be. He was slight for the strength he displayed—a tall drink of water, reminiscent of Jimmy Stewart, Tim Robbins, and Mort Valero.

"Don't go. Look, I'm sorry." Aaron jumped up and yelped. Every other step was a stab of excruciating pain—Barrier burn flare-up.

"You know how it is, you wake up with some stranger breathing down your neck, you throw a few punches before your mind's online. It's not what you mean." He managed to shove past the Dancer just as the partition slid open. "How'd you get past security?" Balanced on his right foot, Aaron blocked the exit. "Not even a footprint on the snoop mat..."

The Dancer wiped blood from his nose and stared past Aaron to the twenty-five wall screens running in silent mode: newsy ad-operas, publicity, old Entertainments, ancient Jolt spots with Ray, and work prints of *The Transformers*. Aaron felt naked. The Dancer tried to squeeze by him.

"You broke into my inner sanctum, I can't just let you disappear into—" Aaron lost his balance and tumbled to his knees. The Dancer stepped over his back, but Aaron grabbed an endless pants leg. "Not so fast." The Dancer towed him toward the outside door, banging his injured foot against chairs and equipment. Aaron howled, and the Dancer halted. They both looked at the aggravated foot.

"Barrier burn," Aaron said. The one bit of backstory Mahalia's gene art couldn't erase. "From when I was a kid."

The Dancer leaned down to him, and Aaron let go of his leg.

"What does the Wovoka want with me at Wounded Knee? See how jacked up I am? I wouldn't be worth dick to your fearless leader—"

The Dancer slapped a cool hand against the old wound. A surge of energy slithered down Aaron's back, under his arms, and made the tight crotch of his jumpsuit itch. A couple of tears dribbled down his cheeks. The foot had hurt like hell before, but never made him blubber—not in front of a total stranger.

"Okay." He took hold of the Dancer's shoulders and pulled him down into a squat. "Why all the cloak-and-dagger intrigue? At least tell me that." The gene-art lizards on the man's silvered face were pumped for action but had nowhere to go. "You don't talk, do you?"

Brown eyes darted about, independent of each other, out of focus.

"Messengers split their tongues."

Muscles up and down the Dancer's body flexed. He snorted like a broken engine, and his face twitched. Spittle dribbled across his chin. The hand on Aaron's foot felt icy, but sweat soaked the Dancer's clothes and drizzled down his face. He opened his mouth and threw back his head as if to scream, yet no sounds came, just hot, sour breath. The lizard scars looked like they might tear his face apart. Throughout this performance, Aaron continued to clutch his heaving shoulders. The man could do every born-again Sioux ritual in the book. Aaron wouldn't be taken in by cheap theatrics.

"I respect you people, I really do," Aaron said as the Dancer cycled through his fit again. "I'm beaucoup grateful for you-all saving my ass. Still, I don't owe you my whole future..." This was the same raft of BS he'd handed Mahalia. He felt sick repeating himself. "I'm spending megabucks, risking my neck for a goddamned story I don't even understand." He pointed to a wall screen where Ray pranced across a high wire as the world exploded. "If I don't get on the case, Mifune Enterprises could crash and burn!" He clapped his hands in front of the Dancer's wandering eyes and startled the man into focusing. "I can't ditch this shoot and wander in the Badlands for spiritual uplift with the Wovoka. I gotta write the climax, shoot the chase, psych-out market censors, and—"

A woman with long black hair burst into flames on three screens.

Hope for Mahalia? Who the hell was he kidding?

39: Council Hall, New Ouagadougou City
(October 14, Barrier Year 115)

> I love numbers and shit, but mappin' the mind as a point on
> a line? Damn, they could at least give you IQ in four or five
> dimensions. I don't even know where you are with one number.
> Can't get close to what you be or what you capable of.
> —Geraldine Kitt, *Junk Bonds of the Mind*

"Just a light show, Major—always the scientist." Jocelyn shook her head as dragon's blood gushed onto the Council Hall stage floor.

The burning crossroads faded, releasing the Major back into what passed for reality in New Ouagadougou. As he snatched his hand from the shower of light, his upper lip and mustache went into spasm. He checked the chronometer in his thumb. Barely a second had passed. Had he experienced a Barrier encounter like those described by Ouagadougian informants...or was he just hallucinating?

"Anybody's expendable," Jocelyn said over her shoulder, as if for the first time. She stood with Daniel Ford in the Stonehenge set. "Have you figured out the reception protocol yet?"

"I've made a stab at it," Daniel said. His thug entourage had gone on without him except two bodyguards hovering at the stage door.

"I'm going with Danny," Jocelyn said. She and Daniel glanced at the Major, who nodded.

"At your service, Madame." Daniel held out his arm like a gallant adventurer in an ancient Entertainment saga. Jocelyn folded herself around him. His black tuxedo with jade syn-silk facing was a perfect match for her green satin, even if the rainbow hair clashed. They sauntered away, up to no good.

First Lawanda, now Jocelyn in the clutches of a suave gangster. Not that the Major wanted to keep count. He repressed this evening's second spike of jealousy. "Close on the queen bee. I'm on special reconnaissance," he rasped orders to his squad then set his Electro to a private channel. Paradigma security glided from the wings and headed through the stage door to the reception with Jocelyn and Daniel. The Major dispatched a flying auto-bomb squad, a fleet of winged buglets capable of subtle discernment. It was hubris to think he had to attend to Jocelyn's safety personally. *Anybody's expendable.* His people were chemical dependents. They'd die for him without hesitation. Before Lawanda, all his lovers had been addicted to him as well. He wasn't used to dealing with free emotions other than Jocelyn's, certainly not his own.

He felt abandoned, cut loose in a power storm. An acid taste filled his mouth. He checked his bio-indexes and brain chemistry. Everything came up normal, except for the shower of red light that had penetrated his skin. On that score he got nothing but error messages. If the dragon's blood was a psychoactive hallucinogen, how had Jocelyn walked through unaffected? Was his breakdown part of her plan? He donned the Eshu mask to conceal his distress, not caring what a spectacle he must seem.

What was the Prime Minister up to?

Jocelyn shouldn't be up to much without him. Perhaps she sensed him straying from the fold, so she was testing him. Could he deliver Barrier access, could he do his extreme duty with Lawanda, or had he confused exquisite lust for love and lost the big picture? The Major didn't want to imagine what would happen if he failed Jocelyn. He'd been wired for loyalty, otherwise she would never have trusted him with life and death power over her. The smart bombs in his head were subtle and perspicacious, yet they allowed only a slight margin of error. So he forced his attention to solving concrete problems—solving the magic could wait.

Lawanda's sister Geraldine and other renegade scientists had cracked a few Barrier mysteries and then disappeared off world in Celestina's ship; thus for corridor access, reliable intelligence reported that the Healers Council was his best shot. Duma was the ruthless ambition behind the Councilors' challenge to Elleni's power and Sidi its pretty face. Hard-line reactionaries in Femi Xa Olunde's camp and lovers of some sort, they would make dangerous allies. Healer sexual relations never made much sense to the

Major, although he was beginning to appreciate their belief in the immense and sacred power of the erotic. He opened a channel on his Electro to contact Duma, then hesitated. Elleni hadn't cooperated with Jocelyn, and neither would Duma or Sidi freely share Barrier secrets, so he'd be forced to… Board ops were shutting down the stage lights, and in the gathering gloom, he saw his weapon hand fluoresce a neon red. He shoved the offending appendage under the raffia fringe of the Eshu mask.

The Major scanned the hall, half expecting someone to notice his increasing deficiency, even behind the Eshu mask. The few delegate stragglers still onstage were too busy jockeying for power to pay attention to a glorified bodyguard/errand boy struggling for sanity. Nevertheless, the Major slipped beyond blue velvet curtains to a shadowy backstage. He needed a low stimulus area to regroup.

Getting a deep breath inside the stifling Eshu mask was impossible. His usually hot hands were ice-cold and tingled as he deposited Eshu on a rickety prop table. Rather than blow drugs, he focused his eyes on the catwalk above the velvet curtains, willed his heart to slow down, and forced his breathing back into balance. He couldn't afford emotional chaos or an impossible red hand that glowed. If he didn't panic, a rational explanation would eventually occur to him.

His eyes played tricks on him whatever direction he looked. Just below the catwalk, he saw a shimmer of Barrier energy sliding across the velvet curtains. A giant ant mask materialized "out of nothing,"—out of a break in normal spacetime—and sprang at the Major. Music erupted from a fifty-stringed Kora strapped to its back. The acrobatic musician who had interrupted the honor tableau vaulted over a prop spaceship. The enormous studded calabash of the old African harp banged against her with uncanny rhythmic precision. A hundred layers of weightless synthetic silk streamed behind her like the icy tail of a comet. Her muscular grace reminded him of Elleni, as did the Kora. The strings were a blur of vibrations, as if she played behind her back. The music was too beautiful. He wanted to scream and drown it out.

The musician touched his shoulder as she drew near, and his rage subsided. No magic realism, she was flesh and blood. A diamond-tipped laser-blade in her left hand reflected moonlight. With lightning reflexes the Major held a weapon to the musician's head, yet hesitated long enough for her to have plunged the laser-blade into his heart.

"A man of some integrity, I see." The insect mask muffled her voice. Only her eyes were clear. "*Es ist ja noch nicht aller Tage Abend.*" She sliced a hole in the stage wall with the laserblade then translated the old German. "All our suns have not yet set."

He kept the weapon at her head while he peered out the impossible opening she'd made. Here he'd been telling Lawanda to remain skeptical, yet look how credulous he'd become! Jocelyn was right. New Ouagadougou was a danger to his mind...

The reception was going full tilt. Ambrose, Entertainment queen bimbo, in all her gene-art splendor and several Los Santos bosses he didn't recognize swarmed around Sidi along with conservative Healer Councilors and Paradigma Undersecretaries and Ministers, Jocelyn's yes-men. Why had Carl Samanski sent Ambrose to represent Los Santos? Another setup, like Lawanda? Jocelyn made an entrance on Daniel's arm and joined this unlikely crew. Sidi drew them all into a sculpture garden where a gong orchestra played among stern wooden visions of the past and future. Jocelyn embraced Sidi with tears in her eyes. Daniel kissed Sidi's fingers and his rainbow hair sparked. Despite a sophisticated surveillance microphone, the Major couldn't catch what they said. Twice Sidi glanced in his direction and smiled as if she could see him at this distance.

"Watch your back!" the ant musician said. She stood behind him, away from the opening. He turned to find a laser-blade at his throat. "Sidi's charm is subtle. You can't resist her if you don't really want to. And if you want to resist, it hurts."

He recalled everyone chanting Sidi's praises and the effort it took not to join in. "Who are you? What do you want? How do you do all this?"

"I thought you'd recognized me." She withdrew the laser-blade and leaned into a statue—a black Asian man dancing in a vertical ring of fire. A god most likely, the statue wore a garland of human skulls and had four arms that essentially were swords. He didn't remember seeing this ancient Indian idol when he first came backstage. A reject from Rama's realm, the statue embraced the musician, its swords slicing through layers of syn-silk.

"Is that Shiva?" the Major asked, struggling after strands of Hindu mythology.

"No, Shiva's consort, Kali, absolute night, mistress of time. I need your help. Come to me." Static snapped across her pitch black eyes. Spacetime stuttered on itself and she disappeared, fading into Kali, leaving behind polyrhythmic harmonies and strong fragrances: cinnamon, jasmine, and the smell of ozone, as from a flash of lightning.

By what force he couldn't say, but the Major was drawn from this vanishing act to peer out the impossible hole in the wall. He watched Sidi hold court with Jocelyn, Daniel, and sycophants from every Zone fawning over her. Panic pushed him into the shadows behind Kali's black marble torso. Lawanda's torpedo words came to him again. *Fire virus don't take no prisoners.* When he stood up and looked again, the hole had disappeared. He ran his fingers over the wall's smooth surface in disbelief. He should have detained the ant woman, interrogated her, but the magic of the moment had distracted him. He wasn't sure she'd even been there. His data glove offered ambiguous witness.

A jackhammer drilled the nerves in his head, and his hands were still ice cold. In fact, he felt frosty through and through. "Damn!" The Major rarely cursed, but as Lawanda said, this Zone give you a foul mouth, so he cursed again and felt a little better. "Damn."

He opened a channel to Lawanda in Los Santos and got static. He couldn't bring himself to leave much of a message. He wanted to *talk* to somebody he could trust with his life, somebody he could trust with the world.

A woman thrust her head through the blue velvet curtains. Gene-art calligraphy danced across her angular face—the stranger who talked with her hands. The Major waved a weapon at her flared nostrils. She signed at him furiously. When he didn't reply, she rolled watery brown eyes at the ceiling then withdrew. Not a native and not a delegate—this unsettled him. He sent a probe to hunt her down in his image banks.

A scrap of syn-silk hung from Kali's razor arms. He plucked it from the goddess, held it to his nose, and caught a whiff of jasmine and cinnamon. "Do what you gotta do." He bit into his twitching lip and mustache until the spasm passed. "And what exactly is that?"

The musician wore an ant disguise, but the eyes, the bearing were unmistakably Elleni's. He would start there. Why get bogged down in all the details, all the noise? Donning the Eshu mask, he strode out of the Council Hall toward the Insect Pavilion in search of Elleni. Villagers claimed they'd caught sight of her on the old super highway, running through *Vermittler* rituals at the Barrier's edge. Wherever she was hiding, he would find her, make her explain all this magic realism to him, and if she were the one putting out the SOS, perhaps do what he could to help her in return.

He ignored the alarms going off in his head. Information always had its price. He wasn't an enemy, traitor, or threat to Paradigma security. He needn't kill himself just yet.

The smart bombs in his head were defused for now.

40:   Cross-Barrier Transmission/Personal
(October 14, Barrier Year 115)

From: Lawanda

To: Major

What is up with you?

I scan your transmission over and over, but you ain't say diddly. I hear you suckin' your teeth, holdin' your breath. I do not believe that after all I tell you, you ain't got nothin' for me but your ole stank stutters and static! How 'bout a conspiracy theory or two, make some sense outa this sick shit over here—you the big analyst!

Hey, I swallow somebody's last breath, I got another soul to keep!

I guess you done forgot how sweet I am and what good lovin' really is. Gone on back to your old tricks, to those folk that be strung out on your ass? Well, I could use me some good lovin' right about now. I mean, nobody back home would believe the freaky terror Santosians swallow down 24/7.

Captain and me bury that Chief Executive Dancer, right next to the Barrier, near her Promised Land. While I'm trippin' out on gang rape and how that Dancer lady *feel* dyin' like that, the Captain get all kinda evidence from the greenhouse. Facts to fight with. Don't know what I'd do without the Captain.

You ever feel like a alien in your own skin?

Mr. Aaron Dunkelbrot could probably help me with that one.

Here's the deal: I been tryin' to conjure that eighth impossible story, but it ain't lookin' good. Gangstas courtin' a fire-virus megademic and don't have a clue. I mean it just ain't real to 'em. I gotta figure how to shake they heads straight. YOU GOTTA BE MEGA-IGNORANT TO TRY THAT KINDA OUTA CONTROL STUNT! You know what I'm sayin'? How you make people feel the shit they doin' when they stuck on stupid? How you keep it real?

The whole gene-art, disappeared-scientist thang smell like a *interzonal* conspiracy. No way gangstas get this deep all on they own—

so you watch yourself over there in Shangri-la, all right? What am I tellin' you that for? Suspicion be your middle name. I *#^!#*

41: On Location outside Nuevo Nada, Los Santos
(October 14, Barrier Year 115)

Raven black hair turned flame red and filled the shot.

"Mahalia wasn't my fault." Aaron turned away from his Electro screens to the sweaty Ghost Dancer. Watching Mahalia burn in the man's big brown eyes was unbearable. The walls of the location trailer closed in on Aaron. The synth-marble floor felt like ice. He shivered. "I got her to your outfit. She was all set, and then I don't know what happened... A traitor has infiltrated the home team."

Moses Johnson. His AD, right hand, the man who'd walk through hell and back for him. Not psycho Dancers or rebel Extras. Not Achbar, Ray, Samanski, or desperadoes in production. As this realization was kicking Aaron in the head, the Dancer coughed his throat to shreds. His watery brown eyes still on Mahalia in flames, he sank to the floor, an ugly tremor distorting his entire body.

"Don't watch that." Aaron switched channels with the remote on his Electro belt, gathered the man in his arms, and patted his back. "Getting bent for somebody you don't even know..." The whole born-again Sioux scene was pathetic. Mutilated for security and with nothing but feathers and silver peace paint, these schmucks were thrust into the real world to do the cult's dirty work. Why did Aaron ever think these guys were sabotaging him?

"Your waist pouch is empty. No more feathers?" Aaron said. The man nodded against his chest. "So you can't go back through the sentinels to Wounded Knee. What do you do when the gig is up, take a flying leap into the Barrier?" The man trembled in his arms. "Sorry."

Dancers believed that when the Wovoka gathered the lost tribes together for a final war dance, the Barrier would give the dead back to the living. The faithful could blow themselves up in the lethal nightmare and expect to rise again on judgment day (or the born-again Sioux equivalent).

The Dancer's head lolled back. Aaron cradled his neck, and hot sweat soaked his sleeve. He felt sorry for the kid, for all the dumb schmucks on suicide gigs, himself included. He hugged the man against his chest, wanting comfort as much as giving it. He'd been as gullible as any half-wit acolyte in a cult melodrama. Moses had played him like Electro-synth.

Aaron surfed his transmission archives. Moses's dirt-streaked face filled screen sixteen. The close-up cut to a wide-angle shot of the bombed sea mammal sculpture. Pigeon feathers floated in the fountain around a body in moss headdress and bloody white robes.

"Not even the right feathers," Aaron said.

The archive was running in mute, but he knew what Moses was saying, *she laughed,* said *we played for the wrong team,* said *Mahalia was on the loose. I told you not to trust spirit warriors getting ready for the end of time. Just 'cause they helped you once, they can do no wrong? What kind of cracked logic is that?*

"Moses, you lying son of a bitch..." Cursing out loud didn't help.

Aaron froze the image. Kamikaze Dancers never blew up Rock Center or told Moses crap. *Moses* bombed the set, murdered the Dancer messenger or whoever she was, and sold the Treaty out. To who, for what, Aaron didn't know, but...

Even with truth beating down the door, he didn't want to believe it.

Moses had saved his life, before the skin job, back when Aaron was less than nobody and saving his life was a waste of spacetime. Four thugs ambushed him one night in the Nuevo Nada Extra camp.

They were working him over pretty bad. Thinking about it, Aaron shuddered, glad he wasn't in that body anymore and his nerves couldn't call up specific torture, glad his skin didn't still crawl with the hours of gangbanging. He had been dying and nobody lifted a finger 'til Moses screamed, "Are we scumbags too? How can we just stand around and watch something foul like this go down?" Then they'd pulled the men off Aaron. Torture seems to go on forever; miracles are over before you know it.

Months later, Moses didn't recognize Aaron inside the skin job, but Aaron remembered the light in Moses's eyes when he covered Aaron's busted body with a raggedy coat. How could those eyes watch Mahalia burn? Aaron remembered choking on the awful smells of the other men, then breathing the musky comfort of Moses's coat. All through the night Moses held his hand, made him drink bitter water. When he was still alive the next morning, Aaron vowed to pay back the life Moses had saved. He'd promised the Wovoka and Mahalia the same deal. Aaron owed a lot of lives, and it was looking like he might have to default.

When the porno-trash came gunning for him the next morning, Moses saved Aaron a second time. If the roles had been reversed, Aaron would have hidden and prayed to any god who might listen to let the perverts be satisfied doing Moses or anybody else. Aaron was the ruthless, soulless bastard, not Moses. The AD wasn't too swift, but he did good shit because it was right, not because he might hit the top ten, or... How could Moses be ruining Aaron's ambitions and bringing Mifune Enterprises to its knees? How could Moses let Mahalia burn? And what the hell was Aaron going to do about it?

Just 'cause they helped you once, they can do no wrong? What kind of cracked logic is that?

The Dancer was in the middle of a silent scream. Aaron shook him 'til their eyes met. "I have mega-problems of my own. I can't help with yours. Take your feathers back and tell the Wovoka I'm sorry, all right?" Aaron's face burned. "I'm no good to some crazy medicine man in the desert, preaching apocalypse now."

The Dancer's fit had subsided. His hands still shook, but his gaze was sharp and clear, and he nodded with understanding. Aaron let go of his shoulders, surprised at how quickly he acquiesced. "I'm glad you see my point. I was beginning to think you were hopped up on Scud." He stumbled to his desk and gathered tail feathers from the vase. "That's a wicked spirit dance you do. I'd love to get it on a bio-corder." He thrust the feathers in the Dancer's waist pouch. "I do appreciate you-all thinking about me."

The Dancer rubbed his face with trembling fingers then pressed the silver stained tips along Aaron's cheekbone.

"What?" Aaron touched the smudge on his face.

The Dancer pointed at Aaron and shook his head as if to say no.

"Me, no? What about me?"

The Dancer shook his head no and smudged Aaron's face again.

Aaron wiped the silver away. "It's not my original skin, is that what you mean?"

The Dancer thrust thumb and index finger at Aaron's heart and then to his own.

"I don't follow you." Aaron shoved sandy hair out of bloodshot blue eyes.

The Dancer repeated the heart gesture, a bit frantic.

"If this is some we're-all-brothers-under-the-skin throwback thing, that's not my style..."

The Dancer's chin fell to his chest and he covered his eyes.

Aaron was baffled. "My people weren't Sioux, weren't Lakota, Dakota, Teton, whatever. They were Seminole—Black Indians. A long time ago. We're all mixed up now. What does any of that mean? What did it ever mean?" He had to avoid a spiritual confrontation. He wasn't about to join lost souls wandering the Badlands of history desperately seeking salvation.

The Dancer slowly raised his head, shaking a hand in front of his right eye, which was almost swollen shut.

"Let's put some ice on that, then I'll let you go." He took the man by the arm and limped to the med-cabinet. The Dancer pointed at Aaron's foot. "It's much better," Aaron said and handed him an ice pack. "Dancer voodoo really works, huh?" The Dancer snorted at this bit of cultural ignorance. Aaron shrugged. He didn't watch his words for anybody.

A loaf of fresh-baked bread sat on his desk, scenting the air with herbs and yeasty cheese. Aaron's stomach was thrilled. "You bring this?" He stuffed a warm wedge from the loaf into his mouth. "Or do I have other angels watching over me."

The Dancer shook his head and set the ice pack to his eye. He was trembling all over. For an instant Aaron thought the bread was poisoned. *Watch your back*, the new demon had warned him, but like Celestina she hadn't told him who to watch.

"It tastes even better than it smells." Aaron broke off a chunk and offered it to the Dancer, who took a sliver and chewed slowly. "What's the secret ingredient?"

A wall Electro squealed with a priority transmission, and they both jumped. Moses's rugged profile filled screen one. Aaron pushed the Dancer out of range and enabled the transmitters. "Don't leave, watch the show first."

The Dancer slumped in the corner hugging himself. He was clearly incapable of going anywhere soon. Aaron turned from him to the Electro screen.

"Moses, you look terrible. What, the world's coming to an end already?"

"I'm down at the south security gate and..." Moses's violet eyes were dull, his skin ashen. "I thought things were going to be different, boss, with Celestina's Treaty, with...everything. A lot of promises tossed around."

Aaron grunted. "We've heard the big-change lie forever."

"Things have a nasty habit of staying the same," Moses said.

"But if you jazz the colors or do zigzag instead of curlicue, people swear it's a goddamn paradigm shift."

"Something like that, yeah." The sun came up behind Moses, providing a halo effect. "Only worse."

Aaron looked over at the Dancer huddled in the corner shaking wild turkey feathers in the air. "Tell me about it, Mose."

42: *Seelenwald,* New Ouagadougou
(October 15, Barrier Year 115)

New O City was like a set for paradise. Ugly had been banned from city limits. Voluptuous curved houses painted by women's guilds to resemble old West African textiles welcomed Ray home. Animal signs, astronomical symbols, and trigonometric arabesques set in visual polyrhythms along walls and windows soothed his jagged nerves. Gardens spilled color and scent onto the road. Illuminated-calligraphy newsstands and graveyard altars to Shango, Ogun, Oshun, and Eshu celebrated life and death. The playgrounds re-minded him of Hundertwasser paintings. Giant spider puppets dangled from the towers of an onion-domed schoolhouse. The main drag twisted through sculpture gardens and past fountains and wa-terfalls gurgling down marbled steps. No buildings blotted out the sky, no skyscraper canyons swallowed him whole—everything was built on what Femi had called "the human scale."

The rise in his spirits surprised Ray. He never got used to how elegant, how sublime every aspect of Ouagadougian architecture was, down to the fire hydrants, stop signs, trash bins, and gutters. In Studio City, where he grew up, public objects this glorious wouldn't have lasted ten seconds. They'd have been snatched or defaced on principle. Despite Elleni's SOS and a passenger at death's door, Ray felt hopeful coming home to such gracious living. Los Santos was hard on his soul.

Most residents of New O City traveled by public transport, human-powered vehicle, or by foot. The disabled zipped around in glorified electric crates. Luckily it wasn't morning yet and the cob-blestone streets were deserted. Respectable Ouagadougians were getting a healthy night's sleep. No one would shout at Ray's smelly pollution or have cause to chastise Elleni for a reckless consort who abused precious resources. He drove right up to Council Hall in his flashy red tank, farting brown exhaust on a statue of Femi Xa Olunde that guarded the entranceway. Femi scowled at his gangster impudence, but Ray wasn't carrying the burning woman one step further than he had to.

She didn't complain when he scooped her up from the sticky cushions. Strung out on Rapture or the Barrier, she was feeling no pain. Ray hurried up the side ramp to the private living quarters, a little dismayed that he didn't sense Elleni's presence. When the great lady was close after so long a separation, he usually felt an itch underneath his skin. The Rapture was messing up his intuition royally.

The hallway knew him and the direction he normally took through the labyrinthine Council compound. A path was lit for him with soft nightlamps that winked out as he passed by. He always wondered what would happen if he didn't follow the lights. Horror stories abounded of wayward guests dying in the corridor maze. Elleni's quarters overlooked the canyon and the lake, but her rooms were a hike from the entrance. The burning woman seemed lighter than before, as if he was carrying ashes and soot, not muscles and bones. Still, approaching the last twist in the hallway, Ray tasted blood in his mouth, and his knees were shaking.

Turning the corner, he jerked as a spiral disk the size of a poker chip zipped past his head. His knees buckled, but he managed to fall against a wall and hold on to the burning woman. The blood rushing to his head made him dizzy.

"Ray Valero! If you are well, I am well." Sidi Xa Aiyé offered a traditional Healer greeting then frowned at the burden he was carrying. Her disks made a corkscrew shape above her head. "You are in need of healing, and Elleni flings herself down a corridor to the stars with so little thought for the ground on which we stand."

Ray almost fell over. He skipped the formal greeting. "Elleni's not here?"

"No." Sidi gestured to the drummers and praisesingers who followed her. Before Ray could protest, powerful arms relieved him of his desperate charge. As Sidi examined the woman, her disks smashed through one another in what Ray took to be a display of rage. "What happened?" Sidi drew back her blackberry lips in a snarl. She could kill him so easily, Ray thought, rip out his mind and dash his body to bits. He batted at her disks as they came too close. "Who is she?" Sidi demanded.

"I don't know." Ray slid down the wall to the ground.

"Well, did you pull her from a burning house or what?"

"Something like that," Ray said as the drummers carried the burning woman down the hall to healing chambers.

"You've risked yourself for a stranger, an Extra by the bar code on her wrist. What would you heroes do without women to torture and rescue?" Sidi's disks buzzed about his head like dragonflies hunting for fat mosquitoes. "Is she important to you?"

He closed his eyes. Could she touch his mind the way Elleni did? "Don't Healers say, we have no miracles to waste."

"That sounds like a universal cliché masquerading as deep wisdom." She bent so close he felt the heat of her skin against his clammy cheeks.

"No, it's German. *Kein Wunder zu vergeuden.* Femi said it whenever I ranked on the fire virus." Ray opened his eyes to disks circling his head and Sidi's cold eyes sizing him up. "Will you help her?" Something about Sidi was like Elleni, only twisted. "You don't need to know who she is to help her, do you?"

"Healers would nurse an enemy back to life, so she could stab us in the back or put a bullet in..."

"Look, I don't have the energy for a fight. Where is Elleni?"

"Everything unravels. So many strangers in our midst." Sidi said. "How can I keep track of her?"

"Strangers are always to blame when there are problems. It's like that where I come from too, a universal cliché."

"Someone has stolen Femi's ashes, his fifty-stringed Kora, and his final image-board. We had yet to run through all his illuminated calligraphy."

"Pinched his ashes? You're kidding."

"Healers have no sense of humor, remember?"

"Your prime suspect ought to be a Ouagadougian native then. Gangsters could give a shit about ashes and a calabash covered with funky goatskin. And they wouldn't know an image-board from an Electro-pad, which blows up in your face if you can't disable the bomb-locks in time. Last I checked, none of the bad boys with big bucks to blow was in the market for dead shaman artifacts."

"You're right." Sidi licked her lips. Her tongue was ruby red. "The culprit's not an ordinary gangster. Too convoluted."

"What do you mean by that?" Electric sparks raced up Ray's spine.

"To bring an alien culture to its knees, you steal the natives' stories and fill them with lies. You desecrate sacred symbols and replace ancestral wisdom with your story of the world. You obsess the benighted natives with being like you, until finally they forget themselves and become you. Why waste bullets when a cultural bomb will do? Stealing the future is an old story, a universal cliché, and Femi died for us, for our tomorrows, for our integrity in the face of..." She paused. Her disks were lined up, like rows of eager missiles ready to be launched. "So it means something to us when his ashes are stolen, even if it means nothing to you."

Ray flashed on his uncle Mort blasting Femi in the head, blasting Chris in the chest; he saw Celestina being cut down by Piotr Osama, then the burning woman with her hair on fire.

"I know you don't like me, but..."

"That's not what I'm talking about." Sidi laughed. "In fact, I'm jealous of Elleni."

"What?" He grinned. Here was somebody better at seduction than he was, and what a babe—ripe fruit with an electric charge. Under other circumstances he could have made a total fool of himself. "You've seen Elleni, haven't you? I think she...needs me. Tell me where she is." He slipped his fingers through hers and squeezed, trying to say with skin what he didn't dare say with words.

Sidi shook her head. "I believe you are a good person." The disks burrowed into her thin ochre braids, almost disappearing, yet still catching the dawn light and spinning it back to him in rainbow flashes. "I will attend your wounded lady." Sidi pulled her hand from his and strode down the hall toward the healing chambers.

"You know, in the long run, being a good person doesn't always matter."

"Just tell me where Elleni is," he whispered at her undulating hips.

"The old super highway near the dead mall," Sidi said without turning. "She's been doing too much Barrier surfing." She disappeared into twinkling lights.

Ray raced out of the Council compound. With the sun rising, he'd have to park the tank and find Elleni on foot. He blew one last hit of Rapture to make sure he didn't pass out before reaching her. When this was all over, he told himself, he'd get off the shit for good.

43: Cross-Barrier Transmission/Personal
(October 15, Barrier Year 115)

From: Lawanda

To: Sweet, Sweet Major

Did I get cut off before? Sun must be comin' up in the New O. Still dark here, but sleep ain't doin' nothin' for me. I'm nightmarin' myself sick. Scope this dream:

> Fire ants be havin' a powwow down by the Barrier, talkin' 'bout "all our suns have not yet set." Giant fire ant with funky dreads like Elleni run thru a dead mall, zappin' killer mites with a Healer staff. Giant ant reach arms, feelers, and wiggly whatnot out at me, tears drippin' from everywhere. She pleadin' with me, like I can help! Like I can stop the genocide and save the race! While I'm hemmin' and hawin', Femi

charge on the scene, flappin' mudcloth robes and poundin' his crystal staff on a ole super highway 'til my head be throbbin'. Celestina pop in too, blazin' through clouds in her silver space ball, fussin' to herself like she a coupla people who don't get along. What is up with that? Councilor Femi jitterbug the Elleni-ant right past one of them ole fast-food grease parlors and drive her smack into the Barrier. Femi be in high-priest mode, exorcisin' demons and shit. Celestina reach down from the clouds, a kaleidoscope of hands tryin' to snatch Elleni, but she be too late. Femi's done the damage, so Celestina just get a handful of air. The ole lady shaman look too sad, like the sky's fallin' and the world's over—'llowed to break my heart. Insida the Barrier, the Elleni-ant got dreads screamin' astral blues right 'fore she explode in a rainbow of sparks.

The melody be sweet but the Barrier's so funky, like a battlefield in high summer, wake me right up outa that nightmare. Who the hell wanna go back to sleep behind that? So I g*#^!#*

44: At the Barrier's Edge, New Ouagadougou City
(October 15, Barrier Year 115)

The Major didn't have time to puzzle the abrupt Electro disconnection or consider the uncanny coincidence of Lawanda's dream transmission.

"*Mo so awon enia mi po,*" a semiconscious Elleni muttered.

She was sprawled naked on the ground at the Barrier's edge, just beyond a stand of scraggly cathedral trees near the ruins of a dead mall. There were no signs of struggle and the area was deserted.

The Major set the Eshu mask on top of an old parking meter and scoped Elleni's bio-indexes with his data glove. Although he couldn't rouse her, he detected no serious injury or trauma. Her skin looked as if it were covered with flecks of colored glass that caught the muted dawn light at oblique angles. With each labored breath, a flush of rainbows cascaded across her flesh. The nipples on her breasts were an iridescent purple, the line of hair from navel to pubis, sapphire-blue. Whether any of this was extraordinary, he couldn't say, as he was no expert on *Vermittler* anatomy. The braid and dreadlock snakes on her head were matched by silky worms between her thighs, several also sapphire-blue. The Major found his appraisal shifting from clinical to sensual. Someone or something had wrestled Elleni to the ground, and she was in no condition to defend herself against his appreciation or disgust. In so vulnerable a state, she called forth a novel combination of lust and revulsion that shocked him. However, since this had been a night of shocks, his guard was down and he indulged these feelings for a moment.

Elleni's bio-indexes seemed weak: her heart fluttered, her lungs were on the verge of collapse. The brain scan was off the charts. The Major's diagnosis of her condition was hampered by his extreme ignorance. *Vermittler* physiology wasn't exactly human, and despite a vast database for comparison, he possessed scant analytical resources. Perhaps this mental state was a variation on REM sleep or deep meditation that required no intervention on his part for her to revive. Whatever her mind was up to, motor activity was suppressed, including autonomic systems, and she was suffocating. Of this he felt certain. Cell asphyxiation was cell asphyxiation, no matter the body. Fumbling through his weapons belt for the med-unit, he chastised himself for allowing flagrant emotions to compromise his efficiency in the face of such an emergency.

Her voice rasped. "All our suns…"

"Yes, the sun is rising, so save your breath."

He put iridescent fingers to her lips. She seemed to smile under his touch. This response pleased him more than it should have. He had been so distracted by her glittering skin, he'd missed the crisscross of Barrier burns covering shoulders, breasts, and thighs, which were now apparent as he leaned close enough to smell cinnamon sweat and taste jasmine breath, close enough to see a hundred tiny burns ooze purple pus. Evidently most of her skin had come into naked contact with the Barrier. For normal humans such exposure would have been lethal. Was this the cause of her present stupor? He shot a demanding glance at the Barrier, as if it might answer his question. The fluid, milky veil hanging across the horizon looked unusually dull in the predawn light. The wind off its flanks made the Major shiver. He felt a sharp pain behind his eyes, and his vision blurred. A black crystal corridor in the Barrier yawned open before him. He tried to blink the illusion away. New Ouagadougou had infected him with magic realism, but if he allowed the hallucinations a few seconds to pass through his mind, he could conquer them with focus. The artifacts of his illusions were another matter, but he would study them when circumstances were less urgent.

He pressed an oxygen mask over Elleni's mouth and nose. He would need to know much more before blowing drugs into her system. A beaded braid, oozing a golden discharge, reached up toward him. The Major involuntarily jerked his face just beyond its reach. Elleni's breathing deepened, and the braid strained in the air toward him—a macabre, pitiful thing, spraying the morning mist with gold sparkles. Despite his unease, the Major leaned his cheek into the agitated hair. The golden discharge splashed against his lips and tasted sweet. As the braid slid across his face and around his neck, he closed his eyes and indulged his senses for a second time. This was much better than magic realism. The hair was a soft bundle of static. Its tiny electric jolts were quite pleasant, if also disconcerting. The Major's fluorescent weapon hand itched as the braid tugged him closer to Elleni. He opened his eyes, and his moist breath wafted across her breasts. Her nipples turned a soft brown. What would a kiss have accomplished?

Elleni coughed and sputtered under the oxygen mask. She batted at the device with claw-like fingernails. Noting what he took to be stable respiratory readings, the Major withdrew the mask, and her eyelids flashed open. Static snapped across her pupils as she focused on him. Recognition flickered in her face, and a nascent smile collapsed.

"Expecting someone else?" he asked, irritated by her evident disappointment.

"Yes." She pulled her hair from around his neck. "But you have come, forsaking festivities no doubt, risking ridicule, hoping for a grand prize, so I shouldn't complain...even if I want to." This brusque speech exhausted her. He proffered the oxygen mask, but she shook her head. "Do you want to poison me? Just give me a second."

Her Healer bluntness reminded him of the diplomatic delicacy of their situation. He sat silently for several minutes, monitoring her rapid recovery through his data glove. Finally he spoke in direct Healer fashion, to cover his amazement. "Elleni Xa Celest, I searched for you all night, in the Insect Pavilion, through the Library of the Dead. What are you doing in the middle of nowhere, unattended..."

"They allowed *you* in the Library of the Dead?" Blood rushed to her face, like dark mud under her yellow skin.

"Honored guests have unlimited access, by order of the Healers Council, even to the Library. I saw ganglords and physicists discussing wormhole theories and ancient Koras, and even a Ghost Dancer taking in the sights." His probe suggested that the sign-language woman with gene-art face markings was born-again Sioux. "Does the Council Center disapprove?" He secured the oxygen mask in the med-unit.

"You wandered through the wisdom of the ancestors with a weapons belt, data glove, and martial art spirit. Even your hands are lethal weapons." She stared at his red fingers. Every hair on her body wiggled. The ones at her crotch, longer than his initial estimate, reached down muscular thighs. What he wouldn't give for a specimen.

"No one asked me to strip, and combat skill can't be checked at the door."

"I'm glad they let you in." She didn't mention his red hand. Could she see it? "What did you think of the mandala arcade, Major?"

"Given my objective, there was no time for proper inspection. Awa Xa Ijala said I might find you here. I left the Library before I could..."

"Awa, yes, she would do that. The others would never tell you how to find me."

"Did someone, some thing," he glanced at the Barrier, "attack you, hold you hostage? You've been absent from all the interzonal proceedings."

Elleni sat up, glanced around the empty road, and then down at her body. She probed an oozing burn on her shoulder blade as her hair crawled across her back. The last shreds of the Major's patience dissolved. The sun was almost up, and what did he have to show for a sleepless night? A "magic" infection and mysteries inside of mysteries.

"I'm not what you expected either, am I, Major?"

He held out her ceremonial robe and trousers. "I found these by the trees."

Elleni squinted for a second at the intricately embroidered white rayon garments, as though she were trying to fathom their use.

"The mist is chilly. You should put something on." He swatted a few ants that crawled along the lapels, grateful to have something other than her body to attend to.

"Don't," she growled and snatched the robe from him. "What was I saying?"

"Nothing much, diplomatic chit-chat."

"Before you came." He raised an eyebrow, so she quickly added, "As you came."

"You were passed out, mumbling gibberish when I found you."

"No, probably just not English." She hugged the robe, straining after a thought. "I have to remember."

A braid reached in his direction, and he avoided it. She struggled to her feet and stared at the Barrier. Why didn't she put the robe on? He'd really rather not see her breasts banging together like ripe eggplants as she flexed aching muscles and tried to remember unconscious mutterings. Obviously her nakedness in his presence didn't disturb her as it did him. He wasn't aware that Healers were so indifferent to modesty. Perhaps this was a *Vermittler* attribute. She dug a stone from the small of her back and pitched it with surprising ferocity at the Barrier, where it exploded into gray spume. She flung her head from side to side, disentangling a few snarled braids. Muscles in her back and buttocks rippled under sparkling skin as she danced from foot to foot. The moment of her vulnerability had passed. Elleni was her usual Amazon self again—the kind of woman a dominatrix would trade in her chains, electric whips, and stiletto boots to be, even for a second.

"You were saying *mo so* something or other."

"*Mo so awon enia mi po.*" She smiled at him. "*I tie all my people together*, says Oshun. She is the warrior woman deity who unifies the world." Her excitement dwindled. "I carry her shield and spear, but not her spirit."

"That wasn't what I was thinking at all."

"Do I want to know what you were thinking?"

"I thought *Vermittler* could read minds."

"You don't believe that." Elleni eased the robe over her wounded skin and winced. He hadn't considered that nakedness might be less painful than getting dressed. "You look perturbed, Major. Do ancient myths disturb you? Or naked thighs?" The white rayon framed her sparkling face and unruly hair. Her head seemed to float in the mist, her body slipping beyond the folds of cloth into the earth.

He refused to let magic realism overwhelm him. The dawn light was playing tricks on him. "The seasonal corridors are open. Any fool can crash a Zone and set off a chain reaction of terror." He activated infrared scanners to warn him of the approach of warm-blooded life forms. He should have done this sooner. "Unattended, in an unsecured sector with swarms of foreign guests, you're an easy target—"

"No." A few braids hissed in his direction. "My Barrier guardian has powers neither of us can fathom." She grabbed the aggressive hair and stuffed it under the collar of her robe. "You're glad to have been of service, but you've come here with urgent questions. You wonder at my absence from the honor tableau. You wonder if there's an explanation…if there's still hope."

The Major's thin mustache twitched. He activated a communications scrambler to block surveillance of their encounter, but held his tongue to see what else she might say, to see if she'd refer to his iridescent hand.

"You want answers. Well, it's simple. I detest high-gloss, hypocritical ceremonies, where important people make you feel good before gutting you."

"Politics and diplomacy must really try your patience then," the Major said.

"I had more critical business to attend to, so I left diplomacy to Sidi and Council."

"This business?" The Major displayed the scrap of syn-silk that the Elleni-apparition had left in Kali's sword arms. "Do you prefer art to politics?"

"Doesn't everybody?" She smiled as he held the cloth to his nose and savored the cinnamon, jasmine scent captured in its threads. "That fabric is my favorite, so light, like a piece of cloud or Barrier wisp." She walked to the Eshu mask, which was slipping from its perch on the old parking meter. She wedged it firmly in place. "Sidi gave you Eshu-Elegba, I see." She slid her hand along the wooden feather/knife that rose above a solemn Eshu face. "Mamadou's work, our most renowned sculptor. Sidi must be charmed by you."

"Hardly." He pocketed the fabric and came up behind her. "Always share wealth you encounter or create so that it spreads out and increases." He quoted probe results on Healer Potlatch. "What can you tell me? Last evening, I saw a woman in an ant mask and a gown of Barrier wisps dance on air. The Kora on her back played itself."

"Impressive. I wish I could have seen it." Elleni stroked Eshu's grinning face. "Do you know the story of this old West African

Orisha?" Her hair seemed to wriggle with delight. "Do you?" She turned and inspected the Major with unblinking eyes.

"I was trying to remember," he lied. He'd had no time to process the results of inquiries into Eshu and the Orisha of old Nigeria. "Does Eshu also dance on air?"

"Good question." She walked again, this time toward the trees. He followed her. "Watch out for mounds. Fire ants get nasty if you step on their homes. Hard as marble too. You could break your foot." Elleni's voice was sing-songy, like a musical caress.

The Major sidestepped a mound. "Teneather boots. Bullet proof, fire-ant proof." He watched his step nevertheless.

Elleni was barefoot. Ants crawled over her feet continuously. "Eshu stands at the crossroads of your life, giving you the face you expect, the lies you'll believe, holding his other selves in reserve. Change is his currency."

The Major's mouth went dry. The coincidence of her words and his crossroad hallucination was uncanny. "Go on."

"Eshu tests you with your own wicked desire and just enough truth. Pour him libation and ask for the wisdom to speak to the gods. Never believe you have outsmarted him, but if you tread carefully the path he has marked, mysteries will unravel." She embraced a tree and looked up into the nightsky. "That's what Celestina would have told you, if she were here."

"Celestina has gone on to dance with the ancestors. This is your wisdom now. She lives on in the changes you make." He'd done his homework on Healer basics. "*Aṣe?*"

Still clinging to the tree, she twisted herself to stare back at him and smile. "Euro-Christian Missionaries to West Africa thought Eshu was the devil." Her contorted spine looked painful. "Eshu is a good gift for you, Major, isn't it?"

"I..." He hesitated, not knowing what she accused him of. "I'm not sure yet."

"You know how to rig a mind to destroy itself. That's an Eshu sort of thing."

"Really? What exactly do you know of interrogation protocol or loyalty implants?" The pain in his head flared again.

"What do you want from me, Major?" Her gaze broke through his skin.

"I don't know." He felt itchy all over. "You called me, remember? So here I am. What do *you* want?"

"You were summoned, yes, but you came because you needed something. Don't waste my time with lies. I don't feel well as it is."

"Lies? You're the one shrouded in illusions, not me!" His anger surprised him.

"You live in lies and the truth is now alien to you. Can you even speak from your heart to a loved one?"

"Minutes ago you were barely breathing, sprawled naked on the ground, and I..."

"Thank you. Did you prefer me like that?"

He would not be baited by Healer self-righteousness. He let anger pass through him, like the illusions. Such passion didn't serve him at the moment. "I need your help," he said softly, "but I can't exactly say how or for what."

"Can you at least say why I should help you?" She matched his gentle tone.

"You are a Healer, aren't you? 'Dis-ease' should be all I need to garner your support. Or have you renounced healing along with politics to prance around naked at the Barrier's edge?"

She wanted to smack him or cry: he'd seen that look on the faces of countless women. Elleni wasn't so alien after all. She took a deep breath and blinked back tears. "You don't know what you're saying." She let go of the tree and moved toward him, yellow discharge dripping from her dreads.

"In Los Santos, gene artists attack malanga fruit and infect your precious fire ants with deadly mites. Lawanda suggested... Well, I've had reports..."—which he should have checked out more thoroughly— "We're in danger of..." He trailed off as a silver eddy of

Barrier energy surged by him and splashed against Elleni's shoulders. It swirled about her and then dissipated.

"Who designed the mites?" she asked as if nothing unusual had happened. "Who's behind this?" He continued to look from her to the Barrier in silence. "Talk to me!"

"Celestina's *Wiederaufbauwunder* is in danger. We might even be facing a megademic. There are extenuating circumstances, and I don't know how to proceed." He managed to say quite a lot without betraying Jocelyn, but his head was throbbing and he felt so cold inside. "What was that just now?"

"You asked for healing." Elleni grabbed his iridescent red hand. "What did you expect, a skin patch, a pill?" Before he could protest, she slipped the data glove from the other hand and pressed his icy fingers onto her hot forehead. She was impossibly fast. "What else do you hear from Lawanda?"

A startling rush of energy passed between them. He couldn't speak.

"Your plans are half-formed. Uncharacteristic, I suspect." Elleni moved through the folds of his clothes to clammy skin. She gripped the oblique muscles that connected ribcage, spine, and pelvis. Her strength was impressive, and the heat from her hands made him gasp. A musky herb scent in her hair made him dizzy. Tiny white bubbles drifted up his nose and burst, clearing his sinuses. A sense of well being permeated him so thoroughly that even the bombs in his head felt inconsequential.

"I am no longer myself," he whispered. She utterly intoxicated him. "The advantage is yours." He felt a strong impulse to tell her everything. "You're doing something to make me talk, aren't you?"

"Only if talking is what you most crave."

"What is it? What do you do? Explain to me how all this is possible."

Static crackled across her eyes. She placed her cheek against his chest, struggling it seemed with thoughts and impulses. Perhaps she had a similar "truth effect" on herself, for he could feel her agitation, her desire to speak what would probably put both their lives in jeopardy. A braid slithered through the tight curls at his temple and wrapped itself around his skull. Its tiny shocks relieved his throbbing head.

"Talk to me," the Major whispered in Elleni's ear as a lover might. "We could share our terrible secrets. Think what a relief that would be." He'd said this often enough to taunt prisoners he tortured or enemies he'd seduced. He never expected to mean it.

"Don't." Elleni shivered with his chill and drew away from him, beyond the range of fingers, hair, or breath. "Not yet."

"Why not?" He reached for her.

"You're not ready."

Satisfying warmth permeated him for the first time since Lawanda left for Los Santos. "You don't think so? This may be the crossroads." He wanted to feel her hands against his skin again. He walked toward her. "You have the power..."

She stopped him with a snarl—from her hair, which continued to hiss at him as she spoke. "I'm on the way down, don't you know? What sort of spy are you?" She caught a handful of snarling hair and twisted it into a reluctant plait. "Sidi is our rising star and Duma the black hole at the center of her galaxy. They are your mission." She sank down to the ground, shivering and twitching. "Sidi would never listen to me, never accept the Barrier's challenge if you were my ally."

The exact significance of Elleni's words escaped him, but she had certainly come close to sharing a terrible secret with him. He crouched down next to her. "Jocelyn would have me destroy what I believe in." He expected the bomb alarms in his head to shriek, but they were mute. Impossible.

"For a moment, we are free." Elleni spoke so quietly, he had to hold his breath to hear her. "Betray your loyalties, and you lose your mind. It explodes on impact."

The Major licked dry lips. "How is it that you know so much about me?"

"Are you such a deep mystery?" she asked and shuddered from head to toe.

He stared at her as the fit faded to an echo.

"Terrible secrets… What are you looking at?" she demanded.

"You."

"How can you see me if you don't know me?"

"Help me," he said simply.

"All right," she replied and fell into him.

They wrestled a moment in the dirt, then the Major watched her face fly apart and scatter in every direction, like radiation from a blazing star rushing off to infinity. Finally his brain refused the riot of stimuli coming at him. Vision, all sensation was lost. He floated in black silence without taste or smell.

What the hell was Elleni doing to him?

45: Faith

> We have devoured the sky, and now it is an angry warrior battling
> inside of us. Until we turn ourselves inside out, peace is illusive.
> —Vera Xa Lalafia, *Healer Cosmology, The Final Lessons*

Forty years ago, Celestina thrust the limp child into the Barrier
and tried to pray, but her throat was too dry for words. The child's
neck snapped as it flailed against the Barrier's lethal influence.
Celestina let go of the young *Vermittler* before the Barrier could
suck them both in. Staggering away from the explosion, she
squeezed her eyes shut, and still the stench from the *Vermittler's*
last moments blazed behind scrunched lids. As she ran far from the
execution site, curses and prayers refluxed across her tongue. *Was
für ein Wunder ist das Leben!*

The death ritual always brought on acute synesthesia—one
sense hijacking another. Sounds were colors, light tasted bitter, and
the wind played dissonant music on her skin. Before Robin and
Thandiwe were lost to each other, they had studied how the brain
shuffled sensory modalities, including pain. Now intense pain—and
joy—brought Celestina back together again, if only for a heartbeat.
She must be close to redemption. Feeling like the worst kind of
traitor didn't make sense. She reached to the stars. Her hands were
blood red, iridescent in the moonlight.

Assassin's hands.

After twenty years of chasing death, Robin was still a refugee
drifting through an alien body and Thandiwe a fugitive host who
had yet to find her way home, murderer and murdered running
through one body. Where could they meet? Where could they rest?
Murahachibu, Celestina did not make sense to herself. Villagers saw
her dance with ghosts, fuss at dust devils by the Barrier, and make
love to herself in graveyards. Femi Xa Olunde, *Geistesvater,* wise
shaman, Council Center, had taken pity on Celestina's worthless
soul. He allowed her a most honorable task, one that no other shaman in New Ouagadougou could do and stay sane.

Holy war.

"We have the right, *the duty*, to defend our way of life against the enemies of our future," Femi said, his breath on fire, his beard and hair like ashes on rich earth. "*Ebo Eje* for redemption. When the people of New Ouagadougou learn what you have done, they will remember you not as traitor, but as the patron saint of tomorrow."

Ebo Eje. Celestina must kill the Barrier spawn. *Vermittler* were false griots, abominations who would destroy the world. Femi had chosen well. Celestina had betrayed and poisoned herself years ago. She was lost, a daughter of the stars, Celestina Xa Irawo, a name snatched from nightmares. For redemption, for the future, she'd perform atrocities with impunity. She could be trusted to keep terror secret.

...But no longer. Elleni should write a suite for the Kora and tell all the world. So Celestina must relive her past, one last time at least, for the future. To die in peace... *Daughter of my mind and spirit, I feel you reach out to me. Can you see who I was? Sing my terrible secrets, Elleni. Dance my struggle, forty years gone by.*

The acid lake by the slumbering volcano burned at cathedral-tree roots. Celestina stumbled to the ground and plunged iridescent red hands into the corrosive water, hoping to burn them brown again. Assassin's hands.

Suicide, genocide. Who are our enemies but our other selves?

Femi had chosen well. Saint Celestina—string theorist, gene artist, *Vodun* and Chi Gong master, who could match her powers? Tonight, before they found their voices and grew strong enough to throw the world off its course, Celestina had flung the bodies of raw *Vermittler* into the Barrier. Dying, their wild spirits had stained her hands. How many times this same ritual? In twenty years, eight thousand one hundred eighty-six, only a few *Vermittler* left. Soon she would finish off Vera Xa Lalafia's perverse symbiogenesis, this artificial commingling of Earth and alien life forms. Soon there would be no *Vermittler*, no mutant lives to snuff out, no threats to the biome, to the future, no Barrier death colors blazing across the horizon to rub her skin raw.

"You will set the world back on its course!" Femi had filled her mind with the fervor of his vision, leaving no space for her own thoughts. She was a refugee, a fugitive, lost to herself. What did it matter what she believed?

The pain on her skin was too great, and the red glow undiminished. Celestina pulled her hands from the acid lake as clouds burst overhead. She fell down among the tree roots, embracing herself. Soft rain was a Kora concerto against her skin, but she couldn't remember how to sing or sigh or what she had just thought or how she had lost her feet her hands her back her breasts her mouth... her body her mind.

And then she was running, stalking gene-art mutants, high in the slumbering volcanoes where rain had fallen as snow. Her arms and hands were wrapped in synthetic skin. A medicine bag banged against her back, a corridor staff provided balance and light in the night. Awa Xa Ijala, daughter of warriors, daughter of heroes, had escaped from the valley with the remaining *Vermittler* to a rock cabin in the cliffs of Fire Mountain.

The last outpost.

Six blood sacrifices to reach eight thousand one hundred ninety-two rituals—two to the thirteenth power, a number Celestina had always appreciated. When the sun rose over the snowy volcanoes, her deal with the devil would be done. The ancestors would flow unbroken into the future. The battle in her skin, in her head, would be over.

The massive rock door slammed behind her. The ceiling rained fire; the floor exploded. She should have been killed. But *Death was afraid of Celestina*—who didn't know that? No magic door, booby traps, or power netting would deter her from Salvation. The rock cabin's vaulted ceilings reminded her of old-age cathedrals, as did the dark chambers, frosty walls, and a bitter wind from nowhere in particular. At first she couldn't fathom which direction to take. The Barrier progeny, however, shone like a beacon in the night. Celestina was a stepchild of the Barrier. Her madness often gave her second sight in a spectrum beyond visual light. Like a honeybee, she danced herself into a magnetic trance that carried her through labyrinthine chambers to the last living prey.

Babes they were. Chubby cheeks, buttery skin—and to think such wide-eyed innocence was the beginning of the end for humanity. Alien invaders in the perfect disguise. Awa Xa Ijala, daughter of heroes, snow leopard, wild woman, shielded them, ready to give her life. Celestina hesitated. She didn't want Awa's blood on her hands. That stain would not redeem her.

"Stand aside," Celestina said softly, waving the corridor staff in the air.

"Not in this life," Awa said. Wisps of blond hair fell to her waist and fluttered in her ragged breath. Icy eyes reflected the staff's sparkling light. Celestina shivered.

A *Vermittler* boy with silvery brown skin clutched Awa's waist and tried not to cry. The Wovoka—Celestina didn't remember what he called himself then—was old enough to understand, old enough to shoot hate from his eyes and hurl curses. "The dead will have their day. They will dance your spirit to dust!" he shouted.

Celestina laughed at ignorant superstition, while sensing the truth in his metaphors. A snake-haired *Vermittler* crawled toward Celestina. Awa scooped her up quickly. Elleni, too young for fear, struggled in Awa's arms. She wanted to play with the stranger. She shrieked and reached out hands and hair toward Celestina.

A willful child.

"Sacrifices must be made. For the future," Celestina said.

"Then sacrifice yourself." Awa pressed Elleni against her fake fur cape until the girl was quiet. "You cannot choose sacrifice for others."

"My dear friend, best friend, twenty years ago, why didn't you stop Femi from ruining me?"

Awa's lips trembled, and she blinked her cold eyes.

"Exactly, you clutch them to your breast now, but you were afraid *Vermittler* might be the end of us. You walked away from the circle and let others decide to sacrifice me. Now you interfere, but it's too late. Femi's vision is greater than ours!"

"Vision? Murdering these children is vision?"

The Wovoka began to cry.

Celestina ignored his tears. "They strike at the core of who we are!"

"Twenty years ago I was a weak coward. I was wrong to let them twist your mind and drive you to madness," Awa said. "I change the past with the actions I take now."

Behind them, a young Sidi burped. Her large almond eyes took in Celestina's every twitch. An amethyst mist revolved above her head, settling on her face like dew. Beside her in a makeshift cradle, freckle-faced twins gurgled and cooed. Bundled up on Awa's back, Phoolan, Elleni's sister, slept peacefully. Her sweet countenance and silky black hair looked almost normal. Innocence was a perfect disguise. Almost.

"Celestina, Saint Tomorrow, avenging Orisha, death angel! You have not kept your promises! Not one! Broken promises everywhere." Voices in Celestina's head and on her tongue echoed off vaulted ceilings, gurgled in the dirt beneath her feet—familiar voices, singing like snow against burning skin, at her again, to order the chaos, to make room for her own thoughts.

"What promises? Whose promises?" Celestina said.

"To find another way." Was this Robin speaking? Thandiwe?

"To never leave me alone." Who, then?

Celestina balled her eyes shut. The corridor staff slipped from her hands and she lunged at Awa. Mind was a pattern of patterns spread across spacetime, emergent, regenerative, and fragile. Her patterns interfered with one another and she was lost.

"They are only children." Awa sounded so unreal, not like the other voices.

"Femi has just about used you up!" Two people shouting as one. "These children are not your enemies…"

"Too many voices." Celestina's words slurred. She opened her eyes. Vision was slurred as well. Faces were smeared across the cave walls. "Did you hear them? Two voices like one?"

"No, what voices?" Awa looked around, her eyes bruised. "Listen to me."

Celestina held Elleni in her hands. What had she done? Awa was on the ground, clutching Phoolan, the Wovoka was an unconscious smudge, and Sidi had disappeared. "Voices. They say...Femi... these *Vermittler* children...not our enemies...salvation."

"Then listen to them." Awa licked blood from her lips. "We can teach these children."

"You can't teach... They are altered biology, foul symbio-genesis..."

Elleni's hair snaked around her neck.

Celestina was of too many minds about everything. "Holy war, biological war, Femi's vision..."

"Has never been yours," Awa said. "The children are singing for you."

The Wovoka had revived and moved his mouth; so did Elleni, and Sidi hidden somewhere. Colors swirled in front of Celestina's eyes, making her dizzy.

"You don't hear them? Two ladies, I think," Celestina said. "Agreeing with you."

"Only your voice," Awa said.

Celestina looked into Elleni's face, into eyes blacker than night, impossible alien eyes. "How can you be sure we do not save the enemies of our future? Can you see tomorrow in their faces?"

"I see tomorrow in every face," Awa said softly. "And it is always a mystery."

Elleni slipped from Celestina's fingers and dashed her head on the rock floor, but Celestina grabbed the child's foot before the image on her mindscape became reality. Elleni squealed in delight. Awa shuddered.

"I am not well." Celestina hugged the child. Cinnamon and jasmine filled her with Kora music. "Even through the recon-skin, the death stain stinks." She thrust a glowing red hand at Awa, who flinched away. Elleni kissed Celestina's fingers, and her dreads brushed Celestina's cheeks and tickled her trembling lips. "Voices in my head torment me, counting by twos to the thirteenth power." Celestina fought gibberish. "What tomorrow do you see in my face?" Awa shook her head. Celestina was engulfed by an alien presence, yet everything that she had been was not lost forever.

The sweet song of dolphins chased away lingering pain, and...

Celestina floated in a magenta sea on the Barrier starship wondering what became of the freckle-faced twins, what tomorrows they had sung. She clutched the soggy roll of parchment that Elleni had tossed into the ocean at her crossover ceremony. The funeral poem crumbled in her fingers and dissolved in the viscous sea, unread. On Earth, the sun rose over an old superhighway, and Elleni dashed away from Celestina.

Child of my tomorrow, do not desert me, be a witness.
Sing my song, daughter.

BOOK V

*To live is to wrestle with despair yet never allow
despair to have the last word.*

Cornel West

46: At the Barrier's Edge, New Ouagadougou City
(October 15, Barrier Year 115)

Elleni phaseshifted.

Desperate for a different Earth, another dimension, she was on the run, trying to get as far from Saint Celestina's bloody hands as she could.

Despite contorting her mindscape and shoving herself through every available portal, she was still crumpled up at the Barrier's edge on the outskirts of New Ouagadougou City. The Major was dead weight, like a hundred G's, smashing her to the surface of this Earth, holding her in the dirt. She wanted to scream at him but lacked the energy. To be honest, it wasn't just the Major resisting magic realism that sabotaged her escape. Elleni was a daughter of this dust, barely human perhaps, yet only human. She had limits. Her stomach flipped upside down.

Child of my tomorrow, do not desert me, be a witness.

Elleni loved Celestina, but how could she ask so much?

Discovering that her *Geistesmutter* had murdered herself, Elleni had been fascinated, titillated even by the prospect of enemy lovers inhabiting a single body and bringing a divided world back together. But who would listen to a ballad for Celestina, Saint Assassin, avenging Orisha, death angel?

What would Elleni ever say to Sidi? It was hopeless. Sidi waged Femi's Holy War against herself. She didn't want to be a *Vermittler*, in the family with the Wovoka and Elleni. Certainly Sidi would never journey down a corridor to act as blood sacrifice and heal a wounded Barrier. How do you heal genocide? Sidi wouldn't trust the future to an alien invader or death angel. She'd dismiss Elleni's vision of an exploding Earth as Barrier manipulation, grandiose lies. She'd hate Elleni for forcing truth on her. And since the Barrier demanded Sidi and wouldn't accept just Elleni, the exploding vision could become reality.

Celestina had almost smashed her brains against the rocks.

"We need to dance on your head so you don't make yourself too big! *Vermittler* are nothing special." Celestina had regularly chastised Elleni for her arrogance. "Nobody leaves this world alive, child. We all die, after one go-round. Everybody's life is precious."

The memory made Elleni's skin crawl: Saint Tomorrow on her third life, dragging Elleni and Phoolan from one remote village to the next, across the Barrier to the Wilderness, to Paradigma and Los Santos.

"See? Who are our enemies but our other selves?" *Geistesmutter*, teaching her "children" many worlds of wisdom, initiating them in the final mysteries…

Elleni was on the run from monster lovers and assassin mothers. If not to another Earth, at least to another story, or she would find the fairies and head off to the bright lights at eternity, drag the earthbound Major with her if need be. The circus at home was making her sick, insane. They asked too much of her. Blind faith. *Mingle the ashes, heal our wounds.*

Maybe you couldn't heal genocide.

Elleni had lost her nerve. She was no impossibility specialist. A star turn in this epic saga was beyond her. Celestina had not chosen well.

Scrambling to save herself, Elleni phaseshifted again, hoping to get so far away as to lose home all together.

47:   On Location outside Nuevo Nada, Los Santos
(October 15, Barrier Year 115)

> In a world of monsters and everyday horror, you want to give a
> card-carrying scumbag a medal for just being a decent guy once in
> his life. I suggest waiting until he at least makes it a habit.
> —Tadeshi Mifune, *Surviving the Future, Last Minute Notes*

Aaron hustled through the ruins of an alpine castle modeled on
mad King Ludwig's fairytale palace, Neuschwanstein. The Ghost
Dancer leaned against him, matching his brisk pace, but sleep-
walking really. Nothing registered in his eyes, and his gene-art lizards had gone into hiding. Aaron would have parked him in the
Achbar's rig, but the kid went wild when he tried to leave him.
Against his better judgment, they headed off together for a showdown with Moses. The Dancer's basketball stature and retro-freak
costume were hard to ignore, so they hit the back way to avoid
arousing suspicion.

Many chambers in Neuschwanstein were opera settings.
Production design's fantasia on Wagner's *Lohengrin* was more
Hollywood/Disneyland than Old World kitsch. Aaron couldn't
recall which *Transformers* episodes went down in the Byzantine
throne room. Crawling over felled columns, he felt as though they
were stumbling through a bad dream. As the director, he should
have known how to wake up, but he didn't. He was lost.

"This way," Moses shouted from an arcade beyond more fallen
columns. He stood under a wedding tapestry, an over-the-top image
of Sir Lohengrin losing his bride. The broad was beautiful, but she
asked too many damn questions. Knights of the Holy Grail were
sworn to secrecy.

"Who's that with you?" Moses didn't look happy.

Aaron paused in the sunlit alcove to catch his breath. "A
messenger."

Moses grimaced and looked down the broken hallway. The
Achbar in red brocade burnoose rode a transparent scooter through

the rubble. Brandishing his Healer staff in the scattered light, he seemed to glide on air. Very *Lawrence of Arabia*, and a definite surprise to Moses. Aaron savored the AD's apparent distress. The Dancer swayed between them, his face dripping silver sweat on the synth-marble floor. Moses scowled at the large wet splotches. Feeling grateful to the mad King Ludwig for his operatic excesses, Aaron eased the Dancer down into a swan boat with wine velvet cushions. The Dancer curled his long legs under him, dropped his head on a pillow, and closed his eyes.

Achbar pulled up on the scooter and dismounted as from a hot-blooded stallion. Aaron turned to Moses. The AD's pinstriped power suit was bagging at the chest, like treachery and double cross had been wearing the muscle off him.

"What's so bad you boys don't want to talk over a secure channel?" Aaron asked.

Moses batted his puffy violet eyes. The rosebud on his cheek was a tight ball. "We got company at the gate, boss."

"More of Carl's thugs chasing down Mahalia?" Aaron said. He fingered the gun under his silver duster. Moses glanced at the weapon's bulge, but surprisingly didn't flinch.

"Carl's got his hands full. Fire-virus breakout in Nuevo Nada," Moses said.

"What?" Aaron dropped the weapon back into its holster and walked around the swan boat. "How the hell did that happen?"

"Thugs blasted greenhouses, so the city's low on malanga, and fire-ants are dying off." Achbar sat down next to the Dancer. "What's wrong with the big guy? Who beat him up?"

Aaron clutched a panel of the Lohengrin wedding tapestry to steady himself. Mahalia's gene-art program was coming back to haunt them. " I should just open my wrists and get it over with."

"Is that all you can think of, yourself?" Achbar checked the Dancer's pulse.

"Samanski has quarantined Nuevo Nada," Moses said. "Everybody in the outlying region is under curfew, except us and Jesus Perez." He paced along the wall, his boots crunching plaster into white dust. "Burb dwellers want to come on the lot. They think they'll be safer."

Aaron grunted. "Like the virus gives a shit about our power nets."

"They think we stockpiled the cure," Achbar said.

"We have." Moses shrugged. "I didn't want us to run short, if anything bad went down..."

"Could you stop crunching?" Aaron said.

Moses halted. Achbar rubbed his bald head, like he was polishing it. Aaron wanted to smack his hands away. Everything aggravated him. Achbar stuck a probe in the Dancer's mouth and accessed the med-unit on his Electro to check bio-indexes.

"This is some fucked up anti-Treaty conspiracy, isn't it?" Aaron said.

He and Moses locked eyes, passing one breath between them, stopping time. Achbar cleared his throat, and Moses finally looked away.

"You're always so smart, boss, such a plot wizard," Moses said. "Took you forever to get a clue about this."

"I trusted you," Aaron said simply. "For real life."

Achbar undid the Dancer's high-necked tunic. "He's got a temperature of a hundred and three, and his heart rate's all over the map. When's the last time you saw a sick Dancer?"

"Just do what you can," Aaron said.

"Not much I can do," Achbar said.

"You never trusted me, boss," Moses said flatly. "You lie everyday, all day long."

"You know about me?" Perhaps Aaron shouted this, but the blood roaring in his ears made it difficult to tell. "Who I was...before?"

Moses nodded.

"Not on the same scale, not even in the same universe. Who's dying on my lie?" Black stars floated through his field of vision, as if he'd been hit in the head.

Achbar stared at them, mystified.

Just 'cause they helped you once, they can do no wrong? What kind of cracked logic is that?

Aaron scratched at the shadow of beard on his face and blinked rapidly, trying to clear his mind as well as his vision. "You've known all along?" he said.

"Yeah. She told me," Moses said.

"Mahalia?" Who else had she told?

"She said I was..." Moses looked around the room, struggling for the memory or the words. "Like your knight in shining armor. You talked about me all the time. And after she fixed you up, you got me out of that Extra camp. She said I should know."

A thunderous shockwave rumbled through the castle ruin and nearly knocked Aaron off his feet. Foam columns rolled into one another and banged against the walls, raising gray dust to the ceiling. For a second, he hoped the set would come crashing down on them and bring this baroque nightmare to a halt. No such luck. Cursing in English and presumably Arabic, Achbar caught the Dancer before he bounced out of the swan boat. Moses was rooted to the ground, rubbing his eyes and arms like a junkie in need of an overdose.

Aaron threw back the tapestry to look out the window. The south gate was just twenty yards from the Neuschwanstein set. A hundred or so plump, well-dressed burb dwellers rushed the perimeter, their pudgy arms and faces shining in the sun. Location security shot in the air above their heads, to no avail. People at the front of the mob were getting jammed into the power netting. Some idiot threw a grenade. As bodies exploded, most of the crowd lurched back. Aaron let the tapestry drop and leaned against the swan boat, sick to his stomach.

Achbar wrestled the shivering Dancer into his burnoose. His struggle on slippery ground with the gangly body seemed ominous, as if the Dancer was getting wrapped in a red syn-silk shroud.

"What do you want us to do, boss?" Moses said.

"Business as usual, huh?" Aaron wanted to bust a cap in Moses. "I give orders, you sneak behind my back, do evil shit, and then grin in my face."

"It's not like that," Moses said.

Aaron jerked the tapestry from in front of the window. Outside, the burb dwellers hurled junk at gate and guards but kept their distance. Several children shrieked. One guy was frozen, holding a boot he'd pulled from a charred foot. "What do you think we should do, Mose?

The AD twisted his mouth to say something then slouched against a giant swan with a mournful expression on its bird face.

"In *Lohengrin*, some dip-shit pisses off the local witchdoctor and ends up with feathers instead of skin. I know just how out-of-it the swan-guy felt." Aaron pulled his gun and aimed at Moses.

Achbar jumped to his feet. "What the hell are you doing with that?"

"Say something to me, you son of a bitch! What's our next move?" Aaron's hand shook. He'd never shot anybody before, but Moses was in close range.

"Why? You never listen to me." Moses sounded weary.

Aaron turned to Achbar and waved the weapon at him. "No sneaky hero shit. This is between me and him." Achbar pressed his palms together as if in prayer and bowed his head slightly. Aaron turned back to Moses. He'd expected more melodrama from the AD, not this eerie calm.

"I tried to tell you things for your own good, but you didn't listen," Moses said softly.

Aaron held the gun with both hands. "I'm all ears now."

Moses's breath was coming hard. They were all breathing hard, watching the tremor in Aaron's gun hand. The Dancer's breath whistled through thick congestion. Outside, some wounded soul wailed. Aaron thought of Mahalia singing the blues to the Barrier one last time and cocked the trigger.

"Tell me something quick or forever hold your peace."

48: Cross-Barrier Transmission/Personal
(October 15, Barrier Year 115)

From: Lawanda

To: Sweet, Sweet Major

Seem like I got cut off twice now. Is your system jacked up? That definitely ain't like you. And this connection feel like a live channel, but you ain't all there or somethin'. Maybe I'm just havin' a jumpy night.

I got a rabbit now, see?

So, last night after gettin' thrown outa nightmares, I prowl 'round my transport 'til the moon rise and chase the stars behind its light. Then I gotta move. I gotta get some sweat goin', some kilometers of perspective, so I'm out, runnin' 'round in Celestina's *Wiederaufbauwunder*, listenin' to birds, feelin' thangs grow. Somethin' spicy smell like home and soothe my soul—a breakfast of miracles, you know what I'm sayin'? The desert in bloom be a tonic to my achin' spirit. I wanna throw off the slimy protective suit, all my syn-silk clothes and Teneather boots, and run 'round bucknaked. 'Cept your Captain be doggin' my heels. Girlfriend say you strangle her if somethin' nasty happen to me. That don't sound like no figure of speech. She say if pollution and radiation don't whack me, gangstas would love nothin' better than to get they funky paws on my naked butt. She talk like I'm a big threat. We just pissin' in the wind far as I can tell, but I think on that born-again Sioux lady dyin' in my lap, and I keep my clothes on and don't run so fast the Captain can't keep up.

I take a last breath in my body. I can't be throwin' myself away.

Forty-five minutes out, Captain say we gotta turn back. Sun comin' up in a few. Extras camped a coupla kilometers away. Joggin' is fun but way too dangerous. Somebody hide in the bush and pick us off like rabbits. Gangstas assassinate me and let Extras take the heat. But I'm sicka bein' diplomatic, talkin' at thangs I don't know nothin' 'bout. I wanna see how Extras be livin' not just how they dyin', and what could be worse than the hospital freak show? The wild child take over and I dash off. For a heartbeat, I think the Captain goin' pull her weapon and cap me, cuz I be way faster than her. I don't turn 'round to see, just hit top speed and follow my nose to the Extra camp. Captain can't order me to do nothin', can't turn 'round herself and go back, she just gotta run after me into danger. I do feel sorry for her.

I dash in the camp—drainpipe and cardboard shacks, patchwork tents and junk car villas, raw sewage runnin' down the middle of the street, balls of barbed wire rollin' 'round like tumbleweed with I don't know what all tangled up in it. Four years of the Treaty, and Extras still livin' in shit, they own and everybody else's. Ain't no other way to put it. I turn down a funky alley, and bam, a gang of teenage thugs got some girl pinned against a tin-can wall; six overgrown boys with battered laserblades eatin' her food and tearin' her clothes to shreds. I freeze. Captain crash right into me and try to haul my butt outa there. I can't move a muscle, sixty-six kilos of dead weight, like I been turn to stone. Captain scope the rape and curse me out under her breath, but that don't get me movin'. Coupla women, lookin' sick and scared, hurry by. I scan a few guys lurkin' in doorways groovin' on the show. One man with matted, greasy hair hangin' down his back and ribs pokin' thru holes in his shirt look like he havin' the time of his life. Jumpin' up and down, squealin', just like how gangstas be. He got a hard-on that I do not wanna see. Like at Paradise Healthway, over half these folks is dark-skinned and they all look sick, wheezin', snottin', and shit. Captain take the safety offa all her weapons. I feel her steely nerves sparkin', her muscles gettin' juiced. I swear to god the hair on her head lay down flat.

Some raggedy ole guy with a few gray hairs pokin' out a blotchy scalp try to scurry by, but can't. He start talkin' 'bout what pathetic human specimens we be, when a girl-child ain't safe in a damn alley with a crust of moldy bread. "Aren't you ashamed," he's yellin' and pointin' at us, "shame on you all!"

"Ah man, shut your mug!" somebody yell. A few ugly grumblin' faces nod.

"Boy-child thinks raping makes you a man!" Ole guy ain't givin' in. "None of us are worth shit."

The junior gangbangers stop what they doin' in unison, like on cue, and look at the ole guy and then at each other. I swear it's a bad scene from a Entertainment. I scan a kid with a beat-up camera hangin' from a ole light pole, filmin'. One guy grab the girl 'round the throat, while the other five guys smack the ole man in the face 'til he on the ground bleedin' from his mouth, nose, and a long gash over his eyes. They slash him 'cross the back then go back to rapin' the girl against the wall. Some little kid standin' in the corner, watchin' and cryin'. A big hand snatch that kid into a rusty sewer pipe. Six guys goin' at her, and that girl don't make a sound. Eyes shoved back in her face, hair matted up in clumps, titties tryin' to bud but she ain't eatin' enuf. A coupla muddy tears dribble out one eye, a gaspy noise squeeze thru her teeth as they pumpin' away. Ancient look on her face as she set her jaw and stare right at me and the Captain, but I bet she ain't broke fifteen. None of the little thugs workin' her over be much older. They ain't gangstas neither. They look just like her, raggedy and sick. Extras—same as the crowd that be watchin'—gangsta wannabes.

Can't believe the evil shit I'm seein' and what I'm not doin' 'bout it. I'm so flipped out, I piss myself. Shame on us indeed. I reach for the Captain's arm. She like ice and shake me off. She need her arm to take aim. I blink dirt out my eyes and spit the funk of the place behind me, prayin' for inspiration motivation, prayin' for courage I know I ain't got, and then the Captain pop one of those boys in the leg. He fall down, bleedin' and screamin'. Spectators look over to us—then everybody split, 'cept the girl, the ole man, and the wounded boy who grab for his homies. The little punks beat him off and keep on runnin'. I hear 'em say laser-blades are for shit against a long-range piece.

Captain mumble somethin' 'bout if I can walk again, now would be a good time to exit, but the wild child in me feel some crazy courage, so you know which way I'm headin'. Captain could grab me or keep aim. She keep aim. The boy crawl in a open shack. Ole man just sit in the dirt moanin', pissin' hisself. Naked, bloody girl press herself against the tin can wall and don't let out a peep. I don't know what I think I'm doin'. Girl stare at me and down to the ground. I look down too. A laser-blade stickin' outa the mud. She grab it and dash toward me. For a second I don't know what's up. I hear a pop from behind and the girl's sprawled on the ground, her right thigh opened up to the bone. She still don't cry and she still comin' at me with that laserblade.

"Girl-child don't stand a chance." The old man mumble to himself, but I hear him.

Captain kick the weapon outa the girl's hand. "Now can we go?" She grab me and walk us backwards the way we came. I stumble into barbed-wire tumbleweed, which slice into the Teneather boot but don't reach my skin. At the edge of the camp, some guy be coughin' his insides out; we jump over him and run. Ain't nobody followin' us, but we run anyhow.

Some days, Major, I think maybe people be too damaged—a steady diet of violence, you know—and we just can't do no better with ourselves. Why that girl come chargin' me with a laser-blade? You live horror, that's who you be, or what?

I'm runnin' like a bat outa hell. Captain ain't sayin' nothin', don't look at me, just run top speed too, almost fast as me. Weapons, scanners, and whatnot bang all up against her for ten kilometers—she goin' have nasty bruises. Didn't know she had 10K of top speed in her. Old folks say, still waters run deep. I just thought it was another cliché they was proud of rememberin'. Captain definitely run deep. We get back to our camp, she toss down her gear, stretch balled up muscles, and throw cold water at her bruises. We both in shock. She be real pissed-off. I cool down away from her, avoidin' the I-tole-you-so bit.

That's when I find this little rabbit in fronta the transport, all dragged out, soggy, and stupid. Somebody'd run over Ma-rabbit and five other little ones. The survivor's hunched beside dead brothers and sisters, her head pressed against Ma's bloody haunch. She be screamin' with all her little body—only she so itsy-bitsy, her screams ain't nothin' but a sweet high-pitched squeak. Almost can't hear her. Sound like a kid virtuoso sawin' on a toy violin. Oh. Maybe you don't know what that sound like. Electro-synth don't come close. Anyhow, I pick up the soggy ball of fur—which ain't like me at all—and start cooin'. Go figure. Rabbit tremble like a hummin' bird, probably think I'm goin' eat her. She brown on the back with a white tummy. I walk toward our transport and the Captain freak. She stand in fronta the power nets, wavin' a big-ass weapon at me. Megademic could be 'round the corner, so she don't want no wild-card germs or bio-waste gettin' in the system. We already too vulnerable. No way she goin' let me bring a rabbit inside. She point the weapon right at us and ask what the hell I think I'm doin'. I can tell she real upset 'bout shootin' those kids and leavin' that ole guy in the mud. They probably die without medical. Neither one of us feel like goin' back with first or second aid.

I tell the Captain she act just like my Pops. When we was kids growin' up, my sister, Geraldine, pick up any ole half-dead mangy thang offa the streets and bring it on home, make it well or let it die peaceful, not out in traffic with cats and creeps makin' fun. Dyin' with dignity, she call it. Soon as she's sure somethin' be really dead, not just sleepin' or fakin', Geraldine cut it up to see what's on the inside. Like she know already she goin' be a scientist not a sister of mercy. I never know what I'm goin' be or do until after I be or do it. But I always help Sis with her crazy experiments. One day Pops say, Lawanda, you ain't no genius like your sister, just regular, so you oughta have more sense than to bring home a damn three-meter snake that 'llowed to eat us for lunch. Pops act like he goin' get ugly, cursin' and wavin' a tire iron at the snake who be food comatose. Stupid thang don't care 'bout nothin 'cept digestin' and sleepin'.

"Three-meter snake...What, a boa constrictor?" Captain ask.

"It was a trick with all the pet hogs, rats, and stuff, but Sis just feed it road kill."

"Is this some sort of ethnic-throwback tall tale, urban legend?" Captain ask.

"Well, maybe snake be only two-and-a-half meters," I admit. "In back country settlements, where we goin' get urban legends from? That's y'all city nerds."

Captain snap outa whatever she was in, lower her weapon, and say, "The first shot, I meant to hit the wall, not the kid. No more stunts like that. We could have been mobbed back there." Then she let me walk into the transport with the rabbit.

Don't be hard on the Captain now—she doin' the best she can with me. I'm not talkin' shit behind her back, this just 'tween you and me, okay?

Rabbit sit in my lap the resta the night. She kinda rumble and purr like a cat, 'specially when she suck liquid protein offa my little finger. Ain't so dragged out no more. It's funny, I look at her and see my pitiful self—talk about ego!

I send a squad to the Extra camp to help those kids and that ole guy, but Ghost Dancers already come thru recruitin' rebels—born-again Sioux ain't just contemplatin' navels and stakin' out heaven. They pick up the wounded and vanish without a trail or a trace. We don't get to rescue nobody and feel better.

So which story is this, Major? You think that girl figure I'm a gangsta all suited up and ready to do worse stuff to her than those boys? Or maybe she think the Captain shootin' that punk goin' make a mess for her later? She coulda been pissed at how long it take the Captain to do anythin'. Captain got rigid priorities. She don't go stickin' her weapon in other folks' mess 'less it be a obvious threat to me... Maybe that girl just hate rich folk who ain't Extras? Uppity outsiders peepin' her pain. Maybe it ain't goin' make sense.

Watchin' folk get shot like at Paradise Healthway is one thang, shootin' 'em yourself be somethin' else altogether. Captain pull the trigger, but it feel like me doin' it. I ain't never hurt nobody like that before, and after bein' such a coward too. You shoot people all the time, huh? What's it do to you? On the inside, I mean?

Look, man, you know I wanna hear from you. Anythin'! So why you transmit but don't say nothin', just alotta deep breathin' and weird shit? Hey, I even take one of them cold memo thangs you do. Better than nothin'. Geraldine and her genius self tip off to the stars in that ET spaceship with Celestina. I miss her somethin' fierce, but she got a excuse for not gettin' in touch. I don't even know if she be gettin' my messages. But what the hell's wrong with the resta y'all? Elleni ain't respond to none of my transmissions neither—it's like she drop off the edge of the Earth. You know what's up with Miss Freaky Thang? Maybe you should check on her.

I'm gettin' all emotional, but that ain't affectin' my ambassa-dorin', so don't worry. Jenassi still doin' his Euro-trash imitation—talk about throwback—look like Sir Armando goin' make a run for it down a seasonal corridor. He be packin' up his contraband booty and dumpin' excess baggage. Me, I'm down for the long haul. It's funny, when I first hit Los Santos, I couldn't wait to *adios amigos*, but after what I seen, wild horses couldn't drag me outa here. Not 'til we turn this mess around.

I been mind doodlin' on all my clues and info. I ain't no genius, but I feel like if I can get to the Knee, I could put it all together, put myself together. Captain think we can find Wounded Knee by extrapolatin' offa ole maps—Barrier ain't changed geography that much. I'm bettin' I can work a deal with 7-Stories, get him on our side. He got a inside track with Dancers and gene artists. I'ma pitch him a Wounded Knee episode of *The Transformers*—that's the kinda outlaw thang Mifune Enterprises get rich and famous for!

One way or another, we goin' make that born-again Sioux ceremony.

Love you, Lawanda

49: At the Barrier's Edge, New Ouagadougou City
(October 16, Barrier Year 115)

> No meaning without experience, no future in advance of living it,
> no absolute, eternal truth revealed either by God or mathematical
> logic. The infinite cannot be reduced to a finite algorithm,
> poetic fantasy, or prophetic Vision. The map of the Universe
> is the Universe.
> —Vera Xa Lalafia, *Healer Cosmology, The Final Lessons*

"Elleni?" A velvet voice spoke in the darkness. "Where are you rushing off to?"

Magenta light scurried through the milky Barrier, and the coppery taste of blood filled the Major's mouth. He'd bitten a hole on the inside of his bottom lip. Branches snapped in the shadows between cathedral trees at the Barrier's edge. The Major was flooded with relief as he regained his senses and dropped back into normal spacetime.

He stepped away from Elleni's prone body, jerking around to face the crackling twigs, his sidearm locked on a human target. Saved by a clumsy assassin from god knows what atrocity with a *Vermittler* witch. He remembered only a few outrageous images from Elleni's black-hole spell—Celestina waved blood-red hands at him—yet as consciousness claimed him, they faded quickly. His own hand no longer glowed neon red. Had it ever? His data glove put out error messages declaring the entire experience a malfunction of its programming. He had to reboot the system.

"Don't shoot!" Ray Valero staggered from the hanging gardens onto the old highway, the silhouette of New Ouagadougou City ghosting behind him.

A spasm in the Major's lips prevented his issuing more than a grunt in response.

"You're quick on the draw." Ray's studded suede jeans and shirt were smeared with what looked like blood—from an external source. His shaggy dark hair was slicked back with sweat. His skin was a sickly olive green. He held his arms above his head in fake terror. "I'm unarmed." Ray smiled mockingly and pounded his chest. "Just a lonely heart and an empty medicine bag." It was slung over his shoulder.

The Major recognized Elleni's painted Barrier-scapes on the bag. Who but she could make the invading enigma look beautiful? He retracted his weapon. Elleni struggled to her feet and would have toppled over, except the Major broke her fall. She winced and held on to him for balance. Her sudden weakness baffled him. She had gone from warrior woman Oshun to ordinary helpless female again. A sign?

Ray took a few steps toward them. "Am I interrupting a secret rendezvous?" His eyes were the color of the Barrier at twilight, tinged with a thin ripple of anger.

The Major forced his twitching lips to cooperate. "Where's your security, Ray? Whose blood is—"

"You don't wanna know."

"You shouldn't walk around without escort!" the Major said, and Elleni groaned.

"Why? We're in paradise. Are you trying to steal my woman, Major, at this ungodly hour?" Ray performed the jealous lover. "Don't answer that." He avoided a dozen fire-ant mounds despite apparent intoxication. "Who but I could possibly lust after such a bizarre specimen as Elleni, the wise and terrible—"

"I thought you were on location." The Major interrupted Ray's drunken insult. He recalled Elleni's iridescent nipples and the silken worms between her thighs and suppressed a shiver of lust and disgust. Of her physical aberrations, only the exploding face had no appeal whatsoever.

"My lady belongs to the world." Ray bowed. "Jealousy is unworthy of me."

Elleni found her balance; she brushed warm fingers across the Major's quivering lips and mustache, and the debilitating spasm faded.

"Isn't she a wonder?" Ray said.

"You're supposed to be shooting in the Nuevo Nada wasteland, making art until winter. That's the buzz." The Major stepped away from Elleni. Ray was a reformed gangster. Jealousy could easily perforate his thin veneer of civilization. No point provoking him. "What brings you to New Ouagadougou City?" Seasonal corridor intelligence hadn't notified the Major that Elleni's star-lover had come through the Barrier. He probed the reports again, just in case he'd overlooked something.

"Making art in Nuevo Nada? Where'd you hear that?" Ray stumbled up to Elleni. She sighed and closed her eyes as he embraced her. The Major recognized the smile that illuminated her face. When he'd first come to her aid, she'd been expecting Valero. "Gossip Electro invents truth, don't trust 'em! I don't know about your spooks, but I wouldn't trust them either. What brings you down to the dead mall so early in the morning, Major?"

"My spies don't lie to me. You're doing an epic, about the history of the Barrier. *The Transformers*." The Major kept the focus on Entertainment.

"Trash," Ray said. "Recon-porno slop. Not art."

"Oh, of course. Tadeshi Mifune is no longer with us." Ray's director of choice had disappeared off-world with Celestina and Company. She was among a select few directors who didn't want to bring back good old gangster Entertainment: he-man heroes, violent sex, and hordes of Extras dying in snuff takes. "Must be hard-going without Tadeshi at the helm."

"Yeah."

The blood on Ray's shirt was recent. Had he acted the hero in real life? The Major's pulse spiked. If Ray didn't come through a seasonal corridor, exactly how did he manage to cross the Barrier without a *Vermittler*?

"I'm confident you can transform even mediocre material into a sublime Entertainment."

"You flatter me, Major. Why?" Ray and Elleni fell into each other and pliéd gracefully to the ground.

"I'm a fan of yours, Ray. I admire your ability to inhabit so many different people. I want you to find a project worthy of your considerable genius."

"I didn't think you gave a shit about Entertainment, Major."

"I always appreciate excellence, in any field."

Elleni leaned heavily into Ray. The Major appreciated Valero's desire for "Miss Freaky Thang," just not what the handsome star did about her revolting aspects. Her breathing was labored, her hair agitated—relapse? She had enjoyed a miraculous recovery until she'd…taken the cold from the Major's body and stripped herself truly naked for him. The illusion of her human face had exploded, and he couldn't see her after all.

"What did you say, Major?" Ray asked.

"The sun's going to come over those trees any second."

Ray looked from the Barrier to the magenta horizon. "Bella," he whispered to Elleni without irony. "Open your eyes, see the new day breaking. Say goodbye to the Major." Ray glanced back at him. "She's not fit for human consumption, but I'm sure you're feeling much better, Major."

"*B'ao ku ishe o tan*," Elleni said, flashing static-filled eyes at the Major. They cleared in a second. "When there is life, there is still hope."

"So true. Thank you." The Major stood at attention.

"I say that for myself," Elleni said.

"But it can apply to us all." The Major bowed as he had seen Healers do and backed away. He lifted the Eshu mask from the parking meter. "I hope I haven't offended you." He managed a smile. Jocelyn was right. Elleni was a powerful lady—he had almost betrayed himself to her—but she was no politician, no threat to Paradigma's security. Certainly not worth risking everything. "Perhaps we can finish our discussion another time?"

"When you're ready. Don't be taken in by swirling discs or other floating parlor games. Let me find a way to Sidi's heart, if I can." Elleni sighed. "It's too dangerous otherwise."

The Major nodded, turned on his heels, and headed toward the Canyon Bridge. The Barrier was the source of magic realism. Elleni and possibly Sidi could manipulate its energy for shaman tricks, such as Elleni's "healing touch." Without understanding why, he knew he had nothing to fear from Elleni. This was an irrational conclusion after a tangle in spacetime, but he couldn't argue with himself about this.

Through Elleni, he experienced indirect Barrier intercourse, which had so far been invigorating. The chill and jackhammer headache were gone. So were fluorescent illusions. His weapon hand looked normal. Macabre images of Celestina still ghosted about just beyond consciousness—nothing he couldn't handle. He noted no signs of sleep deprivation, and his mood was optimistic. Even the bombs in his head had been subdued. The familiar hum at the back of his thoughts was so quiet, the lethal bio-bots might have been incapacitated. If there were ever an opportunity, the Major would study *Vermittler* "laying on of hands" and other magic realist phenomenon...for now he had too much political upheaval to balance out.

He raced along the Canyon Bridge, avoiding low-hanging alora vines with balled up blossoms. Gene-art madness in Los Santos was the real threat to world security. He initiated the hyper-dig mode on his computer for a probe of Robin Wolf, Thandiwe, and disappeared scientists. He contacted corridor security for an update on all interzonal travelers. He queried his spies in Los Santos about Ray's latest art adventure and about renegades sabotaging Nuevo Nada greenhouses. He activated a sentinel search engine for any indirect references to Lawanda. Jocelyn's death warrant for the Vice-Ambassador was premature. The fire-virus threat and Ghost-Dance promise were factors critical to the security of Paradigma. Assassinating Lawanda before she had solved these mysteries would not be in the Prime Minister's best interest. He alerted the Captain to her deadly task, ordering her to frame Aaron Dunkelbrot for Lawanda's murder, yet leaving the date of execution open. Nobody could say he hadn't done his extreme duty. The Captain would be ready at a moment's notice, but the Major indulged in hope. Perhaps he could find a loophole and change Jocelyn's mind about Lawanda. If Elleni could touch Sidi's heart, anything was possible.

The Major flexed the fingers in his data glove. Once again automatic, efficient, back on track. Healers might say that Eshu, the trickster deity watching over the crossroads, had shown him the way. The thought amused him. As he laughed out loud, dark heavy clouds obscured the rising sun. Whirling winds tried to snatch Eshu from his arm. The Canyon Bridge turned from opaque ochre to translucent blue, revealing metallic plastic innards reminiscent of intertwining dragons.

"Warning! Warning!" a sweet alto voice sang out in English and other languages. The alarm voices were accompanied by piercing Tama and Djembe drums rather than a shrill siren. "Rogue cyclone approaching. Wind at dangerous velocities. Given your maximum speed, you cannot go back or forward and reach shelter in time."

"Thanks for nothing," he said, scanning the incoming turbulence.

A blast of wet air almost toppled him. He skidded across the bridge's translucent surface, which now pulsed from blue to magenta. Where did this rogue storm come from? His data glove had given him no warning. He would run a systems check when he reached his transport—if he reached it...

"You must take shelter now!" The warning voices roared. "Your situation is life-threatening!" In front of him, a dragon's mouth opened on a lighted stairway. The Major scrambled toward it. "Leave the mask outside or wear it!"

The Major set Eshu on his head and shoulders and dropped inside the hatchway just as the storm hit with full force. The dragon bridge undulated in the high winds, its strength and elasticity verging on the impossible. The Major clamped himself to the stairs and laughed. After his Elleni encounter, riding dragons through a rogue cyclone seemed like an amusement-park romp. An image-board in his cramped hideaway displayed a schematic of the storm's activity. Everywhere but the Canyon, the sun shone and winds were moderate. The Major smirked. Ouagadougians were not the devout technophobes he had imagined them to be. Techs at Electrosoft Corp would salivate with envy. He gathered data on the bridge's inner workings, then, deploying a communication scrambler, sent Lawanda a terse communiqué. Indirect discourse with his ladylove was safest until he knew her fate.

"The storm has passed." The bridge voices sang out to him. "Slippery when wet." The dragon mouth opened to the outside. "If you are well, I am well." The voices sang their good-byes and faded with a drum flourish.

The Major scrambled out and lifted Eshu from his head. The sun massaged his skin. The air tasted like seltzer with a twist of lime. He sucked in tart gasps, no longer surprised by anything. The bridge's surface was once again opaque ochre but looked as if it had been swept clean and polished. Everything sparkled. The Major jogged the last eight hundred meters across the bridge toward a brand new day.

With such natural spectacles punctuating their mundane lives, no wonder people still believed in omens and portents.

As the Major strode past the Library of the Dead, the lanky Ghost Dancer with the calligraphy face stared at him from the open door-way—accusingly, as if she could read treachery right off his mind. She signed at him. Her hands were big and clumsy; he'd seen more elegant speakers, but he easily perceived her accusatory tone. Who was this Ghost Dancer to challenge him? Ignoring twinges of guilt, the Major trotted a good distance from the born-again Sioux lady before deploying a scrambler and buzzing Duma's personal Electro channel. If not Councilor Duma, he would, when Elleni wasn't around, convince/force Ray Valero to share his Barrier secrets.

A deep voice yawned across a channel connection demanding a good reason for being snatched from pleasant dreams. Duma was not an early riser. The Major hesitated several seconds, frankly doubting his own sanity. He held his weapon hand up to the light, then shook his head. The skin was burnished bronze from hours in the Ouagadougian sun, showing not a hint of fluorescent red. He sighed. Too much spacetime had already been wasted, skittering on the edge of treachery with Elleni. On the Electro, Duma cleared his throat and thumped a reproach in Healer drum-speak.

"Sorry to wake you," the Major said. Foolish emotions and illusions had driven him close to auto-destruct, but as Duma complained that the dew on his eyelids had yet to evaporate in the sun, the Major's habitual discipline kicked in. He noted the quaint Ouagadougian metaphor then proceeded to stack the deck against Elleni, Lawanda, and the Treaty. What else was there to do? Anybody was expendable. He was still loyal to Jocelyn and Paradigma, and Elleni had said it herself: Sidi was the woman of the hour.

50: On Location outside Nuevo Nada, Los Santos
(October 15, Barrier Year 115)

> According to the Romans: *Ars est celare artem*—the nature of art is to conceal, but I think art's about revealing, showing us what we couldn't see in what we always see.
> —Tadeshi Mifune, *Surviving the Future, Last Minute Notes*

Achbar glided between Aaron and his ghost-white AD. Aaron's cocked gun pressed against Achbar's broad chest. Moses stumbled backward into Achbar's scooter, which fell over with a loud clatter. The Ghost Dancer sat up in Lohengrin's swan boat like he'd been yanked from the valley of death to Neuschwanstein. The gene-art lizards chased each other across his face, and he slumped back down in the wine velvet cushions.

"Move. I don't want to shoot you," Aaron said to Achbar.

"Of course not." Achbar didn't move. "You don't want to shoot anybody."

"You're wrong about that."

"And Moses doesn't want a bullet in the brain for his sins," Achbar said.

"What does he want, then?"

"He wants us to take the power nets offline, open the gates wide, and let all the trailer trash from outside Nada join *The Transformers'* cast and crew."

"You don't think that's a good idea?" Aaron said.

Achbar pressed into the gun. "We don't know who or what we're letting in."

"Aren't you the one who thinks we can raise people like Mahalia from the dead?"

"Not us, that's Elleni's gig." Achbar closed his hands around Aaron's and pressed gently until the gun was aimed at the ground. "Miracle workers can be a royal pain."

Moses righted the transparent scooter then shuffled to the window and pulled the wedding tapestry back across the mob scene outside. "I always say, we should save who we can."

"You mean that, don't you?" Aaron leaned against Achbar, who didn't seem to mind holding him up. "But what about her?"

"Mahalia..." Moses shook his head.

"Dr. Selasie first worked against the Treaty, then she had a change of heart. That was a capital offense," Achbar said. The sly old thug knew all about it.

"I'm not gonna shoot him—he isn't worth the bullet," Aaron said

Achbar released his gun hand.

"Look, the bitch signed her own death warrant. What was I supposed to do? Let them put my ass in a sling too? They wanted Entertainment-quality terror, one flashy hit to freak the other scientists, to keep 'em in line, so I did it."

"Just like that, huh?" Aaron said softly.

Moses shouted. "I've done worse shit, for you."

"That's a lie."

"I just don't tell you, but you know I'm doing it. Somebody's gotta do it."

"My dirty work, anybody's dirty work, it's all the same…" Aaron dropped down on a fallen column.

"But this fire-virus thing… They didn't tell me…"

"They? Who is this 'they'?" Achbar asked.

Moses looked around anxiously, his tongue worrying the inside of his cheek.

"What? You think the damn swans are snooping our tête-á-tête?" Aaron snorted.

"It's clean here, trust me," Achbar said. "I swept this whole area."

"It wasn't supposed to be like this," Moses said, leaning against the tapestry.

"What'd *they* promise you? Immunity? Immortality? Your own studio?" Aaron asked. "Burn the bitch alive or we'll turn you into a slug?"

Moses shivered. "I don't like torture."

"Yeah, well, neither do I," Aaron said.

"Then we all agree on something," Achbar said.

"It wasn't me, you know, who saved you that night." Moses blurted this out.

"What are you saying?" Aaron jumped up

Moses ran his fingers through a tangle of blue curls. "You don't want to hear it."

"Cut the high drama and just spit it out!" Even Achbar was losing patience.

"I was hiding out while those punks were doing you in the old studio subway, and this woman started calling the rest of us fucking cowards, and she tried to pull 'em off you. They cracked her head open, but all of a sudden, everybody was out on the platform, me too, screaming at 'em. It was a crazy mob thing. Those four punks took off down a tunnel, or we would have splattered 'em all over the walls. When the dust settled, I was so scared they'd come back and pick us off one at a time… I didn't want to be alone, that's why I stayed with you the whole night. We all sort of huddled around you. In the morning when the punks snuck back, they got scared off by all the people *behind me*. I'm not a shining knight who saved some helpless broad getting boned by gutless thugs."

Aaron felt like he had been skinned alive with a laser-blade.

"Helpless broad?" Achbar squinted at him. "You were a woman?"

Aaron saw himself tumble down in the Achbar's mind.

"A black woman from Angel City," Moses said. "Can you believe it?"

"Shut up," Aaron said.

"Dr. Mahalia's a genius—you have to give her that." Moses kept blabbing.

Achbar stroked his mustache. "Nobody even tries full-body gene art. Sex-change is still slicing, dicing, and hormones—if you can afford it."

"You do such a good act, I have to regularly remind myself who you really are," Moses said.

"You sound pretty brave to me," Achbar said to Moses then squeezed Aaron's shoulder. "I was a hit man from age fifteen. Since healing I haven't wanted to kill anybody, 'til today." He glanced at the AD. How much Achbar had known before was unclear, but he knew everything now. Aaron cringed. Having the big Arab on his side didn't ease the shame.

"We gotta keep moving. What's the plan?" Achbar asked, like Aaron was still the director, calling the shots, like nothing had changed between them.

"Right." Aaron couldn't let Moses ambush him with old-age retro-BS. He couldn't fall into any black holes—that's what his new demon said. And Achbar had his back. "Who you working for, Mose? They're reneging on promises right and left—Mahalia, the fire virus, the whole gig is spiraling out of control. You're going to strangle in your own net, so come clean."

Moses looked as if he might launch into another confession, but the med-unit on the Dancer shrieked an alarm. Moses closed his lips over half-formed words. Achbar hurried to the swan boat. His face as he read the results was too grim. The Dancer's gene-art lizards had turned purple and yellow. Aaron would have sworn they writhed in agony. Achbar cursed out the med-unit in Arabic or some other dead language.

"What the fuck are you saying? Talk English so somebody can understand," Moses yelled.

Aaron didn't need a translation. Fire virus. Laying a Dancer low—who would have imagined that? Dancers didn't catch the virus. Everybody knew that. The Wovoka promised immunity, immortality. How else could he get all those people to join his whacked-out cult? And he'd delivered immunity—until now, that is.

"Wow." Aaron had held the Dancer's shoulders, swallowed his breath, drank his sweat. He'd watched his eyes wander and his muscles spasm, all the while thinking the guy was a bad actor in fake ethno-drama. *You see what you expect to see.* Aaron felt stupid that he couldn't tell a born-again trance dance from a viral seizure, early stage. But he was in good company. The little bugger had outsmarted the Wovoka, breached location security, and even foiled high-powered interzonal conspirators.

Aaron started to giggle. Maybe it was everything hitting him at once: Mahalia, Moses, the conspiracy...and a dead girl he carried around inside, Stella Jackson. He couldn't quite remember what Stella looked like. He pressed his tongue against front teeth—her nervous gesture, not his. He didn't have a gap anymore.

Moses and Achbar argued over mutations and symptoms. Aaron tuned them out. He listened inside, for what his demons might say. But for the first time in a long time, his mindscape was as quiet as an empty soundstage. Celestina and her posse had deserted him. Only a gap-toothed ghost girl huddled in a corner, wheezing, trying to find her lost breath in a stranger's mouth.

Panic attack.

Aaron's throat was closing up. Somebody's Electro squealed, and his head pounded. He didn't want to swallow his own saliva. He wanted to vomit up his insides and peel off contaminated skin. Moses touched his shoulder, and Aaron put the gun to his head, ready to blow his brains out. The Dancer's whistling breath startled Aaron, threw his aim off. He fired at the domed ceiling. The bullet grazed Moses's ear and temples. He choked down a scream, grabbed at the wound, and staggered back.

Aaron stared at the gun and then Moses's bloody blue curls. "Sorry," Aaron said. Achbar was right—he didn't want to kill Moses, certainly not before he got the lowdown on the conspiracy. "Why?" he asked.

"I don't fucking know... I like to back the winning team, how's that?" Moses tried to work up tears.

Aaron was dry, as if he'd swallowed a desert. A few tears wouldn't make any difference. "Who's behind all this?"

"Jesus Perez," Moses said.

"The soybean weenie? He's nothing, chump change. Even Lawanda bagged his ass." Aaron backed Moses against the wall, the gun at his cheek. "Give me somebody bigger, somebody with brains."

"Danny boy," Moses said quickly, eyeing the gun.

Something didn't sync up. Aaron glanced at Achbar. He looked skeptical too as he reached toward Moses's wound with recon-skin. Moses flinched and pressed himself into the tapestry. Achbar wiped away blood and pressed the bandage from temple to ear.

"How did Danny get turned around?" Achbar said.

Moses winced. "I don't know. Danny's in touch with people in every Zone working to bring the Treaty down."

"Spilling your guts, and your head didn't explode—no chem-implants?" Aaron said. "Handsome Danny must really trust you. How'd you work that?"

"They ran out of Paradigma implants. Ours are for shit. Danny didn't want a zombie." Pungent sweat drenched Moses's under-arms. "He said he has electronic spooks and if anything goes wrong, he'll know and... The location is wired. They could take us out anytime."

"*Was* wired. I don't work a bomb site." Achbar waved his Healer staff.

"Danny's in New O City hooking up with double-crossing pricks from all over the world." Aaron thrust the gun back into its shoulder holster as Achbar nodded in agreement.

Moses's Electro squealed again. They all jumped. "That's Lawanda. She's at the north gate. Says she has to talk to you about a Wounded Knee episode. Says it's urgent." Moses slid down the wall to the ground.

"Lawanda in your conspiracy too?" Aaron asked even though he knew she wasn't.

"No, Armando Jenassi's our boy. Lawanda's on a short list." Moses sighed. "Somebody big wants her out of the picture."

"You're real helpful all of a sudden," Aaron said.

Glancing at the Dancer's vacant eyes, Moses looked genuinely terrified. "It wasn't supposed to be a full-blown fire-virus breakout."

"You actually thought they could control this shit?" Aaron shook his head.

"Yeah..." Moses said. "But without Mahalia, I don't know."

"What about the other scientists?" Achbar said. "Could they contain the breakout?"

Moses closed his eyes. "I don't know."

"Like somebody said, all our suns have not yet set." Aaron took a deep breath. "Open the south gate, let these people onto the lot. Get 'em treatments—placebos if you have to. That'll give us time. We should all do treatments. Achbar, neutralize the rest of Danny's electronic spooks. Leave a few or it'll be too suspicious. And Moses, I want you to tell Achbar everything, all the sordid details. Even stuff that's not important."

"I'd rather tell you." Moses picked at his nose.

"I might want to shoot you, and then where would we be?" Aaron had to get away. He couldn't stand the sight of either one of them right now.

"Never leave a trail that your enemies can follow back to you." Achbar lifted his Healer staff and paced a circle in the dust. "If this were Danny's conspiracy, he'd have better cover."

"I'm not lying, all right?" Moses said. "Perez deals through Danny. Trust me on this."

"Danny must be the fall-guy then." Aaron said.

"So who's calling the shots?" Achbar asked.

"That's the trillion dollar question." Aaron pushed past Moses to the scooter. "Don't let this sack of shit out of your sight."

"What about him?" Achbar stood by the Dancer in the swan boat. He evidenced the slightest trace of fear in the face of the virus, or perhaps it was just healthy respect.

"Get him to your rig while I meet Lawanda. Can I borrow your scooter?" Before Achbar could reply, Aaron leapt on the transparent vehicle and headed off through the rubble for a rendezvous with Paradigma's Vice Ambassador.

51:   Cross-Barrier Transmission/Personal
(October 15, Barrier Year 115)

From: Lawanda

To: The Major

Old folks will tell you, shit or get off the pot. You understand what I'm sayin'? The sky is fallin'. Hello. I can't be waitin' 'round for you or nobody to give me permission to do the right thang. Is anybody home? I tell you all this significant shit and you transmit less than nothin':

To: Lawanda

From: The Major, Head of Sagan City Secret Services

Situation—critical.

Anything you do might blow up in your face. I can't be responsible.

Keep me posted about ALL new developments, however insignificant.

Check the reckless antics—they are not cute.

Wait for orders.

What the fuck is up with that? Man, you a piece a work. Spit in my eye and try to act like you washin' it out. I love you and all, so much 'til it hurt. I could really use one of your torpedo kisses that start in my mouth, zip down my spine, and explode out my toes. I wanna taste your sweet breath, suck your tongue, and have all your skin against mine. I want you insida me, a heat seekin' missile, settin' me on fire.

But my momma ain't raise no fool. I can read between the lines. You like a junkie, tryin' to kick a violent habit, still surrounded by your ole cronies who be mainlinin' the shit. Well, who you think I am? One of your chem-implant zombies that get off on witholdin' mindfuckers? See, I know you, how you operate. Jocelyn's makin' it hard for you, ain't she? I bet her team's against the Treaty so you tryin' to play both sides. That's rough, cuz then you got everybody firin' on your ass.

Well, sorry, I ain't waitin' for no orders from a two-timin' loser. It's me or the PM, you better make up your mind and quick. You won't be hearin' from reckless me no more 'til you do. You understand what I'm sayin'? I ain't goin' be sleepin' with the enemy.

I give you this one last chance. How's that for cute?

So, scope ALL the new developments.

(I see you tryin' to figure if I'm goin' lie, or what I'm not tellin', or why I'm tellin' you anythin' at all. You can't psych me out like that, so don't even bother.)

This mornin' Jenassi disappear with a caravan of loot, ain't leave a trace or a trail, just like the motherfucker wasn't never here. (I be way past watchin' the curse words, so filter what you can't handle.) Jenassi ain't warn me 'bout all the danger we in, say good-bye, nothin'. One of his security get caught in a curfew in Nuevo Nada, and Jenassi leave him cold. I wouldn't be leavin' nobody behind in this nightmare, even folk I can't stand.

News flash: fire-virus breakout hit Nada and Extra camps on the outskirts of the city. A ugly scene. People at they worst, dyin' from each other steada the disease.

To top off the mornin', I get a second invite from Jesus Perez, that jive turkey whose soybean assets I data-chilled way back when. Piss-ant gangsta be throwin' a party in honor of the Treaty for politicos and the glitterati—ganglords, stars from every studio, drug mavens, and contraband queens. I'm the guest of honor. Can you believe it? Man must think I'm a retard. Even if I could trust his ass, which we know I cannot, I wanna get to the bottom of thangs, not party while Rome burn. I don't bother RSVPin'. Captain check it out tho and word is, some Dancers goin' show at this party, tryin' to hook up rebel folk for the Knee. You always be tellin' me to keep my options open…

Anyhow this afternoon, me and the Captain is outsida the north gate of *The Transformers* location shoot waitin' for Mr. 7-Stories. Captain ain't too happy with my choice of allies. She poutin' and shit, talkin' to herself, and lookin' terrible. Her skin's ashy, hair dull, cheeks sunken in. The bad-ass edge be gone from her step. I ain't never seen her like this. Discipline stretched way too thin. This gangsta Zone's finally even gettin' to her. Tell you the stone truth, I don't look too fly neither. I lost ten kilos and shaved my hair down to fuzz, like a Extra at the end of the line.

The guard at *The Transformers'* gate can't leave his post to escort us in, but he buzz Dunkelbrot's assistant director who tell us just to wait, somebody be down.

"Why Dunkelbrot?" Captain ask me over a private Electro channel for the umpteenth time. "Dunkelbrot's a gene-art reactionary— not a rebel! He and his crew could be behind the whole anti-Treaty plot!" She sound tired, irritable.

"Yeah, well, don't seem like his kinda plot, and he the only gene-art lead we got." I'm repeatin' myself too.

Captain groan, but she don't disagree cuz just then, our flyin' auto-bomb squad come down with somethin' nasty, and it be rainin' slimy silver fish. They crash, flop 'round on the ground, and spew buglet guts on our Teneather boots. The security man flip, dash in the guardhouse, and turn up his power net shieldin'.

Captain look real distressed. "I've never seen them all break down at once."

"Maybe the whole squad ate some bad shit and got sick."

"You think?" she say and start vacuumin' up the remains.

"I'm just talkin' trash," I say. Her takin' a obvious joke so serious ain't good.

"Auto-bomb squad consists of independent agents with individual codes and experience-modified bio-processors operating in a loose federation of cells, like terrorists." She sound kinda like you, Major, only real sad.

"Uh huh." I'm workin' the buglets offa my enviro-suit, they real sticky. Rabbit poke her head out my pocket to see what's goin' down. I scratch her head and say, "I don't get the terrorist bit."

Captain stare at the rabbit, disgusted. "What is there to get? If you infiltrate or blast one cell, the other cells aren't affected!"

"You could've meant they be kamikaze suckers ready to die takin' out a target."

"Well, that's obviously a part of their operating system!" she yell. "Beyond obvious. Without the altruism loop, an auto-bomb squad would be useless, just out to save their own little..."

"Why you trippin'?"

"Who's tripping?" Her face look distorted, muscles goin' every which way, her mouth workin' like a machine gun. "I just don't have time to patch up the yawning gaps in your feeble education." She at the dead-end of her patience, but I don't mind. That's when you find out who people really be.

"Don't lie," I say, "You pissed. And this ain't 'bout my ignorance of buglet behaviors."

"You bet I'm pissed. I've been sent down a corridor to hell on this loser mission with an incompetent superior who mind-doodles diplomacy and bug-bot equipment that self-destructs. How would you suggest I feel?"

This the most real conversation we ever have. "I know I make it hard for you sometime," I say.

"Sometimes?" Buglets be flyin' in from everywhere, croakin' mid-air, like a plague of sick locusts splatterin' us with slime. Rabbit burrow deep in my pocket away from the shit storm. "*All* the time making it hard." Captain grunt and drop to the dirt, checkin' out buglet remains. "Diversity should be our best secret weapon…"

And then *snap!* I gotta tackle her 'fore she be trippin' into the friggin' Barrier!

Mystery shit happen again. A dreamwalk to the Barrier thru a crack in spacetime. Alluva sudden, me and the Captain ain't nowhere near *The Transformer*'s north security gate no more, gotta be at least a hundred kilometers away—rollin' 'round in the wasteland. Skyscrapers and coolin' towers in Nada clutter up half the sky. It's gettin' dark, afternoon done tip out on us. All along the horizon, the Barrier look like it swallow black and blue tornadoes. The wind offa the ugly funnels blast us with sand. And scope this, somethin' sides me be under my skin, in my head—a boogey, just like before, only not quite. Time's stretched way outa proportion. 'Tween one breath and the next, a woman's singin' me ole-age blues. I seen her once before, a cloud of fuzzy red clown hair and pale skin glowin' in twilight. She was runnin' from thugs *into* the Barrier. Lady from the underground choir. Now she float out a black crystal corridor with a little boy ridin' on her shoulders. His big brown eyes is smilin'. I remember him in Paradise—the kid that explode from the fire virus. I got his mind-doodle on my transport wall. He all healed up, just some funny-lookin' scars on his tummy. He reach a hand out to me and whisper so quiet I gotta lean in to hear what he's sayin'. "They said you were coming. I didn't believe them. Nothing ever happens like they say." Kid's voice ain't nothin' but air. "You're not a dream, are you?" He ask, then him and the blues singer dissolve into champagne bubbles 'cross the horizon. A Ghost-Dancer man with silver skin and electric eyes, walk thru bubbles, nod, then disappear too. It's the Wovoka. I'd swear my life on it. A religious fanatic bringin' folk back from the dead to talk to me. Now that's what I call a new development!

I ain't havin' a psychotic snap, so don't even go there. This shit's as real as anythin'.

A heartbeat after I tackle her, the Captain got my arms pinned, my neck in a vise grip, and I'm 'bout to be history. "It's me, Lawanda. Watch the rabbit!" I try to shout, but she's chokin' me. "You don't wanna break my neck, do you?"

Captain blink her eyes real fast and purse her lips like SHE AIN'T SO SURE. I know I been pissin' her off since we come to Los Santos, but this creep me right out. She scan the empty wasteland with her mouth hangin' open. Her white hair is full of static, standin' on end, at attention. She drop me in the dust, don't say, 'scuse me, sorry, nothin, just, "Why'd you tackle me?"

"You were 'bout to be crispy crunchies," I say and point to the Barrier behind her. Stringy licks offa the lethal thang be gropin' in the dark, reachin' for us.

"Damn!" Captain jump up and pull me outa range with her. "How the hell did we get out here?" She ain't happy 'bout our Barrier dreamwalk. "I don't like this. Where are we?" She start fussin' with my bio-computer, jackin' it into her Electro.

"Born-again Sioux believe the Barrier's goin' bring back dead ancestors," I say, kinda thinkin' out loud.

"I don't believe this." Captain let a breath whistle thru her teeth.

"Me neither. It carry us here, but not our enviro-suits or—"

"No, no. That compound of buildings to the east beyond that rock outcropping. See that?" She point.

It be twilight dim and I barely scope some smudges on the horizon. "I guess."

"That's Jesus Perez's villa."

"Talk about a special invitation! How far we got to go?" I start bookin' in Perez's direction, of course. The wild child's in charge. "One last stop before the Badlands."

She don't chase after me like usual. I turn 'round to see what's up and gotta swallow a scream. Captain look like all her disks done crashed. She sink into the dirt and don't move, 'cept her upper lip be steady twitchin'. I run and stick a probe in her. It be talkin' 'bout ain't nothin' wrong. Med-units have a rigid definition of sick. I buzz our squad and tell 'em to meet us at Perez's place, transmit to 7-Stories and make up a fast lie why we disappear from the gate. I pitch a Wounded Knee episode at him and tell him he better meet us at Perez's or else.

Like I got somethin' to back a threat with.

Last time the Barrier mess with us like this, Captain have to just 'bout carry me back to our quarters. This time I'm doin' the carryin'. We be half way to Perez's place. I'm pausin' to catch my breath and transmit to you. Captain ain't sayin' nothin', just starin' back at the Barrier. She seen them ghost folk in there too, I bet, just won't say.

Sittin' here, tryin' not to freak, and it hit me. You musta ordered the Captain to do some awful shit and she don't wanna do it. That's why she all messed up. The auto-bomb squad in her head be mobilizin' against her. If the Captain don't do like you say, them implants will splatter her brains to kingdom come, huh?

I got an awful feelin' you set me up for target practice and since you the enemy, it don't make no sense givin' you the inside story like this. I know I'm takin' a big risk here, but I ain't got nothin' but big risks to take. I want you to know what's up, in case I don't make it outa Perez's party alive. I figure it could go either way with those thugs. Or maybe the Captain'll do me steada herself.

You gotta follow up my Barrier encounter no matter what side you on, no matter what transpire 'tween the Captain and me. Elleni got her hands full with Sidi and that messiah-wannabe Duma, a puddle to Femi's ocean, all right. See, this ain't just petty politics. Somethin' beyond scary, somethin' miraculous be goin' down.

I'm appealin' to the scientist in you.

I know I ain't make up everythin' I feel about you. You and me were s'posed to be a dream team, Major. *We were goin' feed starvin' babies, stop wars and extinctions, turn the tides of history...*

You talk more shit, but I'ma hold you to it.

Lawanda

52: At the Barrier's Edge, New Ouagadougou City
(October 16, Barrier Year 115)

> You understand the truth you grasp but not the truth
> that grasps you.
> —Vera Xa Lalafia, *Healer Cosmology, The Final Lessons*

"Do you see tomorrow in my face?" These were the first words Elleni had uttered in god knows how long.

Ray stared at her with all the focus he could muster, which in his wasted condition wasn't much. It had been a while since he'd blown a hit of Rapture, and he was crashing. Elleni leaned against him, her face barely a breath away, her braids wriggling through his hair. Prickly sparks soothed his feverish brain, but still he could think of nothing useful to say.

Since the Major had gone, she'd been jacking them through the Barrier, phaseshifting, to where a minute could seem like a year (or at least several hours). The sun had been trying to rise for an eternity, but the blazing red disk had gotten snagged on a gnarled cliff. A monkey's screech hung in the air like a bass foghorn. At his feet, a hot spring gurgled up out of broken asphalt, sluggish in their spacetime, a disorienting comfort. Ray guessed that Elleni was mucking around with reality to give them privacy—with time to burn, they were as good as invisible—but he hated her jacking his mindscape. It was just too weird.

"Tomorrow—in your face?" he repeated stupidly, not knowing if she was asking a literal or figurative question. Normally he was sharper, catching her nuances, riding her metaphors with ease. Just now, he was hanging from a slender thread. Some hero-to-the-rescue he was. "I don't know what you mean." They had more important things to discuss: snuff takes, Treaty conspiracies, fire-virus epidemics. Yet he couldn't get himself to broach these weighty issues either. He just wasn't up for any real-life adventure. His eyes fluttered shut.

"No, look at me!" She squeezed his hand until it hurt.

"Piano, piano," he said and stared at her. He could never quite capture Elleni in his gaze and after every separation, it took all his senses to know her again.

Static flared across her pupils. She looked different than he remembered, even if he never remembered exactly how she looked. He could taste change on her breath, smell it in her hair. Her skin was like a stained-glass mosaic, catching the light at different angles, shimmering. Whatever she touched held a faint after-sparkle. He traced the curve of her lips then marveled at his glowing fingers. Something like that, he would have noticed before.

"What happened?" His voice was husky. "I'm driving a corridor, and there you are, shapeshifting through the Barrier, instead of buzzing my Electro? Never done that before." The bangs rioting on her forehead told him he was hot, on the right track.

She tried to dodge him. "Hard to say. English is so…limited."

"Cold comfort. Does that mean you can't or don't want to tell me?"

"You really wouldn't understand."

"Shadow man, zero substance. Too much gangster to appreciate Healer subtlety."

"Why do you always repeat that?"

"Because maybe it's true," he said. Elleni bit her tongue, ruby red like Sidi's. Spots of blood seemed brown against it. "I'm sorry, look—"

"It's what *they* say about you, Sidi, Duma, and the rest, but never what I feel."

"So prove it, talk to me," Ray said, "Trust me!"

Elleni's hair hissed at nothing in particular, releasing a pungent mist that made him sneeze. Her ruby tongue reached for words, then she clamped down on it. Maybe Ray never remembered how she looked, but he remembered how hot and delicious her mouth tasted, even when she flicked half-truths at him.

He sighed. "Ah, Bella, you have ominous secrets that frighten even you." A line from a *Transformers* episode, but he had to say something—she looked so desperate. A yellow tear dribbled down a skinny braid. He hugged her, and she winced. "Tell me what you can, how you can." He kissed her, savoring icy, tart lips and then a hot, bitter tongue, cinnamon and coffee, without the sugar. He pressed her against his heart.

Elleni winced again and pulled her mouth from his. "I phaseshifted with the Major. He was an anchor, like you, but he couldn't really see me. So, not like you at all." Ray wasn't sure he could "really see" her either, but he didn't argue. Her nipples hardened and pressed against his chest. "*Er kann eben aus seiner Haut nicht heraus.*" She sounded wistful.

"How about phaseshifting from old German to English. That's not a long road."

"He can't break out of his skin," she said. "To see me, it isn't words that are lacking, but experience, full-body knowledge…"

"Full-body? What were you and the Major up to?"

A rude question. She didn't answer. Jealousy made Ray stupid. Elleni's tastes were ecumenical, downright indiscriminate, but how could she want that loose-dick, rod-up-his-ass, nazi Major? Ray could have had anybody, yet he'd turned down every temptation for her: Sidi, for godsakes; sweet Danny; that transport attendant; and hordes of horny people he didn't even remember. That Elleni didn't feel exclusive about him tore at his guts. A stupid response, but he couldn't help it. At least he didn't give himself away. He splashed her with water from the hot spring and flashed a thousand-watt grin.

"Too bad for the Major," he said. "I can't get enough of seeing you." She brushed a hand across his face. "But you gotta do something about those claws, babe, you could take out an eye." He tickled her fingertips with his tongue, and she laughed.

"*Augenfeuer*, fire in your eyes, for me. You bring me back, like no one else." Elleni pressed him into the gravel on the old highway, which felt softer than it should have. She sat on his stomach and held his arms to the ground. Her hair slid under his shirt, down his back, and across his chest. Sapphire-blue dreads smelled of seaweed and rainstorms. They slithered across his face, playing his nerves with tiny electric jolts. Despite anxiety, exhaustion, and withdrawal, despite a virus burning in his lungs, he felt aroused. Elleni's longing for him was like a hot wind, a cyclone gathering force. All he wanted was to lose himself in her body—a few blinding orgasms and fourteen hours of sleep—then they could worry about tomorrow, then he could play hero.

Shimmying out of his suede shirt and tight leather pants, he noted the bloodstains and almost lost his erection. But Sidi had promised to heal the burning woman, and Elleni was kissing his eyes, her dreads purred in his ears, and he was a better real-life lover than hero any day. So rather than dwell in tragedy and spoil the precious time Elleni had stolen for them, he reached for romance, his best genre.

Elleni didn't complain.

Ray splashed hot spring water into her hair and coaxed snarled dreads into relaxing their grip on brambles, weeds, and a few crazed beetles. Bloody tatters of a syn-silk scarf dissolved in the fragrant steam. Ray soaked her scalp and massaged away tension. Her sighs were like Kora music. He undid the magnets down the front of her tunic with a practiced flick of his thumb, and the ceremonial robes slipped from her shoulders. As he was about to spill hot water between her breasts, he gasped. No wonder she'd winced when he hugged her. Scream would have been more like it. Purple pus coated the inside of her robes. Her skin was covered with Barrier burns.

"What happened?" An image of the burning woman writhing in the dust clouded his senses. "Couldn't you sculpt-sing a corridor? Did the Barrier collapse on you?"

"No, I...don't stop, the mineral water will help, I think." She took his hand and splashed the fluid against her skin. "Do this. I'll be all right. Please."

He showered water over her shoulders, breasts, belly, thighs, and buttocks, as if he could put out the fire that had already burned her. Elleni's wounds drank in the hot liquid then sealed up, disappearing into the stained glass mosaic of her skin. She sighed, a chord so deep his bones resonated. He drenched her again and again and again. Finally, she grabbed his hands, her strength making him tremble against her.

"It's enough," she said. A shower of sparks passed across her eyes. "Enough."

His body quivered. "What's that prayer, for actors, that Celestina told me?"

Elleni stiffened at the name.

"Sorry," he said. "I know how you miss her."

"We all miss her," she said. "*Şotito şododo şoora ma şika*—perform truth, perform righteousness, perform kindness, avoid cruelty."

He repeated the Yoruba prayer, an actor's thing, dropping the words deeper than he could think, letting the sounds and rhythm soothe him until he became the words. She didn't ask for an explanation, just held on to him, waiting.

"It always sounds so simple," he said.

"Simple is hard. Everyone knows that."

"On location, they set a woman on fire, not a pyrotechnician, a scientist in a snuff take, and she almost died, but..."

"But you saved her?"

He shook his head. "I don't know," he whispered, "maybe, maybe not."

She drew him to her. "Feel me." Her skin was hot and slick with spring water. She didn't wince at his touch. "I won't break, not even from pleasure." He looked at her skin doubtfully. "Passion heals. Everybody knows that." Her voice caressed him.

"But sometimes we forget…"

She slid her body across his. He felt muscles rippling under her skin, blood rushing through her veins, and nerves charging and discharging. All was pleasure, no pain, a praisesong to his body—which he could never quite remember, because when they were together, he was different, his thoughts, his possibilities. Santosians believed shamen bewitched their lovers. Not true. Together they were just better than he was alone.

The snarl of hair at her crotch was sapphire-blue. He slid between her thighs and felt light break apart and scatter across his skin. A magnetic rush in his groin made him shout. He was glad no one could hear. She rocked against him with such urgency, he could barely contain himself. But he didn't have to. At their third orgasm, broken glass filled his mind, sparkling, cutting up his thoughts, setting off lines of poetry, sultry rhythms, a mix of metaphors painful and beautiful, nothing he could linger in.

"Ṣotito ṣododo ṣoora ma ṣika." His own deep, resonant voice startled him.

"You're so easy with love," Elleni said, hands circling his waist, breasts pressed against his back, and chin resting on his shoulder. They were sticky with each other's sweat and smelled of jasmine. When he squinted, his skin looked like stained glass, too.

"What do you mean?" he asked. Ouagadougians had a different hit on lust, love, sex, and whatnot. Spirit notions got tangled up into everything. Ray wasn't against their way of sorting it out—it was just too convoluted for him to get his mind around. "I've loved only two people my whole life, so you got me beat on that score, Bella."

"OK, stingy with love, but easy in someone's body. No ugly on you to get in the way." He felt her impulse to push him away and hide her breasts under whining hair.

"Ugly?" In Los Santos, people would have squandered fortunes and risked death for jewel-toned hair and stained-glass skin. Gene art was all the rage for those who could afford it and the envy of those who couldn't, but having sapphire locks and electric eyes naturally still meant you were a freak. Ray tried to remember his first encounter with Elleni. A big-assed, big-tit, muscular broad with freaky hair, dodging bullets, spouting poetry, and living like "every moment was a jewel in the necklace of eternity." Who said shit like that? Elleni wasn't a dog, but nobody he would have looked at twice, except for the gangbangers on his ass and the fire virus tearing him up. Running-for-their-lives adventure romance—that's how their thing started. He had laughed at Elleni's heart-on-her-sleeve intensity and thought to use her, a joy ride to nowhere in particular, and then move on. He cringed at this memory, at his shallow gangster sensibility. But it hadn't turned out that way. "What ugly?"

He cupped her breasts and kissed her nipples until they were hard again and iridescent purple, then with tongue and lips followed the blue line of hair from navel to pubis bone. He lost sense of time. Her climax seemed to go on forever, one of the positive features of their spacetime bubble. Still, he could never tell if he satisfied her.

"Am I the exotic jewel in your heart?" she asked.

"Huh?" He didn't want to go down that corridor. What did it matter how he loved her? He doused his head in the spring. It was hotter than before and scalded his face.

"You make love like you want to eat me whole and leave nothing for anyone else."

"Busted." He held up his hands. Yeah, he was obsessive and possessive. "Is that so bad?" He fanned fiery cheeks. He was burning up inside.

Her hair curled around his waist. "I don't want to be forbidden fruit."

Ray shivered at her words. "Is that what you think or what *they* think? Gangster out of Sin City suffering acute jungle fever, chasing down Healer witch—and what's your problem? Slumming…sleeping with the enemy…"

She put her hand over his mouth. "It's too hard, impossible. I want to run away."

Ray registered her shift in tone. This was what she wasn't telling him. "Where to?"

"Farther than you can imagine." Her eyes turned a dull black. "Leave this universe behind."

"Why?"

"There's something I have to do, but it's hopeless." She reined in her hair and slid away from him. "I want to get away before tomorrow explodes in my face."

"So, you've been jacking us into the Barrier, stalling." He grabbed his clothes. "Hey, tomorrow hasn't happened yet. I say give it a chance." Ignoring the bloodstains, he stuffed himself back into tight leather and suede.

"You're a great actor," she said.

"So you've noticed."

"But I can tell you're ill." She traced sharp claws from his lips down his throat to his chest. "Are you going to tell me about it?"

"Why don't you just read my mind and snoop all the dirt?" He smirked. She looked so stricken, he almost retracted the question, but he was desperate for an answer. So rather than apologize, he grabbed his jaw and shook out tension.

"If I channel the Barrier to touch your mindscape, for that instant you "read" me as well. The corridor goes both ways. I can't sneak around in your mind and spy on your spirit. The Barrier holds our thoughts together, and what you don't want to share is murky terrain."

Although he couldn't have expressed it so well, he had experienced some of what she described. "Like I'm in your skin and you're in mine," he said, and she nodded. He felt ashamed. "You never explained it to me like that before."

"Not for the uninitiated. I tell you now because, to hold this burden alone, is too much, I need—*Igi kan ki s'igbo*—one tree does not make a forest."

"Sorry for the backhand swipe," he said. "It's just freaky having somebody..."

"A glancing touch, a quick exchange, no real danger, but anything deep or prolonged, and *Vermittler* are inside-out, very vulnerable. If you close down or confuse the corridor, I could lose the way back to myself and scatter into the cosmos."

"Really?" He wanted her to touch his mindscape now, so he could feel all this, but he'd been such an asshole about it, he didn't dare ask.

"I'm flying off in every direction, and you always call me back. I do trust you." Her voice softened, and she stroked him with cool hands. "Your head is too hot."

He sighed. "I'll trade my story for some normal spacetime."

"Fair enough." The smile faded. She stared at him with unblinking black eyes, the detached bug look. Her dreads dripped patience. He batted the bubbles away, yet still told her everything: the stolen medicine bag, bombed-out greenhouses, burning woman. He even mentioned seductive Sidi at New O City and Barrier encounters with a middle-aged Chris. He edited few details. She hadn't sleazed his mindscape—it felt good to tell her everything, and nothing surprised her. As he spoke, the sun climbed above the cliffs, the gurgling spring was a geyser, and monkeys dangling from vines screeched high-pitched alarms once again.

"I worry that Sidi's right about Los Santos and Paradigma," Ray said. "Warrior Zones, a plague on..." Blood drained from his face. They sat in placid sunlight on the old highway, a few hundred yards from the Canyon Bridge, while a rogue cyclone raced along the cliffs, scouring canyon walls with violent swirls of debris. Cathedral trees along the edge twisted their bushy crowns into knots before snapping loose and exploding into the whirlwind. A torrent of gray-green water rinsed the rock faces clean. Ray leapt to his feet, scanning the dead mall for a sewer or an old subway to take cover.

"A seasonal corridor has collapsed." Elleni slipped into her robes.

Seasonal corridors usually dissolved back into the Barrier without such *Sturm und Drang*, and they never closed this soon after opening. Ray appreciated Elleni's calm but couldn't duplicate it. As he watched the cyclone approach, adrenaline bypassed his intellect. He grabbed her and started to run for the mall.

"No, wait." Elleni dragged her feet in the dirt. "The Barrier is changing, and it calls for *Ebo Eje*, for blood sacrifice to mark the transition. This is a sign. Watch."

"Blood sacrifice?" He couldn't drag her anywhere she didn't want to go, and he certainly wasn't going to leave her behind. "Are we safe here?" A jaguar howled and twisted in the air above them, desperate for solid ground. Ray ducked reflexively.

"As safe as anywhere," Elleni said, but she was talking about something else.

The Canyon Bridge was like the single string of a giant Kora plucked rapidly by an invisible hand. Vibrating, it screeched and roared but did not break. Ray turned his back on this violent display. The words he tried to utter were snatched from his lips.

Elleni spoke with her hands. "We can't run away in this."

"You haven't told me everything," Ray signed awkwardly, glad that he'd pestered her into teaching him the basics. "What're we going to do?" He longed for a hit of Rapture.

Elleni shrugged then watched with unblinking eyes as the rogue cyclone slammed into the Barrier, and its force vanished. Monkeys screamed from every tree and vine.

How much blood did the Barrier need, Ray wondered.

53: Barrier Wasteland, outskirts of Nuevo Nada

(October 15, Barrier Year 115)

Aaron revved the transparent scooter way too fast for twilight near the Barrier. Phantom horizons faded in and out of view, interfering with his perspective. Dust devils stung his eyes and tried to choke him. Visibility was zip. One minor glitch in the crappy roadbed, and he'd be mincemeat. He just couldn't get himself to slow down. Lawanda had pitched a Wounded Knee episode of *The Transformers* at him, but he didn't know enough about the Wovoka-Celestina conflict, and there were too many holes in this plot already. Lawanda said meet her at the Perez soirée or else. Since when did Miss World Peace threaten him? Waltzing into Perez's home territory, Lawanda could get herself killed. She didn't have to be on anybody's hit list. Perez's bad boys would smoke her just for fun and sell her body to the highest bidder. Aaron ratcheted the engine up another notch. He was determined to make an entrance when she did.

Jesus Perez claimed he lived near the Barrier for the sunsets and midnight light shows. Actually the wasteland location made it hard for other ganglords to snoop Perez's operations or mount a decent ambush. There was nowhere to run, nowhere to hide, just desert, and the Barrier interfering with high-tech sabotage. Perez could steal soybeans and peanut butter from starving Extras. He could murder people and deep-freeze them for Paradigma's organ market. He could stage orgies and death porn for the glitterati. He could do any evil shit to his heart's content. Aaron didn't give a damn about all that. Live and let live. But he couldn't stand by and watch Perez take Lawanda out the way he stood by while they set Mahalia on fire.

Save who you can.

Crashing this party *sans* the A-Team was dicey, but Aaron had an edge. He was nobody to Perez, an Entertainment "art freak." They wouldn't be expecting an ambush from his direction. He'd stage a distraction, hook up with Lawanda before Perez's squad had a chance to regroup, then they'd improvise their way out.

Aaron laughed at this slim scenario. Who was he kidding? His mad dash into the desert had little to do with Lawanda. He was on the run from Moses, Achbar, and Stella Jackson, his Extra self. It galled Aaron to no end that chump change like Jesus Perez thought he could get away with stealing Aaron's right hand, sabotaging *The Transformers*, and using Aaron's location shoot for a snuff take. More than anything, Aaron wanted revenge.

The Lawanda storyline just gave him a noble sheen.

Stella wasn't impressed. Aaron had almost forgotten his Extra self, couldn't remember what she looked like 'til just now. She hung in a corner of his mindscape, poking her tongue through gap teeth. Raw emotion rolled across her body for all to see. Not a pretty picture. Since Aaron had dumped her for a deluxe makeover, Stella had watched him betray anybody and anything and forge ahead, eyes on the prize. She waited for the crash. The Moses and Mahalia saga signaled the beginning of the end. Stella broke out of shadowy memories for the *coup de grâce*.

He snarled at Stella. "Don't hold your breath, sugar, I'm not over yet."

The sun was a giant blood orange on the horizon. Aaron was heading north but caught the show from the corner of his eye. Anything to distract him from Stella. In the Barrier, explosions of color chased each other for miles. Golden shadows danced across the road. Tadeshi Mifune called dusk the magic hours, the absolute best time to film. As usual she was right. Aaron would have given anything to get a Barrier twilight on film. Nobody but Tadeshi had the tech to do it. In fact Tadeshi, courtesy of witchdoctors and nerds, had bio-corders that captured an actual piece of the frigging Barrier. Serious genius machines. Aaron had used one to record Celestina's crossover ceremony. If he could get his hands on equipment like that again, he'd be invincible. Tadeshi took her souped-up bio-corders off world. The bitch wanted to hog all the glory. He couldn't blame her. That's exactly how he'd be. That's exactly how he *was*. Without a ruthless, killer focus, he would have never made it from half-dead Extra trash to Entertainment boss. He would have never dared to make *The Transformers*. When he got to Wounded Knee, he'd get the Wovoka to say what he had against St. Celestina, what kept Dancers from signing off on the Treaty. Making story sense of shit that didn't make sense—that's what he was good at.

Aaron didn't see the rabbits scurrying across the road until it was too late. He would have just run them over and cursed at stupid nature, except the animal chasing the rabbits or maybe even chasing him was too big to run over with a scooter. A black cat, like from a safari movie, with glowing eyes and flashy teeth bounded onto the road. They crashed into each other at an odd angle and with such force Aaron had no time to think, no time to understand what was happening. He soared through the air, tangled up in the scooter, with a nasty growl ringing in his ears. Air bags inflated around him. As they plowed back into the ground, he heard bones snap and saw the cat's neck twist to a funny angle, then go limp. The animal died before he did. He registered that and passed out.

54: Cross-Barrier Transmission/Personal
(October 16, Barrier Year 115)

To:	Lawanda Kitt, in response to your Cross-Barrier Transmission
From:	The Major, Former Head of Sagan City Secret Services
<u>Re:</u>	<u>Cancellation of Diplomatic Mission</u>
Question:	Is there any possibility of trust between us?

Assumption: Your suspicion is grounded in an accurate assess-
                ment of my political loyalties and the disposition
                of my duties to Jocelyn and Paradigma in the
                name of democracy, economic growth, and world
                stability.

Observations: In our system, everything is exploitable and
                anyone expendable. Thus whatever I say could
                be construed as manipulation. Only in the final
                analysis of future events will the "truth" of this
                communication be ascertained. Although you may
                discount this transmission, I must make an attempt
                to reach you, as I hold you in the highest regard
                and am ultimately responsible for the danger you
                find yourself in. If I engaged in poetry, I would re-
                sort to metaphors that aroused emotions, empathy,
                and projection, but I've always been suspicious of
                analogies. What does a sentimental story or clever
                turn of phrase prove but the cunning of the artist?
                Would you believe me if I could rhyme the truth
                or bring tears to your eyes? You're too intelligent.
                I'm still loyal to Paradigma, Jocelyn, and a future
                of liberal justice and scientific bounty, yet by mov-
                ing against Elleni and the Treaty, I feel the Prime
                Minister is about to commit a fatal error, which
                will endanger us all. I'm doing what I can to save
                her from herself. And although certain loyalty
                devices hamper me, I have not, curiously enough,
                been incapacitated.

Note: Our (yours and mine) ultimate objectives are con-
                gruent if not equivalent. Since I encountered your
                formidable and immanently logical challenge to
                Paradigma's official policies, I've been forced to
                reconsider many deeply held assumptions—expos-
                ing myself to grave danger. At first I tried to blame
                you for my fall from favor. I tried to blame you for

my increasing inefficiency, for my susceptibility to Ouagadougian magic realism.

In fact I have only myself to blame. *I* ignored the evidence at hand. *I* refused to believe the plot against me. Jocelyn, Daniel Ford, and Sidi Xa Aiyé counted on my arrogance. I watched them conspire my demise, yet still imagined myself as central to Jocelyn's vision, even indispensable. This was indeed a poetic fantasy.

Recommend: Exercise extreme caution. Jocelyn has terminated your mission, and I'd suggest leaving Los Santos if at all possible or better yet disappearing among the Ghost Dancers. I cannot transmit to the Captain's Electro channel. The access codes have been changed. She is dangerous. Leave her behind or, better yet, use last-resort protocol to dispose of her. Do not under any circumstances indulge in sentiment.

Re: Is there any way out of my Current Situation?

Assumption: No one is infallible. This recent cadre of despots, thugs, and demagogues scrambling for a stranglehold on the world will also fall prey to the excesses of power and other human weaknesses that particularly affect dictators and criminals. I haven't given up hope. However, I do not underestimate the ubiquity and subtlety of the forces against us, how long their demise might take, or how much damage they can effect in this time.

Observations: Our immediate circumstances are congruent if not equivalent. Jocelyn also sacrificed me for the good of Paradigma. The ambush was elegant. I will try to offer as detailed a description as possible.

At a private meeting to discuss interzonal relations—actually to discuss deposing Elleni—Duma

Xa Babalawo plied me with exotic refreshment and live art. (Babalawo means "father of mysteries" and is a Yoruba high priest.) My guard was down, my security team and auto-bomb squad off protecting Jocelyn. Councilor Duma, knowing of my interest in ethnopharmacology, offered me a traditional fruit drink purported to guarantee long life when consumed first thing every morning. He called it *ein echter Zaubertrank*, a real magic drink. I am usually suspicious of oxymorons, particularly from dead languages, yet...

The room was too hot, too sumptuous, every surface a tapestry, no rest for the eyes. The unrelenting polyrhythms of Duma's drummers and praise-singers were hypnotic. I felt suffocated, irritable. Yet why shouldn't one's security and top advisors also be musicians? Duma showed me the fruiting bodies and roots used to make the *Zaubertrank* and explained that individually the juices were unremarkable, not even tasty. Only in combination did they find their flavor, their potency. I've heard hundreds of Ouagadougian informants make similar claims, so I didn't really listen. Instead I speculated (irrationally) on Duma's physiognomy: tall, sinewy, with lentil-sized freckles scattered across face and arms, small gray eyes, and flat silver hair pulled back in a tail. Not unattractive, but he displayed neither wit, nor fiery spirit, just a rather pedestrian mind and a conservative nature. Healers eschew the warrior spirit and flaunt their peaceful society. Since Duma and I ostensibly played for the same team, what threat could he be? Sidi was the one to watch out for. I'd been lulled into complacency.

As Duma prepared the drink, we lounged on the floor, there being no proper chairs, just pillows and cushions covered in opulent fabrics. An image-board was tucked in a niche at floor eye-level. Duma explained that it was Femi Xa Olunde's last masterpiece and that he studied it now for insight and guidance. These supposed technophobes are actually bio-computer wizards. Femi was a master of artificial bio-intelligence, inventing several organic machines. Ouagadougians are brilliant political strategists. Playing on our prejudice, they can hide in front of our faces. Dark Matter, indeed. I asked if Femi's masterwork shouldn't be in the Library of the Dead. Duma shrugged. I was too fascinated with the display to press him. On the image-board, winding corridors through the Barrier transported us to what Duma claimed was another universe. As subtitles for the images, there was a stream of physical equations and chemical projections. Duma insisted that Femi had captured a piece of the Barrier itself and that what we observed was more than speculative visual art or crude simulation—but a truly fascinating marriage of art and science. I could tell that Duma believed what he said. Yet, if Femi's image-board pierced the enigma of the Barrier, why was Duma so free with this information? I considered stealing the device and unmasking Healer duplicity but filed the theft option for later action. I had come to plot against Elleni. Betraying my ally of the moment was impolitic.

As Duma poured us each a drink of his magic elixir, my habitual caution had me almost refuse. On second thought, I felt it would be bad diplomacy to shun his hospitality. The drink must be prepared fresh each morning and could not be stored. After surreptitious sampling, my data glove

offered no warning, and in the close atmosphere
of Duma's private quarters, I was very thirsty. The
drink tasted cool and refreshing. Councilor Duma
consumed his portion in one gulp. We barely had
time to speak. The entire fiasco lasted only eight
and half minutes. However, as I swallowed the
Zaubertrank I did hear him say I behaved exactly
as Jocelyn predicted. For an unguarded instant I
was flattered, then thinking myself an arrogant
idiot, I lost consciousness.

Duma stole my data glove and weapons belt and
dumped me with the Eshu mask on the road between Shinjuka and Oberammergau, the villages
where Elleni grew up. Trying to read road signs
and listening to passers-by, I felt suspended between old Japan and Germany. People were cour-
teous, offering food, shelter, and English words of
wisdom—reminiscent of ethnic-throwback settlers
at home, but with an Ouagadougian overlay. I declined their generosity.

I encountered no violence or even mild hostility.
Still, without weapons, surveillance tech, or scrambler, I'm an easy target for assassins. Without my
data glove, I feel like a naked intellect, adrift in
sensations and anecdotes. Indeed it's as if I've lost
myself. A novice would not have been fooled as I
was. One consolation: I've finally had time to think
about what has been happening to me, vis-à-vis
you, the Treaty, and Jocelyn. Ergo this long transmission. What Duma did not suspect is that I had
hidden my Electro in one of Eshu's mischievous
heads. This channel is still secure. Unfortunately, I
did not also think to stash a weapon in the mask.

Note: The data glove will do them no good. Without
regular contact with me the system will eventu-

ally auto-destruct, jettisoning all information to
hidden reserves (see attached codes). I've retreated
to *Seelenwald*, the forest of souls. According to my
informants, only Healer acolytes come here, to
talk to the dead. Duma did not of course divulge
how they intend to use me, but Jocelyn sees simple
assassination as a waste of resources, so I suspect
it's a frame job. For what, I can't quite fathom.
Without the data glove, my reasoning seems foggy,
my judgment flawed.

Searching Eshu and my clothes for bugs—electronic—I found a snippet of sapphire-blue braid,
Elleni's hair, wrapped in a scrap of syn-silk. At
first I thought they intended to pin her assassination on me. But on calmer reflection, I believe that
Elleni gave me the hair during a curious encounter
we had with the Barrier (which I will describe
at a later date, assuming this is not our last communication). I was fascinated with her hair and
indeed coveted a sample, but I never expressed this
directly to her. The lock of hair still "lives," not
with the force the things exhibit on her head…or
elsewhere, but if I move in a particular direction,
toward the west volcanic mountains to be exact,
it becomes very agitated. Despite how ludicrous it
might seem, I have decided to follow the hair.

Recommend: Delete my transmissions. It's unfortunate that
we couldn't make a live connection. Take care of
yourself. Remember, nobody will care that you
pursue miracles. As Celestina said, long life is
sweet revenge.

Afterthought: I did "talk more shit," as you said, but do hold me
to it, all right? It seems obvious now, but in the
beginning of this fiasco I didn't realize how far
Jocelyn would go. I thought I could protect you

from such extreme measures. I denied the risk I
was taking with your life, with my own.

My given name is Honoré, after a favorite French
author—my parents secretly hoped for a poet,
albeit a realist. Not a lot of poetry in me, but the
dreams were true.

55: Fire Mountain, outside *Seelenwald*
(October 16, Barrier Year 115)

We still yearn for a Metatheory, a God who never lies, whose
simple, absolute truth will guide us from nothing to everything
without once falling down. Unfortunately truths are false and lies
are true. Anything that we are absolutely certain of doesn't matter
and everything that truly matters is uncertain.
—Vera Xa Lalafia, *Healer Cosmology, The Final Lessons*

Elleni shuddered on a rock ledge of Fire Mountain. The cold
and damp made her hair irritable, quarrelsome, even clumped together in two, long plaits down her back. Celestina's hidden fortress
loomed before her, a stronghold for secret shame and sin, but also
vision. Inside, Elleni hoped to find an image-board speculating on
gene art and symbiogenesis or mandalas meditating on the Barrier
and its transformation—wisdom that Celestina left behind that
might protect the Treaty from gene-art conspirators or persuade
Sidi to join Elleni in a Barrier quest. She knew it was a rogue corridor chase, probably ending nowhere, but what else could she do?
Wait around for the world to blow up? For the thousandth time,
she hoped she didn't understand what the Barrier had shown her,

hoped the shattered Earth sucked down a Barrier corridor was an exaggerated metaphor that she insisted making literal. That hope blurred quickly.

Elleni shook her quarreling braids, which spit snow at the rock door barricading Celestina's mountain hideaway.

"Thanks." Ray wiped slush that had missed the door from his eyes. "Is the hair action going to help us get in?"

Elleni shrugged unruly locks down her collar. She drew fingernails across the door, and sparks skittered over the rock surface. Ray shivered. A blizzard had chased them the last ten minutes up the dormant volcano. The wind knifed along the cliffs and out into whiteness, carrying their body heat toward a purple-haze Barrier. Her monster lover looked agitated, desperate, clinging to the mountains in raggedy Mandelbrot shapes as it reached through snow clouds to the stars. Time was running out.

"Dashing between seasons like this is hard on us mortals," Ray said. "Maybe Celestina left a key under the mat?"

"Why would she do that?" Elleni had no idea how to open the door, but she didn't want to tell Ray this. Then she'd have to tell the entire sordid story. Awa brought her to Fire Mountain as a baby, to save her from Celestina. Decades later, Celestina brought her back to study Healer Cosmology and Vera Xa Lalafia's *Final Lessons*. Working the Treaty swallowed most of the time, then Celestina was shot before Elleni completed her studies. Her *Geistesmutter* hadn't even trusted her with commands to open the door. Perhaps she thought Elleni paid attention when they went in and out. No such luck. Elleni only paid attention to what interested her.

Ray had come up Fire Mountain to Celestina's intellectual fortress for miracles. Elleni couldn't even open the door. Actually, she didn't want to. Celestina, *Geistesmutter*, had almost smashed Elleni's brains against these very rocks. *Sing my song, daughter.*

The urge to run away, to leap off the cliff into cold whiteness and beyond, overwhelmed Elleni. She tried to touch Ray's mindscape but was too agitated; or else he was closed to her, consumed by his own worries. Suddenly she turned from the door, screamed a melody in the sound beyond sound, and soared into the air toward the Barrier. Ray lunged for her, his hands flailing in a gust of snow.

Disoriented, she hesitated. This diva melodrama was ridiculous. She'd already tried phaseshifting into oblivion but hadn't had the courage, the discipline, the whatever, to shake off her demons and give up home altogether. Still didn't. Staring into Ray's furious eyes, she backflipped onto an icy boulder and grabbed hold of a carving above the door. Ray gripped her around the waist, steadying her in the wind. He didn't say anything, just squeezed her hips into his chest. His heart pounded against her buttocks. Fear that he could have lost her filled the air, stinging her nostrils. His touch soothed her, grounded her, brought her back from whatever nth dimensional edge she teetered at. He was awkward and naked with her, his self squeezed tight against her self.

"I hate snow and a wind that takes skin off your face. On this ledge, one slippery patch of ice and it's *sayonara*. Not the place for fancy stunts," Ray said. "How'd you talk me into climbing up here?"

"Me? I've been avoiding this place." Embarrassed, she pretended to investigate the entire overhang above the door. Truth be told, she was so tangled up in lies and betrayals, chasing monster lovers and fleeing death angels, she wouldn't have been at Celestina's door trying to do anything without Ray. "This was your idea. You said let's give tomorrow a chance." She strained on tiptoe to reach a carving cut in the overhang. "What I want to know is will tomorrow give us a chance?"

"You find a key up there?" Ray asked.

"Do you see a lock on the door?" Elleni's fingers recognized Eshu at the crossroads. He scowled, grinned, leered, and teased, his heads facing every direction. If she poured him libation, Eshu might help her find a way. "A warning, blessing, and a challenge." Her voice was weary, her muscles slack. "Figure it out or die trying."

"Just to get in?" Ray whistled. "Can't you sing to it?"

"It's a rock, not the Barrier. And Eshu watches, he's the guardian of this gateway."

"Eshu doesn't like singing?"

"Eshu loves singing!" she snapped. "But it's not so simple. Has anything ever been simple for us? Well, perhaps you had the world handed to you, but—"

"No," Ray said.

"But I've been fighting all my life with righteous folks who spit at me with disgust, who want to throw me away." Even Celestina.

"Not me."

"That's not enough. You don't make up for…" She gestured in the wind. "*Murahachibu*—waiting for tomorrow to blow up in my face, everybody's tomorrow. And I don't even know if I care. Celestina cared, at least I think she did, finally, but… Today feels as nasty as the rest of my life."

"And yesterday?"

"We stole a few minutes. What is that in a lifetime?"

He looked mortally wounded. "So you're going to beat 'em to it, throw yourself away, me too, make us *Muraha*-whatever, is that the deal?"

"No." She slammed her fists against the door, "the deal is, walk naked into a Barrier black hole for people who wished you'd never been born!"

"Hey, babe, we don't have to go up against Celestina's booby traps." Ray grabbed her fists then glanced at her monster lover, rippling through the snow. "If she's got the door bomb-locked to the Barrier…"

He hadn't understood what she said. Still, with the awful secret spoken out loud to him, her mood backflipped out of despair. "We're doing this. With Celestina's bio-computer—her image-boards—I can run a better simulation on the gene-art mites."

"Quick-change artist, all over the place," he grumbled, "slow down, Bella."

"Know all the directions. To meet Eshu's challenge is to be renewed."

"Renewal's good," he said, squeezing her belly. "No more high-wire stunts, okay?"

"Sure." Of course, once inside Celestina's learning sanctuary, the ceiling might torpedo them or the floor could blow up. That would be more than a test of their spirits.

Elleni glanced down at Ray. He looked terrible. Frost hung from his nostrils, his breath was a wheeze, and his skin puffy and discolored. After taking him to the Insect Pavilion for a fire-virus cure, she had dragged him through miles of the Library of the Dead, seeking solutions to the gene-art threat. *No more enemies.* When that search led to dead ends, she had thought of questioning the burning woman but hadn't wanted to run into Sidi or Duma. So they retired to his vehicle. After a few hours of fitful sleep, she woke Ray and made him drive the mini-tank beyond *Seelenwald* up into the volcanoes where winter came in late September. She couldn't bear facing Celestina's fortress alone. The old east road deteriorated quickly and they had trudged the last narrow stretch on foot with snow squalls chasing them. They weren't dressed for winter. Ray didn't complain, but it was too much exertion for his fragile system.

"I'm so sorry," Elleni said. "I shouldn't have brought you…"

"Let you come up here alone? No way. I know how much Celestina meant to you."

"Do you?" Jumping from the boulder, she whispered, "*Mojubar*" and drizzled melted snow on the ground. "*Omi tutu, ile tutu, ona tutu, tutu Eṣu, tutu Oriṣa.*"

"What are you saying?" Ray pulled her under the overhang and out of the wind. He blew on her hands and rubbed them warm.

"I pour libation. Cool water, cool house, cool road, cool Eshu, cool Orisha." She translated the Yoruba as best she could. "*Tutu*— cool—isn't just temperature, or being hip, or wise, or propitious, it's all of that. Beyond English."

"You open this door with a prayer?" He eyed the enormous rock wedge.

"Not directly. I open my mind with prayer."

"But isn't there somebody else who knows the door, how to do it?"

"Yes," she said. "Celestina."

"No, I meant someone alive."

"Celestina lives in me. If I quit fighting her, maybe she'll trust me."

"With what?"

"*The Final Lessons!*"

Ray shook his head, "This is a dead woman we're talking about here."

"Memory is the master of death."

Ray whistled and shivered. "Cold comfort."

"Best I can do in a blizzard." She should get him inside, let him rest. Let him heal. "*Tutu* Celestina."

Memories flooded Elleni. Celestina always emptied her mindscape and went blank as stone before pressing into the fortress door. Elleni never thought much of this until now.

"Celestina said once, shedding who we are to cross a threshold into a new life. What better security?"

Ray looked doubtful, but Elleni leaned against the door and emptied her mindscape as she might for trance. Her braids unraveled and locks floated about her head like wisps of syn-silk. Without passing out, she lost sense of herself, until blank as the rock itself, she was no one in particular.

56: Promises

> Swing low, sweet chariot, coming for to carry me home...
> I looked over Jordan and what'd I see?...
> A band of angels coming after me,
> Coming for to carry me home...
> I'm sometimes up, I'm sometimes down...
> But still my soul feels heavenly bound,
> Coming for to carry me home...
> —Celestina Xa Irawo, "Preamble to the Interzonal Peace Treaty"

Ten years ago, Celestina went home to Sagan City, Paradigma, for the first time in over sixty years, to head off disaster. Thoughts of betrayal and murder brought on acute bouts of synesthesia, so Celestina avoided thinking about Robin making love to Thandiwe, all the while squirreling away stolen Barrier secrets. Robin had planned to break secret-society silence and usher in a brand new day, a second Renaissance. Surely betrayal was justified...

The *Final Lessons*, the Promised Land, coming for to carry me home, sing my song, Elleni.

Communing with the Barrier, the great shaman, Vera Xa Lalafia, had mastered artificial symbiogenesis, bringing together diverse life forms in the Barrier to create novel forms with emergent capacities. Vera was midwife to the first *Vermittler*, whom Femi hailed as alien abominations. Her Barrier experiments constituted the last volume of the *Final Lessons*. Robin had only glimpsed fragments of this masterwork, but what tantalizing fragments! She gave no thought to the catastrophe releasing incomplete knowledge might cause. Robin left an encrypted data cache at Sagan Institute, the ⚌Promised Land⚌— A challenge to hackers, to the curious and the competitive, a time-bomb. Thandiwe had poisoned Robin before the scientist threw the world off its course, but Celestina had never destroyed Robin's data cache. She merely banished it from memory.

Had she left a loophole on purpose?

A wily hacker accessed Robin Wolf's ⚌Promised Land⚌. Elegant security measures had protected the data cache for over half a century. Yet someone got in deep without triggering the auto-destruct protocol, and one of Robin Wolf's electronic spies alerted Thandiwe Xa Femi to a visitor at the site.

I'm bound for the Promised Land
My Lord! What a morning, my Lord! What a morning!
When the stars begin to fall!

The hacker, Mahalia Selasie, tracking Robin's electronic spy, sent a greeting to Thandiwe or whatever Ouagadougian had been so friendly and *open* with a Sagan Institute scientist in these chilly times. After a flurry of cryptic Electro transmissions, Celestina surmised that Dr. Selasie was engaged in Barrier research at Sagan Institute. A member of an underground choir in Paradigma, she was familiar with the ethnic-throwback music Robin loved so much. This coincidence (few scientists ever joined underground choirs) allowed her to discover the musical codes that decrypted Robin's files.

June bug has a golden wing, lightnin' bug has a flame
Bedbug has no wings at all, but he gets dere jes the same

"I wish to become fluent in the language of God," Dr. Selasie told Celestina, ostensibly referring to gene art and symbiogenesis. "There are a few fine points of the music that escape me." If snoops scoped their transmission, she made their job hard.

Celestina wasn't sure what to make of Mahalia Selasie. She agreed to meet her in person at Tombouctou Observatory and Galactic Library. Alone. Both promised to keep the meeting secret. "If God knows everything, what use language? Nothing to tell and nobody to tell it to..." Celestina warned her. Would she have to kill this cheeky scientist and destroy Robin's data cache? How to keep all her promises...

"Take me with you." Elleni leaned against the cold rock door of Celestina's learning sanctuary. They had arrived at Fire Mountain only two hours ago and already Celestina was readying herself for a journey across the Barrier to Sagan City. "Storming the technocrats' citadel with my *Geistesmutter* as guide, why not?"

Celestina scowled into swirling snow as she rifled through her medicine bag. "This isn't a journey for you." She and Elleni had traveled to Paradigma many times but avoided Robin Wolf's old stomping grounds in Sagan City. They stuck to outlying cities and throwback settlements, never entering the capital.

"Didn't I survive Los Santos's wicked ways, spirit in tact? Surely Sagan City can offer no greater temptations than Sin City…"

"I must go alone, to heal the past with actions I take now," Celestina said.

"In other words, you're not going to take me or tell me why not." Elleni's hair hissed and vaporized snow. "Why did you drag me up here then?"

"I was of many minds on the matter." The trip to Sagan City terrified Celestina. The choices she faced might shatter the fragile truce that held her together. She couldn't risk exposing Elleni to whatever she might become.

"I'm not a child anymore," Elleni said, "waiting on your whims to see the world."

"Go to Sagan City on your own then, just stay clear of me." Celestina pulled white rayon robes with magnetic clasps from the bottom of the bag and offered them to her.

Elleni wouldn't take the shimmering fabric. "When will we finish Vera Xa Lalafia's *Lessons* then?"

"I made these for you, for Council Ceremonies. Femi can no longer complain that you're hard on his eyes."

"I still won't be welcome." Elleni plopped down on an icy boulder.

"Be at home in yourself." Celestina stood behind her, holding the robes above her head. "Self cleaning fabric…"

"They're so afraid of me, so…" Elleni shivered.

"They fear their own weaknesses."

"It's a mystery how I even got on Council, the way they rant and rave."

"Let their petty tirades roll off you, like beads of sweat dripping from taut muscles."

"I disgust them. I make their skins crawl and their stomachs roll. Femi most of all. I swear, he would snap my neck if he could."

"Probably." Celestina staggered away from her. "Make them feel safe, play to their strengths, and—" she hesitated— "let them eat all the glory. Let them gorge on it."

"So you've said a hundred times." Elleni sighed and snatched the robes. "Treat them as fools, not as equals."

"Is that what I said?" Celestina grunted, then continued to rummage through her medicine bag. "I thought I said lead them."

"You manipulated half of New Ouagadougou to get me on Council."

"The people, not Femi, called you to service. No Healer surpasses you. Keep your eyes on the prize."

"You manipulate me, to keep me from quitting—for a Treaty that's not even written yet."

"Not just what we write, but what we do. Here." Celestina tossed a bag of bells and beads at Elleni for her hair, and Vera Xa Lalafia's thread-metal ring.

Elleni tried the ring on every finger. It didn't fit any. She dropped it back into Celestina's bag. "I don't want trinkets. I want adventure, I want… Talk to me!"

"These are acid-proof, silver- and brass-coated in fiberplastic, the heavy kind you like." Celestina stuffed the hair ornaments into Elleni's medicine belt. "My medicine bag will be yours some day. You'll have Vera's ring soon enough."

"What good is your medicine bag if I don't understand anything?"

"Walk me to the seasonal corridor."

"Why bother with a seasonal? I can take you wherever you want. Or you can make a corridor yourself with a Barrier staff! What's the matter with you?"

"At the moment, I don't have the voice, the stamina, to sing my way from New Ouagadougou to Paradigma. That'd wear out a chorus of Healers. I'm an old lady, subject to fits. No need to show off. I'll take a ride, save myself the effort, and arrive in full strength."

Celestina picked her corridor staff from the snowy ground. "Act like the woman you are. Not much more to the Final Lessons that you don't already know. Experience is what you need now."

"Are you afraid to share your sacred secrets?" Elleni stood in front of Celestina. "Afraid that with the magic of Vera's lessons, I might surpass you? Do you fear *Vermittler*, like Femi and all the others?"

"Fear you?" Celestina laughed until tears ran down her cheeks. In the cold they turned to slush. "What could you possibly do that would hurt me more than what I've already done to myself—other than fail at your life?"

"You always act like I'm going to fail, like you can't really trust me..."

"What do you know about trust?" Celestina had already trusted Elleni with the world. "I've done all I can. It's up to you now." Celestina pushed past her *Geistestochter*, impatient for her own destiny. She headed toward the old east road, overgrown and neglected, but the shortest route down Fire Mountain. "I have no sacred secrets and, as Healers say, magic is your own affair." She glared at Elleni, who trotted along beside her. "There aren't any recipes for wisdom. If you don't know that, you haven't learned anything at all from me, and I'm ashamed for both of us." She had taken a great risk letting Elleni come this far. Awa said teach them, but Celestina had been afraid to think all her thoughts. Who was she to teach anyone?

Elleni bit her ruby red tongue and turned sparking eyes backwards. Her hair looked like fat snakes copulating on her skull. Celestina shuddered despite herself. Elleni registered every minute cringe and drew away to the edge of the cliffs. Celestina wanted to apologize, wanted to hug Elleni and take back stupid reflexes, but her mind went blank. Her body was chaos. Whose feet, whose hands, whose back, breasts, mouth were these... Elleni streaked ahead, disappearing into a snow squall.

Though Celestina came back to herself, they climbed down Fire Mountain and passed through *Seelenwald* in silence. Celestina boarded a cross-Barrier transport to Sagan City, Paradigma, without looking back. They didn't hug or say a proper good-bye. Elleni couldn't forgive her for a momentary lapse, and Celestina never told Elleni how much she loved her. Such was their last encounter until Piotr Osama shot Celestina signing the Treaty.

Angels

Coming for to carry me home

Down a Barrier starway, like the sweet song of dolphins.

BOOK VI

The visions we offer our children shape the future.
It matters what those visions are. Often they
become self-fulfilling prophecies. Dreams are maps.

Carl Sagan

57:   Archive Transmission/Personal
   (October 16, Barrier Year 115)

From: Lawanda

To: Herself, and whoever might find this if I get dusted

Me and the Captain be 'bout a kilometer from Jesus Perez's digs in the Nuevo Nada wasteland. Sun's outa the picture completely. It's way past midnight. The Barrier look pale blue against a blue-black sky. A sky within a sky, silver and green clouds streakin' thru. Kinda unusual. No ghosts, tho.

I know what I oughta do, I mean, if I had any sense—last-resort protocol, toggle a damn switch, and dust the Captain's ass, but... Set off her body implants myself? No fuckin' way. Not after all we been thru. How many times she done save my booty? Not just that, she's my girl! I ain't never been ruthless. I guess that's why people play me so easy.

The Major be a high-level bullshit artist, try to ambush you with your own shit. What am I s'posed to do with that sob story of his? Feel sorry cuz Jocelyn don't love him no more? The man get religion now they be sacrificin' his ass too. So I should turn the other cheek, forgive him for settin' me up, and just go on and trust him?

Well, if somebody piss on my head I ain't never goin' call it rain.

I tell the Captain I gotta park her here, where there's still some cover: a big ole rock formation, look like a beached whale with flukes and stuff wavin' at the stars. Just beyond the whale is a exploded transport. I bet some sucker be tryin' to sneak on Perez and get bombed to shit, and Perez leave the twisted metal carcass here, so everybody know the score. Gangsta monument. I lean the Captain against the rocks and make excuses, tell her any closer in than the beached whale and the Barrier be jackin' up her scrambler and she be a sittin' duck for ambush. Captain don't wanna hear nothin' 'bout me leavin' her behind. She act like I'ma unload her and never come back. Shit, if that was the plan, I'da dumped her heavy ass three hours ago.

"Why drag you halfway 'cross the wasteland?" I tell her. "You too sick to be my security, not too sick to be my friend. Why risk us both on a wild-child whim? You rest up and help with the getaway to the Badlands, to Wounded Knee."

Captain's eyes get big when I say alla this. She be sweatin' somethin' awful, givin' off a fishy smell. I wipe her neck and face and stick a probe in her mouth. Med-unit say it ain't fire virus or nothin' like that, which I already know. It's a auto-bomb squad up in her head. I be hopin' for suggestions from the tech-doctor. *Nada.*

"Your brains goin' blow?" I blurt this out—can't be pussyfootin' 'round no more. "What the Major tell you to do that you ain't doin'?"

She bite down hard on her laser-blade but don't answer, and I don't push. My naggin' probably aggravate the mess in her head. I figure, if I ain't in her face, maybe the auto-bombs'll let up a bit. I plan to leave her the bio-computer and the weapons belt. (I'd shoot my own foot steada the bad guys.) A scrambler and my Electro's all I need. I promise to hook up with Ghost Dancers first thang. They can be my shield against trigger-happy thugs.

"You hold the rabbit for me?" I reach the little ball of fur at her, but she won't take it. "That's all right," I say as rabbit crawl down my sleeve and nestle in my warm armpit. A cold breeze be whippin' 'round the rocks. "I be back," I say and turn away.

Captain is one stubborn lady. She grab my shoulder—she still got a steel grip—and talk a mile a minute at me 'bout what could go wrong, what I gotta look out for—detailin' the sneaky gangsta MO and who all I done pissed off. She try to scare me with graphic crap. Perez'll wanna fry me for the soybean hijack and data-chillin' his shit halfway to bankruptcy. He'd probably love nothin' better than to chop me up and sell the pieces. Like she forget I been to Paradise Healthway or swallowed that Dancer's last breath. I seen enuf ugly to take the gleam outa anybody's freedom daydream. I know what I'm up against. I gotta do this, even if they goin' try to cut me down to nothin'. I been so scared the whole time here in Los Santos that maybe Jocelyn and the Major set me up: starry-eyed ethnic throwback, who ain't got enuf sense to come in out a fire-storm. I just knew, before I got down to anythin' real, somebody was goin' pop me off. Never dreamed the Captain would be the somebody after my ass.

Anyhow, now that I know for sure that Jocelyn and the Major been playin' me, there's this hollow place inside, where the fear should be, where the love should be. Man done tore my heart right out and took the fear too.

"In other words, I can't talk you out of this wild scheme?" Captain ask.

"I have me a Barrier invite to Perez's party. What I got to lose?" I start to leave.

"Wait!" She fumble with the med-unit. "Wait, wait."

"I'm waitin'."

Captain blow a arsenal of drugs and put a skin patch under her arm. She swallow screams and double up. Then—*snap!*—she lookin' a whole lot better, prancin' 'round, her feet barely touchin' the ground.

"Damn, girl, I thought your get up and go had got up and gone," I say. "Whyn't you do that sooner?"

"Don't ask."

I hate it when people say that, cuz then I think the worst.

Captain see me poutin' and talk shit, "This drug protocol is only good for a few hours of reprieve, and then..." She wave her hands in the air. "You're not walking into a viper's nest with just a rabbit for defense." She flex her muscles and run fingers thru matted hair 'til it stand up in stiff little spikes. I don't know what to think. She still kinda flaky 'round the edges, but I wouldn't be messin' with her. "Let's go!" She roarin' at me now.

"Major tell me to dispose of you. That what he tell you 'bout me?"

"Not exactly." Captain look like she swallowin' somethin' bitter.

"Well, I ain't studyin' him."

Rabbit crawl from armpit to 'tween my titties and burrow like she makin' a nest. I nip that and stuff her in my front pocket.

Captain sneer and shake her head. I guess rabbits just don't float her boat. We head 'round the whale. I pause at the bombed-out transport so I can archive it with my thoughts. In the Electro flash beam, ten or so bleached out skeletons sneer at me too.

"We should do our business and get out of there," Captain say.

"You don't have to tell me."

"I'm just saying. No talking jags, no wildcatting."

"Who me? Look, how hard can it be to find Dancers? They stick outa any crowd."

"The dream team's ETA is in seventy-seven minutes. If we don't find any Ghost people by then or rebel Extras, we'll make our getaway anyhow." She shrug, like her ole self, ready to walk on water and box with God. "Then it's Wounded Knee on our own steam."

"Okay." I give her a high five.

"You know, we're crazy." She be powerin' up her weapons. "You can't help yourself, but what's my excuse?" She walk ahead, taut and jittery, uniform squeezin' her butt, boots skimmin' the sand. Still, a fine figure of a woman. "The Major said close to the Barrier the scrambler won't hide us, but it should confuse the bastards. I think we can trust him on that." She stride right for the danger.

I wanna give the Captain a hug, but she worse than the Major 'bout folk touchin' her. Maybe that's cuz she never know who she might have to blow away.

"Wait up," I say.

So that's all for now.

58: Fire Mountain, outside *Seelenwald*
(October 16, Barrier Year 115)

"Elleni," Ray said. "All that hype, and you make it look dirt simple!"

Bright lights burned Elleni's eyes, and the rock she'd pressed against was air. *Coming for to carry me home.* How to forgive herself, forgive Celestina? Fire Mountain's fortress door slid open. Elleni would have fallen on her face, but rough, garlicky hands caught her. The smell of curried goat, *Weißbier*, and black-eyed peas made her stomach rumble. When was the last time she'd eaten a good meal?

"Awa Xa Ijala, daughter of heroes, greets the Center of the Healers Council, Elleni Xa Celest, granddaughter of the stars." The old shaman's voice echoed off vaulted ceilings. She hugged Elleni in a fleece blanket, smothering her in the aroma of gingered sea-vegetable and hickory-smoked tempeh. "Awa Xa Ijala greets Elleni's consort, Ray Valero, larger-than-life-Entertainment star and impossibility specialist." Awa shouted Elleni's praisesong at Ray as she wrapped him in a blanket. "Dream technicians, I've been expecting you. Time for reprieve dwindles. Healing will soon be impossible." Awa didn't need to remind Elleni of what terrified her.

"*Tutu* Awa Xa Ijala, a surprise to find you here." Elleni bowed, irritated but relieved. Well-versed in the *Final Lessons*, Awa would have disabled Celestina's booby traps. She was liberal, their one sure ally on Council. If Ray could just perform enough Healer etiquette not to offend her rigid sensibility…"Cool Awa. An honor."

"If you are well, I am well." Ray bowed and kissed Awa's fingers with a cinematic flourish. "The days between us are too many." His voice as he spoke Ouagadougian idioms was molasses, dark and sweet. Awa smiled at his gangster charm.

They stood in a brightly lit entrance chamber. Tunnels branched off in several directions, the largest arcade ending in a bruised blood Barrier. Hot springs warmed the rocks under their feet and fed a pool in the center of the chamber. Twenty-five image-boards mounted on the walls, gurgling and cooing like hungry bio-computers, mimicked the Barrier's subtle activity. Images morphed one into the other so quickly that even Elleni could barely distinguish between them. Ebony corridor staffs and intricate sand mandalas hung between the boards. Celestina's fifty-stringed Kora was mounted above a synth-marble table laid out with a feast that brought water to Elleni's mouth and tears to her hair. *You have come home, daughter. No more enemies.* Celestina's presence suffused the chamber.

"You neglect yourselves," Awa said, "as is the custom with the young and the restless, so I have prepared a meal."

"Middle-aged and restless," Ray said.

Awa laughed and filled tall glasses with *Weißbier*. Foam trickled down the sloped sides. She scooped it to her mouth with dye-stained fingers as she sliced pumpernickel biscuits with a laser-blade. "Sit!" She pointed toward the carved stools tucked under the table. "What you attempt requires much sustenance. Orgasms and peach-fuzz tea won't carry you." She laughed as Ray blushed and Elleni's locks shriveled. "Eat! The food won't ever be this good again! Then you can tell me how together we might try to save the world from itself."

Awa ladled large portions of curried goat, peas and rice, tempeh, and a bouquet of dirt- and sea-vegetables into their plates. Ray was about to shove an entire biscuit into his mouth but hesitated while Elleni whispered prayers to the living and the dead. Awa winked at Ray. "If we are mindful, it tastes better."

Barely chewing, Ray swallowed the biscuit and started in on the goat. Elleni cringed at his thug table manners. "Best food I've ever had." He spoke with a full mouth. "In Los Santos, even stars eat too much recon-slop. A real privilege to join your table, *Tutu* Awa, cool Awa."

Awa grabbed his hand. "Then take your time and enjoy."

They ate slowly and in silence to honor the food with full-body attention, even Ray. Awa filled their plates several times. Elleni had to loosen the medicine bag belted at her waist. When they were stuffed, Awa covered the leftovers with fiberplastic. Purple Barrier tentacles swirled across the chamber and splashed against the table. Ray squirmed on his stool.

"Why have you come?" Awa asked, glancing at the enigmatic tentacles with chilly respect.

Ray swallowed a last mouthful of *Weißbier*. He'd come for miracles, though he certainly wouldn't admit that to Awa. Elleni had also come for miracles but didn't want to admit it either. No one mentioned the Barrier tentacle. "I bring an offering, a question." Elleni put the injured ant Ray had brought her on a specimen tray under the largest image-board. It disappeared into the wall as she typed her query.

While they waited for a response, Awa inspected first Ray then Elleni for signs of dis-ease, prodding, poking, and sniffing. Ray endured this probing with more grace than Elleni. Awa's white hair, sculpted in the shape of a half moon and held in place by a beaded wand, tickled Elleni's chin as the old shaman listened to her breath. Tipsy from two glasses of *Weißbier*, Elleni barely squelched an urge to snatch the wand with her teeth and unravel the coif. She burped to cover a giggle fit. Examination completed, Awa leaned back against a Healer staff and sucked her teeth in disapproval.

Ray spoke before she did. Awa's feast had recharged him. "Winds of change blow off the Barrier and threaten to undo us. The warning signs are clear: rampant Barrier fever, passageways to the Wilderness, collapsing corridors, rogue cyclones. Does Awa Xa Ijala come to Celestina's mountain sanctuary for the wisdom to set the world back on its course?" Effortlessly he mimicked Ouagadougian rhetorical style. The sensual gestures and lilt in his voice were that of a native. Elleni smiled to herself. Hardly a shadow man.

Awa cut a look at Ray so sharp he winced. "I'm not so arrogant as to believe that I alone can turn the world from disaster. A pebble can start a rockslide, a butterfly change the weather, and a shout bring on an avalanche. To trigger a cascade of events requires no messiah if forces converge around you. Yet, never underestimate inertia."

The wise-woman-to-acolyte mode relieved Elleni. Awa pricked Ray's arm and sucked blood from a vein into a conventional gelatinous bio-computer. Infecting itself as a shaman might, then accelerating and charting the course of the dis-ease, the organic smart machine would offer its analysis of the experience. "I did that already," Elleni said.

"And?" Awa asked.

"A previously unknown strain of fire virus, highly contagious in the tertiary stage, aggressively displacing other strains. Mutation or gene art, I don't know. It follows a curious life path."

"We'll see if Celestina's bio-computers confirm your simulations."

"Then I'll try it on myself," Elleni said, "if there's time." Awa nodded.

Ray dropped his Ouagadougian overlay. "No fucking way!"

Elleni hadn't meant to blurt out her plan in front of him. "It's my decision."

"Jacking yourself up with a new strain—it's a stupid decision."

Awa cut her eyes at him again, this time without respect. "What do you know of shaman techniques that you make such judgments?" she asked.

"The damn virus is burning up my lungs," Ray said. "You almost died the last time. You can't be serious."

"But I am." Elleni had found the first fire-virus cure by infecting herself with Ray's dis-ease. He'd never forgiven her for risking her life for him, for everyone infected.

"Way too dangerous," he said, rude, presumptuous, and possessive, "even for you."

Awa sucked her teeth, got up from the table, and walked to the hot-spring pool. "You do not write her future. You do not choose what danger she will face. No one should make that choice for another." The old shaman glared at Elleni, plunged her hands into the steaming water, and splashed it against her face.

"Don't worry." Elleni wanted to calm them. Ray's passion was an anchor, not a control. The new fire-virus strain already infected her. She could let it pass through or settle in. "I'm called to other things first. We'll unravel this knot another time."

"What other things?" Ray asked.

"You can't imagine…" Orgasms and peach-fuzz tea, rich food, beer, and heated emotions had intoxicated Elleni, made her hair dizzy, loosened her tongue. Before she could catch herself, she flaunted her impending sacrifice. "I have an invitation to eternity, to dance naked with the Barrier and all the ghosts it has swallowed. Healing the past and the future, as the Barrier's consort…"

"Consort?" Ray slid his stool away from the table and almost fell over. He was tipsy too. "Like how a shaman gets it on with a virus, or do you actually fuck the Barrier?"

Awa glided past Ray, shaking her hands, sprinkling him with spring water. He folded his arms across his chest and tapped a foot on the stone floor. Awa took the Kora down from the wall. "The ghost Celestina speaks to you still?" she said.

Elleni shook her head. "No ghost: Celestina lives."

"Indeed." Awa handed her the Kora and placed damp fingers on Ray's thigh. He stopped tapping. "What does she ask of you?"

"Too hard to say." She rested the Kora's sounding gourd against her belly and grasped the smooth handles on either side of the strings. It was like hugging a pregnant friend. It had been too long since she played. She caught a faint whiff of Celestina, coconut and desert rose. Plucking the strings absent-mindedly, a melody emerged. Her fingers cramped, and she stopped. She glanced at Ray.

"Go on, please," he said. "I won't interrupt, and Awa speaks all your languages." Awa's eyebrows arched, but she didn't contradict him. "We got you covered, Bella."

Elleni winced at his term of endearment. Her hair oozed tiny white bubbles, yet she wanted to hide, to lie, but lies were difficult to negotiate and very lonely. "Celestina asks me to write a suite for the fifty-stringed Kora…" Ray leaned into what she was saying. "To sing her terrible secrets and dance her struggle. To heal the Barrier."

"A griot's task." Awa nodded.

"You saved my life, Awa, perhaps in this chamber?" She traced the ground with a bare foot. Yellow tears dribbled down her braids. "Did Celestina almost smash my skull on these rocks? Would she have killed other *Vermittler* babies here and washed her hands in that pool?"

Awa closed her eyes on the image.

Ray was ashen. "Celestina? What are you taking about?"

Elleni broke off playing. "You know this song, Awa. How can she ask me to sing it? Who would want to hear?"

"I don't know all of it," Awa said, eyes still shut. "Who knows the whole song?"

Ray took a humble breath. "I want to hear whatever it is."

"I have too many painful questions," Elleni said.

"Anything we are certain of doesn't matter," Awa said.

"As if a song could heal the past." Elleni's voice trembled.

"It might," Ray said.

Awa nodded. "A griot sings, and we listen to the unspeakable."

"You started, Bella. Don't think, just keep going." Ray hummed the melody for her after just one hearing. Awa watched him, clearly impressed. Elleni wanted to fight the melody, smash the Kora, but sympathetic strings tingled beneath her fingers. The gourd resonated against her belly with Ray's deep tones. He could mimic anything he'd heard once. He was the actor, the minstrel, the griot. Music never came easily for Elleni. Learning to sculpt-sing the Barrier had been torture. The first time she heard her full voice carve crystal archways, she'd sobbed for hours, until her hair was singed from too many acid tears.

Play it for us. Celestina's voices echoed through the cave.

Elleni's fingers plucked the melody again. Ray shifted to harmony, and Awa added an alto drone. The Kora music was like hot mineral water poured on Barrier wounds. It made the story possible. Elleni recounted the epic of Saint Celestina, death angel, avenging Orisha. In the refrain, the Barrier devoured the Earth.

At the end of the tale, Elleni's throat ached, and angry dreads fussed on her shoulders. Awa's laser-blade was too far away or she would have sliced the maddening locks from her head and been bald, light-headed. Too much sex, too much food, drink, and phase-shifting. No control. She attacked the Kora, reprising the chorus. Her hands flying across the strings were like a mosaic of broken glass. Ray stroked her hair until it settled down. In the glow of the Barrier, his hands were stained glass too.

"I'm used to keeping my own council," Elleni said, continuing to play the Kora.

"Today is not yesterday," Awa said. "*Igi kan ki s'igbo.*"

"One tree doesn't make a forest." Ray smiled weakly. "Won't take her own medicine."

He was right. Elleni sighed, ashamed of herself. Was she afraid she couldn't do what had to be done, or did she lust after fame and glory for herself alone? A "messiah wannabe" was how Lawanda once pegged Duma. Was Elleni any different? "I...we have to mingle ashes, persuade Sidi to join her enemies and go beyond old stories. She must walk naked and silent with me into the Barrier as *Ebo Eje* or we lose this Earth." She played an explosion on the Kora.

Ray's jaw dropped. "You mean the Barrier would actually blow up the Earth? Like in your song? The real deal—not a metaphor?"

"I'm not sure," Elleni said. "But how will we get Sidi to sacrifice herself, if the Zones are...the way they are. If Paradigma and Los Santos are so corrupt, violent, if they threaten to contaminate us and steal our future."

Awa lifted her eyebrows and flared her nostrils. "Is Sidi so naïve as to believe New Ouagadougou is free of corruption and violence?"

"Sidi fears letting outlanders write her future," Ray said.

"And she has no love for me—"

"Well—"

"So the Barrier will swallow the world, and it will be as if we never were." Elleni let the Kora slip from her hands.

Ray and Awa caught the instrument before its gourd shattered on the rock floor. They stared at Elleni as if from far away, as if she had spoken a language no one could be bothered to remember. An image-board squealed a long thin note. Startled, Ray jumped away from Elleni and fell against the table. His *Weißbier* glass shattered on the rock floor.

"Sorry about that." He squatted down to gather the shards.

Awa grunted and looked toward the Barrier, then at Ray. "You'll cut yourself."

He shook his head and displayed a napkin. "No problem."

Awa hung the Kora above the table and pulled an antique dust-sucker from the wall. She nudged Ray aside and vacuumed up shattered glass. Elleni wanted to scream at their mundane interaction, yet somehow she managed to remain quiet: even her dreads were silent.

Awa pulled the beaded wand from her hair. The half moon coif quivered, then fell apart. Thin white braids cascaded down beyond her waist. Awa waved the wand at the squealing image-board, and it was quiet. "The convolutions and complications come down to the same question."

"What would that be?" Elleni's voice was as icy as the draft from the rock door. She hadn't closed it tightly, and the air made her shiver.

"The Barrier demands two *Vermittler* for *Ebo Eje*, yes?"

"It wasn't satisfied with me alone." Elleni glanced at Ray who had cut his fingers on the *Weißbier* glass. He sucked blood surreptitiously.

"What is *Ebo Eje* again?" Ray asked.

"Celestina thought the Barrier would require two *Vermittler* to make sense of our world," Awa said. "She hoped when the time came there would be several to call on."

Elleni's eyes sparked. "You mean any two?"

"Any two *Vermittler* who are willing," Awa said.

"It doesn't have to be Sidi?" Elleni tried to contain her relief.

"Is this the blood sacrifice you mentioned earlier?" Ray grabbed Elleni's hand; his blood oozed down her arm. "You're going to do it, aren't you? Worse than infecting yourself with a damn virus. Do you die? How much blood?"

"With the Barrier, it's hard to discriminate literal from figurative. Maybe no blood."

"When were you going to tell me?" he asked softly.

"I tried. Do you even understand?" Elleni said.

"You mean, do I agree?"

"Do you agree?"

"No." The look in his eyes was too intense.

"It's like acting." Elleni spun around and hugged him from behind. "Sacrifice makes the ancestors and Orisha immediate, makes forces we can't hold in our hands real. We sacrifice to reach into eternity. I think the Barrier asks that of me."

Ray pulled away from her. "If it's any two, why you?"

"Why anybody?" Awa said.

"Fancy bullshit." He kicked water from the hot spring against the door.

Awa stepped away from their quarrel.

"I was born to this," Elleni said.

"Oh, it's fate now and you're resigned?" Ray circled her.

"You encouraged me."

"I didn't mean to. What do I know?"

"You said, don't run away, give tomorrow a chance. That's all I'm doing. That's all this is."

"Somebody else's tomorrow."

Elleni shrugged. "Everybody's. You would do the same if you were called."

"Sure, when I'm a big Entertainment hero, I run out on people all the time, to save the world, but..."

"Be my real-life hero, now." She snagged him, her claws digging into his back.

Ray sputtered, dropped his head, and took a deep breath of her. "I don't like tragedy. I want us to ride off together into the sunset. Options, goddamnit, a sequel."

"The Wovoka. He's a *Vermittler* too. I could ask him to go" She looked around for Awa to confirm her idea, but the old shaman was hidden in the shadows. "That's an option."

"The Wovoka's crazy enough to go out there pretty far, but this?" Ray pulled away from her and slumped against a wall.

"You'll carry our story further. Memory is the master of death."

"Just like Chris, running into the Barrier, leaving me to a shitty life, telling me to make good for her too."

It wasn't the same at all.

Ray's eyes were wet. "What's it like doing the Barrier? Better than mundane reality, like mega-special effects SV, huh?" He balled his fist and tapped his chest. "I don't mean that much to you, do I?"

She stepped toward him. "If I can't come back, I shall miss you."

"You *want* to run. Regular life, *our* life's too hard for you, so it might as well be noble when you run. Then you're a hero, not an escape-artist coward." The nastiness in his voice—the truth of it—burned as much as the Barrier had against silent skin.

"Please, don't do this, don't make me *Murahachibu* in your heart." Elleni reached her hand toward him, but she couldn't step close enough to touch.

Ray looked past her to the door. A snowman squeezed through the crack and stumbled to the ground. Elleni recognized the Eshu mask he carried. The Major had followed them to Fire Mountain. Awa stepped out of the shadows, blew the snow off the Major with the dust sucker, and wrapped him in a fleece blanket. She touched the door with her beaded wand, and it slammed shut. The Major shivered and gulped warm air. Awa tried to pour a tonic down his throat. He resisted, reaching for Elleni.

"It's all right." Elleni took his hand. "Drink it." She stroked his trembling lips and cheeks.

Ray pressed himself into the wall. "What are you doing here, Major?"

"On the run," he said and closed his mouth against the medicine.

"Sidi claims the Major stole Femi's ashes, his final image-board, and fifty-stringed Kora." Awa arched an eyebrow at Elleni.

"Lies," the Major said.

"Perhaps, but..." Elleni shook her head.

"Duma drugged and framed me. He stole Femi's board. He showed it to me in his chambers at Council. I don't know about the Kora or the ashes." The Major held out a lock of sapphire blue hair in a scrap of syn-silk. "I followed this."

Elleni touched a bare spot at her neck.

"He's too cold, we must warm him up," Awa said. She motioned at Ray, who didn't move. "We should use body heat. Come close."

"This is not happening." Ray walked over to them and leaned against the shivering Major.

Awa pulled icy clothes from the Major's body. "Skin to skin is best."

"Naked?" Ray said as he watched Elleni undo magnetic clasps.

"How else?" she replied.

59: Barrier Wasteland, outskirts of Nuevo Nada
(October 16, Barrier Year 115)

> We're a generation savaged by the megademic, snuff takes,
> and the organ market. We can't just ignore all that and hope
> for the best.
> —Tadeshi Mifune, *Surviving the Future, Last Minute Notes*

Something smelled awful enough to make Aaron hold his breath. But that didn't do much good because eventually he had to take a deep breath, and the putrid stink filled him up, 'til he vomited it out. And then everything smelled worse.

A hand tapped Aaron's shoulder, and someone repeated his name. His head was ringing. Every bone, muscle, and joint hurt like hell, but his time wasn't up yet. *Not getting out of this mess that easily*, Stella muttered inside his head. The crash hadn't shut her up. Aaron forced his eyes open to a dark wasteland. The sun was gone, but the Barrier was still a riot of color. He squinted at a flash beam in his face.

"You all right, boss?" Moses asked, blue hair falling in his eyes, rosebud scar balled up on his cheek, recon-skin erasing the bullet wound on the side of his head.

Aaron tried to curse, but his mouth didn't work, maybe it was his throat too. Stella laughed. *See how much good running does you?* Aaron scowled.

Moses thought the look was intended for him (who else?) but pretended not to see it. "Bounced all over. You're real lucky, boss." He grinned, just like old times.

Aaron coughed. The scooter was dust underneath him, and he was jammed between collision balloons. The fool didn't know what lucky was.

"You could have broken your neck." Achbar slashed a laser-blade through the dense fiberplastic that had saved Aaron's life. The balloons deflated. "Don't move." Achbar thrust a med-unit probe into Aaron's ear and scanned his body.

"How many fingers?" Moses held up three.

"What the hell are you guys doing here?" Aaron's voice rasped; talking hurt like shit.

"You're welcome," Achbar said and eased him to standing.

"Lawanda sent me the same message she sent you," Moses said. "Girlfriend wanted to be sure to reach you."

Achbar patted Aaron down. For a big guy, he had a gentle touch. "You didn't think I'd let you crash Perez's alone, did you?"

"And the Achbar couldn't leave me behind," Moses said.

"No, I guess not." Aaron stepped upwind of his vomit and the dead cat. The ground slipped about underneath him. "Whoa." He reached out to hold it still.

"Mild concussion." Achbar grabbed Aaron's flailing hands. "A few strained muscles, a lot of bruises, and you almost choked on your vomit."

Aaron shoved Achbar and the probe away. The med-unit squealed in protest.

"It wasn't done yet."

"I don't care." Aaron tried to clear his throat. "We don't have time for all that. We have to move. How long was I out?" He stumbled toward Achbar's transport.

"Don't know. We found the accident site ten minutes ago." Moses followed after Aaron. "Didn't know it was you at first, but Achbar wanted to stop anyhow."

Achbar leaned over the twisted remains of the big cat. "This is a jungle species, not a desert animal, extinct for seventy-five, a hundred years in the inhabited Zones." He muttered to himself in Arabic.

"What's that you say?" Moses asked.

"A jaguar from the Wilderness," Achbar said. "The Barrier must have opened up a corridor to the Wilderness."

"Shit," Aaron said. The ground kept shifting under his feet. Moses reached out to steady him. "Back off." Aaron snarled. "You think I'm delicate all of a sudden?"

Achbar grabbed Aaron before he banged into the transport. "No, we just don't want you to fall on your ass and scramble your brains some more."

Aaron wanted to snap back something nasty, but Achbar thrust him on the transport lift, and then they were inside the main compartment with nothing to fight about. Achbar shooed several pigeons into their cages and plucked flowers and leaves from a vine that crawled across the ceiling. He crushed them in his hands.

"Skip the blessings and rituals," Aaron said. "We got to move." He was too dizzy or he'd have started the vehicle himself. "We can't hand Lawanda to Perez. I promised to look out for her!"

"Nice of you. Deep breath." Achbar thrust his hands in Aaron's face.

"What is it?" Aaron sucked in a spicy, sweet aroma.

"Alora." Achbar stuffed flowers and leaves into his mouth. "Chew slowly, it'll straighten your head. We're not leaving until we're sure about you."

Aaron didn't have the energy to protest, so he chewed. It didn't taste half bad. *Swallow it, fool, then you can get a move on*, Stella said. Achbar pulled a curved sword from over the viewscreen and slashed through the air. "I'm chewing, I'm chewing," Aaron said.

"Good." Achbar plunged the scimitar into a scabbard at his waist. The weapon disappeared in the folds of his lavender and mint green burnoose. His tunic and pants were the same colors in billowy syn-silk, and he wore those funny embroidered slippers that curled at the toes. "Party clothes," Achbar said. "We must be ready for them, and they must suspect nothing unusual." He took hold of an ebony Healer staff studded with blue and green crystals. "A good disguise, don't you think?"

Aaron nodded. As usual the man looked grand, star quality. Was that an Arab thing or a hit-man trick? Aaron looked down at his vomit-stained jumpsuit and shredded duster. "You got something I could change into?"

Achbar indicated a storage closet. Undressing, Aaron's head cleared. The room stopped spinning, and the pain rippling through muscles and joints was damped down.

"You have to mix flowers with the leaves. Separate they're lethal," Achbar said.

"Oh yeah?" Aaron burped up a sweet aftertaste. "You learn that from Healers or hit men?"

Achbar shrugged. He placed the Koran at his heart and slipped a gun up his sleeve. "Something for the guards to find."

"Good idea," Aaron said. With Achbar and Moses, he'd have more than an edge against Perez. *If Moses doesn't doublecross you*, Stella reminded him.

"You gonna get dressed?" Achbar asked.

Aaron chose purple and brown. He didn't have Achbar's bulk, but with the loose-fitting style, that didn't matter. When he finished dressing, he felt as sharp and focused as a laser-blade. Sharper than he'd felt in months. "Alora's top flight. Better than Rapture." He glanced around the transport. "Where's Moses?"

"Don't panic, I have his Electro, and he can't get far on foot." Achbar checked the viewscreen. Moses was off the road, running through the wasteland. "What the hell are you doing?" Achbar said to the screen. Aaron pulled his gun and headed for the door. "Wait," Achbar shouted. "It's both of them. We'll catch them in no time." He started up the vehicle.

Aaron holstered the gun. "Both?"

"Your Ghost-Dancer pal. Not falling down sick anymore. Remission of some sort. An odd strain of fire virus."

Aaron cursed under his breath. "We don't have time for this!"

"Perez is less than an hour from here. You want to leave them?" Achbar hovered above the steering frame, ready to adjust.

"No, I was just bitching."

Achbar had to drive slowly because of the uneven terrain. Even so, they caught up with Moses in less than a minute. He didn't say anything, but jumped aboard. The Ghost Dancer was farther out, clocking ten, fifteen miles an hour. The transport was doing only twenty.

"Where the hell is he going so fast?" Aaron asked, peering out the viewscreen.

"He asked us to take him to the Promised Land," Achbar said.

"How? I thought he couldn't talk," Aaron said.

"He left these for you." Achbar dropped a waist pouch stuffed with wild turkey feathers in Aaron's lap and a drawing of the Barrier at twilight, with the Dancer's request in neat block printing on the bottom.

"Immortality, that's what he gets if he dies there," Aaron said, looking over to Moses. "Were you going to run into the Barrier with him?"

"I don't know what I was doing." Moses slid down a wall and hung his head. His motion triggered image-boards on either side of him. Arabic words morphed into exploding planets.

Aaron shook his head. "You're pathetic. The Wovoka didn't promise redemption for everybody. You have to be born again. You have to believe in something, a power beyond the petty day-to-day. Otherwise it's the usual burn-in-hell scenario."

"Dancers don't believe in hell," Moses said stubbornly.

"Hell is here, hell is now." Aaron donned the waist pouch for good luck.

"What is this, old movie wisdom? *Daughters in the Dust, Dancing with the Wolves*, that ancient slop you watch over and over. Like you're a genius *auteur*—Frankenheim, Juarez, Tadeshi Mifune—a big shit who's hit the top ten of all time so we better listen to your drivel? I can't stand your hipper-than-thou crap. Why don't you just shoot me or shut up." Moses strode in front of Aaron. A close shot, the hairs in his nose and the spit on his teeth caught the light. "Did you join the rebels, do anything righteous? No, you're no better than me, *Stella*, an Extra sleazing around on borrowed time. Barrier wouldn't redeem your ass either. You'd fry, and that, as they say, would be that."

The transport lurched to a halt. "He's about to do it." Achbar interrupted their lover's quarrel. Grateful, Aaron shoved past Moses to a viewscreen.

"It's suicide. Are we going to try and stop him?" Aaron asked.

"Why steal a man's belief from him?" Achbar pulled a bio-corder from under an image-board and jumped out the side entrance.

One of Tadeshi's genius bio-corders.

Aaron and Moses followed him outside. This close to the Barrier, Aaron's foot would usually have been on fire. All he noted was Stella's gap-teeth tingling. The Ghost Dancer turned and bowed. They all bowed back, even Achbar with the bio-corder. The Dancer touched his face: most of the silver had sweated away; the gene-art lizards had crawled to the ridges of his high cheekbones. He put one hand to his heart and with the other made shapes in the air. They all nodded as if they understood, then he turned back toward the Barrier. His legs trembled, and Aaron worried that he was too scared to run in or getting sick again. Aaron exchanged glances with Moses and Achbar. The Dancer stumbled to one knee.

"*Aboru, Aboye, Aboşişe,*" Aaron said. Celestina's prayer for the Treaty. Did the Dancer know it? He must, everybody did. Famous last words. "May what we offer carry, be accepted, may what we offer bring about change."

Nothing happened. Time dribbled away. Aaron wanted to scream, but his throat hurt too much. Close to the Barrier, his mood turned even nastier than before. "This is pointless," he said. "Let's just leave him." But he didn't move, and neither did Achbar and Moses.

Finally, the Dancer stood up and without flinching walked into a burst of green and silver. Aaron thought he saw a crowd of people gathered around the Dancer's lanky figure, but the image was lost in a wave of turbulent color ricocheting across the horizon. While Aaron was looping through Perez revenge scenarios and trying to figure how he could get his hands on Achbar's bio-corder, Stella was relieved the man got to choose his time and his own way to go.

60: Fire Mountain, outside *Seelenwald*
(October 16, Barrier Year 115)

"Stealing Femi's ashes would afford me neither tactical nor strategic advantage."

The Major's ragged tones grated on Ray. He, Elleni, and Awa lay naked on spring-heated stones huddled under a blanket against the Major's clammy skin, warming him back to normal.

"The thieves are obviously people who would use my demise to shift the balance of power in their favor. Interzonal conspirators."

Ray took a deep breath, pressing against the Major's muscular (gene-art enhanced?) chest and abdomen. The Major kept looping through the same conspiracy crap. The poor slob was in over his head and couldn't admit that arty technophobes and mumble-mouth villagers had outsmarted him. Ouagadougians were very principled people and totally slick. They always gutted you for a righteous cause with beaucoup ceremony and flourish, yet for all the polyrhythmic mumbo-jumbo cover-up, it was still just a snuff take.

"Don't you get it?" Ray shook his head. "You're a sacrifice, man, *Ebo Eje*, to Sidi's future."

Elleni glanced at Ray, tears glistening on her dreads, but she didn't speak, sign, or touch his mindscape. How was he supposed to know what was going on inside her? Osmosis? Fortune cookies?

"I claim sanctuary," the Major said.

"We can't help you. More than we already have." Elleni used her queen voice. Bad omen.

"You're Council Center," the Major said, his lips still blue. A faint dusting of beard was like snow on his sunken cheeks. His hazel eyes were shot with blood and he smelled stale, like a musky dressing room. How long did this skin-to-skin warm-up routine take? "You must intervene on my behalf," the Major said.

Awa sucked her teeth like an ethnic throwback. She'd been doing that all night, obviously appalled by rude, crude outlanders who gave orders like they were in charge of the future.

"I'm sorry." Elleni slid away from the Major and slipped into her robes. He eyed her shimmering breasts and belly, than glanced quickly at Ray.

"Why should she intervene for you?" Ray backed away too. He wiped the Major from his skin before donning his suede shirt. "I know you're guilty of something, and I bet Sidi's got mega proof."

Blood had returned to surface tissues, a pink flush under yellow-ish brown skin, yet the Major still shivered. Awa wrapped him in fresh fleece blankets. "Your clothes are almost dry," she said, patting the uniform, which lay on warm rocks. She must have gotten dressed when Ray blinked. Her hair was even back up in a crescent bun. She stuck her hand into the steaming pool at the center of the chamber. "Not too hot. Good for your blood." She beckoned the Major toward her and pointed to the water.

The Major stood up stiffly, holding the blankets tight against his body. "I did contemplate stealing Femi's image-board," he hobbled to the pool, "but I never got the chance." He scanned the chamber and its twenty-five image-boards with obvious lust. He'd steal those too if he could.

"Celestina's. She studied the Barrier." Elleni sounded like she wanted to give the nazi creep a demonstration, like he'd appreciate it, being an intellectual giant and all.

Ray sucked his teeth like Awa. "What other dastardly deeds were you contemplating, Major?" He scoped panic fleeting across the Major's body before martial discipline geared muscles into neutral. Elleni probably missed it. She was too busy looking for the good in everybody, even terrorist scum.

"Duma stole my data glove and dumped me in the middle of nowhere, naked and blind," the Major said. "I jogged through *Seelenwald* wearing Eshu. I came upon lovers frolicking in the bush and martial artists engaged in training rituals. They ran at me, pounding drums and screeching horns, to attack—I thought. I sent a few flying through the air, luckily I didn't kill anyone, and they cheered. I was mobbed. They poured wine on my boots, stuffed flowers in my pockets, danced a mock battle, then disappeared up into cathedral trees. I 'borrowed' a transparent scooter parked in a clearing beyond the trees. Nobody came down after me. I drove up this mountain until the storm blinded me. I didn't want to sail off a cliff, you understand, so I walked the rest of the way."

"Sounds like quite a melodrama," Ray said. "*Castaway Without a Data Glove.* It would make a good episode for *The Transformers.*"

Awa stuck a vial under the Major's nose. "Drink this."

"Is it some sort of *Zaubertrank*?" The Major drew away.

"The magic you must work for yourself. These herbs simply bring more blood to your extremities." Awa put the vial in his hand.

He looked to Elleni, who nodded. What did she see in this latter-day fascist? The Major drank the medicine and stuck a toe in the hot spring. Awa tugged at the blankets. He clung to them. Despite a well-endowed, flashy physique, the man was modest!

Ray laughed. "We've already seen everything."

"No need to get my blankets wet," Awa said. No arguing with her.

The Major submerged himself in the warm water without exposing his goods or soaking the fleece. Awa walked the blankets out of reach, but the Major was too busy working Elleni to protest. "I am falsely accused. Why would I steal dust? How can you refuse to help?"

"Maybe you don't care about auctioning Femi's ashes." Ray pressed him with Sidi's rap. "Maybe jacking up Ouagadougian culture's your thing. Politics, not greed."

"Such strategy would be an effective cultural bomb. However, you overestimate my tactical foresight. Jocelyn beat me to the punch. Now she can finish off the Treaty, New Ouagadougou, and me with one bullet."

"Why would the Prime Minister want to dump her head of security?" Ray said.

"To, and I quote her, 'rout the throwbacks and thugs. For civilization, democracy, free market, and science.' Anyone's expendable." The Major's eyes darted about as if Jocelyn could hear, as if the truth might kill him.

"She sounds just like Femi," Awa said dryly.

"Oh yeah?" Ray said. Femi and Jocelyn seemed about as different as two people could be.

"Duma and Sidi follow Femi's course," Elleni said.

The Major smacked the water. "I demand asylum. I'm ready. You promised to—"

Elleni shook her head. All her hair turned sapphire blue and strained against her scalp.

The Major drew away from her. "You do what you believe. You're the good guys."

"You don't really believe that, do you, Major?" Awa smiled at him.

"You're a spy and a terrorist who all of a sudden got cold feet. Why should you get asylum in paradise?" Ray said.

"He didn't take Femi's ashes," Elleni said. "Yet, innocent or not, I can't help."

The Major reached for Elleni. "Jocelyn, Sidi, and Duma want to bring the whole world down."

Awa nodded. "They grasp at the same tomorrow."

"So, helping you, I give Sidi fresh ammunition against me." Elleni backed away.

"What made you defect to us 'good guys,' Major?" Ray said.

"I can't support fatal errors." The Major's face twisted in pain.

"Don't blow your brains on our account." Ray grimaced.

Elleni ran fingers through the Major's hair, and he relaxed. "They plan to assassinate Lawanda Kitt and frame Aaron Dunkelbrot— my fatal error." He took a breath. "Which I intend to correct."

"How can you correct anything?" Ray shook his head.

"They who?" Awa said.

"Sidi, Duma, and Jocelyn along with chameleon Daniel Ford, have fabricated a gene-art catastrophe. If I can get to the Captain..." The Major trailed off.

"Sidi's behind the designer mites?" Elleni stumbled back into Awa.

Ray strode to the edge of the pool. "Danny's in on it too?"

"At the control center." The Major let spring water cover his head.

"No way…" Danny had been apolitical 'til he came up against Celestina, then it was like he'd found God. "Where's your proof?" Ray squatted down to the water and shook the Major's shoulder. He reemerged, tight curls glistening like black opals and pearls. In the Barrier light his right hand was iridescent red. Ray blinked several times to be sure.

"I speculate that Sidi has entangled Daniel and Jocelyn in her… disks." The Major glanced at Elleni.

"Danny's got an outlaw streak, but not megademic deep," Ray said.

"Sidi gets people to do what they already want to do," Awa said. "It's her talent."

"Sidi swore to honor life. She wouldn't use her talent to…" Elleni sputtered.

"Healer voodoo?" Ray said. "I don't buy it. None of it." He flashed on Danny's sweet skin and tongue, muscular embrace, hot breath and hotter thighs. Kid really knew how to make a person feel great, not the mass-murderer type. "You're trying to fuck with us, Major, but we got your number. No wonder they're after you!"

"Don't shoot the messenger." The Major raised his hands high.

"I betrayed Thandiwe, my best friend, stood by and let Femi drive her insane, turn her into an assassin." Awa stroked Eshu's faces. "I don't know what my excuse was, saving New Ouagadougou? Maybe I was jealous of Thandiwe. Or maybe I was simply a coward paralyzed by fear. Who are our enemies but our other selves?" Awa's words knocked Ray down ass-first on the rock floor by Eshu. "Are you all right?" She caught his head before it banged into a boulder.

"Alter egos," Ray said. He'd been a snap away from doing anything Sidi asked. He was a coward, an anti-hero just like Danny. If he hadn't hooked up with Elleni first, maybe he'd be burning people alive, too.

Cold comfort.

61:   Cross-Barrier Transmission/Personal
(October 16, Barrier Year 115)

From: Lawanda Kitt, on diplomatic mission to Los Santos

To: Elleni Xa Celest, in New Ouagadougou

My mouth be writin' checks my ass can't cash! Done run outa credit! Me and the Captain be jitterbuggin' into Jesus Perez's gangsta fortress on a Barrier tip. Suicide mission. Captain could blow any second. I'm on her hit list, but she ain't subscribin' no more. No tellin' what Perez's bad boys goin' do. Aaron D might show for our side, but I ain't holdin' my breath.

Sorry I only transmit twice before, and now it's the eleventh hour. Course I ain't heard diddly from you since you took off for the New O to mingle ashes and left me in Entertainment LaLa land. I sure hope your system ain't jacked up, cuz this could be my last crack at you, at anybody. Anti-Treaty folks got us comin' and goin'. Duma up on the world channel, colorless eyes, big-tooth grin, hollow cheeks, talkin' lame shit 'bout he only a spark to Femi's lightnin' bolt or a spit in Femi's flood, but he'd keep the world on its course. Yeah, what course is that? Auto-destruct? I know you can take care of business, you got the Barrier at your back and a medicine bag of tricks. Who wanna mess with alla that? Me, I'm just over here twistin' in the wind. Then it hit me. This action-adventure Entertainment ain't just 'bout me. I should tell Elleni what's up 'fore it be too late and I can't tell nobody nothin'.

Sorry for the afterthought.

Jocelyn and all them two-faced motherfuckers be cookin' up gene-art madness, 'llowed to bring on another megademic. Rebel Extras and born-again Sioux ain't takin' the shit sittin' down. They plannin' a big powwow at Wounded Knee. The Wovoka s'posed to raise the dead or some out-there mess. I hope he do it too, cuz if he don't, I don't know. Barrier talk at me, try to explain what's what, but I ain't no *Vermittler* like you, into figurin' visions and transgressin' my way thru reality. Barrier dump a boogey on me, and it's like mind doodlin' with a wild child who be accessin' a trillion channels at once. Talk 'bout attention deficit, Barrier be downloadin' half the universe and want me to check out the simulcast. Somethin' bound to get lost in translation.

I'm at Perez's party tryin' to hook it with Ghost Dancers then I'ma get my booty thru the Badlands to Wounded Knee. You oughta put in a appearance at the Knee too. Seriously. It's a gatherin' of forces, and if you ain't a force, Miss Shaman *Vermittler*, I don't know what is.

Now, I know you got mucho problems, and this transmission probably sound lame—I ain't got the juice to lay it on you like I wanna—so you just have to trust me. I'm transmittin' a map to the Knee that the Captain and I do up and a drawin' from this dead kid I just (less than three hours ago) see in the Barrier, alive again. (I figure I can tell you this trippy shit without you freakin'.) That's his head on fire in the drawin'. Don't them two ole ladies on the dolphin look like Celestina? And check the title: "Barrier claims gene-art traitors at Wounded Knee." What do gene-art traitors got to do with Celestina? Between the visions and the dreams, it's a little dodgy. How you tell if the clue train don't go your way no more?

Well, I believe *we have been called.* I thought those prophet folk made up that spirit-in-the-dark mess. Not the supernatural jazz, I mean feelin' like your soul's on the line. Celestina steady whisperin' in my ear (no magic, she be transmittin' thru the Barrier or the Barrier transmittin' thru her—even I can figure that). She say, *I can't. It's you now. Do it, heal us*, like somebody gotta do what she couldn't. I get the feelin' it's Earth shatterin', you know what I'm sayin'? The highest stakes. And I just wanna bust out wailin'. I feel like Celestina took a bullet for nothin'. I let her down, let you down too, Elleni, everybody. I fucked up the whole Treaty thang, a total bust and for a no good, triflin' son of a snake that any self-respectin' retard ('scuse my French) would know was a player. It's whack, what I still love 'bout the lousy sucker is how possible he make me feel, like I can do anythin', even change his nasty ass. This ain't no excuse, I just want you to see how it is. I know you don't want no sorry neither, so I'ma just keep on keepin' on 'til somebody wipe me out the picture for good. Least I can do.

Never thought I'd kick it in a funky place like the Nada waste-land, smog coatin' my mouth, death itchin' my skin. (Left my enviro-suit somewhere.) When the end come, I been seein' my ole-lady self in Sagan City, hooked up. Folk in the settlements so proud of me, they makin' up big fat lies. Grandkids doin' more good than I ever dreamed of. History on our side again. Then I turn out the lights, sigh one last time, and it's eternity... But I guess you don't get to say how you go.

Sometime, behind your back, I be callin' you Miss Freaky Thang and all that, but see, that ain't nothin' but ignorance. You my girl. So I catch you at Wounded Knee, all right? Maybe with you riffin' offa Barrier images, we can still turn this mess around and Celestina won't have taken that bullet for nothin'.

Old folks say, put your house in order, then no matter how, you go easy.

Lawanda

62: Fire Mountain, outside *Seelenwald*

(October 16, Barrier Year 115)

> We are not a chosen people nor have we been abandoned, we are just unfinished. Past glory inspires us, yet nothing works the imagination like terror, except perhaps hope.
> —Celestina Xa Irawo, "Preamble to the Interzonal Peace Treaty"

A high-pitched wind whistled through Celestina's rock cabin. Ray had been a coward since forever, a fake hero who couldn't even save himself. Old news, so why hyperventilate? The Major sulked in the hot spring and Awa inspected Eshu. Elleni stood against a wall, talking to herself, hands chattering at a furious pace. Her personal Electro, twisted in a sapphire braid, beeped softly, somebody checking in. The sand painting above Elleni made Ray gasp. He recognized the black satin hair and windowpane eyes. It was the burning woman—before she caught fire. She hugged a middle-aged Celestina and a pale woman with a sparse buzz cut—something about her also recalled Celestina. Could this image be Thandiwe and Robin with the burning woman? Ants crawled at their feet, and a sea mammal soared in the mist behind them. Celestina—on the way from assassin to peace angel... Ray's butt was going numb sitting on the hard rock. He made himself stand up.

"Sidi gave you this mask at Potlatch, didn't she?" Awa asked the Major, who nodded. She pulled the beaded wand from her hair and ran it along Eshu's many faces. "You're not the only one skilled in espionage."

"I didn't find any bugs," he said.

"Watch that jungle fever, Ouagadougians are slick, man." Ray glanced at Elleni.

"Eshu himself is a beacon." Awa tapped an image-board by the door with her wand. It displayed a schematic of the activity on Fire Mountain. "More visitors, vehicles from Council and Paradigma by their looks, coming up the south side."

"An ambush!" The Major, modesty out the window, jumped from the hot spring toward his uniform.

"Yeah, well, we just have to be slicker." A knot released in Ray's stomach. "*Şotito şododo şoora ma şika.* I'm an actor, time to act."

"Is there a back way out of this place?" The Major wiggled into pants and jacket. "If not asylum, at least give me a head start. I know you don't want my blood on your hands." Ray helped him stuff swollen feet into unyielding Teneather boots. "Do you?" The Major reached toward Elleni.

A single braid on the crown of her head hissed green spittle. Sparks from other locks framed her face. Ray almost expected her to zap the Major with a Barrier bolt. Instead she grabbed a corridor staff from the wall and thrust it into Ray's hand, signing about love, dusty daughters, and spirits riddled with holes. Her hands talked too fast for him to get more than the gist, and she hummed a weird melody in his ear. "Repeat it," she signed. "Life and death hang on the intervals." A few notes were almost too low, yet after two tries, he could sing it exactly. Still speaking with her hands, she marched him and the Major to a tunnel that ended in the Barrier. "Sidi's closing in. I don't want her to catch either of you here." Ray nodded. They were on the same channel. As Elleni continued, her relief flooded over him. "The song and the staff will get you through the Barrier and back on the east mountain path. They're coming from the south and won't check the old road right away. Take the mini-tank and get out of New Ouagadougou. Cross the Barrier to Los Santos."

"All right," Ray signed back, "but I'm not going to let you throw me away."

"Okay, okay." Elleni pushed them on.

Ray held his ground, signing clumsily. "I'm going with you. All the way to anywhere. We're best as a team, as a forest, like the old Yoruba saying. If you don't let people help you, it won't work."

Elleni's eyes turned inside out, as if truth chased behind her and she just had to look back to catch it. The Major almost puked at this, but Elleni didn't notice.

"What exactly are you saying?" Elleni signed slowly.

"Hell, I don't want to be running the rest of my life. I chose my danger, not you." Ray's fingers tensed on "danger." He was determined to follow her down a black-hole corridor. The Barrier had sent him invitations too, via his sister, Chris. "You're not the only one willing to sacrifice."

"Indeed." Elleni blinked her eyes back to normal and switched to spoken language. "You two meet me in the Badlands, at Wounded Knee...for a Ghost Dance with the Barrier. The Wovoka's calling for a gathering of forces."

"The Wovoka? I didn't think you were serious. He's a fucking head job." Elleni flicked static in Ray's face. "All right, all right, but I'm down for the whole dance."

"Look for Lawanda there," Elleni said, and the Major perked up.

"What if he's part of the conspiracy?" Ray said, scanning the Major.

"Not part of anything. You're all I've got." The Major's voice was husky. Humiliation or humility?

"He's one of us now," Elleni said.

"Well..." Ray couldn't go that far.

"They've left their vehicles and started up the last stretch on foot," Awa interjected. "If Sidi is with them—"

"I feel her," Elleni said.

"She'll be able to open the door," Awa said. "She is also Celestina's *Geistestochter*."

"I'll hold them until you're away." Elleni pressed her mouth against the Major's. Ray tried not to care. What did a kiss matter anyhow? He was Elleni's anchor. "Your best self," she said, and the Major's lips were brown again.

Awa thrust the scrap of syn-silk with Elleni's sapphire blue hair into the Major's hand. "You don't want to forget this." The Major stuffed it into his pocket.

"Keep each other safe." Elleni hugged Ray, tangling her hair in his. "My real-life hero." She touched his mindscape, and for a fleeting instant they were jumbled up inside one skin.

"We can do this." Ray kissed Elleni passionately. He scoped her from tip to toe, trying to capture her with his eyes. In vain. She blurred as he turned to wave a good-bye to Awa. "Thank you for the food." He snatched biscuits from the feast table then ran with the Major down a tunnel that eventually ended at the Barrier. Its tentacles splashed against naked flesh, burning their cheeks and hands. Ray let the pain clear his head.

They had been underway barely two minutes when the floor and ceiling behind them exploded, knocking them off their feet. The Major turned to look back, but Ray dragged him on.

"What was that?" the Major said.

"Celestina's booby traps. The posse won't be able to follow us," Ray said.

"Yeah, but what about up ahead?"

"Trust me." Ray couldn't bother with doubt, not for this role.

The Major picked up speed. Ray matched him. The tunnel was longer than it looked; and then suddenly the Barrier's undulating surface was upon them. They skidded to a halt two steps from getting fried. Panic skittered across Ray and added its force to his resolve.

"Now what?" the Major said.

Ray opened his mouth. He had to hit acting focus. "Showtime."

"Right." The Major rolled his eyes and clenched his fists.

A skeptical audience was perfect incentive. Elleni's melody filled his body and slid off his tongue. As he sang, he touched the crystal head of the Healer staff into black and purple Barrier swirls. The Major scoped the device with naked envy. An odd light filled the crystals and muddied their vibrant colors. Below the staff, the Barrier turned white, and snow blew against their faces. Ray should have snatched blankets instead of biscuits.

"Is it safe?" the Major asked.

"One take's all we get," Ray said.

The Major pulled a face.

"Let's just go for it." Ray rushed into the blowing snow.

The Major wasn't far behind.

63: Perez's Mansion in the Nuevo Nada Wasteland
(October 16, Barrier Year 115)

> We done let the poetic spirit in folk languish, like bein' human
> mean togglin' a damn switch steada imaginin' yourself 'cross
> spacetime and back. Check me on that, all right? The square root
> of bullshit is bullshit.
> —Geraldine Kitt, *Junk Bonds of the Mind*

Except for power nets and Electro screens, Jesus Perez's cavernous mansion looked like Tara, inside and out. Aaron tried to remember the story of *Gone With The Whatever* but could only recall fragments. He wasn't a fan of the enduring blockbuster and felt zero nostalgia for knights and ladies or masters and slaves. The candelabra in the foyer dripped pink wax onto his nose. He shook it onto the parquet floor.

"What the hell am I doing here?" he said, expecting Stella or some demon to fire off a snappy retort, but his mindscape was like a dark, empty soundstage. He was flying solo for this mission. Handing over his gun, he sauntered through the weapons detector. Moses deposited an empty pistol and followed close behind.

Achbar hesitated at the metal archway sniffing the air. "The story will reveal itself."

"Yeah, right," Aaron said. Who would they have to kill to get out of this alive?

"What does this detector do to the cells of my body?" Achbar asked the guard, whose bulldog face and wrestler physique had been enhanced for maximum terror.

"Fuck if I know," came the nasty reply.

"It's not going to kill you, Achbar," Aaron said. He could smell the testosterone.

"Man, don't be playing around." Moses was right. They couldn't afford an explosive scene at the top of this episode.

"Why should I trust your radiation?" Achbar said.

"Just take your ass through, you're holding up the line." The guard was in Achbar's face, muscles bulging, gold teeth flashing. "People want to party. They don't wanna think about all that."

Unfazed, Achbar stretched out his arms. "Search me with your hands. Gently, please, and take your time." The bulldog guard rolled his eyes at an equally ugly companion with lightning bolts flashing on his cheeks. They grumbled but complied with the Achbar's wish. Notoriety had its benefits.

"What the fuck's your problem?" Moses said. "There's a epidemic down the road. A riot—"

"Shut up. I'm trying to check out the show." Aaron pointed to a band in the front hall. They were slipping in and out of key and falling off the beat. It was painful. Good live musicians were hard to come by—everybody was into Electro-synth. A mostly dark-skinned choir huddled on the stairwell and did their best with the lousy band, singing as if their lives depended on the next outrageous harmony. On mute Electro screens behind the tenors and altos, shadow people plucked fluffy white stuff from extinct vegetation like they were doing Tai Chi. Lawanda Kitt was the guest of honor for this glitterati shindig. Was this throwback nostalgia supposed to make her feel at home or put her in her place?

A soloist scatted around the deadly instrumentalists. Like Elleni sculpt-singing a Barrier corridor, he teased out a harmonious portal where before there had been only a dissonant, lethal blur. His mellow bass baritone sent chills up Aaron's spine.

"I could use singers like that," Aaron said. The faces in the choir were unfamiliar. "Where'd Perez find these guys? Very good for a bunch of unknowns."

"Too good. They've already been discovered," Achbar said as Lightning Bolt leafed through the Koran. "You read Arabic, do you?"

The guard grunted and dropped the book. He probably couldn't read anything.

"Perez must have exclusive contracts, huh?" Aaron said.

Achbar shrugged. The portable contraband detector found nothing suspicious in staff, turban, or pointy shoes. "You know Perez better than I do."

Achbar was trying to tell Aaron something in front of everybody and with electronic spooks listening in, but what? As Aaron surveyed the choir again, the rosebud scar on Moses's cheek twitched. Achbar insisted Moses would be useful. Fat chance. Aaron should have killed the scumbag traitor when he had the nerve. He could rat them out at any moment. Except, Moses didn't know why they had come. Aaron didn't know either. It wasn't just a rescue and revenge mission. He was trying to prove something. But what? To who?

A soprano soared above soggy horns and drums, then dropped low enough to vibrate Aaron's breastbone. She sounded so much like Mahalia it hurt. Singing for her life too. Aaron applauded the performers' desperate skill as Lightning Bolt relieved Achbar of the gun hidden up his sleeve and Bulldog unsheathed the scimitar.

"Is that sharp?" Lightning Bolt growled.

"As a butter knife." Achbar ran a thumb along the edge then displayed unbroken skin. A distant explosion made the floor ripple under their feet. The lights dimmed. "Rebel Extras trying to crash your power nets?"

The guards exchanged glares. Lightning Bolt jerked his head at messages coming down his Electro then headed for the door. Barely glancing at Achbar's genius bio-corder, Bulldog waved the threesome on. "You're clean."

Moses whined. "Now what? Are we gonna get trampled in the riots?"

"Dunkelbrot," Perez shouted from a second floor landing. He was dressed as a southern gentleman circa 1850 and stuffing his face with barbecue goat. A pale woman in a fright-green hoop skirt and bonnet hung on his arm and giggled. "A devout workaholic, I didn't think anything could tear you from your shoot," Perez said.

Aaron forced a smile. "Surprise."

Achbar grinned up at Perez too. "I persuaded Aaron and Moses to quit slaving on their masterpiece and join me in some fun."

"Two Arabian knights." Perez nodded at their burnooses, then scowled at Moses's bedraggled pinstripe suit. "What's with you? Don't like to dress up?" Moses scratched his ass through baggy pants. "You gotta look like a gangster every minute?" Perez laughed.

Achbar roared and slapped Moses on the back. The AD winced and coughed something fierce.

"Where's the rest of your squad?" Perez scanned the foyer.

"Somebody's got to mind the store," Aaron said.

"Too bad." Perez set down the barbecue goat rib and leaned over the banister. "We could use more party people. Roads are a nightmare. Virus panic."

"We heard," Aaron said evenly. "Samanski's on the case, though."

"People need outlets, not just curfews and quarantines." Perez kissed his southern belle and squeezed her tits 'til she squealed. "Do you know this Lawanda broad?"

"Not really. We had a few tussles." Aaron glanced at the coughing Moses. If he was coming down with the fire virus, maybe they were dead meat already. "We should get him some water."

"Don't let me keep you from the party." Perez waved them on.

As Moses's coughing fit eased, they walked toward the smell of barbecue, hush puppies, and dancing bodies. In the ballroom, Entertainment stars were draped over everything. Perez flaunted the next generation: baby-faced wonders with fancy scars, sparkly skin, and impossible bodies. A sleek couple sporting blue-green snakeskin and feathery hair slithered around a fake horsehair couch. Above them, naked men and women gyrated in cages: buns of steel, torpedo tits, thunder thighs. Fragrant sweat dripped from velvet skin, scenting the air. Aaron shook his head. Nothing really imaginative or rad, too commercial, too ad-opera chic, but these clueless slobs risked their lives for designer gene-art glamour. Lucky if they lasted out a shoot. Most would be dead in a month.

"I'm getting great footage," Achbar said. With lenses mounted in jewels on belt, sleeves, and turban, he had impressive multiple perspective. "How you doing with all this?"

Aaron took a deep breath. "One minute like warmed-over road kill, the next like a clear horizon, visibility into the next day."

Achbar grunted. "Alora winding down."

"What's the plan, boss?" Moses said.

Aaron laughed. "Fun. That's the plan. This is an all-you-can-eat kind of party. We've been working way too hard. Reaching for the top ten of all time and our lives are just slipping away."

"Yeah, right," Moses wheezed softly.

A blue-black butler with a cap of white-blond hair tap-danced toward them. He balanced a tray of drinks, avoided the runners of plush carpet, and rapped to the beat of his lightening feet on the real hardwood floor. From what Aaron could scan he was doing old style Jamaican Rastafari rap—the power of Jaa, nappy hair, and jungle sex.

"I think they're getting their colored folks mixed up here," Aaron said to Achbar.

"Oh, is that it?" Moses said disingenuously.

Achbar shook his head as the dancing fool proffered his tray. "I don't drink, and these two are keeping me company,"

The butler cursed them out Jamaican style, snapping his feet and popping the fingers of his free hand. Another stellar performer. What kind of casting call had Perez put out? "No spice in life without at least one vice, gentlemen," the butler said with a wicked grin. "From arsenic to old lace, from Sudden Death to Rapture, whatever you're after." He slipped back into Jamaican rap and followed them as they wandered out of the ballroom, obviously one of Perez's spooks trying to tag them for surveillance or drug them. Not even subtle, he ignored the other guests, dancing with them through courtyards, past pleasure stations and sexcapade suites. His fast-talking cycled back to straight English. "...all on the house. If I don't have it, somebody around here does."

They stood in a gazebo framed by oak trees trailing Spanish moss. At a mobile bar, a rugged Samurai type punched up the designer drug display. "What's your poison?"

Moses picked at a nostril. "What you got?" His face was drenched in sweat. He looked ready to guzzle or blow anything.

"Get your fingers out of your nose. You know I hate that," Aaron said.

"So just tell me how I figure in." Moses wiped his hand on a sleeve.

"We're on a contact high." Achbar eyed the drugtender's sword.

"Ming dynasty," Samurai said, but it looked more old Hollywood than old China.

Watch your back. Aaron jerked his head around, scanning the gazebo. A tall woman with long black braids, prominent nose, and gene-art creatures roaming her face, glided through Spanish moss and slipped between Aaron and the butler. The enormous instrument strapped to her back bumped into Aaron's thigh—some sort of old-age harp on a gourd, Elleni played one. A Kora? The sound of the strings was so delicious, his mouth watered. "Sorry," he said.

The woman turned to gaze at him, but said nothing. Everything about her was familiar. She wasn't a member of the band or an up-and-coming starlet. Even in a simple moss green tunic and pants, she was exquisite. The butler ignored her. Aaron stared into her eyes, transfixed. The gene art on her face coalesced on the diagonals above her nose into two lizards frolicking at a crossroads. Suddenly she turned and strode on endless legs into the trees. Silvery Spanish moss fluttered to the ground at Aaron's feet.

"Damn, you look like you've seen a ghost." The butler laughed. "I got something to put the color back in those pretty cheeks."

"Beat it. We don't want any of that shit," Aaron said. "And we don't want to be snooped either."

Achbar waved his scimitar to punctuate this sentiment.

"Sorry, I didn't know I was dealing with divas." The butler tap-danced off to a less threatening party. The Samurai wheeled his bar in the same direction.

"Fuck!" Aaron rubbed his throbbing eyes. It seemed the head-on collision with the jaguar had released his demons into the world.

"You're not losing it," Achbar said. "She looked just like our Sioux friend, like a twin or something. Come on." He headed after her. "She's a Dancer too, want to bet?"

Aaron was right behind him, then halted. "Where the fuck is Moses?"

Achbar didn't stop. "Mr. Johnson slipped away while we were distracted by ghosts and tap dancers."

"You mean you let him get away?"

"I hope he'll be all right, a lot of shady characters skulking around tonight. Not a party you'd want to do solo. Virus breakout makes people desperate. Are you coming? The lady with the Kora is the hottest thing I've seen around." The man had snake venom for blood.

Aaron took a deep breath. "Lawanda hasn't arrived yet."

"Exactly. Might as well do something while we wait."

64: Fire Mountain, outside *Seelenwald*
(October 16, Barrier Year 115)

Elleni watched Ray and the Major race away to the Barrier. Just like Lawanda, her mouth was writing checks her ass couldn't cash.

As a girl aching for love and glory, she dreamed of riding the Barrier's alien flash of spirit into divinity. This romantic image had carried her to multiple orgasms on countless occasions. When the Barrier actually claimed her as its conduit to a living Earth, however, would she falter? Would she ache for Ray's sweaty touch, the fire in his eyes, the poetry on his tongue and fingers, the sweet anchor to her wayward spirit? Would she long for Lawanda's sassy wisdom, the Major's blunt intellect, and Awa's chilly reserve, or even Duma's disgust and Sidi's scorn? Such craving might shatter her resolve to face *Ebo Eje* with the Wovoka. Elleni was a daughter of this dust. Perhaps that's why she'd failed before. And even though she finally felt at home in Ray's heart, he couldn't make this sacrifice with her. Celestina and sister Phoolan had already streaked away down a Barrier starway leaving a hole in her spirit. Now she'd have to be ripped from Ray as well. The Barrier indeed called for blood sacrifice.

With her beaded wand, Awa tapped a rhythm celebrating menopause on the tunnel walls and pulled Elleni away from the opening. Celestina always configured security using throwback musical codes—Robin's influence? The ceiling torpedoed the floor, which exploded into a shower of rocks. Ray raced on without once looking back; then dust and rubble obscured Elleni's view.

"We have guests." Awa shook Elleni gently.

The rock door slid open and Sidi, wrapped in flame-red fleece, staggered from a white whirlwind into the dim entranceway. Her almond eyes and full lips were open, vulnerable. Eshu must have offered her a disarming vision. Sidi's disks careened into the chamber and bounced off a Barrier tentacle. Elleni's locks got tangled in the disks' hypnotic rotations, and Sidi's way of seeing phased in and out of her own. This double perspective made gravity confusing. As the ground tossed Elleni toward the sky, she tasted with Sidi's tongue, felt with Sidi's skin. Sidi's heart fluttered in her chest. More than just touching each other's mindscape, Elleni was dissolving into Sidi. She clutched her breasts and belly in a wave of disgust. Her own? Or did swallowing Elleni whole revolt Sidi? Trying to dislodge Sidi's disks, Elleni shook her head so violently she thought her neck might snap. At a hiss from Sidi, the disks returned on wobbly trajectories to orbit her head.

Blood dripped from a gash in Elleni's forehead. As she and Sidi struggled back to standing, an auto-bomb squad swooped into the chamber. The bug-bots flew down dark tunnels and crawled along walls and ceiling, clumsy compared to Sidi's elegant disks. Duma entered followed by Sidi's troupe of drumming and singing advisors. They wheeled a patient in on a gurney, which surprised Elleni, as did a brigade in gargoyle Electro masks and bulky enviro-suits. Hired guns, multi-channeling through someone else's reality-scape, they bumped into walls and fell over boulders. Two stumbled into the hot spring and declared, "all clear." Jocelyn and Danny, sporting spotted fake fur, stomped through the door. Elleni tied her hair down with pendants from her medicine belt. No hissy fits or she'd chop it off.

Confused bug-bots zigzagged several times across the gelatinous underbelly of an image-board. Finally they flopped onto their backs, waved thread-metal legs in the air, and exploded. Danny's gargoyle squad cocked their weapons. Jocelyn's guards furiously toggled switches. Tiny explosions filled the air with gray slime. Dodging dead and dying bug-bots, these fierce warriors looked like clowns.

"Celestina always had impressive defenses." Sidi pursed her lips at Elleni.

Awa walked between Elleni and the intruders. "You insult us with a cold draft and a swarm of ill-programmed vermin."

"On the contrary, the Barrier challenges the bug-bots' reality paradigms and rather than jeopardize the mission, they auto-destruct." Jocelyn nodded to her team leader, who frantically recalled the squad. Most exploded en route.

Duma contemplated Celestina's gurgling image-boards, corridor staffs, and sand mandalas. "How long has all this been hidden up here?" He clutched Femi's staff to his chest.

"Rivals the Library of the Dead, na?" Sidi whispered.

"Where's the Major?" Duma wiped bug-bot slime from his face and flung it at the hot spring.

Awa ignored Duma. "You enter without invitation, Sidi Xa Aiyé."

"Celestina said I was always welcome." Sidi shrugged. "We track a terrorist and in our haste to warn you of the danger, we appear to act rude."

Awa snorted at this.

"Where is the Major?" Duma asked again, standing by Eshu. "Don't waste our time with lies." The air around him turned electric blue. "Where have you hidden him?" Duma brandished Femi's staff.

Elleni slipped past Awa and confronted Sidi. "I have no energy to fight you."

"Then don't," Jocelyn said. "Turn the Major over to us and resign."

"Council is no petty bureaucracy. Our Centers do not 'resign'!" Awa snorted at Jocelyn again. "You're not in Sagan City where leaders come and go on the wind."

"Who is this?" Elleni bent down to the patient in the gurney. A burn victim, swathed in synthetic skin, she rested on air cushions. Elleni touched her lips.

"A traitor," Jocelyn said.

"To whose cause?" Elleni gazed at Sidi. How would she rationalize megademic?

"We're one world now, na?" Sidi said. "Healers, scientists, and gangsters—the good doctor has betrayed us all."

"Why have you brought her here?" Awa asked.

"We didn't actually know where 'here' would be," Sidi said, "but—"

"She's dying. We did what we could," Duma said.

"You are New Ouagadougou's premier Healer. Who can deny it?" Sidi bowed to Elleni. "Perhaps if we had gotten her to you sooner..."

Elleni hit trance in a millisecond, channeling Chi vital essence to the tortured woman and calling back her dwindling life force. She effected a momentary reprieve, not a miracle. Elleni felt flames roll across her skin but quickly shook off the sensation.

"She asked to be buried in the Barrier, like a Ghost Dancer." Duma didn't conceal his contempt. "We intend to honor her request."

"One of ours," Jocelyn said. "She and her underground choir of scientists disappeared. I was touring Healer intellectual facilities when Duma realized who she was, so I offered assistance."

Fingering the Eshu mask, she grinned. "A scholar like the Major could never bring himself to abandon such a valuable artifact. And deprived of his data glove, I predicted he'd come to you for aid, Elleni." Jocelyn smiled as Sidi held up the Major's thread-metal glove. "I expected your consort would also be at your side and before Sidi granted this woman's burial request, I wanted to question Ray, since he'd brought her in for healing. I was curious about his Barrier crossing."

"I'm sure." Elleni slipped away from the burning woman and thrust her fingers into the data glove. Jocelyn and her entourage stepped back. The glove tingled against Elleni's flesh, not entirely unpleasant.

"He programmed it to explode on an alien hand..." Jocelyn said.

"Sorry to disappoint you, but Ray and the Major left just before you came." Elleni gestured with the data glove. "This tunnel eventually ends at the Barrier. We'll take your patient that way. She hangs by a slender thread. I've done what I could. Still, there's no time to lose."

The burning woman had revived somewhat. She reached for Elleni and muttered gibberish. Her breath was rotten; teeth rattled in her mouth. Guards grimaced and drummers played a rhythm to soothe her.

"Hand over the Major, then do whatever voodoo you want for the lady." Danny spoke for the first time. He rummaged through the leftovers on the feast table, swallowing biscuits and dumplings whole, like Ray. "We know you stashed him in here somewhere."

"Do you accuse me of lying?" Elleni glared at him.

"I do, Madame." His mouth was full of goat. "Nobody came down the road."

"Ray speaks well of you. He was disappointed by the company you keep," Elleni said.

"I could say the same to him," Danny said.

"Did you think to come in and collect the Major like discarded trash?" Awa asked.

"He stole Femi's ashes," Sidi said.

"And his final image-board and fifty-stringed Kora," Duma said. "We should never have let outlanders in the Library of the Dead."

"You're the one who should be banned from the Library, Duma," Elleni said.

Duma's eyes darted about; his hologram colors turned gray. "You think I'm a novice and you can corridor around in my head?"

Elleni's dreads slithered up her neck despite the heavy pendants. Duma retreated. "I don't need to read your mind to smell your lies."

"Enough prattle." Sidi shifted to a Healer dialect. "So Duma stole the board and *you* the ashes…Still, the Major came to destroy us. He must suffer the consequences."

"How many must suffer the consequences?" Elleni said in the same dialect, phaseshifting with Sidi out of human standard time.

"New Ouagadougou has a right to defend our future." Sidi shouted, unperturbed by the slow motion scene behind her.

Elleni shouted back. "By burning people alive, unleashing a fire-virus megademic?

"That was Jocelyn and Danny's idea, technocrats and thugs warring against their own people. What more proof do you need?"

Elleni stared at her in disbelief. "Do you forget who you are?"

"You're the great Healer, Elleni, Chi Gong and *Vodun* Master bringing back to life enemies who stab you in the heart as reward."

"I prefer that to murder any day."

"Like Celestina." Sidi circled behind her. "You aid and abet murderers. How innocent does that make you?"

"Should I have let the fire virus burn out *your* life force?"

"In your place——" Sidi's disks formed a spiral above her eyes—— "I would have."

Elleni hugged herself and spoke carefully. "No matter how you twist it, just because I saved your life, I'm not responsible for the evil you do."

Sidi stroked Elleni's arms and forehead. Elleni flinched. Sidi whispered in her ear. "Why should I sacrifice Ouagadougian generations for a horror-Entertainment future?"

"Do you know what you are?"

"Should we twist our bodies with gene art, guzzle Jolt, dress up in junk, think junk?" She stroked Elleni's neck and throat. "Should we squander everyone's resources? Would you have me poison tomorrow?"

Elleni leaned into Sidi's feathery fingers. "Femi declared you an abomination, would have seen you murdered as a child, and now you follow his..."

"Femi would have murdered me? Why?" Sidi dug her fingers in Elleni's hair.

"You're a *Vermittler*." Elleni pulled free. "A Barrier griot."

"A *Vermittler*, like you? Is that what you think?" Sidi laughed, a beautiful, scary sound, and hugged Elleni from behind. "The Barrier wounded me, marked me as a child." She turned Elleni to face her. "I was precocious. Celestina healed me, honored me with these disks, allowed me powers from the *Final Lessons*, Barrier access even."

"*Vermittler* don't need Vera's lessons to access the Barrier. Femi ordered Celestina to murder all the 'wounded' ones. She spared you and me for Peace."

Sidi shook Elleni's shoulders. Disks collided, spraying a fine mist into their eyes. "Lies, and if not, Celestina was incredibly naïve, wasn't she? Peace, on such a scale." Sidi laughed again and Elleni was chilled. "I am no *Vermittler*."

"But—"

"Maintaining our own humanity is difficult enough. New Ouagadougou certainly can't humanize Paradigma or Los Santos."

"Perhaps they will humanize us."

"Imperialists are not the route to our humanity. Europe cannibalized Africa and the Americas, remember?" Sidi shoved Elleni away. "Are you a colonized Extra with only Entertainment history and ad-opera futures?"

Elleni stumbled to her knees. "I meant, our *struggle* with them... Who are our enemies but our other selves?"

"A waste of spirit to struggle with Paradigma and Los Santos... and then they'd define us." Sidi dropped to her knees, kissed Elleni's forehead and eyes, and grasped her hands, utterly sincere. "Don't help technocrats and thugs rape our spirits. Join us."

No one except the Barrier had ever asked Elleni to join anything.

"Our ancestors didn't have the benefit of hindsight," Sidi continued. "Let them not have suffered in vain. Let them be *Ebo Eje* for us, for our children. Whatever Femi's excesses, he died for us. This time, this war, I say let the colonialists feed on each other instead of our future. Let's make our story beautiful, you and I, no enemies."

"I don't know." Elleni muttered. Sidi's passion and sincerity made too much sense. Who could argue history with her? Celestina would have had a rebuttal, but... Cool hands brushed her cheeks. *Tutu* Sidi got people to do what they already wanted to do.

"Join us." Sidi's voice was mangoes and cream. "Do you think this savagery is what I want? Fire-virus megademic, snuff takes? With Celestina's Treaty the Barrier no longer shields us from contamination. Tell me a better choice to save New Ouagadougou and I'll make it."

"Maybe I'm wrong and you're right." New Ouagadougou City exploded in Elleni's mindscape. She tasted burning flesh and smelled spirits on the run.

"Let Paradigma and Los Santos destroy themselves. There'd be no blood on our hands."

"But what's to stop New Ouagadougou from becoming just like...them." A bristling braid gripped Sidi around the neck. "How are your tactics better, any different than theirs? Didn't Femi always say, playing on the enemy battlefield, you are the enemy. They define us already."

Disks sliced through Elleni's hair, and an explosion of pain broke her concentration. She found herself phaseshifting, but it was like smashing through concrete with Sidi bearing down on her.

"This is suicide," Elleni said. They could end up anywhen—mountain time, star time, taking an eon to blink or worse. Sidi's disks retreated from this thought. The pain faded and Elleni groped toward familiar markers. Trying to regain control, she skidded back with Sidi toward human standard time.

65: Perez's Mansion in the Nuevo Nada Wasteland
(October 16, Barrier Year 115)

> Eat breakfast by yourself, do lunch with a friend, give dinner to your enemies.
> —Tadeshi Mifune, *Surviving the Future, Last Minute Notes*

One minute the born-again Sioux lady with a Kora strapped to her back was right in front of Aaron and Achbar. The next, some pale has-been was trying to talk his way into action-adventure Entertainment, forcing Aaron to get rude and crude, and a blue-black porch monkey was telling them to chill out. Picturesque darkies were turning up everywhere; shucking and jiving spies, they didn't fool anybody.

Aaron and Achbar walked by peach and cherry trees, brought back from extinction courtesy of Celestina's *Wiederaufbauwunder*. Aaron plucked a fat peach and took a bite. Delicious. He wolfed it down and snatched another. "Ungrateful sons of bitches," he said as peach juice dribbled down his chin. He swallowed a handful of sour cherries but avoided the buffet tables loaded with southern grease cuisine and death-by-chocolate dessert spreads. He wouldn't risk poisoning for a taste adventure.

Lawanda was taking her time about making an entrance. Didn't the stupid broad want to get rescued?

"Now what?" Aaron asked Achbar.

The big Arab was deep in his Electro, multi-channeling. He shouted over the noise in his ears. "The Dancer headed past the fruit trees for the side entrance, I think."

"I'm all turned around." Chasing ghosts, he and Achbar had gotten lost in a maze of gardens, stables, and gazebos encrusted with southern-belle kitsch. No way could he find the front or back door or any kind of quick getaway. "So why are we following the Sioux chick?" The smell of burnt goat filled the back of his throat, making him almost lose the cherries.

"Plague victims are crashing seasonal corridors. More riot break-outs." Achbar stopped under a tree, so heavy with fruit it leaned to one side. "Mobs and Rebels headed our way." He'd hacked Perez's private channels and was snooping uncoded dirt.

"Tell everybody, why don't you." Aaron scanned the shadowy grove. Only a few bio-corders, no human backup.

"My Healer staff disrupts electronic snoops." Achbar pounded it into the ground.

Aaron sighed. "Look, I don't like the menu, don't like the script. Nothing to do but wait for disaster." Astral blues drifted over the trees. "Lawanda would go for live art." Heading for the music, he tripped over water hoses spraying trees that would have died in the desert air.

Achbar stood in his way. "We're getting close."

"To what?" Aaron stepped around him.

"Word is that gene artists holed up here at Tara are responsible for the new plague."

"No wonder you were so eager to join this mission."

Achbar touched the feed in his ear and looked baffled. "Perez may have an antidote for the malanga blight or the mites dogging fire ants."

"I don't give a shit about that." Water from a sprinkler soaked Aaron's parched skin, but didn't soothe him. "A little rescue, a little revenge, that's all we're doing here. Don't get fancy. I'm not sticking my neck out…not my style."

"So what are you doing here?" Achbar asked, a scary edge to his voice.

"I made promises. Against my better judgment, but…" Aaron really couldn't say why he was there. It felt like compulsion, insanity.

"This is a suicide mission." Achbar drew his sword.

"You're such a hero type, on a high moral plane. How do you put up with me?"

"I used to be very quick to give up on people." Achbar was slicing his scimitar through the air in figure eights. "I gave no second chances. In a flash, you were a goner."

"But somebody saved your ass when you were an unrepentant thug, and now hanging with me is like payback." Aaron stepped into a sword swipe. A clump of hair fell to the ground as the scimitar whistled by his head. "Butter knife?"

"Illusions rule." Achbar turned his wrist and the blade was at Aaron's throat. "The first 'thugs' were an assassin cult of the black Hindu goddess, Kali. Thugs wormed their way into a stranger's heart and then, when he let his guard down, killed and robbed him. Believe what you will of me." Achbar hacked at the cherry tree.

The tap-dancing butler fell to the ground with a severed branch. Before the butler could scream, Achbar stuffed a drug-soaked handkerchief into his mouth and tied his feet and hands in an excruciating contortion. The butler's eyes rolled up in his head.

"Bad actor, bad spy," Aaron said.

"Let's move. He'll only be out a couple hours," Achbar said. "Perez has an underground lab."

"Time's running out—" Aaron headed for the music— "and I still don't know who to trust." He froze mid-stride.

Lawanda and the Captain sprinted across the peach grove. Lawanda's butt was skinnier than a week ago and her once thick Afro was scraggly fuzz. Her bruised neck looked as if somebody had choked her. The Captain's hair stood on end. Sweat soaked her clothes, face, and hands. Her skin color was all wrong.

"What the hell happened to them?" Aaron said.

"Not a word on Perez's private channels," Achbar said. "And Lawanda is ignoring her Electro."

Lawanda dashed onto the veranda. Aaron moved to follow her.

"Careful." Achbar jammed Aaron behind a tree. The Captain aimed a long-range weapon in their direction. "You can practically see that one's nerves fraying."

"Great. The Captain'll ice us before we can rescue them," Aaron said.

Lawanda threw open the French doors on the big-house veranda and standing on the sill let the choir's music stream over her. In sync with the meter and melody, she marched into a library set, outfitted with walls of books and a blue globe spinning in the breeze. The Captain closed the doors behind them.

"Come on." Aaron raced up the steps. As he turned to see if Achbar followed, the Sioux woman stepped from behind a pillar on the veranda, and he crashed into her. She staggered back, the Kora screeched, and Aaron tumbled to the ground. She reached behind her and dampened the strings. Gene-art lizards perched on her cheekbones hissed at him.

"Who are you?" he whispered as Achbar helped him up.

The Dancer touched his lips then pulled him and Achbar behind a pillar. Lawanda and the Captain's shadows danced on the curtains as they crept through the library.

"She doesn't talk," Achbar whispered, "but I bet she can write."

"We're going to lose them." Aaron pointed at the library.

"The Captain might shoot us if we barge in there after her." Achbar offered the Dancer a magic pad. She hesitated, and her lizards disappeared into her hair. Definitely more sophisticated than the usual gene-art skin job. "Take it." Achbar put the magic pad in her hands. "Clue us in."

She grasped the thin stylus and scribbled quickly, in Arabic. Achbar translated. "Who I am does not matter, a grain of sand, a wisp of smoke. We are all friends of the Wovoka. The ceremony at Wounded Knee comes very soon. On foot, impossible deadline. Do you have vehicles to transport the underground choir? I've taken Femi's Kora from the Library of the Dead. This will be a formidable Ghost Dance. The ancestors will grace us." Achbar paused.

Aaron shook his head in disbelief. "She really say all that or did you spice it up?" Achbar shrugged. Aaron sighed. "Got to hand it to 'em, Dancers never give in."

"I don't know if we'll all fit," Achbar said. "Twelve scientists plus us, Lawanda, and the Captain, tight squeeze."

"Scientists? Those are Mahalia's people singing in there, and you plan to rescue them."

The Dancer grabbed Aaron's cheek and turned his face to hers. Her fingers burned his skin; the lizards spat at him. Her eyes were streaks of lightning. She thrust a finger at his chest.

"Me? Help?" He tried to pull away. She gripped his jaw. "You're crazy." She looked so much like the other Dancer come back from the dead, he wanted to hug her or shake her. He drew a feather from his waist pouch. "Twins—you and him?"

She blinked her eyes and dropped her head. He took that as a yes.

"Listen to me. We can't do all this."

"Why not?" Achbar said.

"Are you brain dead? Steal the whole goddamned choir right from under Perez's nose?"

"Here's how you get your hands on some really good singers!"

"I didn't come here for all that. I came here for Lawanda."

She made a sign in the air and then to the pouch.

"What does she want? To know what happened to him?" Aaron asked.

"Of course," Achbar said. "Wouldn't you?"

The Dancer took Aaron's face in the palms of her hands and stared into his eyes. "We can't do it," he said softly. "Too many bad guys, not enough of us. You get me?"

She shook her head and thrust thumb and index finger at Aaron's heart and then to her own.

"Friends of the Wovoka?" Aaron put his hand against her heart. "Your brother died on the stupid word of a crazy man, understand? The Wovoka's no medicine man, confidante of the gods, magic spirit, whatever! He's just another psycho politico playing an angle."

Again she shook her head, slapping Aaron with a braid.

"Your brother got sick with the fire virus and walked into the Barrier."

The lizards fell from her temples and tumbled down her cheeks.

"I'm sorry, that's how it was."

Her knees gave out, and she slumped in Aaron's arms. He patted her back awkwardly. What could he say? He looked over to Achbar who offered no assistance.

"He didn't look sad. Real peaceful, actually. The Barrier was twilight colors and there were people inside, coming to carry him over."

She pushed away from Aaron, scribbled on the pad, and thrust it in his face. Achbar translated. "Without faith we are not human. Dreams are the maps of our souls; we follow them to fulfillment."

A loud crack split the night. Lights inside and out went dark. Tara's machines and security systems whined down to silence. The band cut out abruptly. The singers improvised a graceful ending. Party guests hooted, excited by the sudden darkness. Then terror set in, and the screaming voices became shrill.

"Power jam," Achbar said. "Finally, it begins."

Action-adventure dialogue always worried Aaron. He looked across the wasteland. Nuevo Nada had also gone dark. "Perez's personal generators should have kicked in." Something didn't sync up.

The woman scribbled again on the pad. Achbar translated. "Rebel sabotage. I can see in the dark. Are you with me?" She ran through the library into the foyer before they could answer, and fast. They had a tough time keeping up.

Amplified voices called for order as guests stampeded the front hallway, trampling one another and screaming. After a volley of shots, silence ensued. Electro flash beams streaked across the faces in the mob. "Single file or get shot in the head." Aaron recognized

Bulldog and Lightning Bolt barking death threats as he and Achbar followed the glowing Kora on the Dancer's back and wound their way through frozen mayhem.

The choir hadn't moved from the stairwell. The Dancer disappeared among them.

"Without power nets, it'll be open season on this place," Aaron said.

"But if the nets come back online, we're prisoners again," Achbar replied.

"Whatever we're going to do, we better do it now." Aaron scanned the shadows. "How the hell are we going to find Lawanda?"

Moses, trussed up in a sheet, rolled down the stairs and banged into Aaron. Gunmen on the second-floor balustrade were locked onto him. Red laser lights danced across his body. With their gargoyle Electro masks, shooting in the dark would be child's play.

"I never trust traitors," Perez yelled from above. "Kill him."

"Hold up!" Aaron said. Laser beams played across the crowd as gunmen tried to locate him. "Give me a gun, I'd like to shoot him too!"

"Dunkelbrot?" Perez shouted. "Good lord, man, what's gotten in to you?"

"Music," Achbar yelled and the sound of the Kora was so loud, so profound, everyone was thrown off balance except Achbar. He slashed the ropes around Moses with his scimitar and thrust the Healer staff over their heads. A blistering energy pulse from the staff's crystal head seared through the darkness. Aaron winced in pain even after squeezing his eyes shut. He heard bullets sink into wood, fabric, and flesh. Screams bounced around the foyer as all semblance of order collapsed. The mob was on the move again. Eyes still shut, Aaron careened with the choir toward a cold draft.

"Hurry, through the lab!"

Someone pulled him into a doorway underneath the stairwell.

Darkness was a tonic for his eyes. Moses collapsed into him, sticky with blood. "Thanks, boss," he said. Without thinking, Aaron pulled him down a passageway past refrigeration units and operating theatres, following the glowing Kora. Moses was dragging a leg, and they were falling behind, so Aaron heaved him over his shoulder, fireman style. They weren't going to get far like that, but Aaron just couldn't leave the bastard. More gunfire and a familiar roar behind him—Aaron glanced back to check. Achbar hung in the doorframe, brandishing the Healer staff. Aaron wondered if he'd gotten everything on the bio-corder. This would make a hell of a final episode for *The Transformers.*

"You're a goner!" Perez screamed.

"In your dreams!" Achbar said, letting loose one last pulse of deadly white before slamming the door shut.

66: Fire Mountain, outside *Seelenwald*
(October 16, Barrier Year 115)

"What the hell was that?" Jocelyn asked Danny.

Elleni had managed barely a second with Sidi, yet phaseshifting at such close range disoriented everyone else in the chamber.

"Barrier Fever." Awa rapped on the door. The wind sprayed snow against their feverish cheeks. "You are not acclimated. You must finish your business and leave."

Sidi rubbed her forehead. Elleni stuffed severed braids into her medicine belt. She tried to catch Sidi's eye, but it was hopeless.

Awa barged between the two *Vermittler.* "Will you banish the Major to the Wilderness or give him to his own people for punishment?"

"From my POV, it's a capital offense." Danny poured himself a *Weißbier.*

"Please, all of you, help yourselves to food," Awa said. After a moment of hesitation, everyone but Sidi, Duma, and Jocelyn crowded around the table. "What sort of hosts betrays the guests who honor their house?" Awa asked.

"If the guest is a thief, he can no longer demand hospitality," Duma said.

"Are you one of the Barrier's griots?" The burning woman spoke in an almost normal voice, startling everyone, and she tugged at the data glove on Elleni's hand. "I have a story for you to sing." Elleni bent down to her cracked lips. "Robin and Thandiwe had Barrier intercourse. They knew symbiogenesis. Femi was wrong. A lavish symbiotic affair, the Promised Land. Let me die there and live again."

Elleni looked at Awa. "How could she know Robin and Thandiwe?"

"They died before she was born," Awa said.

Elleni touched the woman's lips. "Mahalia Selasie."

Sidi nodded. "How do you know her?"

"I thought she was dead," Elleni said. Mahalia's breathing was so labored, Elleni attached an oxygen mask. With acupuncture needles from the medicine bag at her waist, she modulated Mahalia's Chi to relieve pain, to help her hang on.

"Who are Robin and Thandiwe?" Sidi said.

"Follow me and I'll show you." Elleni pushed the gurney around the hot spring and headed down a tunnel with the burning woman. They had to hurry, no more reprieves.

Danny reached for a weapon tucked close to an armpit. Gravy dripped down his chin. Sidi's disks surrounded him, and he froze. "Only one door out of this cave. All passageways lead to the Barrier. If the Major is here, we'll find him eventually," she said.

"He's nobody to dick around with," Danny said.

"We're safe." Sidi and her entourage of drummers followed Elleni.

"Don't worry," Jocelyn said, "we can take him in pieces, as a last resort, you understand. I'd prefer him alive."

Paradigma security stayed behind wolfing food at the feast table, but everyone else hurried down the tunnel. Sidi jogged alongside the gurney, her disks hovering above Elleni's hair. She moved in time to the drummers' beat. Jocelyn, Danny, and his squad of thugs tramped off the beat behind her.

"*Schnee von gestern*!" Duma said as he argued with Awa in old German.

"Yesterday's snow indeed. How do you put up with him?" Elleni asked Sidi.

Sidi almost smiled. "How do you put up with Ray? Love is a mystery, na?"

"That's the excuse," Elleni said. "You know how much I... respect you. Joining you would be like a dream." Elleni wondered if being so beautiful, so beloved would make it harder to give up the world? "I want us to..." Elleni halted. She and Sidi stood skin-close to the Barrier, Mahalia between them. All Elleni knew of the Wovoka were rumors and visions. She'd much rather face eternity with Sidi.

"What do you want?" Sidi asked.

"Join me," Elleni said simply.

Sidi's nostrils flared, and a disk darted for Elleni's mouth. "You're serious aren't you?" Sidi said. "And what are you a part of?"

"Let me show you Thandiwe and Robin's story. Let me prove to you who you are."

Before Sidi could speak, Elleni drew on Barrier energy and phase-shifted. She contorted her mindscape and shoved herself through familiar portals, dragging Sidi and Mahalia with her. She begged the Barrier to show Sidi what it had shown her of Saint Celestina.

Mahalia was thrilled to pass beyond pain. Sidi, however, resisted Elleni's mad dash through alien dimensions. Sidi was an untutored *Vermittler*, yet the strength of her will surpassed Elleni's; she pulled the three of them back through the tricky portals toward Earth normal. Doubts weakened Elleni's resolve. She flailed about, but could not get them back on course. Thandiwe and Robin beckoned her, to no avail.

Elleni feared that Sidi would shatter her mindscape and scatter it through the cosmos, but then Mahalia wedged herself in the gateway portal. Her body was spent, not her will. She had a surprising affinity with the Barrier and refused to return to pain. She was bound for the Promised Land.

They stalled.

Angels? Coming for to carry me home?

Daughters, I try to heal the past with the actions I take now, but I see the future in your faces. Heal us.

Celestina's voices called to them from a distant portal. Not even Sidi could resist.

67: Spirit Daughters

> My race is run, the end's unclear
> Oh Death
> Won't you spare me over to another year?
> My head's too hot, my feet way cold
> You've run my life right outa my soul
> The children pray, the preacher preach
> Oh Death
> Won't you tell me mercy ain't outa your reach?
> —Celestina Xa Irawo, "Preamble to the Interzonal Peace Treaty"

Ten years ago, Celestina went home to Sagan City to prevent Mahalia Selasie from opening the ⚛Promised Land⚛ to the uninitiated, revealing Barrier secrets, and throwing the world off its course. After decades with no blood on her hands, Celestina was prepared to kill Selasie if persuasion failed. As she boarded the cross-Barrier transport, Thandiwe and Robin abandoned their sixty-five year truce, and war broke out under her skin.

Daughters of my mind and spirit, I bear my wounded soul. You three must do what I could not. Finish this song and dance, heal the universe in yourselves, and set me free.

The trip through the seasonal corridor and customs passed in a blur. At first Robin occupied Celestina's mouth and Thandiwe dug in behind her eyes, then Robin retreated to her guts while Thandi seized her breath. Celestina was weapon and target, ambushed at every turn.

"Tombouctou Galactic Library and Observatory. End of the line, you'll have to get out now." The driver blew his nose against his sleeve. "We gotta get ready for a return run."

Celestina stared at his chafed nostrils.

"Hey lady, you sick then or crazy?" Seasonal corridors drove some people potty. "You got coverage?"

Celestina shook her head but couldn't move her legs. Her breathing was funny, her tongue too fat. Neither backbone wanted to hold her up, but somebody's heart pumped blood at a furious pace. The driver got a burly maintenance woman with a purple neck rash to deposit Celestina on a bench in the transport hall. Celestina proffered a vial of bag balm for rashes and chafing, but they declined and hurried off.

Mustard smog wafted through station windows. A clot of tall buildings scraped most of the sky away, leaving a few taupe smudges. Everything was familiar but all wrong. She vomited behind the bench.

"Shit, do it in the lavatory!" Hurrying along a sticky walkway, she tried to remember a poem about promises to keep and miles to go before you sleep but came up blank. So embarrassing, so painful to have forgotten more than you could ever learn again. Vibrations rattled her corridor staff, jarring her wrists, jarring all her bones. "The city roars—you remember that. Rumbles through the empty spaces inside." Speaking settled her stomach, and she wasn't the only unfortunate in the station talking to conflicting selves. "You fit right in." She smiled at her compatriots. "So don't start with the evil megalopolis crap. You love the city, the roar, the funk—vibrating with life." She stopped and gazed out the north entrance.

A market square teemed with militia wielding fiberplastic stunners. Dis-eased pedestrians dodged half-dead beggars and danced over smelly bodies, while merchants in impromptu booths promised bottomless bargains and infinite profits. Bulbous fire ants swarmed over everything. Rock-hard fire-ant domes wrecked havoc with vehicle chassis.

"Loved this, did I?" Her medicine bag whacked aching hips. Turning from the market exit, she headed toward Tombouctou. She didn't remember such a cavernous, crowded transport station. "It's been awhile. Things had to change." She ducked down an alley, away from the hordes.

The stench of so much dis-ease made her head ring. Her synesthesia was flaring up. She hadn't been plagued with that in thirty years—since her last stint as assassin. "If Dr. Selasie won't listen to reason..."

No wavering, no second or third thoughts, this was a murder run.

"Tour's over there." A greasy-faced tech blocked her path. "Can't get to the Observatory this way, it's off limits." He scoped her syn-silk robes, feathered headdress, bare feet, and corridor staff. "From Ouaga-what'sit, huh? Speak English? Where you trying to get to? This maintenance alley goes nowhere."

"Emerald City." The first glimpse of the Observatory's towers reminded her of ancient Entertainment. "We're off to see the wizard."

"Not this way you're not."

She spritzed him with cathedral-tree balm. He slumped to the ground, and she propped him against a workbench and walked on. He'd remember her as a vivid dream.

At the security gate, a wall Electro projected an old Entertainment hit just for her. Ray Valero rode a Mustang scooter, guzzled Jolt, and saved the world. He promised a taste of before-the-whole-world-was-like-the-Third-World, when humanity ruled the Earth and reached to the stars. Stifling a shudder, she disabled the power net-ting and galloped through the gate on four feet. She was grateful that Robin still had low-priority systems clearance and a hacker's spirit. "You're missing, not dead, Wolf—" she almost smiled—"but don't get cocky."

As she headed down a cobblestone alleyway, security robots chal-lenged her—boxy little buggers with squeaky voices and wheels that turned to feet when necessary. "CRANIAC—the best security in the world!" She disrupted their programming and raced into the plaza.

Selasie was late. Spinning around to take in everything at once, Celestina got snarled in her robes and tumbled to her knees. Space-age pagodas, the tallest structures in the world, loomed above her. Fifty stories up, hanging gardens with flowers always in bloom flowed over balconies. Cathedral trees in glass cages teemed with weaver ants, braiding their metropolises in the tree's bushy crowns. On both sides of the tower complex, fields of white radio telescopes planted in crushed, blue gravel called to mind giant water lilies. But Electro-billboards were blank, and the sliding walkways and lifts stood idle. Tombouctou's glory days were long gone.

Heart and breath out of sync, Celestina started to leave without seeing Selasie.

"Thandiwe." A gravelly voice called to her from shadows.

"No. Celestina." She tried to catch a breath from one mouth or another. "Not Thandiwe." She waved the corridor staff against that name.

"As you wish. You're alone."

"Am I? Who says?" Celestina pulled her selves together.

"You came solo on the transport—very trusting, or more dangerous than I thought."

"Probably both."

"Where shall we talk? Have you taken the tour?"

"I'm no tourist. Let's go to the Great Hall."

"It's a hike and just too…unpredictable." A catch in the throat—unspoken pain?

"We'll take the slide-way." Celestina scanned for the speaker's hiding place. "The Hall has a marvelous view of the Barrier."

"View? The Barrier's practically in the room with you!"

"They can't snoop us there. Too much interference."

"Nobody ever bothers to snoop me."

"That could change. Show yourself. I'm alone and unarmed."

"Still quite lethal I suspect."

"And you're not? If we risk nothing, we gain nothing." Celestina leaned against her staff and waited.

After sufficient time to scan for weapons or even scope Celestina's DNA, Dr. Selasie strode out of a wall. She wore a taupe jumpsuit and a gray utility belt jammed with state-of-the-art tech. She was less flamboyant than Celestina had expected.

"Thandiwe would be very old, as old as you," Mahalia said as the hole in the wall faded. "And flaunting her age."

"If she were alive." Celestina struck the wall with the Barrier staff. It was solid. "Thandiwe died, sixty-five years ago."

"I know all about her and Robin Wolf."

"Not how they end up. Let's move, before the robot fleet revives." Celestina marched toward the slide-way behind the plaza.

"They were lovers, weren't they?" Mahalia matched her pace.

Celestina didn't answer. Using Robin's access and the corridor staff, she tapped a power grid and brought the slide-way back online. "Watch your step getting on."

"Wolf pissed a lot of people off," Mahalia said as she jumped up beside Celestina. What mythology had she created around Robin? "She was a bit of an intellectual gangster."

"For all the good it did her. This'll take us right up to the Hall."

"I'm impressed." Mahalia grinned as they sped toward the Observatory. "You're quite fit for an old lady, but aren't you worried about an ambush?"

"No." Celestina cinched the robes billowing about her with a syn-silk belt. "Why? Did you have one in mind?"

"No...I was thinking more of escape."

"Aren't we all?" Celestina said grimly.

"I'm not just a dreamer..."

"*Schade.*"

Mahalia shook her hair in the breeze. "I'm suffocating here."

"In Paradigma, you mean? Life closing down on you?"

"Women are still outnumbered almost five to one at Sagan Institute and haven't been awarded a single Astral Prize since... forever."

"Yes, well, we do have to keep our eyes on the prize."

"Don't condescend to me. What do you know of my life?"

"Infatuated with Robin Wolf. Desperate, reckless, and brilliant. How's that?"

Mahalia turned toward their rapidly approaching destination. "That doesn't cover everything."

"Yes, I forgot arrogant. How else could you have gotten this far?" The slide-way ended at a glass lift on the ground floor of the Observatory. Celestina stretched stiff neck muscles as she disabled the security grid, which took all of two minutes.

Mahalia eyed her. "I didn't know Healers had expert espionage training."

"You don't know anything about Healers."

"But you know everything about me, about us. Deep secrets even."

"There's no point in maintaining a facility at tip-top security if hardly anybody's interested." Celestina shrugged. "I can hack into Tombouctou because they left the door wide open."

Mahalia raised a skeptical eyebrow. "Oh, is that it?"

The frosted glass glowed pink as the lift asked their pleasure.

"Take us to the top," Celestina said. They rose above mountains of books, stacks of gold and silver disks, and banks of gelatinous bio-computers oozing yellow goo and noxious fumes. "Rotting, you see? Nobody cares."

"It's pathetic how we let ourselves go," Mahalia said. "Why don't they just tear the place down, bulldoze it over, make a park?"

"Strategic ambiguity. It still looks impressive. Keep your enemies nervous."

"No, politicians are terrified of the Barrier. They don't want to get near the place."

The lift deposited them directly in the Great Hall of Images, a cavernous chamber at the top of the towers. The only light came from the Barrier, blazing behind a window at the far end. Celestina strode to the bronze plate inset dead center in the synth-marble floor. The metal was warm against her bare feet. A strand of weaver ants hung from the ceiling just above her head, and despite her somber mood, she smiled. Her totem insects had come to welcome her.

"Not much to it, huh?" Mahalia hesitated behind Celestina. "I've never been in the Great Hall, just heard about it."

"It's as if I've never been here either." Celestina let her medicine bag and robe slip to the ground. The Hall's prickly atmosphere felt delicious against bare back and arms. "But the stories are so vivid, I feel like I'm home."

"My father worked here, before they axed the basic research program, before I was born." Mahalia walked slowly toward her. "Back in your day."

"Is my day over? I hadn't realized."

"He always promised to bring me here, but never got around to it."

"Your father was a dreamer, big on ideas, but no action hero. Small minds hacked at his spirit. He died a broken, bitter man, before his time. You've sworn never to be like him. That's why you've never come here." Celestina laughed. Robin had worked with a young Gregor Selasie. Mahalia's father?

"If you have such contempt for me, why did you come?"

"Join me." Celestina clutched Mahalia's hand and swallowed her bitter laughter. "We could work together for an Interzonal Peace Treaty."

"I'm flattered." Mahalia squeezed Celestina's rough fingers. "But I'm not your girl. Try Ed Lopez or Geraldine Kitt—an ethnic-throwback genius. Or Jocelyn Williams. She has decent vision for a politician."

"Why not you?"

"I'm a scientist." Mahalia pulled free. "That's all I ever wanted to be."

"After your father died, you pledged to honor his vision, but you've been wasting away in petty intrigue and bureaucracy-hell."

"You hacked my private files?" Mahalia bristled.

Celestina danced on the plate, praying for a way out of murder. "Think of the intellectual exchange across the Barrier if—"

"Peace is still in the fantasy stages. I'm on the verge of an actual breakthrough—maybe to another universe! I'll never be this sharp again. I can't waste myself waiting around for dimwit politicians to see the light." A weaver ant dropped from the ceiling and landed in Mahalia's bangs. She shook her head violently, and the ant crash-landed on the ground. "My father *and* mother waited around for Peace and Enlightenment, and it killed them both. I want time in my prime, not ten years from now, not after I'm dead."

Celestina snatched up the dazed ant before Mahalia could squash it under her foot. "Yes, after you're dead, it's hard to appreciate...time." The ant stung Celestina four times. "You remind me of me."

"Now *that's* arrogant."

Celestina pocketed the angry bug. "The intellectual gangster bit."

Mahalia narrowed her eyes as she considered this, but the sight of hundreds of ant strands dangling from the ceiling startled her. "The Hall's infested."

Celestina grabbed her leg to stop her from squashing an ant running in circles. "They won't bother us. Weaver ants are my totem insects."

"Sorry, I didn't realize..."

Celestina pounded her staff against the bronze plate.

"Are you cursing me out in Healer drum-speak? I'm not as ignorant as you think."

"No. I've been holding out on myself," Celestina said. "But no more."

A Barrier tentacle arced across the room and splashed the crystal head of the staff. Mahalia jumped from the now hot bronze plate back onto the synth-marble floor. Colorful arabesques morphed across translucent walls and ceiling.

"Are you doing that?" Mahalia's windowpane eyes glistened.

"The Barrier is." Celestina's voice cracked . "I'm rusty. I haven't corridored in the Barrier since Thandi died."

"Died?" Mahalia snorted. "Let's quit equivocating. I know Robin Wolf studied the *Final Lessons*."

"The fragments she'd stolen from Thandiwe."

"*Vermittler* and the Barrier itself are genetic transformations, products of symbiogenesis." Mahalia gasped as Celestina snagged a second Barrier tentacle with her staff and hurled it against the wall.

"Go on, go on, talk! It grounds me," Celestina said. Her hands shook. "This is more difficult than I remember."

Mahalia licked her lips. "In an extension of Gaia Theory, Wolf saw the Barrier as an emergent life form; not an organism, but like Earth, composed of interconnecting ecosystems—a trans-organism, only operating on a vast, intergalactic, inter-dimensional scale."

Mahalia knew too much, but not enough. Celestina shuddered all over. "How very interesting."

"Not to anyone at Sagan Institute," Mahalia said.

Celestina grabbed Mahalia's arm so forcefully, she broke the skin. "Symbiogenesis is the creative engine of evolution, not genetic drift and fierce competition between random mutations. Biodiversity is a result of competition *and* cooperation." Her head lolled about as she whirled the staff overhead. "Join me, or…"

"Or what?" Mahalia stood stone still, curiosity overcoming fear. "As devout mainstream biologists, my colleagues dismiss a radical theory of symbiotic evolution."

"Well, only a very brave person can abandon her ideological home for an alien world." A third Barrier tentacle rushed through Celestina, and her body became translucent. She felt like a ghost hovering between worlds, waiting for a portal.

"The damn bio-corder's on the fritz." Mahalia fumbled with devices in her utility belt, and a light sweat bathed her face. "What are you doing?"

"Too long since I trusted myself to the *Final Lessons*," Celestina said. Colorful arabesques morphed across her body.

"What do you mean?"

"I've been avoiding my mind. Time to initiate myself to all my secrets."

Experience was the true teacher. That's what Mahalia needed to persuade her. As strands of weaver ants reached for the feather at the nape of her neck, Celestina pulled Mahalia onto the hot plate. "*Şotito şododo şoora ma şika,*" she said. "Perform truth, perform righteousness, perform kindness, avoid cruelty,"

The bronze plate was a pool of sparks. Spacetime fractured, and the Great Hall vanished. Electric rainbows arched above their heads and scurried under foot. Corridor walls hurtled by at enormous speed, twisting and turning so violently, the women were thrown off balance. Explosions of color cascaded across their bodies as other travelers passed through them. Sketches of life, alien and delicious, streaked across their mindscapes. Mahalia reminded Celestina of Kali, absolute night, mistress of time, surveying infinity. If they survived, Celestina would throw this vision in sand: Robin, Thandi, and Mahalia at eternity's gate—a mandala for Indian goddesses and scientists.

Forgotten mandala images from the Library of the Dead flooded Celestina. Thandiwe had repressed so many sweet memories, hiding any hint of the *Final Lessons* from Robin. For too many years she had been afraid to think her thoughts and ashamed of her treacherous selves. Celestina had been a poor *Geistesmutter*, unable to guide her daughters through tricky corridors and dangerous portals so that they might always find a way home.

Perhaps Sidi, Phoolan, and Elleni would forgive her. *Sing my song, daughters.*

Mahalia hollered a blues wail. The hurtling walls were still. Countless corridors of light ended at a black-hole crossroads. Celestina and Mahalia teetered at the edge of darkness. Mahalia balled a fist and held it to her lips as she sang. Tears streamed from her laughing eyes as she watched a universe give birth to itself out of the blackness. The jagged signatures of distant galaxies warped into impossible patterns then burst into clear constellations. A blue planet swathed in feathery clouds loomed close enough to hug. Voluptuous brown landmasses framed blue-green oceans teeming with life. Earth, a delicious bio-mosaic, was caught in a Barrier stranglehold. Massive eruptions shattered the watery face of the planet, burst a kidney-shaped continent, and hurled clouds of matter out into space. Mahalia's song fizzled in her throat. In no time the riot of Earth's life became a dull whimper, and the planet's core exploded.

"What are we seeing here?" Mahalia asked, face ashen, eyes bloodshot.

Celestina spoke with several tongues. "The Barrier calls for *Ebo Eje*."

"How does that work?" Mahalia flinched as the Barrier sucked up the shattered bits of the planet, leaving only a red slit.

"We could sacrifice ourselves and save the day or throw the world off its course."

Mahalia grabbed Celestina's shoulder and shook her. "Don't talk action-adventure nonsense."

"Right. Who do we think we are?" Celestina continued in two voices. "Who are you, Dr. Selasie? Robin never got to all the *Final Lessons*. Thandiwe betrayed everything she knew. And me? *Mo so awon enia mi po*. Who am I to tie all my people together? Certainly no Oshun, no divine warrior woman to ride people's spirits into tomorrow! That's too much to ask of this stepchild of the Barrier. I'm a thief, traitor, and assassin, a coward longing for death. Why mingle my spirits with eternity? Let *Vermittler* be *Ebo Eje* and join with the Barrier, they were born to it. I can't." She yelled into the darkness. "I just can't. Do you hear me? Let someone with a clear spirit save the day." She collapsed. "Only a brave person can abandon her ideological home for an alien world."

"Admit it, you're her, aren't you?" Mahalia whispered. "Robin's Healer informant, Thandiwe Xa Femi?"

"Worse, my dear, I'm Thandi *and* Robin."

Mahalia pursed her lips and blinked rapidly. "How is that possible?"

"Less possible by the second, and still I have miles to go and promises to keep."

"The Barrier did this to you. Double Consciousness, I've seen references... Give me full access to the *Final Lessons*. It's a treasure trove of the old knowledge lost during the Barrier wars. I could make sense of—"

The corridor crossroads and black-hole vista collapsed. Mahalia jumped off the bronze plate as her Teneather boots began to smoke. She stomped at the fire on her feet as the Great Hall of Images slammed into focus around them.

Celestina tried to stand up but couldn't. Desperation drained her. "I've shown you all there is. Vera Xa Lalafia said the *Final Lessons* are...an experience, what you make of your life, what you add to eternity."

Mahalia shook her head.

"How your life goes beyond this moment, from the ancestors to unborn dreams." Celestina was of too many minds, breaking apart, about to fly off in a thousand directions. "It was either share the secrets or kill you." Her eyes clouded over. "You must understand, or..." Her mouth her feet her organs her heart her soul began to slip away.

"I don't know what I understand," Mahalia said.

She gathered Celestina up in smooth hands and held her together with a song. And a choir sang near and far, yesterday and tomorrow, a crossover ceremony: Lawanda's astral lament, a dolphin's ululation, the Major sucking death from her lungs, and Elleni's funeral poem dissolving in a magenta sea:

Go down angels to the flood
Blow out the sun, turn the moon into blood!
Come back angels bolt the door
The time that's been will be no more!

Pheromone harmonies played tricks with her ears. Celestina's eyes fluttered open. Weaver ants sashayed across her nose, glided on her breath, and crawled in her ears. A colony swarmed over her and Mahalia, circling from hair to bare feet with vague intent.

"Snap out of it." Mahalia stood beside Celestina. Ants poured out of the ceiling in long strands, impossibly fast. Mahalia tried not to gag as old-lady soldier ants marched across her lips, fierce creatures with jagged pincers. "They're *your* totem insects, *do some shaman thing* before they decide to sting us to death!"

"Don't worry, no death today. Mercy." The ants revitalized Celestina, inspired her.

"I could get hysterical." Mahalia swallowed down a convulsion.

"We smell like home. Stay close to me."

"Where do you think I'm going?"

Celestina headed for the window at the end of the hall, her feet barely grazing the floor. "Whatever you do, don't fall on them," Celestina said. "You're their queen."

"Uh huh." Mahalia matched Celestina's graceful movements.

The transparent fiberplastic window didn't open and was shatterproof. Celestina raised an ant-covered hand to its streaked surface. "How'd they get in?"

"Who cares? I can't stand this another second." Mahalia's jazzy voice had gone nasal.

Celestina spotted a door onto a balcony. It was slightly ajar. "Two seconds more."

"No!" A fat ant tried to crawl up Mahalia's nose. Celestina flicked it aside with her tongue.

"Keep moving," she said before Mahalia became utterly paralyzed.

The door swung open at their approach. Celestina thrust Mahalia into cool twilight and tapped her with the Barrier staff. Mahalia quivered, and the ants fell away. Celestina did the same for herself, then watched as the ants regrouped.

"What now?" Mahalia's skin was gray. She had the wild eyes of a stallion about to bolt.

"Come on." Celestina ushered Mahalia back inside, careful not to crush a single ant. They pressed against the balcony door until a whoosh of air told them it had been sealed. Mahalia gulped a breath and gingerly patted herself down several times. Then she scratched herself violently.

Celestina gathered up her robe and medicine bag. "This will help." She offered Mahalia bag balm. "We've been here too long. It's getting dangerous. We should leave." She took in the Hall one last time.

Mahalia smeared ointment everywhere. "No arguments from me."

The lift plummeted, leaving Celestina's stomach on the top floor. Mahalia's cheeks were still ashen, but by the ground floor, her breath had evened out. "You came to kill me?" she asked.

"Maybe," Celestina said. "Standing at the crossroads and Eshu plays me for a fool. What did you have in mind for me?"

"I was kind of open-ended too."

They rode the slide-way back across the plaza in silence. The CRANIAC robot guards were beginning to revive; Celestina neutralized them again. After three tries she got the power nets back online. Nothing hindered their exit out of the security gate. They jogged down the maintenance alley past the sleeping tech and stumbled into the station just as passage to Los Santos was announced. Tourists and commuters barged into them, forcing them to the center of the waiting room.

"The ҉Promised Land҉ spiraled into auto-destruct yesterday. Your data cache is nothing but static."

"That was the least I could do," Celestina said.

"I take it they wouldn't welcome me with open arms in New Ouagadougou."

"You'll have to assimilate the *Final Lessons* on your own," Celestina said dryly.

"You'll get better people to help with the Peace Treaty."

"Better than you? I don't think so." Celestina dropped a sluggish weaver ant into her medicine bag. "You're fearless."

"Symbiogenesis is not on the screen in Paradigma, so I'm taking my underground choir to Los Santos. They'll let me do what I want."

"Promises, promises."

"I'm not naïve. I won't just be a gangster stooge."

"I'm sure you believe that." Celestina brushed rough fingers across Mahalia's forehead. "What a young fool you are. I could shatter your spine with a thought, and it could end here and now."

"Is that what you did to Robin?" Mahalia blinked back tears.

Celestina tasted alora poison in her mouth and Femi's staff slashing her brain with hot Barrier tentacles. "I became her." She hugged Mahalia. "Even a twilight civilization chasing down decline can be reborn. In the Barrier, you saw what I saw. You're my *Geistestochter* now, one spirit, no enemies. We tie the world together."

"Yes. Your first Treaty negotiation." Mahalia pressed Celestina to her heart. Audio-Electro proclaimed the impending Friday evening power-outage and final boarding for Angel City. Reluctantly, Mahalia broke from the embrace and hurried toward the Los Santos transport. She turned, bright eyes flashing, hair dancing against insolent hips, and smiled at Celestina. "I'll surprise you in the end."

"Please do. I'm counting on it," Celestina said, and then the crowd swallowed Mahalia whole.

BOOK VII

We have what Martha Graham has called "blood memory" that transcends those things that can be put into words and must instead be understood in the marrow of the bones, the rhythm of the heart, the fullness of the womb.

Pearl Cleage

68: Cross-Barrier Transmission/Personal
(October 16, Barrier Year 115)

From: Lawanda

To: Elleni

It's all my fault. Didn't know what I was walkin' into. Captain jump right in front of my sorry ass. She take a spray a bullets liberatin' one of Perez's transports for our getaway. I don't even get nicked. I hear slugs slam into muscles and snap thru bones. Bulletproof vest don't do her much good—gangstas got shit that crack thru armor. I'm lucky they can't afford smart bullets, go right thru one body and fuck up somebody else. Captain's vest save me. All this time, I been stuck on myself and riskin' her life.

Wild-child foolishness stop right then and there, but it be too late. Captain throwin' me in the transport, her whole left side all crumpled up, and she be leakin' too much blood. Dyin', and for what? I ain't accomplish diddly squat in Los Santos. This Zone be a bigger mess now than when I hit the scene. Feel like my heart goin' explode.

I'm thinkin' high-speed auto-drive goin' save our asses—for a minute. Then the sick motherfuckers be on our tail. What's the point? They can't catch us, but we can't shake 'em, either. I try to stop the Captain from bleedin' her life away, but the med-unit say it don't look too good, tellin' me how long we ain't got, like a oracle or some crap. I don't want no death prescription/prophecy. I'ma live this thang one second at a time, in the now, not worryin' 'bout the end. 'Sides, ain't hardly no blood left in the Captain, her heart be pumpin' will. Who know how long that can last?

Done run outa gas and be sittin' up against a wind sculpture with the Captain in my arms. She ain't never been what you call talkative, and you know how I hate quiet. Rappin' back and forth with someone, that's when I'm home free. Captain savin' everythin' she got for her next breath, ain't wastin' nothin' on words.

Sister Shaman *Vermittler*, we sure could use you doin' *Vodun* and workin' Chi miracles like you do.

Lakota call this place *mako sica*, bad land. I hear that. Beat-up gullies and cliffs, desolate beauty, kinda lonely in the dark. Make you wanna reach out and touch someone you love. The chill in the air bitin' at skin—enuf to make your teeth chatter. Captain shiverin' so hard, feel like she goin' shake my bones outa whack. The sun ain't rise yet, but it's comin' fast, horizon be on fire. That should warm us up.

A silver moon's floatin' like a feather 'tween this umbrella rock column and a big booty boulder, look like a giant bending over, lettin' her naked cheeks catch the breeze. Mighty booty! Gotta smile at a sister so bad, she eat volcano ash, wash it down with a river, and pick million-year fossils outa her teeth. Badlands indeed! We surrounded by all these booties, steeples and spires, a cathedral of rocks, and the echoes of engines.

Perez's squad on the case.

I figure 'tween all the steeples and booty, this as good a place as any in the world to die. So I just fall down and wait for the sun to come. Captain want me to leave her here. Say she goin' die one way or another. Say the drugs she blow to counter auto-bomb squad in her head be lethal. Ain't no escape clause. I been knowin' that. But I can't leave her to kick it alone. Where am I goin' from here, anyhow?

Perez's soirée was a bust. 'Fore we could hook it with Dancers, all hell break loose. Random power jam! Then rebel Extras sabotage Perez's private generators. Folk in revolt bust thru useless power nets, trash his whole movie-set mansion, "Tara" or some shit. Up in flames. Extras blamin' Perez for virus breakout. He ain't do this nasty all by hisself, but I peep the underground labs 'fore Extras torch Tara. Ants and mites, human organs, and babies on ice. Babies! That's what Jocelyn, Danny, and Sidi be up to. Totally out of order, the Major too. I don't care how they try to dress it up.

I be paralyzed, scopin' this shit. Captain drag me outa there, say it's not good to look on so much ugly, 'specially when you can't do somethin' immediate. Dream team ain't make the ETA with our transport and not a blip on the Electro. Security codes all changed up. I figure our own side against us now, plus these rebel Extras be really off the hook. I don't blame 'em, but me and the Captain ain't part of they revolution solution, so we just gotta move outa the way. In the middle of mayhem, I scan Aaron D. and posse, seem like they thick with the rebels, rescuin' folk and shit. Big Arab tear it up with that twisted sword of his. Aaron got on burnoose and billowy pants too. He be dodgin' bullets to pick up wounded Extras and carry 'em to they transport. Risk hisself over and over, but Captain ain't trustin' none of these gangstas for a ride. She say Dunkelbrot's posse be a good diversion at the vehicle corral. While they showin' down with Perez's mob, we try for a getaway to Wounded Knee.

Busted. Perez ain't studyin' Aaron D. Sucker chase us six hours at suicide speed, 'til funky stolen transport's runnin' on empty. Captain say we all goin' be stranded in nowhere. Wounded Knee be off the map—Barrier distortin' the geography. We could zoom right by and never know. Sound hopeless to me, but the Captain steady schemin'. We redirect auto-drive, slow down for a beat, jump out, then let the vehicle just go on off by itself. We head for the hills, but don't get very far. Captain's not heavy—my muscles just too run down to carry her. Course when stolen transport finally hit empty, Perez and Co. get wise and be trackin' us like a mad dog.

Captain whisper her name to me, but I can't say it or spell it, sound old Hawaiian or somethin'. She ain't got the energy to be repeatin' herself so I pretend like I know what she say. Then she tell me they comin' and I gotta leave now or she'll never forgive me for wastin' her last breath. Tell me put a wall 'tween us and go now cuz I gotta *feed starvin' babies, stop the wars and extinctions, turn the tides of history...*

"Those goons just sound close," I say. "Anyhow, it's better to go down together than to go down alone."

"Better not to go down at all," she say.

"I ain't talkin' 'bout this," I say. Engines gettin' close now. "Look where we are."

Sun blaze over bronze mesas, offer us a grand view. Talk about wind sculpture! Badlands is serious gravity art, umbrella rocks balanced on spindly columns and booty boulders undulating across the horizon, flashing red and gold back at the sun.

"I can't see," Captain mutter. "My eyes are gone."

I describe everythin' best I can. Rabbit crawl out my pocket and nibble her nose 'fore I can catch it.

"Booty boulders?" Captain got tears in her empty eyes and be strokin' the rabbit with her pinky, so I guess she don't mind. "You can draw with words and still make me laugh. You're a much better storyteller than diplomat." We both laugh at that.

Engines cut out. We can hear voices comin' this way.

"It was all worth it. Thank you." She kiss the rabbit and push it toward me.

"Ambassador Kitt!" Perez got a voice amp and boom his shit to kingdom come. "You don't have to keep running. We didn't come to kill you. We've got medical for the Captain. She's lost a lot of blood." He pause. "Jocelyn Williams would like to talk with you."

"Get out of here now! The scrambler will confuse them." The Captain rally, like she pumpin' the last of her will. "Don't get stuck on stupid," she quote me. "Run as far as you can and when you hear me scream, use the last resort protocol. I want to go out like a volcano. That's my dying wish. Go find the Ghost Dancers and make a difference. Don't you dare waste me and get caught!" Breath rattle round in her throat. "Do what I say for once, for ME!" She pass out, her head fall against my belly, but she ain't all the way gone, yet. Perez and them be almost within spittin' distance.

I s'pose I can't argue with a dyin' wish.

Neither can you, Elleni. This feel like a live channel. You screenin' transmissions? Trance dancin', riffin' off the Barrier's multi-image chat? You don't have to talk back to me but get your butt to Wounded Knee for all of us.

Lawanda

69: Fire Mountain, outside *Seelenwald*
(October 17, Barrier Year 115)

Angels.

Sidi ripped Elleni and Mahalia from the Barrier's Celestina-archive before they knew what was happening. The return trip was so hot, Elleni's dreads got scorched. Soot from their crumbling tips stung her throat and eyes. A thousand stabs of pain made her gasp as Sidi dumped them at the brink of human reality.

Revolution solution.

Elleni ached to open a live channel to Lawanda, but magnetic pulses wrecked havoc between her thighs, sparks on her tongue obliterated words, and static scrambled her mindscape, clouding every sense. No matter how she tried to focus, the entrance chamber of Celestina's rock cabin remained a cacophonous blur. Elleni leaned against the gurney, clutched Mahalia's gummy fingers, and registered a flicker of Chi—though not enough of Sister Mahalia to guide her back to human.

What could you possibly do that would hurt me more than fail at your life?

Sidi denied her Barrier griot identity, yet her *Vermittler* genius already surpassed Elleni's. Phaseshifting through tricky portals, Sidi didn't need anybody to bring her back home—no wonder the Barrier called her to its bosom.

"No," Sidi said.

Far away or close, Elleni couldn't tell.

"Why would I lie?" Awa was hoarse. "Celestina's image-boards commune with the Barrier all over the world. I have studied the rhythm of its fluctuations. Whatever the Barrier intends to do, it will be very soon."

Elleni tried to pull herself together. Lawanda's message repeated in her ear, the Major's data glove tingled against her fingers, and Ray's last kiss lingered on her lips, but she needed flesh and blood to bring her home.

"We won't have this chance again," Duma said.

"I agree." Danny's flat Los Santos twang. "Seize the time."

"You would do this in cold blood?" Awa said.

"*Vermittler* threaten our future," Duma said softly. "Under the law—"

"*They* threaten our future?" Sidi laughed, a scary sound. "Shit on the road and you meet flies on your return."

"What do you mean?" Jocelyn asked.

"You are too casual with death warrants, Duma," Sidi said.

"Are you changing your tune, Sidi?" Jocelyn asked.

"Power concedes nothing without a bloody struggle. You want the ocean without the awful roar of its fierce waters, you want a blazing fire that doesn't burn." Duma passed off Frederick Douglass's wisdom for his own. "You knew we might be forced to extremes, Sidi. Even in New Ouagadougou."

"Exactly," said Danny. "Let's do the bitch while she's out of it."

"The Promised Land," Sidi whispered. "A leap of faith." Her face broke through the veil of chaos for an instant, but Elleni could not read her expression.

"Listen to me!" Awa was shouting. "A dark cloud, a wound in the Barrier, is spreading over the Black Hills in Los Santos. Elleni must attend to—"

"Don't give me Healer mystic bullshit!" Danny was shouting, too.

Scuffling feet.

"Are you threatening me?" Awa said.

"Restrain yourself, Danny boy," Jocelyn said. "This isn't a gangster hit."

Grumbling in the background. The storm troopers were restless.

Awa sucked her teeth. "Barrier fever. You should all leave, before you do something you regret."

Danny talked over Awa. "In Los Santos we don't give trouble a second chance. Fuck that, nobody hardly has a first chance."

"Awa's right, this is ill-considered." Jocelyn's voice shook. "The Barrier's—"

"Think too much, it's like standing still, you're a target," Danny said. "Grab the image-boards and staffs." Elleni was certain she heard him cock a gun. "Out of the way, old broad, unless you want to be part of the fireworks."

"You're giving orders?" Jocelyn said.

"When will such an opportunity present itself again?" Duma said.

"I don't believe this," Sidi's disks punched holes in the atmosphere and the acrid smell of ozone filled Elleni's nose. Prickly magnetic squiggles off the Barrier made her dizzy.

"I won't walk away," Awa said. "Not this time. Not ever again."

Please, don't do anything reckless. Elleni tried to touch Awa's mindscape.

"Come on, Ford, put the gun down!" Jocelyn's voice was shrill. "Put the goddamned gun down!"

"I hold the circle with Elleni," Awa whispered.

"This ain't the time to take a stand, but suit yourself," Danny said.

"You're a fool—" Sidi's words got lost in the scuffle, but her disks gathered around Elleni. Bullets ricocheted off the violet spirals and clattered against the walls. Djembe drums bellowed, and lute strings wailed.

"I warned you," Awa said. There were holes in her voice.

Elleni tasted blood on the air. As a Barrier claw slashed a dark blur to thin wisps, screams echoed off the vaulted ceilings.

70: The Badlands

(October 17, Barrier Year 115)

> The Last Days... People be past masters at imaginin' the end of
> the world—Armageddon, Ragnarök, Götterdämmerung, Apocalypse
> Now, the Big Crunch—doom and gloom in the twilight of the
> Gods—but folk're hard put to imagine a new day where we get on
> with each other, where we tear it up but keep it real. Why is that?
> It's an ole question, but I gotta keep askin'.
> —Geraldine Kitt, *Junk Bonds of the Mind*

The Major stood in a crowd of born-again Sioux, hidden by the
Eshu mask, crying himself sick. He had to be dreaming. Naked
data-glove fingers tingled, recalling a ceaseless interplay of percep-
tion, information, and analysis. A black hole sucked the sun beyond
the event horizon. This spectacle aroused curiosity, not sadness.
Something else pained him. He jerked awake.

The lethal buzz at the back of his mind had gone silent. *Was für
ein Wunder.*

The Major glanced at Ray, hunched in the driver's seat of the
plush mini-tank, and wondered if he looked as wrecked as the
aging star. They could both use a year of R&R. "We there yet?"
he said—and then remembered the shockwave from beyond his
dream that had yanked him to consciousness. "What was that?"

Ray frowned at the viewscreen. "Explosion. Twenty minutes
away."

The Major squinted at the unfamiliar instrument panel.
"Opinion or fact?"

"I wasn't at ground zero, but I saw giant boulders tumble down
and a cloud of sand and flames shoot up in the sky. Could have been
rocks doing the nasty, getting all hot and bothered. Dawn in the
Badlands, who knows, but..."

"Any vehicles?"

"Not in the vicinity." Ray grabbed his chin and shook his jaw
up and down.

"Survivors?"

"Human metabolism's not jumping out at me."

"This is a sophisticated rig."

"Glad you approve." Ray worked the command board.

"What're you doing?" the Major asked.

"We're going to check it out."

As they shifted course, the Major gripped the animal tapestries on the dashboard. He was not in command, more like a refugee/prisoner than a guest/passenger and at the mercy of a reformed gangster. Despite their silence, the smart bombs in his head might still be operational. The margin of error for the Wounded Knee mission was slim.

"Tell me it's too risky, we should stay on task." Ray pulled the Major's fingers from a syn-silk menagerie of extinct mammals. "But don't wreck the merchandise."

"You're a living legend. Recklessness is your *modus operandi*."

Chuckling, Ray powered up weapons and stuffed flowers from a plant hanging over the seats into his mouth.

"I'm glad you at least are amused," the Major said.

Ray thrust flowers under his nose. "Alora, Healer remedy, clears your head."

"No thanks."

Ray jammed the whole stalk into his mouth, barely chewing before swallowing. "What would anybody want to blow up around here?"

"Curiosity is a dangerous luxury," the Major said.

"I thought you were some big scientist, snooping out any and everything, or is that just the ad-copy?" Ray downed a frothy brew from his medicine bag, followed by what appeared to be live ants. Fire-virus cure? His pupils dilated, a light sweat broke out on his neck and brow, and the sneer slid off his face.

"I'm not...who I used to be," the Major said.

"Welcome to the club."

As they wound through a maze of canyon walls, the roadbed disintegrated, and the mini-tank slowed. The Major's throat tightened with the dream sadness again. Desperate, he buzzed Lawanda's

Electro but got nothing, not even static, as if the channel had been expunged. A sign? He quashed his panic and focused his attention on the geological marvel flashing across the viewscreen. Wind and sporadic rain had carved windows, arches, and pipe-organ columns in the bare rock. The stratification of volcanic ash, clay, sand, and silt told a seventy-five-million-year story.

"Hell of a party," Ray said as they neared ground zero. The blast had toppled sandstone mushroom caps, amputated red clay fingers, and shattered volcanic ash minarets. Displaced boulders littered the road, forcing the mini-tank to a halt. "FYI, I swept for mines and anything bomb-like. *Nada.*" Ray patted a gelatinous blob tucked under the front viewscreen. "The bio-computer doesn't lie to me if I feed her right."

"We shall see," the Major said.

Ray tossed an enviro-suit at him. At least paranoid gangster-types took healthy precautions before their reckless acts. As the Major snapped his helmet in place, Ray jumped out the side hatch. The blast site was a black gouge in sand—no signs of life or even recognizable debris.

"Let's look around," Ray shouted over the Electro. The Major shadowed him wordlessly. What did Ray expect to find that the bio-computer had overlooked? Ray read his mind as if it were an open screen. "Crazy, I know but..."

The traces of secondary explosion events radiated out from ground zero for a hundred meters. Debris had smashed into a crimson rock wall that looked like a mortar and pestle. They stared at it for several minutes without blinking.

Ray undid his helmet and sucked a deep breath of canyon air. "The cold feels good," he said, and the Major followed suit. Dark clouds blew in on a chill wind from the north. Ray scooped up a shrapnel souvenir. He rubbed a soot-blackened pendant against his enviro-suit sleeve. "A volcano or something...with writing on it."

The Major snatched it. "It says 'Mokuaweoweo Mauna Loa.'" He shuddered. Clamping down on non-professional bodily reactions was getting harder by the second.

"Mokuaweoweo what?" Ray repeated the name with ease.

"Mokuaweoweo is the caldera—mother crater—in Mauna Loa, a Hawaiian volcano," the Major replied. "Mauna Loa means 'long mountain.' She said she should have been named for Mauna Kea, 'white mountain,' a snowcapped volcano. Her hair's been like snow since twelve, but nobody could have predicted that at birth."

Ray squeezed the Major's quivering shoulder. "Who we talking about here?"

The Major shrugged Ray's hand away. "This belonged to the Captain of Lawanda's security. She never took it off. Mokuaweoweo Mauna Loa is her…was her name. I gave her the pendant after…" He flashed on beads of rain cascading across brown velvet muscles, white hair slicked close to the scalp, and the hint of a smile in her dimples and at the corners of her eyes. She'd won their marksmen contest by one impossible shot in a moving vehicle, during a storm. She had had a knack for beating the odds.

"You and Mokuaweoweo were lovers?" Ray said off-handedly.

"She's dead now, so what does it matter."

"Somebody loved her, somebody will miss her." Ray sounded like a two-bit web-gram.

"Lawanda most likely triggered last-resort protocol, but the Captain expected to get blown and packed other explosives."

"The Captain and Lawanda ambushed each other? Doesn't sync up." Ray shook his head. "What's wrong with your hand? It's all red."

The Major snarled. "Lawanda's probably dead, and somebody loved her too." He spit the words through clenched teeth. "Both of them, blown to bits, right here."

"We don't know that," Ray said. "*Habeus corpus*, before we accuse the Captain, before we accuse anybody, right?" He put his hand on the Major's shoulder again.

The Major pinned Ray's arm behind his back and shoved his face into the dirt. Before he could snap Ray's arm out of its socket or break his neck, the action-adventure hero threw sand in his eyes and jammed a knee into his balls. The Major laughed at the pain, lost his footing in the gravel, and Ray rolled free.

"What're you doing?" the Major asked. "You know a few studio moves and you think that'll stand up against real training?"

"You're talking shit, man." Ray stood up, rubbing his arm. "Get a grip."

"I told them to kill each other!" Dust devils and puffs of snow blew against his feverish skin. Ray backed away from him. "No Jolt-opera jingle for that, huh?"

"I know about murdering someone you love." Ray had tears in his eyes.

"I read the file. How old were you, twelve?"

"Fourteen." Ray bowed his head. "The weather's getting ugly, let's go." Half the sky was storm clouds spitting snow, the other half azure with a blazing sun. Ray took the Major by the arm, as if they were old buddies helping each other through rough times. "Wounded Knee's where Elleni said we'd find Lawanda."

"No. *They murdered each other because of me.*" The Major flung Ray at the nearest boulder. Ray twisted in the air, vaulted through a sandstone archway, and landed on his toes. The Major felt fleeting relief until Ray headed back for him. "You don't know when to quit."

"I know Lawanda would want you to quit farting around and get yourself to Wounded Knee!"

"I'm warning you. I can't count on myself."

Ray snatched up their helmets. "I'd leave your fascist ass right here, but if I did Lawanda would hunt me down, from the hereafter even. Elleni, too. So what'll it be? You gonna kill me? Or you gonna let me help you back to the damn mini-tank?"

The Major had Ray's own laser-blade at his throat. "I'm a merciless killing machine."

"Celestina said, we change the past with the actions we take now. Live each moment like it's forever."

"From web-gram to Healer aphorism." The Major released him. "Lawanda said you could sell a man his own piss as the champagne of bottled beer."

"She told you that? Rough character—can't put anything over her."

"I was willing to sacrifice Mokuaweoweo and Lawanda. How's that for love?" He sagged. Ray hoisted him out of the gravel. "Tell me she's not dead," the Major pleaded as they stumbled back toward the mini-tank.

"I need back-up at Wounded Knee, man, can't do this real-life adventure stuff all by myself." More pop psych, but Ray played it sincere. "Let's just keep going."

The Major corralled disorderly thoughts and raging emotion. He was a good actor too. "Okay. Okay. You can count on me."

71: Fire Mountain, outside *Seelenwald*
(October 17, Barrier Year 115)

Jocelyn broke the silence. "Is he dead?"
Vision still failed Elleni. Had the Barrier attacked Danny?
"You-all leave now," Sidi said.
The draft from the open door made Elleni itch as storm troopers rushed into the storm. Sidi's breath bathed her face, fetid mangoes and sour cream. Elleni reached for her with hair and hands. Sidi buried damp cheeks in wounded braids, and allowed herself a single whimper. Elleni wasn't the only one who needed flesh-and-blood contact.

"I'm sure we can salvage something," Jocelyn said. "All is not lost."

Sidi's heart thudded against Elleni's. "No. All is not lost."

"He's going to bleed to death," Jocelyn said.

"I'll take care of him," Duma said.

"*Deine Seele ist billig*," Awa said.

"What's she saying?" Jocelyn asked.

"His soul is cheap," Awa said. "He will not dance with my ancestors."

Anchored to Sidi, Elleni corridored back to human. The *Vermittler* sisters clutched each other in a foggy tunnel just beyond the entrance chamber. Beside them in the gurney, Mahalia faded, and an angry Barrier crackled at their backs. Awa leaned against a bloodstained wall as gargoyle troopers dragged a body past her, into the blizzard. Jocelyn retreated behind them, clutching spotted fake fur against her chest.

Danny stared at the gun smoking in his hand. Tufts of rainbow hair had been scraped from his scalp. Blood streamed from a gash in his neck as if one of Sidi's disks had almost slit his throat. "I won't let rebel Extras take center screen and X our way of life."

"Quiet." Duma, his limp silver hair splattered with blood, sealed Danny's arteries with recon-skin. He turned to Awa.

"Stay away from me." Awa held up a warning hand. "You are no enemy, but no friend either."

"What holds you to these people?" Elleni asked Sidi.

"We must lead everybody, not just those who agree with us," Sidi said.

Elleni nodded as the Major's glove sent stabs of pain up her arm. "Do you lead them or they you?"

Sidi shivered but did not answer.

Duma gathered Femi's staff from the ground. "This is not defeat."

Sidi snapped at him. "What are you still doing here? Leave now."

Duma opened his mouth to speak, but instead scooped the wounded Danny into his arms and hurried out into the snow.

"Danny tried to shoot me?" Elleni passed quivering fingertips through Sidi's disks. A delicious tingle cascaded up her arms.

"Yes." Sidi drew away from their intimate encounter. "The Barrier slashed one of his comrade thugs, and I..."

"You blocked the bullets," Elleni said.

"Danny sees you as a threat to his gangster way of life," Sidi said.

"And *Tutu* Sidi gets people to do what they already want to do, na?"

Sidi bit her lip. "Duma wanted to shove you into the Barrier with Dr. Selasie, before your strength returned."

Elleni's hair bristled. "Send me back where I came from, where I belong? What?"

"I had hoped it wouldn't come to this." Sidi brushed soot from Elleni's face. "I'd blame Barrier fever, but I know Duma."

Elleni grabbed Sidi's hand before she could stroke her cheek again. "Let the Barrier do the dirty deed, then not his fault that he must take my stool at Council."

"Deep desire can be appallingly shallow." Sidi shook free of Elleni. "*Billige Seele.*"

"Challenge Duma and Danny's cynical politics—"

"I don't care what Awa thinks the image-boards proclaim, I don't see what you see." She hesitated. "I have risked you for *my* vision. For that I am sorry. Forgive me."

"I don't know if I can," Elleni said in spite of her desire to do just that.

"You saved me once from the fire virus. Now, I saved you." Sidi pressed her hands against Mahalia's gurney. "We're even."

"No," Elleni said. "I was never in a league of murderers trying to kill you."

"Pro-Treaty forces would kill New Ouagadougou. What's the difference?" Sidi said.

Her words smacked Elleni. "I see your point, but..."

Mahalia shuddered on the air cushion. Her last breaths rattled in her chest.

"Help me with this. She's our spirit sister after all." Sidi's almond eyes were wet.

Elleni nodded and then whispered to Mahalia. "To the Promised Land."

Mahalia seemed to smile as they rolled her into the Barrier. *I'll surprise you in the end.* Her voice from another time, from now.

"*Mojubar Egun.* I give homage to the ancestors. Greet them for me," Elleni said.

"*Dide dide lalafia.* Arise, arise in peace," Sidi said.

"*Was für ein Wunder ist das Leben,* but this day it is hard to rejoice, even in miracles." Elleni and Sidi spoke this line together as Mahalia crossed over. A shower of sparks and fragrances that Elleni couldn't place filled the tunnel. She thought she saw a chariot of angels, but when she blinked, they were gone. The Barrier was riffing on images from her mindscape.

Sidi turned from the dazzling display and headed into the blizzard.

"Where are you going?" Elleni ran after her. "I thought…"

"What?" Sidi's disks lined up like missiles ready to attack.

Elleni stepped back. "Revolution solution…" She quoted Lawanda helplessly.

Sidi laughed at her. "You thought we spirit sisters might take up Celestina's torch?"

"Is that so funny?"

"Answer this," Sidi said and continued to walk away. Her disks whirled so fast, their rotations hurt Elleni's eyes. "Why should the Barrier bother to destroy us? Obviously, *we* can do that all by ourselves. Why should the Barrier call for *Ebo Eje*? *We* require human sacrifice, not an extra-dimensional behemoth capable of…" She waved her hands to indicate the unfathomable. "Why should the Barrier be concerned with us at all?"

"I can't answer that." Elleni stumbled around the hot spring.

"Exactly." Sidi gathered up her flame-red fleece and hovered in the doorway. "I don't doubt the visions you've seen, just the meaning you would make of them. The Barrier is beyond our petty human melodramas."

"You think I haven't questioned myself?" Elleni was riddled with doubt. "But this is a critical moment. We must risk action before full understanding."

"There's no time, these are the last days: is that it?" Sidi groaned. "Have you swallowed cargo-cult, Ghost-Dancer mythology? Manna will rain from heaven and evil will be vanquished if you and I make the ultimate sacrifice, walk naked and silent into a Barrier black hole—and if not, the Earth will be destroyed!" Sidi shook her head.

"We all see a different story." Elleni tried to step closer, but whirling disks sliced through the air in front of her face, forcing her to draw back quickly.

"Who knows if we ever understand what we see?" Sidi said softly.

"Come to Wounded Knee. Perhaps the answer is there."

"You believe there's an answer hidden somewhere, waiting to be found by us?"

Elleni shook achy dreads which, despite lacerations and burns, hissed at Sidi's disks. "I don't know what I believe."

"That's your problem, not mine." Sidi thrust her arms into the red fleece coat. "I'm sorry I couldn't stop all the bullets." As she disappeared into the white out, the blizzard filled the cabin.

Elleni shivered more from Sidi's absence than from an icy wind blowing against bare skin and wounded hair. She stared into the maze of snow squalls, desperate for a miracle, desperate for Sidi's change of heart. She ached to see flame-red fleece blazing through the storm as Sidi came racing back. Acid dripped from Elleni's injured hair. She'd known all along that Sidi would never join her for *Ebo Eje*, and yet secretly she'd fantasized their suicide run into the Barrier, a transcendent erotic adventure, with Sidi utterly bewitched by Elleni's Barrier prowess and selfless courage.

Her braids hissed in her ears. That fantasy was more suited to Ray. On fire with jungle fever, of course *he* would go all the way to anywhere with Elleni. She had always been so pathetically grateful for his jealous passion...but what beside Jolt-opera reruns and stuntman thrills and spills did he have to recommend his spirit?

Elleni flicked yellow tears into the hot spring. She couldn't keep straight why she was doing anything. Was she a messiah wannabe like Duma, hungry for glory and fame? A dutiful daughter, sacrificing herself to the legacy of her late, great *Geistesmutter*? A Barrier junkie, who, at the behest of a monster lover, contemplated *Ebo Eje* with the Wovoka—a megalomaniacal demagogue? Was she an action-adventure hero trying to save the world from a planet-eating enigma? Or *Murahachibu*, dying to prove them all wrong?

As usual, Sidi was right. Elleni was drowning in uncertainty.

"Don't let Sidi destroy the faith you have in yourself, in peace. *Keine Feinde*," Awa said, tapping the door shut with her wand. "No enemies, not even yourself. Those who love you are not deluded." Had she touched Elleni's mindscape? "You must hurry to Wounded Knee. I know a short cut. I took the Wovoka when he was young."

Elleni looked at Awa and gasped. She hadn't noticed the blood staining the old woman's hair and robes. The bullets Sidi's disks had not stopped had found their mark in Awa's body.

"Flesh wounds. Don't worry about me." Did she lie? Elleni moved toward her, but Awa thrust the beaded wand at Elleni. "For your medicine bag."

Elleni took it reluctantly. "I am honored, but—"

"A shout or even a whisper can bring on an avalanche."

A thunderous roar, as if from a collapsing snow mountain, shook the door.

"What are you doing?" Elleni said.

"Stealing some time." Awa's eyes flashed. "What are a trillion snowflakes against their techno-wizardry?" She leaned against the wall under the sand painting of Mahalia hugging Thandiwe and Robin. She glanced up at them and smiled. "That is how I like to remember them. How will you remember me?"

"Alive," Elleni said and glided toward her.

72: Cross-Barrier Transmission/Personal
(October 17, Barrier Year 115)

From: Lawanda

To: Herself

Still hangin' in, but don't know what I'ma do without the Captain.

7-Stories and his bad boys scope me dashin' thru the Badlands and just haul me up outa there. Nosy motherfuckers don't even ask why I'm on the run with neon blue slime all down my coveralls, all over everythin'. Sittin' up in those booty boulders and bio-computer fart-blue antidote goo on me and the Captain. Perez be tryin' to poison gas our asses, and we done lost our enviro-suits way back when. Sister Geraldine program for all kinda funky sabotage. Everybody savin' my booty, like I'm so special.

I scramble up in the Achbar's transport squawkin' and shakin', like Death doin' the Funky Chicken. The hunka bio-junk I'm luggin' wheeze somethin' awful. Achbar put a cool hand on my hot cheek and say, "We're on our way to Wounded Knee."

"Pull yourself together. We'll talk later." 7-Stories brush lips 'cross my forehead in a half kiss then give me a quick hug, like he 'fraid I'ma break. "Good to see you."

I know he dyin' of curiosity. I mean they had to hear the explosions—beaucoup echoes feedin' back in that canyon maze 'til it sound like the end of the world, but the man restrain hisself, try to show respect. Achbar hand me a wad of protein sticky while 7-Stories clear out a corner of the transport for me to cry myself silly. Pigeons over my head coo at me.

I don't ask who these folk crammed up in there be or why they headin' where I'm headin'. What the fuck, you know? I just feed the bio-computer protein sticky and feel sorry for myself. Nasty little beast so hungry, 'llowed to suck my hand off. Almost pitch it out the viewscreen. Ain't got no space for temperamental organic antics.

The Captain be just ash on the wind now that her flame's died down. And I'm the one that do it to her. I be creepin' on the other side of a booty ridge when I hear her scream. I know Perez be torturin' her so the longer I procrastinate, the more she goin' suffer. She already suffer too much on my account. How can these be her final moments? Knowin' I can put the Captain outa her misery make it easier, but I wouldn't recommend last-resort protocol to my dog. What kinda twisted sucker sit 'round and think up nasty shit like that for a person to do?

My hands won't stop shakin'. Rabbit poop in my pocket, and I don't even care. Transmittin' to my damn self, cuz the Electro's all locked up on this scrambled input from a node that the bio-computer claim don't even exist. Now, how am I goin' be hallucinatin' Electro transmissions and recordin' my hallucinations? Bio-computer don't usually be trippin', but ghost sonata broadcast overload the memory with encrypted slop, and bio-computer block other transmissions, dump files, and compress shit to make room for imaginary code! Damn genius machines in cahoots, workin' me.

Captain'd be all over this mystery, bustin' truth outa nothin'. Yeah, well, she dead and I gotta finish this adventure on my own even if I feel like nothin', all icy and hollow without the Captain, without the Major. I book outa that canyon and don't even grab a bit of her to hold onto, for when the smoke clear. But the cathedral rocks catch her last breath. Badlands be filled with her spirit. Couldn't ask for a better monument.

Ain't got no fond last memory of the Major, but I miss his ass all the same and worry what nasty they doin' to him too. Ouch.

Achbar say we drivin' off the map. Barrier distortin' everythin', comin' and goin'. Seem like we gettin' nowhere fast then we bump right into the shit. 7-Stories be offerin' Wounded-Knee sentinels a buncha feathers. Stony-faced guards crack up, "Feathers get you here, they don't get you in, what do you take us for?"

The Achbar be tight with these rebels tho. He say ain't one unstable compound in our group and the Wovoka be expectin' us. Guards go for it.

With all the hype and heat, I step outa the transport and don't know what I expect at Wounded Knee—bloody ground scream-in'? But it's just a windin' creek, rollin' grasslands, and a cemetery for the Minnicoujou-Lakota massacred long ago. Seventh Cavalry chase down unarmed women and children for miles, leave battered bodies frozen in agony, then after the blizzard thaw, dump 'em in a mass grave. Cavalryman on the big gun cop the Congressional Medal of Honor for uncommon valor.

Cold.

Maybe I think I'ma taste blood on the wind, smell injustice in grass and dirt, hear echoes of wasted lives. Spirits in the dark, lost one bitter winter night, they musta find some peace by now. Hope so anyhow. I don't know who I think the Wovoka goin' be, mad-man or saint, or what folk he goin' call back to life from the Big B. Massacred Indians, Jesus Christ, Sitting Bull, Buddha, Martin Luther King, Nelson Mandela, Celestina Xa Irawo, my dead Nana, or drylongso great people nobody even know? The Captain maybe? I ain't expectin' magic. The Barrier be all over spacetime—life and death miracles ain't outa its reach.

I'm breathin' deep now, cuz this a holy place, a gatherin' of forc-es. Folk're on the case beatin' back the madness. I feel my spirit soar for a minute, then *snap!* born-again Sioux fall out to greet us, some in white robes with moss headdresses and silvered faces, others in great coats and furry caps, and a sharp-featured brother sportin' a war bonnet of blue-eyed turkey feathers. He have almost nappy green hair, electric eyes, and silver skin that flow like a river. The Wovoka. He nod at me and make me shiver. Everybody huggin' and kissin', like it's a party and we're honored guests. Wovoka don't touch nobody, 'cept you feel him sneakin' thru your skin and havin' a look-see. And that skin of his, damn, it never settle down, like he ain't all in this spacetime either. Make Miss Freaky Thang look like a home girl.

Snow blowin' down my back, and the sun's still hot on our faces. The weather don't know what season to be. Lady from Achbar's transport with gene art crawlin' 'cross her face got a Kora like

Elleni's, fifty strings on a calabash big as a booty boulder. She kiss the ground then start playin', a torrent of beauty that vibrate bones. Crowd get still—her music draw us together, everybody feelin' everybody else. I get a hush in my soul.

"In memoriam. We remember Mahalia Selasie, as she remembered us." The Wovoka kinda throat sing, different notes piled on top each other. Seem like he got a voice amp projectin' his five-tone talk right into my head. "Before she left us this final time, Mahalia said to me: never a good day to die, but I have lived long enough."

Scattered voices keen that line. I figure it mean Mahalia was ready to die for what she believe. I look 'round wonderin' who the hell she was, but feel too stupid to ask, cuz everybody be actin' like, course we know Lady Mahalia and ain't it a damn shame what happen to her. Don't wanna break the circle, so I join in the general grief.

"Mahalia gave her life for the tomorrow she saw in your faces, all her relations. We hope she made it to the Promised Land and was born again in unfolding mystery."

Religious talk always sound trippy if you not inside it, but I vibe the general spirit, even act like a believer. Why piss on they parade? Everybody start singin'—all kinda harmonies and polyrhythms. I find me a alto niche and hold forth. This girl limp up to me, clappin' her hands and starin' hard in my eyes. Ain't no bigger than a minute, tryin' to look grown up and evil, like who do I think I am, bustin' into they ceremony. I freak and chomp my tongue. She the girl from the Extra camp those punk gangsta wannabes were doin' up against a tin-can wall. Captain shoot her in the thigh but I guess she survive. Good for her. Soloist let loose on top of us. Have mercy! Make me cry all over again. Feel like a memorial for the Captain too. I look that girl in the eye. Captain could've killed her. The life she leadin' this minute be a gift. The life we all leadin' be a gift.

"Mahalia said she'd surprise us in the end, and what a surprise!" the Wovoka say as folk from Achbar's transport throw on underground choir robes and start singin' somethin' us regular mortals can't touch.

Mahalia ain't the only surprise. The Healer from Paradise Healthway, Zumbi Xa Dojude, color in his cheeks, stringy yellow hair in swirls and curls, break thru the crowd, squeeze and spin me 'round 'til I fall down dizzy. Even his slack eye be bright, like he on track again, no fakin', a real medicine man. His hands make me feel good.

"I took your advice," Zumbi say, helpin' me up.

"Oh yeah? I don't remember givin' you no advice."

"I had to stop shuffling Electro outprint, stop being a good boy feeling sorry for myself. Then I could start being a real Healer. So obvious, but..." He hug me again.

"I can't take no credit for that," I say and look over at the girl. "I guess you all rebel Extras now. Celestina would be proud."

Zumbi stare at me like I have lost my mind. "Don't you remember? That day at Paradise, you and your Captain lead the charge."

"Charge? We were gettin' the fuck outa..."

Zumbi laugh. "No. Nothing was the same after that. No more sitting down and waiting to die. You're such an inspiration to the people of Los Santos, not just me. Standing up to Jesus Perez and all those mobsters, defying Jocelyn Williams! You leave a trail of rebels behind wherever you go. No more flying under the radar and hoping ganglords or twisted shamen won't catch us making a difference. You're a breath of fresh air for tired spirits." Healers really know how to brag on somethin'.

"Quit talkin' shit," I say. I wanna believe him, but damn. I feel like such a flop.

"No matter what curves they threw at you, nothing slowed you down." Zumbi gettin' choked up now. "Walk into danger and walk back out."

"Stop," I try to interrupt, but he ain't havin' it.

"Ambassador Kitt, specializing in the impossible! Why else would Prime Minister Williams put a death warrant on you? She's no fool. She wouldn't waste time on—"

"Death warrant?" I can't quite get my mind 'round what he sayin'. Course, he don't know the whole story—but for a minute, I don't feel like a total waste of spacetime. "Yeah, I guess we don't have to let the bad guys call all the shots."

"Where's the Captain? Did she…turn on you?" Zumbi ask.

"No way." I wanna tell him what happen, but I can't. My heart jitterbug in my chest. "Loyal to her last breath. A inspiration to me."

Before I bust into tears, my Electro go wild and bio-computer be fartin' and sparkin'. Ghost sonata message decryptin' itself. S'posedly a transmission from Geraldine, from all the way down a Barrier starway. She get the scared bunny messages I send, just take her a while to figure how to send somethin' back.

Is this transmission a scam or the genuine article?

No time for deep mystery from never-never land. Talk 'bout unstable compounds, Ray Valero just hit the scene and look like he goin' blow all over Mr. 7-Stories.

73: Wounded Knee
(October 18, Barrier Year 115)

> People be wizards of adaptation, like ants and bacteria. We turn
> deserts, eternal night, and outer space into paradise. Oughta be
> able to handle peace, right?
> —Geraldine Kitt, *Junk Bonds of the Mind*

Aaron ran away from the acolytes congregating around the Wovoka. It was too much like a casting call for horror Entertainment, and the last thing he wanted to hear was a sermon on Mahalia Selasie. Not even Stella could stomach it.

The Wovoka pranced onto a ridge above Wounded Knee Creek and opened his zombie jamboree by insisting that he, like his Paiute namesake, was a man of peace dancing down violence. As he memorialized Mahalia and castigated ganglords and politicos for their savagery, Ray cut across the rolling hillside and without so much as a *fuck you!* chased Aaron down and thrust a laser-blade into his neck.

"Have you lost your mind?" Aaron froze. The Wovoka brought out the absolute worst in people. "Why slit my throat?" Blood pooled in a gully at his collarbone. Ray, his weapon hand trembling, wheezed like an asthmatic in a smoker's den. "What're you doing? This is totally out of character."

"Don't be cute." Ray spun Aaron around and knocked him to the ground face first. "The fucking snuff take. Major said her name was Mahalia Selasie."

"I was trying to *save* Mahalia. Getting her to you, I mean."

Ray tangled Aaron's arms in his duster and pinned them behind his back. "You played me."

"Moses, Perez, and Danny Ford—they played us both."

"So how come you're still walking, and she's burnt to a crisp?"

"You didn't get her to Elleni?"

"Answer my question." Ray pressed his knee into Aaron's spine.

The Wovoka stopped preaching, and his multi-kulti soundtrack faded. A gang of feet surrounded Aaron, but no one intervened. So much for world peace.

"I'm just a lucky son of a bitch," Aaron said.

"You think?" Ray leaned his full weight into Aaron's back.

"Okay, okay, I could have done better by Mahalia, but I'm not the bad guy." The world blurred, like a spastic was shooting the scene around Aaron with a hand-held bio-corder.

"Dustin' him won't bring nobody back from the dead," a woman said. Sounded like Lawanda. As she talked, the pain in his back let up. "Murder's the worst kinda high. Feel good a minute then like utter dog-do the resta your life. Don't waste your spirit. Revenge oughta taste sweet." Definitely Lawanda. She pulled Aaron out of the dust.

Ray bore down on her. "What Zone do you live in?"

Lawanda's peach-fuzz hair brushed Aaron's chin; her palms pressed against Ray's chest. "Redirect the shit storm, you know what I'm sayin'?"

A pungent organic stink cleared Aaron's vision. Who the hell besides him would be shitting his pants?

"What's it goin' be, Ray?" Lawanda put her hand on the laser-blade. The crazed star looked like the pages of his script had gone blank. Aaron shuddered. Ray never liked to improvise. "A creative boy like you can do better than this." Lawanda had the nerve to laugh. Aaron didn't see what was so damn funny.

Ray, always the lady's man, chortled with Lawanda and pocketed the laser-blade. "I wasn't gonna take him out anyhow." He backed away.

"Bullshit." Aaron couldn't find the back of his breath. "I'm dying here."

Lawanda considered the neck wound. "You'll live." She turned to Ray. "What the fuck is up with this gangsta stunt?"

"I don't believe I just did that." Ray shook his head.

"Blowing too much Rapture." Lawanda pulled recon-skin from Ray's medicine bag and wrapped it around Aaron's throat.

"No... All my impulses got blown way out of whack," Ray said, "all the way to...another character."

The Wovoka had revved up Ray's bloodlust, but who in the zombie jamboree could hear that their god was a demon? "Talk about getting lost in a role," Aaron said.

Ray scowled at this assessment then wrinkled his nose. "What is that smell?"

"Rabbit pooh," Lawanda said. She ripped the pocket off her coveralls, held the shit-bottomed creature by the scruff of its neck, and tossed the contaminated fabric in an organic waste bin. A yellow-haired Healer hosed them down.

"I didn't know how pissed I was," Ray said to Aaron. "At you, at myself. Watching her burn was rough."

"Mahalia walked on the wrong side of bad people," Aaron said. "Not our fault."

"Just because I didn't ice you doesn't mean I believe your BS, Aaron." Ray paced. "Something had me acting like the Major, or…"

Lawanda lit up like a searchlight at the Major's name. "You seen him?"

Ray gaped at Lawanda. "You're alive!" He scooped her up and squeezed her against his chest. "Major and I thought you got killed in that canyon blast."

"Where is he?" Lawanda was breathless when Ray set her back on the ground.

"Looking for you. On his way over here, I think."

Scoping the crowd for the Major, Lawanda could barely contain herself. "Man's in the doghouse with me. I am so through with him."

"Uh huh," Ray said.

"No, really. The shit he pulled is unforgivable. Just as soon slug him as hug him."

Aaron shivered and wiped snow from his eyes. *He* had snatched Lawanda from the jaws of death in the Badlands, not the macho Major, and she hadn't even thanked him. He sat down on a rock and pulled off his boot. The Barrier burn throbbed like shit. His gene-art body felt itchy, wrong. Probably all in his head, but where else did a person itch besides in the head?

"Mahalia played us all, boss," Moses said and tumbled down to Aaron's level. He clutched his wounded side and took shallow breaths.

"What're you doing out here?" Aaron asked, grateful for distraction. "Trying to bleed to death? Get up out of the mud."

Achbar stood above Moses, scratching his eyebrows, thumping his staff in the slush. "Insisted he had to talk to you himself, live, in a storm."

"Fuck the blizzard! I know you maybe won't believe me, boss." Moses clutched Aaron's hand. "I had to warn you anyhow…they tracked us in here…"

A shot rang out. Moses's violet eyes lost their shine, and his lips went slack; brown blood drizzled through electric blue curls. The gene-art rosebud on his face opened in a brilliant blaze of fuchsia. Achbar cursed in Arabic. A smothering chorus of gasps and people hitting the ground behind Aaron confirmed the worst. A bullet had pierced Moses's skull and lodged in his brain, killing him swiftly. Aaron tumbled across the lifeless body and screamed silently on Moses's chest. Aaron hadn't saved the treacherous bastard for him to die like this.

"Mose snuffed Mahalia," Aaron told Ray, who cowered in the slush beside him. Aaron scanned the congregation for the shooter. "I thought these born-again Sioux were turn-the-other-cheek, not eye-for-an-eye."

"They're not the ones shooting at us," Ray said.

Up on the ridge, Jesus Perez, soybean king and organ robber baron, held a handgun to the Wovoka's head and aimed a long-range automatic piece at the congregation of unarmed Dancers. "Blink wrong, and your fearless leader's history, like Mr. Moses Johnson there," Perez shouted. He had traded southern-gent attire for assassin fashion—a sleek polymer jumpsuit, weapons belt loaded with explosives, and a duster lined with poison vials. Kill Perez, you'd kill yourself. "Are we all on the same screen?" Perez asked.

No reply. Lizards were crawling over the Kora player's face and arms, gnashing their teeth and flicking tails. What that meant Aaron couldn't guess. As the Wovoka scanned the congregation, his face hardened. He was a dragon who could blast adversaries from the inside out yet had taken a vow of peace

As the crowd stood up to face Perez, the Achbar was working his Healer staff. Aaron and the Kora player stepped between the big Arab and Perez's automatic piece. Stella tap-danced across his mindscape, grooving on crazy courage. But Aaron was thinking of *The Transformers*: the final episodes were writing themselves. The bio-corder jewels on Achbar's turban, belt, and sleeves sparkled in snowy sunlight. He was shooting the climactic showdown. Why should Aaron risk losing precious footage? This would definitely be the hit of all time—if anybody walked out of Wounded Knee alive.

"Man, Jesus, you really stuck on stupid, comin' up in here all big and bad, like you think your balls be atomic bombs or some shit." Lawanda never knew when to be quiet.

Perez grinned. "We've been trying to find this nest of rebels for years. Followed you, Lawanda, and got Wounded Knee plus a few bonuses."

Lawanda stuck out her lips and rolled her eyes.

"I wasn't sure *you* had the balls to blow the Captain yourself. Sent in the bomb squad to loosen her tongue, just in case. I was a safe distance from the blast, like yourself. Got some soot on my duster is all."

"Probably lost half your squad and a shitload of weapons," Lawanda said. Ray yanked her arm. "He goin' shoot me anyhow, why go down quiet?" Lawanda shouted. "I been pussyfootin' 'round psychotic motherfuckers way too long."

"Yes, I have lived long enough too. And you?" the Wovoka said to Perez.

"I'm hoping for triple digits, like Healer Witchdoctors." Perez grinned.

Was this a kidnap gig or a stun run? Aaron counted four desperados with automatic pieces and gargoyle Electro masks backing Perez. Probably another five or six tucked away and a getaway driver. Perez wouldn't waste the Wovoka 'til they'd gotten somewhere secure. That didn't mean he wouldn't waste other people right now.

"You haven't opened fire. What do you want?" the Wovoka asked.

"We want you alive," Perez said.

"We *who*?" Lawanda was either fearless or clueless.

"We also want Mahalia's underground geek choir alive, Ambassador Kitt, and unfortunately Mr. Achbar Ali, rebel ringleader."

Dancers shifted to a tight circle around Achbar and Lawanda.

"No?" Perez fired into the crowd.

Blood spurted skyward as several people were hit. A silver-faced man next to Aaron screamed and fell. Hit in the chest, he took some time to croak; Aaron didn't watch. Ray threw up. Real violence always made the boy-wonder sick to his stomach.

"I suggest you cooperate," Perez said. "From my POV, most of these people are expendable, and as I have demonstrated, ghost shirts still don't stop bullets."

"Fine, we're outa here then. No massacre," Lawanda said.

Ray wiped his mouth and stood behind Lawanda. Aaron scrambled for a plan. He and Ray exchanged glances.

"No need to waste more lives. Of course I'll come with you," the Wovoka said. "Where's your vehicle?"

"Whoever said the Wovoka wasn't a reasonable man?" Perez turned to Achbar. "We're in my dream, Mr. Ali. Lift that staff above your head, and I'll blast your arm off and the Wovoka's reasonable head. Don't anybody get fancy with hidden weapons."

"Dancers don't do weapons," Lawanda said.

Achbar grunted, but didn't move. Perez looked sour. Fanatics outnumbered bullets, so he probably counted on cooperation for the sake of the Wovoka and the other heroes of the revolution. Perez certainly didn't want to blow himself up. Aaron scanned only three gargoyle guards now. The fourth had disappeared.

Perez aimed the automatic at Lawanda and cocked a trigger at the Wovoka. "Put the staff down with your Arab sword, Achbar, now."

"Scimitar," Achbar said. He lowered the staff to the ground in excruciating slow motion.

Another gargoyle guard got yanked behind a bush.

"Whatever you think you're doing, you're too late, Jesus," the Wovoka said, not pronouncing the J like an H as in old Spanish. "Kidnap and murder are pointless."

"I don't know," Perez said. "It depends on who I kidnap or murder."

The Wovoka's eyes were red sparks, his face a glinting, silver mask as he shook snow from his feathered headdress. "Too many bad ad-operas, Jesus. Most great leaders are opportunists riding the tendencies of a generation, surfing the force of a great mass of people, all the way to glory."

"You ready to watch your dreams go up in smoke?"

"Dr. Mahalia created a non-lethal fire-virus variation that protects us from the killer version. She infected as many people as she could. Gave it all away." The sly dog finished his memorial sermon with a gun up his nose. A murmur of triumph rippled through the crowd. "Her gene-art version is a hundred times as contagious as—"

"Shut up!" Perez said. "And you hustle!"

"What's the hurry? We Indians have no plans of dying out," the Wovoka said.

The crowd inched its way closer. Achbar got his sword thoroughly tangled in his robes and sashes. Lawanda sucked her teeth and moved to help. Ray danced from foot to foot in a band of restless braves. The Kora player strapped the instrument to her back.

Aaron's muscles were sludge; his mind wasn't much better. Thanks to Mahalia, the anti-Treaty conspiracy was in shambles. Instead of power-playing, Perez would probably torture and humiliate the Wovoka, Achbar, and Lawanda. He'd demand ransom and let his goons massacre obedient Dancers. Make a party out of scotching the rebellion even if his team couldn't win.

Aaron was paralyzed. Trying for a getaway was suicide. And Stella Jackson wasn't going to lie down and take it up the ass. She'd rather take a bullet or eat poison gas than stomach gangbanging and massacre. Gap-tooth bitch was screaming in his mindscape: *Aaron Dunkelbrot is up there with Tadeshi Mifune and Carl Samanski. Studio bosses and ganglords of that caliber never got caught in a dead-end story line like this.*

Aaron switched on his voice amp. "You don't own the future, Perez,"

"I'll blow us all, the Wovoka first," Perez said.

"Bullshit bluff. You said yourself you wanted to live into triple digits."

A cloudburst of snow blotted out the sun and made everything fuzzy and cold. The Kora player plucked an explosion on fifty strings.

"No more snuff takes!" Aaron said. "*Wokiksuye Cankpe Opi.* Remember Wounded Knee." Aaron's voice-amp blasted these words in every direction. As bullets sliced the air, he raced up the winding path toward Jesus Perez and didn't notice the crowd surging around him.

74: Wounded Knee

(October 18, Barrier Year 115)

The Major grabbed the gangster's pulse rifle and ripped off his tactical mask. Before wrenching his enemy's neck, the Major stared into frightened gray eyes. He remembered relishing a victim's last look: triumph quivering between his fingers while his opponent pleaded for life—as if the Major were a god. His right hand ached red at the thought. Bitterness filled his mouth. He tasted the poor man's stomach rising and his throat closing. Their hearts pounded the same deadly rhythm. This was not how it used to be.

"If you are well, I am well." Elleni embraced the trembling captive from behind. Blue sparks from her hair sizzled against his sweaty skin. The Major refused to be surprised at her sudden appearance. Instead, relief cascaded across his nerves. A braid zapped the thug's temples. His eyes rolled up in his head, and he crumpled to the ground. "He'll be out several hours," she said. Her skin shimmered like a mosaic of broken glass.

"How did you manage that?" the Major whispered.

She put a finger to his lips and pointed in the direction of another hidden thug. The Major nodded and indicated a double-flanked approach. Sparking dreads entwined his left arm and pulled it to her breast. She smiled and slipped his data glove onto cramped, achy fingers. The power pack on his belt booted the system. Her prickly hair lingered against his arm. A jet stream of emotions threatened his equilibrium for the nth time since daybreak. Without the glove his mindscape had been a desert, quicksand sucking away thoughts and insights before he could understand himself. With it, he could direct the blinding clarity he now felt in fingers, head, and heart toward the sniper in the bushes.

Elleni had disappeared. If not for the data glove raging against his fingers, he might have thought her an illusion. Dragonflies fluttered by his nose, a coyote scampered over the hills, and an energy surge ghosted on his data glove before it became fully operational. A violet disc swooped past his head. Hallucination, or…? Elleni appeared ahead of him, walking down the barrel of a gun, talk-singing a language he didn't recognize.

"Damn," he said softly. Taking one last second to assimilate to the data glove and grab the fallen man's weapon, he raced to back her up.

Before the Major could get a clear shot, the sniper squeezed off several bullets in Elleni's direction. Her bedraggled locks snagged the tiny missiles as a frog might snatch flies off the breeze. Her hair turned blue-violet as it consumed the metal. The Major accepted the evidence of his senses and vowed to analyze the event later. Disarming the rattled sniper was easier than processing magic realism.

The man sputtered gibberish—"Gagen leasad ha snukka poius"—and lost control of his bodily functions. Elleni dispatched his consciousness with charged hair.

"I walked a Barrier shortcut to get here. The bullet trick I picked up from Sidi. And disrupting the flow of Chi, I learned from Celestina." She smiled sadly. "Okay?"

The Major nodded. Instead of declaring a systems malfunction, the data glove concurred with his impression of the bullet incident.

Elleni had somehow enhanced the glove's reality interface without setting off auto-destruct. Mysteries within mysteries.

"Who are these bad boys?" she asked.

"Hired killers, ultimately in the pay of Jocelyn Williams." The smart bombs at the back of his thoughts did not protest the course he had chosen against the Prime Minister. "I suspect money, not faith, moves them to sabotage Celestina's Treaty."

"I'm sorry I didn't trust you sooner." Elleni sighed. A sapphire braid snaked through his tight curls.

"You were right not to," the Major said. "Trusting me had lethal consequences."

"I was a foolish coward not to risk it. Hoping for miracles. Sidi has cured me of that," Elleni said. The Major sensed the import of her words without understanding their full meaning. "Try not to kill anyone, all right?" she said as a braid stroked his cheek. Pleasant shocks made his face tingle.

"Easier said than done, when they're trying to kill you."

Beyond a few guards at the perimeter, Wounded Knee security was non-existent. Obviously the Wovoka didn't expect an ambush. Barrier interference was effective cover. Ray had only found Wounded Knee with Celestina's staff.

"They trailed somebody who knew the way," Elleni said, anticipating his next question.

A thug fell out of a tree, twisted an ankle, and slammed his head against a rock before he could ambush them. "Fortunately, these gangsters aren't military grade." The thug was a dark-skinned man with white-blond hair; the Major recalled seeing him tap dance in Entertainments. Did he do terrorism on the side? The Major took cursory med-unit readings. "Concussion," he said. Elleni dropped powder from her medicine bag down the man's nose and stuck thin needles into him, all in the blink of an eye. She was in warrior-woman Oshun mode. Without a single shot or blade thrust, they dispatched seven thugs in thirteen minutes and secured the hill behind the cemetery.

"Have you seen Lawanda?" the Major asked. "I searched for her, but she wasn't anywhere."

"I've seen only you and the gunmen." Her eyes turned inside out, a repellant habit that nevertheless made him smile. "I feel the Wovoka and two other *Vermittler*—too many patterns to find Lawanda."

"Other *Vermittler?*" Before he could mention his Sidi hallucination, purple Barrier tentacles slashed through Elleni's body. She lost her balance and careened into him. The Barrier ripped at the sky, roaring like an ad-opera monster. The Major kept panic at bay by stroking her cheek. "You okay?"

"Nothing bad. See?" She somersaulted to her feet. "An invitation."

They continued on. Snow fell up from the ground; sunlight streamed from the rocks. Barrier tentacles vaporized clouds. The world was upside down. The Major let disorientation fuel his imagination. The data glove picked up one long-range weapon within a hundred meters. Beyond that, he got uncertain readings. Intrepid, yet not improvident, they raced out into the open.

On a ridge above them, Jesus Perez held a gun to the head of a silver-faced Dancer, who, according to the Major's data glove, faded in and out of existence at regular intervals.

"The Wovoka," Elleni said.

Behind Perez, Ray slid on the ground and knocked two guards off their feet. As the gangsters scrambled for weapons, Dancers engulfed them. Perez aimed an automatic rifle at the mob just below him.

"No more snuff takes," they yelled. "*Wokiksuye Cankpe Opi.* Remember Wounded Knee."

"Buddha, Christ: perhaps these men never took a breath." The Wovoka's voice echoed across the hills. "But Buddhists and Christians changed our world. The Ghost Dance does not need me." He began a slow dance around a dazed Perez.

In the crowd below this spectacle, the Major scoped Lawanda, alive. Thread-metal thin, no hair to speak of, bruised and blotchy, yet still throwing her hips around as if she were Queen Somebody. The Major had a good shot at Perez. He aimed—then hesitated, telling himself he didn't want to trigger a bomb. In truth, he didn't want to kill anybody. He nodded to Elleni. She would take care of Perez. He cut through the throng of Dancers for Lawanda.

"Watch your back!" Elleni yelled and clambered up the cliff face.

"If I gotta go, I take some of you sons of bitches with me!" Perez said, but the automatic weapon misfired. Lawanda slipped from the Major's view. Perez tried to fire again then dropped the rifle from a bloody hand. He thrust the Wovoka between him and the mob. "I mean it, I'll kill the freaky bastard." His handgun shook as he looked in vain for backup force. "I walk out of here now or the Wovoka's history." Perez fumbled with bombs on his belt. The crowd hesitated.

Jocelyn had betrayed Lawanda, Paradigma, Celestina's Treaty, and the Major to team up with this low-grade thug? To be honest, the Major wasn't much better than Perez or the Prime Minister. He was certainly not the enlightened visionary of his fantasies.

"It's the chorus that sings the great ideas. We simply strive to inspire. I'm your hostage no longer. I walk away." The Wovoka slipped through Perez's grasp.

The Major glimpsed Lawanda's face at the front of the crowd. Anguish cramped his leg muscles, but he pressed on through the mass of bodies. Elleni scrambled onto the ridge and streaked for Perez. The data glove signaled a weapon being powered up, yet the Major ignored the warning. The sniper was a dead shot. The bullets, however, ricocheted off a beaded wand in Elleni's hair. Before the gunman could get off another round, born-again Sioux overran him. Impossibly fast, Elleni slammed into Perez as he squeezed the handgun trigger. His bullet missed the Wovoka, ripped apart a billowing blanket, smashed into the calabash gourd of a Kora, and burst through the Major's armored vest. It shattered ribs and charged through his organs. However, spasms in his calf muscles were the Major's undoing. He collapsed one meter from Lawanda.

"Honoré," she shouted and raced to him.

75: Wounded Knee

(October 18, Barrier Year 115)

> We've raided all the tombs. Sucked every image bone dry.
> Nothing left to steal.
> —Tadeshi Mifune, *Surviving the Future, Last Minute Notes*

"In fall, the sun sets too quickly. Perez and his band have little chance to survive a long night," the Wovoka declared. Surveying the bleak horizon from a windy ridge, he gestured at a burnt orange slit that dissolved into blackness.

"Fine with me." Ray could give a shit if Perez and crew survived or not. Dumping them in the wasteland was way too generous. He rubbed his throbbing temples. "Just answer the question."

"I cannot go naked and silent through the Barrier with Elleni," the Wovoka replied.

"Why not?" Ray knew he was doing this all wrong, but he wanted to punch the smug bastard, so yelling was a compromise. "You're a *Vermittler* like her."

The Wovoka grimaced as the Barrier crept up behind them. "Really?"

"I don't get all of what's going down, but I get that."

Muddy purple turbulence scattered sand and snow and cut the night sky into jigsaw fragments of navy black. Ray had never seen the Barrier on the move like this. He stumbled away from the encroaching front, which halted a few yards short of Elleni and split open. She was hunched over the wounded Major, oblivious. Her eyes had turned inside out, her hair stood on end, and her skin seemed to be breaking apart—Barrier fever and god knows what else jacking her up. Lawanda stared at Ray with desperate eyes. The Major's sweaty head rested on her belly, and his blood burbled between her fingers. Aaron, Achbar, and a Dancer holding a Kora vigiled with Lawanda but looked as if they wanted to bolt away from the blackout maw growing in the Barrier.

A voice in the distance sang soft prayers in Yoruba, something about healing. The singer sounded like Sidi. Wasn't Sidi one of the bad guys, in league with Perez? Wind from the Barrier opening sent stinging dust up Ray's nose and across his eyes. The singing stopped and now he wasn't sure. Perhaps it was Lakota and not Yoruba after all. He barely knew either language.

"We don't have time for some big metaphysic discussion," Ray said. He rubbed his eyes and leaned his head against Celestina's staff for moral support. "Got to move, before——"

"You are ready and willing. Why tell me how to live or die? You should go!"

"Elleni doesn't want me. She doesn't need me."

"My destiny does not take me to the Promised Land." The Wovoka shook his head.

"It's crazy to ask, I know." Ray sighed. "You were gonna let that jack-off Perez shoot you—you even said today was a good day to die, but now you won't do *Ebo Eje* with Elleni and save your people!?"

"Elleni Xa Celest wants payback? She should have saved the Major and let my life be forfeit then." The Wovoka folded his arms across his chest, like a tobacco store Indian. "I'm not your enemy or your slave. I am no image you make in your head."

Centering on his breath, Ray deleted funky *Vermittler* and Indian clichés. "I'm no fucking good to Elleni in there. Not my gig, I wasn't in the vision." He pointed at the blackout corridor. "Be mad at me and all my ancestors, but have you seen this thing swallow the planet? I wouldn't ask otherwise."

"Celestina's gloom and doom." The Wovoka fingered the jeweled head of the staff.

Ray moved it beyond the Wovoka's reach. "You still hate Celestina?"

"What could a death angel hope to see but the end of days."

"The rebel Extras are on her side, fighting for the Treaty."

"Today a small victory, tomorrow much work." The Wovoka's face blurred out of focus. "Celestina wanted to throw me in the Barrier once. But she spared me."

"I know," Ray said and brought the man up short for a nanosecond.

"It was then I took a vow of peace. I call the spirits of the dead. I am not Celestina's acolyte." He headed for the cemetery.

"Why'd you call us together? Were you just ego-tripping, or trying to get something done?"

The Wovoka halted. His body faded in and out of regular space-time. He turned and strode back so close, Ray felt the sharp cold of his liquid silver skin.

"What? You gonna twist the flow of my Chi?" Ray leaned toward him. "Some vow of peace, jacking people up 'til they're ready to riot."

"You are what you are and do what you do. I cannot change that." His cold breath burned Ray's face.

"Dumping Perez in the wasteland instead of killing him outright, your hands don't stay clean. Living, you get blood on you, even saints," Ray said. "Every rare once and awhile you get a shot at something beautiful."

"Like *Ebo Eje*, yes? A spineless weasel like you, who comes on cue while others are raped to death and burned alive, what do you even have worth sacrificing?"

"Y'all quit trippin'. Hurtin' my head," Lawanda said.

"Is that all you got?" Ray lowered his voice. "Hey, *I'm* going too."

"And you think that will wash your soul beautiful?" The Wovoka laughed.

"No. I don't even want to go, but it's the best I can do." Ray brushed away tears. He was terrified at the prospect, but he couldn't back out now. "What's it gonna be?"

The Wovoka snorted a Barrier filament. "We've spilled enough blood for you."

Ray groaned. "We who? Born-again Sioux? Rebels? Lakota? *Vermittler*? Extras?"

"Exactly. There's already been enough *Ebo Eje*." His face morphed through myriad expressions. "You understand my dilemma."

Ray sagged against Celestina's staff. His heart ached. "Yes, I do."

"I have my own vision to follow. I leave you and Elleni to follow yours." The Wovoka moved past Ray to the black crystal arch, taller than a skyscraper and still growing.

"The calabash is cracked," the mute Dancer signed, "but Femi's instrument still has music." She set the Kora by the Major and strummed a broken melody.

"I can't heal him," Elleni said, blinking her eyes to normal. "Can't even hold on to him much longer." Ray couldn't stand hearing the defeat in her voice.

"Ain't no point in draggin' it out then," Lawanda said and hugged Elleni.

Ray snuck a glance at Elleni, but she wouldn't look at him, and neither would Aaron or Achbar. They were as quiet as dead men.

Lawanda struggled to lift the unconscious Major. She looked so thin. "Help me get him to the Barrier, he say he want to cross over to the Promised Land."

Ray couldn't move—an actor's nightmare—thrust into the climax, his blocking and lines a blank, and everybody else playing the moment to perfection. Aaron, Achbar, and the mute Dancer helped Lawanda carry the Major. Elleni hoisted the cracked Kora on her back and followed them to the blackout corridor. He'd never seen her look so devastated. As if the bullet that nailed the Major had broken her apart, too.

They set the Major at the edge of the black crystal arch. Aaron and Achbar backed away. The Wovoka clasped Lawanda's hands. "Inside, a person does not live as we do now. The Barrier holds his memory, even lets that memory transform, age, but the person, he cannot walk the Earth again. And the memory lasts only as long as we remember."

Ray imaged his sister Chris racing through alpine meadows. This lifted his spirits a notch. "Yes, that's it," he said.

The Wovoka scowled at him, then turned back to Lawanda. She stuffed a drawing into the Major's jacket. "Honoré don't put much stock in a afterlife, but goin' out down a discovery corridor, that's his kinda funeral."

They were all near tears, even cold-fish Aaron. Ray's stomach knotted on itself. "Someone loved him, someone will miss him," he blurted, wishing he had more to say. The nazi Major had turned himself into a hero, taken out Perez's crew, and then run right into a bullet, saving Lawanda's life. Ray was drained—no good eulogy came to him or anybody else. They were all drained. Elleni stumbled into him. He tasted jasmine sweat, cinnamon breath, and sour defeat.

"I know what you're thinking," he whispered. "Celestina would've saved the Major. Maybe, maybe not. Don't blame yourself."

"Who else to blame? Failing at my life," Elleni said in a brittle voice.

"We just throw him in, is that all?" Lawanda hugged the Major to her, shaking her head. "Ain't there some kinda ceremony?" She forced out an astral lament. Others joined in.

"Don't give up," Ray said to Elleni under the music.

"I haven't given up, it's just..."

"And don't lie to me."

"I'm going down that corridor!" Yellow tears drizzled from her battered hair. "But what's the point? If I can't even heal the Major, how can I...alone..."

"I'm going too."

Elleni cut him a laser-blade look.

"You told me sacrifice is like acting. Let's go for it. Act like we're the dynamic duo the Barrier's been waiting for."

"There isn't that much acting in the world," Elleni said dryly.

"You don't know that. At least we can help the Major to his final destination, see what my sister's been up to, do our part for humanity." Ray acted like he believed what he said. He slid his hand around Elleni's waist, as if playing a love scene.

"I never said I wouldn't go." Elleni stared up at him with unblinking eyes. "This is not a Jolt-opera, you know?"

"I haven't done one of those in years." He kissed the dreads fussing on her forehead 'til they quieted down. "I choose the danger, I choose my best self, I choose you. Maybe we're not enough, but hey, we showed up." He ached for her to touch his mindscape, but she didn't.

"So how we goin' do this?" Lawanda said as the song ended.

"I offer you my medicine bag." Elleni thrust it at the mute Dancer and began to strip. "Ray and I must take off our clothes."

"I will hold this until you return," the Dancer signed, then clutched the bag.

"*Mojubar*," Elleni said, "*Omi tutu, ile tutu, ona tutu, tutu Eşu, tutu Oriṣa*." She poured libation to cool spirits and opened herself to whatever would transpire. As Ray peeled off his clothes, he hoped the incantation worked for him too.

Before he could change his mind about this freaky suicide march, he and Elleni stumbled naked into the black-hole corridor. They held the Major upright between them. Lawanda didn't cry as they departed, but dug her fingers into Aaron and Achbar, her Arabian knights. Guiding Ray and Elleni, the Wovoka and mute Dancer stepped into the Barrier for a moment then back out, unscathed. But they were *Vermittler*—the Barrier's own. To his relief and surprise, Ray did not get immediately fried. He gripped Celestina's staff in the crook of his arm. It offered a whisper of light. The Kora banged against Elleni's back, setting off strange chords, and the Major's data glove beeped softly; otherwise, it was quiet on the set.

Ray meant to tell Elleni he loved her with an open heart. But a tall figure in red dashed into the corridor behind them, groping to find a way. Elleni didn't notice.

Ray held out his hand.

76: The Promised Land

There aren't singular atoms, lonely souls, or Final Lessons.
You're never done. Everything stretches beyond you.
Who knows what will be true tomorrow? We look with the
eyes of the ancestors into the faces of our children. Isn't it
wonderful to be blessed with uncertainty?
—Vera Xa Lalafia, *Healer Cosmology, The Final Lessons*

No journey, no time, no single body, no body at all.

Celestina had said *mind was a pattern of patterns spread across spacetime, emergent, regenerative, and fragile.* Elleni swirled through a multitude of patterned patterns at the crossroads of the Barrier mindscape. More dimensions than she could hope to count sliced into one another, passing through her without turbulence, raging storms, or dazzling electromagnetic spectacle. Soothing blackness filled the Barrier intersection, permeating her with infinite possibilities, dissolving identity. In every direction, she sensed tiny points of light, of life. Her heartbeats were universes being born, her breath galaxies spiraling off to uncertain destinies. If she squinted her mind, she could just make out where she had come from, but the darkness and the peace blanketed her thoughts, and the distant familiar light faded.

"Did you expect special effects?" Someone spoke, but not out loud, a familiar voice interrupting her dissolution into darkness, calling her back to herself. "Is that why you dragged your star-lover with you?"

"He wanted to come." Elleni tried to phaseshift to the speaker's mode, but she could find nothing or no one to anchor her.

"A real-life hero then, risking Barrier annihilation for love."

"Who?" Elleni said, losing the thread of this memory. "Who are you?"

"Who are you?"

Elleni couldn't quite remember.

"Elleni Xa Celest! Floating at the Barrier crossroads where dimensions and realities collide, caught in a storm of alien beings, about to lose herself to everyone else—a ripple in the mindscape."

Sidi Xa Aiyé. Elleni was sure of it and reached for her.

"You feel other people so intensely, that's your problem and your gift. I am the exact opposite. Everyone feels me." Delicious Sidi eddied right through Elleni.

"It can't be!" Elleni said.

"The Promised Land," Sidi said softly. She appeared out of a swirl of snow in flame-red fleece. Her violet disks resting on ochre braids were so vivid in the darkness, Elleni was almost jolted back to her body. "I make a leap of faith to the crossroads of eternity," Sidi said. "The Barrier calls *Vermittler* to negotiate meaning, griots to make sense of a cosmic library of the dead—you told us some such grandiose nonsense. I didn't want to believe you."

"What are you doing here?" Elleni asked.

"What do you think?" Sidi smiled at her.

The Barrier was testing her resolve with pathetic fantasies. "You're not really here."

"I'm no Barrier illusion. Feel me." Sidi flowed through Elleni again.

"Why would you come?" Elleni's heart fluttered. "I barely got myself here, and I believe." Stars and companion galaxies raced away from her, leaving her alone with the Sidi apparition.

"I'm a wanderer at the crossroads, honoring Eshu, rejoicing in ashe, in the power to make things be." As Sidi spoke lines too good to be true, faces from every direction scowled, cried, simpered, glared, grimaced, smiled, glowered, sneered, bawled, beamed, smirked, barked...

"Stop." Elleni tried to shield herself from the tantalizing images. A real shaman would revel in this sacrifice, in this opportunity to enfold her spirit, her voice, and her vision in the Barrier mindscape. Eshu roared and spun his faces into one: Sidi, so beautiful it hurt to watch her. "I know I'm not very much, but I showed up," Elleni said.

Sidi's disks sliced up this apology. "I saw New Ouagadougou in flames."

Explosions devastated the Insect Pavilion. The Library of the Dead crumbled. Femi's statue exploded.

Sidi groaned as graphic images surrounded them. "You are always so literal. It was nothing that dramatic. People moved back into the dead malls, led Jolt-opera lives, and let everything else go." The fleece coat slipped from Sidi's shoulders. "You were right. We mustn't let enemies define us." If she'd come, why hadn't she come naked? "I came because I had to explore this Barrier mystery for myself."

"You waited to the last minute. How can I trust this change?"

"I was on my way back to you when Awa buried us in an avalanche. Still, I followed the shortcut to *Cankpe Opi*."

"You were at Wounded Knee?"

"I saw your 'revolution solution.' I sang for Honoré, poured libation to all of your spirits." She paused. "I saw what connects you to those people."

"No, Eshu dances on my head. You're the last bit of my ego holding on." This Barrier-generated fantasy was excruciating. Elleni tried to empty her mindscape. "I'm ready to sacrifice myself, to make human sense of the Barrier."

"When I saw you stumbling down that black-hole corridor... I raced into the Barrier after you. Ray snatched my hand or I would have lost you, lost the thread. A brave boy, reckless, like you." Sidi laughed, and Elleni felt her body returning, taut skin, heavy bones, snarling hair. "When we were young, you were never really good at anything." Sidi smiled. "Nobody ever liked you. You were so clumsy, off-key, and off-color. It used to make me livid, yet you didn't care. You were satisfied with yourself. And nothing stopped you."

"You were kind. That was enough," Elleni whispered, sensing her tongue again, thick against the roof of her mouth. Blizzard cold blasted her skin.

"No, I was amazed by you. Still am." Sidi slipped the broken Kora from a shivering Elleni and wrapped her in warm fleece.

"Uncertain, you walk into the jaws of a monster, you risk all that you are. What if you're utterly, catastrophically wrong?"

"I loved you, and you were my enemy. Was that wrong?" Elleni said.

"No, but I could never manage that. I always liked to be certain... I envy you." Sidi stroked Elleni's trembling cheeks. "You've won, Elleni Xa Celest, and yet you don't gloat." She sighed. "My leap of faith: you won't betray New Ouagadougou or anyone else. I see the future in your eyes. The choice is clear."

Elleni's hair crawled across her shoulders, hissing at shadows, daring her to believe. "You intend to remain at the crossroads as the Barrier's griot?"

"That's the story. At Barrier command central—how better to honor my vision?" Sidi kissed her eyes.

Elleni luxuriated in the sensation. "How can I accept this?"

"Don't you want to?" Sidi screwed up her face. "Or would you rather the Barrier swallowed the Earth whole?"

"You never believed that would happen," Elleni said.

"The Barrier prowls our mindscapes and warns us with our bleakest possibilities, perhaps to prompt us to do what we need to do. A mystery that I have an eternity to fathom." Sidi kissed Elleni's lips. "I'm not a metaphor called up to torment you. You must go, now, before you can't anymore."

Child of my tomorrow, be a witness. Go out and sing our song. Celestina's voice.

"Go where?" Elleni stood on solid ground once more. "Don't we do this together?"

"Yes, inside and out. So much work to be done in all the Zones, a network of souls... Tell everyone of our bond."

"I'd tell the whole story." Elleni was a Barrier griot after all. "But..."

"This will heal old wounds and turn many hearts toward you."

Was this the healing Celestina had called for?

A force tugged Elleni away from the crossroads. Was the Barrier about to spit her out? "Why should I trust you, even if you aren't an apparition?" Elleni gripped Sidi's hand.

"We must trust each other," Sidi whispered, slipping through Elleni's sharp fingers. "I need you, to remember me, to tell this story—Celestina's story—and lead us into the future." A rush of beings hurtled past Elleni toward Sidi: angels, demons, and dry-longso aliens that defied her imagination, griots all converging at the crossroads. "*Mo so awon enia mi po.*" Speaking Oshun's praise poem, Sidi's voice was like rain falling through wind chimes. "I tie the people together. You do too."

"This crossroads swallows all that you are." As the Barrier burned Elleni's skin, a hand gripped her around the waist and dragged her toward a snowstorm.

"I will add myself and do what I can," Sidi said as she faded away.

"I don't want to lose you."

"Think of me at the center of the Barrier mindscape, translating truth, interpreting one being for another, bridging realities."

Ray shouted Elleni's name.

"I'll haunt you from the crossroads, I promise," Sidi said.

"Bella!" Ray shouted.

Elleni turned toward his voice and could almost make out his face, then turned back to Sidi. "Are you certain?"

"No, but you always pushed me to be better than I am. Here's my chance, na?" A violet disk sliced through a hissing braid. Elleni winced as Sidi grabbed the wriggling hair. The disk landed on Elleni's forehead. "Certainty is overrated. Think of the mysteries I shall unravel."

"Who knows what will be true tomorrow?" Elleni said with relief and regret.

"It's what we both want." Sidi signed farewell and turned away from her.

"*Keine billigen Seelen,*" Elleni whispered. "*Kein Wunder zu vergeuden.*" She had to gasp for breath. "No cheap souls, no miracles to waste."

Faces cascaded into Sidi from every direction, enveloping her. Elleni thought she saw Honoré, his eyebrows arched in wonder, but then she was too far away from the avalanche of beings to read any expression. Actually some had no faces at all, but she had no better word in all the languages she knew to describe her experience. She would have to invent new languages. A vortex had sucked Elleni far from the crossroads, yet the familiar lights of home were still dim. A nasty magnetic pulse throbbed between her thighs, static filled her mouth, and she coughed sparks and lightning bolts—and with each breath, heartbeat, and thought, she scattered herself across the cosmos. Ray gripped her belly; her cheek slid across his scratchy beard. She drew him in on a deep breath. He tasted more delicious than she remembered.

"Don't let go!" Elleni fumbled for him.

"I'm trying, babe." His molasses tones slid across burning skin and soothed her.

77: Cross-Barrier Transmission/Personal

To:	Sweet Lawanda
From:	Honoré
Re:	?
Question:	I don't know if you'll get this or not. My data glove seems to think so, so I will trust in it.
Observations:	Plunging down this strange Barrier corridor, I have regained consciousness and am feeling no pain. I have yet to suffocate, explode, or even expire from the bullet wound. Not quite over yet, I presume. I am moved through the corridor by a gentle force,

mindful of my fragile biology. Destination unknown. My senses have been corrupted. I smell
movements and hear things that make no noise.
I "see" a spectrum of light beyond the visible.
Gravity is minimal. I float like a mote of dust on
the breeze. A dolphin gurgles across my eyes, an
old woman's two hearts beat swirls of colored magnetism across my skin. She races faster than light
toward a sandy blue shoreline. Astounding, but my
experience is congruent with the data-glove readings. The system appears to be fully operational;
Elleni engineered extensive Barrier enhance-
ments. My exchanges with her were deeper than I
thought. Please give her my regards. I "sense" her
presence, but can't reach her.

I don't have much energy, but I wanted my last
thoughts to be with you. If you get this transmission, I hope it will not mean more grief for you,
but rather function as some last bit of myself that
I can offer.

I am truly sorry for all that I have put you through.

What I experience inside the Barrier defies description, certainly for one such as myself, lacking
poetic facility. It's as if I glimpse worlds, universes,
dimensions beyond our own, different rules, different languages, different mindscapes. A plan
unfolds before me, an ordering, but its exact pa-
rameters elude me. I try to add your eyes and your
sensibility to mine as wonders course by me. Even
if I fall short, the effort makes the experience all
the richer.

Assumption: My strength is finite, failing actually, and perhaps
you don't want to hear a technical travelogue.
(See attachments for direct data dump on Barrier
observations.)

Notes: I wish I knew what you would like to hear.

I miss the sound of your voice, the energy and force of your being, those spontaneous bursts of eloquent metaphors. I miss the regular infusions of sassy hope. Thinking of such things makes it hard to concentrate. That I shall never experience you again, never touch you, never make up for lost time, never show you how I have changed, never find out what I am capable of...

I don't know how to end that sentence.

Simply put, that I am losing you is unbearable.

I did the best I could to correct my fatal error, but...I have looked death in the eye too many times to have any illusions.

Knowing you, I don't feel I was a waste of consciousness.

Please forgive me if I break off here.

Recommend: Live well, live poetry, live science.

78: Wounded Knee

(November 27, Barrier Year 115)

"Is it ever going to stop snowing?"

Aaron didn't know what to do with himself. Limping beside Achbar along Wounded Knee Creek, he sounded like Stella, inside and out. His body throbbed as if he was all Barrier burn. An entire white sky falling on him couldn't chill out the pain.

A blizzard of days had passed since Elleni, Ray, and Sidi disappeared into the black-hole corridor. Maybe it had been weeks since the crystal corridor irised shut on Sidi's red fake fur and the Barrier morphed into a smoky screen across the snowy horizon. Achbar got great shots for *The Transformers*. All Aaron had to do was shoot filler and edit the episode together. It was a guaranteed hit if even one of the heroic trio returned. Awa Xa Ijala kept telling him, patience, they'll come back, any minute now.

When would that minute be?

Aaron stumbled into a six-foot drift. He flailed valiantly but couldn't figure how to swim the snow to the surface. Achbar hauled him out butt-first, then they both tumbled down an icy incline. Achbar roared like a kid as they plowed into other hapless tumblers.

"What're we doing?" Aaron blinked tiny icicles off his eyelashes.

An hour ago Stella Jackson had broken into his head, said she had to see him on a ridge above Wounded Knee Creek, or else. He already felt insane, but she wouldn't shut up 'til he and Achbar dashed out of the transport. He felt stupid obeying a dream demon, but everyone, even Lawanda, who'd been off grieving hard for the Major, had come out in the blizzard to stare at the Barrier. It was like miles and miles of a blank Electro screen.

"Me, part of the zombie jamboree!" Aaron shook his head and leaned against Achbar, who brushed snow off their fleece burnooses. "Are you supposed to wear those turkey-feather bonnets in nasty weather?" Aaron asked, pointing at the Wovoka's bedraggled born-again Sioux finery. Achbar shrugged; he had hit-man patience. Lawanda squeezed Aaron's furry mittens as she strode in for the show. Up on the ridge in front of the Barrier, Awa Xa Ijala plopped onto a stool and hugged layers of fake fur around her bony figure. The Wovoka paced beside her.

"The Barrier speaks to us with story," Awa said.

The Wovoka turned to his audience: Extras, underground choirs, rebels, acolytes, ambassadors, Dancers, Ouagadougians, reformed gangsters, and Entertainment crews. "Let us remember those we have lost, and then let us act."

Aaron glimpsed Lawanda's puffy eyes and tear-stained cheeks and then turned to the blank Barrier. He conjured his mother and brother, lost a lifetime ago to the organ market, Celestina, cut down by an assassin, Moses, shot in the head, and finally Mahalia burning alive in playback. A face he'd almost forgotten ghosted in front of him on the Barrier screen—Stella Jackson, naked and grinning. She leaned across the ridge right into him.

He smelled the nutty oil she used on hair and skin. "It's really you."

They were close enough to touch. Wounds from torture and rape on her face, neck, breasts, and belly had healed to angry brown scars. This was not his body anymore, but still painful to see. Aaron enveloped Stella in his burnoose. Her rough hand on his cheek was forgiveness for throwing her away before she could find herself. Her lips on his forehead was that awful strain in the back of the throat, behind the eyes, before tears. He had lost so much abandoning her. Stella's heart thudded against his and then she was gone. Aaron hugged his own chest.

He could never have her back.

Sadness ripped through him and was amplified in the crowd as the storm clouds rolled away. The snow petered out, and the sun glared at them. Aaron was dizzy. A legion of demons rushed out of a Barrier long-shot right behind the Wovoka and Awa. Countless familiar faces, beloved strangers, anonymous angels of every age, shape, size, and color danced across the Barrier, a giga-mass of ghosts talking at once, growing larger than life, as they zoomed into close-up. Aaron strained his senses, yet couldn't understand the jumbled words the ghosts spoke. In extreme close-up now, their faces blurred into one another, unrecognizable, a collage of patterns and splotches of color.

"The crazy SOB wasn't lying!" Aaron said through tears.

Achbar smiled. "The Wovoka really called up the dead."

The Barrier's smooth translucence ruptured. Splotches of ghost faces morphed into corridors, into all manner of Barrier openings:

imposing boulevards with sapphire and ruby walls, ominous dark avenues, and rusty little alleyways. Aaron and Achbar raced with the crowd up the ridge.

The ghosts offered them an invitation to the future.

79: Wounded Knee
(December 22, Barrier Year 115)

The crystal head of Celestina's staff crumbled and scattered on the wind. Elleni tumbled from the Barrier into Ray. Snowy ground on a ridge above Wounded Knee Creek cushioned their fall. The air was frigid, even with the sun blazing above. Sidi's fleece coat was as warm as it looked and large enough to shelter them both.

"Winter has come," Elleni said, her burning hair soothed by the snow.

"We're alive," Ray said.

"It would seem."

"I thought I'd lost you, lost everything."

"You held on like a jealous lover." She smiled.

"Sidi glided through me, and then..." Ray shivered. "You were dissolving in my arms. Should I have let you go?" He squinted at the sky. "The sun is up already?"

"*Was für ein Wunder!*" Time had gone quickly for him. "So hold me now again," Elleni said.

Ray was eager to oblige. His skin felt like butter, his heart slow and stately like a Djundjun drum. The terror had lifted. "We made it, Bella, all the way to anywhere and back." He covered her face with kisses, pausing at the violet disk that vibrated just above the bridge of her nose. "Sidi's still in there, isn't she?"

Elleni nodded. A shiver of pleasure emanated from the disk. She didn't yet know how she felt or what story to make of her last moments with Sidi.

Ray narrowed his eyes. "Was she the *Ebo Eje* the Barrier wanted?"

"I don't know. There were many, many who sacrificed with her." She felt the rush of beings across her body and for an instant lost herself to their delicious strangeness again. "I promised to carry Sidi's vision into the future with my own."

"That's a trick," he said and gingerly touched the rotating disk. "Are we safe now?"

"Of course not."

"No, I mean, the Barrier's not going to blow us up or swallow us or whatever..."

She squinted at her monster lover. "We all see a different story. We don't know the Barrier's intentions. But I believe it got what it wanted. Celestina, too." The Barrier was calm, a river of smoked glass with several jagged archways leading into broad sculpted corridors and tiny breezeways. "What happened here?" The countryside below was covered with people for as far as she could see.

"Looks like a winter carnival." Ray gazed at giant banners, acrobatic musicians, holo displays, and larger-than-life puppet-bots.

"From all the Zones," Elleni said. "When did they get here?" People streamed out of the new Barrier corridors as they spoke.

"If you are well I am well!" Lawanda scrambled up the icy hillside. The mute Dancer glided beside her, carrying Elleni's medicine bag. The Barrier tapestries Celestina had woven had begun to unravel. Elleni would have to create new designs.

"Thank you," Elleni signed and pressed the bag to her heart. What would Celestina think of her Barrier quest? Would she be pleased?

Lawanda offered warm dusters and Teneather boots. "We been waitin' on y'all." She squeezed them tight. "Damn, it's good to see you. Where's Sidi?"

"She's…not coming back," Elleni said. Lawanda sucked her teeth, and the Dancer stiffened, but Elleni closed her eyes and said no more. Cheers aimed in their direction startled her eyes back open. Security prevented a crowd from rushing up the hill. Ray shook his head and donned the ultra-thin, super-warm duster. Elleni clung to Sidi's coat. She didn't bother with boots; the cold felt good to her feet.

"Fans," he said.

"Rebel Extras, underground choirs, Ouagadougian villagers," Lawanda corrected him.

"How many bio-corders running?" He blasted a fake, kilowatt smile at Aaron and Achbar struggling up the hill. They weren't as fit as Lawanda.

"Welcome home!" Aaron bear-hugged Ray as if they were long lost buddies.

"This is quite some welcome," Ray said.

"We were worried," Achbar said. "You've been gone two months."

Ray's eyes widened. "That long? Set the shoot back, huh?"

"The world has changed while you were away." Achbar proffered alora blossoms and leaves. Elleni gobbled them gratefully. She felt weaker than she realized, despite having so many good souls to anchor her.

"Elleni thanks you," Ray said, chewing the alora. Achbar smiled indulgently at her.

"Yes, I do," she said. "You're all dressed up." He and Aaron both wore embroidered turbans, laser-cut boots, and velvet burnooses.

"To honor you." Achbar put his palms together and bowed to her. Elleni matched his gesture, but looked puzzled. How did they know to expect them?

"Awa consulted Celestina's image-boards." The Wovoka came around a snow bank and answered her thoughts. "She insisted you'd return today, and she's been right about every other strange Barrier phenomenon, so…" He sounded almost jealous. "Otherwise I would have left for the Badlands long ago. Too many politicians here."

"What is all this?" Elleni waved at Healer Councilors in ceremonial regalia, flanked by Sagan City ministers in drab power suits and born-again Sioux in moss headdresses and robes.

"Word got 'round y'all was doin' a special Barrier quest," Lawanda said.

"Aaron broadcast it," the Wovoka said, leaning against a snow bank off to the side.

"We persuaded the Wovoka to let people from every Zone join our vigil, live." Achbar's eyes twinkled as he fingered his mustache.

"Big powwow. Jocelyn Williams and Carl Samanski want to talk to you," the Wovoka said. "Prime Minister Williams is a political miracle."

"She could survive a nuclear blast in her underwear," Lawanda said.

"She and Armando Jenassi get the prize," Aaron said.

Elleni was not surprised.

"How did you persuade the Wovoka?" Ray asked. The Wovoka grunted.

"Look around," Lawanda said. "Newfangled Barrier openings in all the Zones—like expressways to everywhere. Inside you almost hear somebody scattin' astral blues to Kora riffs."

"Sidi, sculpt-singing," Elleni whispered as Lawanda was talking. "Or Mahalia."

"These corridors don't wink out, you understand what I'm sayin', so folk be steppin' out, gettin' with each other, callin' for a world council at Wounded Knee."

"Revolution solution," Elleni said.

"A new world," Ray said.

"When the walls come tumblin' down," Lawanda said. "Folk even hittin' the Wilderness Zone. 'Cept for shamen, ain't nobody been there for a hundred years."

"A few corridors at Wounded Knee are a mystery." Achbar pointed with his staff. "All the probes disappear. We don't know where these passageways go to or when or who might come down..."

Lawanda grinned. "But the good news is folk ain't runnin' up and down these Barrier causeways killin' each other."

"Yet. Don't get too happy," the Wovoka said.

"Yeah, 'cause when the party's over, the backlash starts." Aaron said. "So what happened to you-all in that dark hole?"

"I can't, not right now," Elleni signed to Ray. The giddy, heady feeling of success had passed. With all these open corridors, the balance of power would shift. She was overwhelmed by the weight of the future, the enormity of the tasks at hand. The alora made her exhaustion profoundly clear. The Barrier was more than one mind could think, more than she could comprehend alone in her skin. And the future as well.

"Come on, there hasn't been another one like that. What's the buzz?"

"Nothing to tell," Ray said smoothly. "Two months, huh? Could've been an hour."

"What about you, Elleni?" Aaron shoved hair out of his eyes. "You gotta give me more than that!"

"No, we don't." Ray blocked Aaron from Elleni.

"Turn down the testosterone." Lawanda pulled Aaron away.

"Tell him that," Aaron said, rubbing a thin scar on his neck.

"You boys got enough adventure down the hill for ten episodes." Lawanda pushed Aaron and Achbar toward a school of sea-mammal puppet-bots that juggled squealing young people on their noses. "Scope the daredevil kids."

"Sounds good," Achbar said. Aaron didn't look one bit interested.

"Who else Ray and Elleni goin' talk to?" Lawanda was in Aaron's face. "Let 'em catch a breath, eat somethin' sinful, get they feet back on the ground, then *snap!* Mifune Enterprises get the scoop of the century, and everybody's happy."

"Finally a sweet-talking diplomat," Aaron said. "A Renaissance woman."

"We leave you to rest." The Wovoka slithered through Elleni like a wave of Barrier energy. He tapped the crossroad experience from her bones and muscles and off her nerves. Elleni was too tired to mind his rude invasion. "Impressive," he said, then strode into the hills. The mute Dancer touched her hand and walked off behind him.

"I want to know for myself, not for some broadcast scoop," Aaron said.

"We're blasted right now," Ray said, pulling Elleni away, "nothing personal."

"Wait, while you were gone, the Wovoka convened his Barrier ghostfest."

Elleni nodded. "A promise he made a long time ago."

"Right before the new corridors opened, all these people, dead people…people we carry around in our heads, showed up like a waking dream, ghosting across the Barrier, talking up a storm. Nobody could understand what they were saying, it was like in code. I thought the dead would have big things to tell us. But they just got bigger and bigger 'til you couldn't make them out anymore, scattering off in every direction, and the Barrier broke open. Corridors to everywhere, everyone welcome."

"Not one of your seven stories, huh?" Lawanda said, gently.

"I saw this spectacle from inside the Barrier," Elleni said.

"You went into the belly of the beast," Aaron said, "so I thought you could explain—"

"*Was für ein Wunder ist das Leben.*" Elleni spoke the Ouagadougian prayer for the dead. "We make sense of the ancestors, not vice versa. They could barely imagine us."

"I can barely imagine myself," Achbar said.

"I'm a control queen. I like answers better than questions," Aaron said.

Elleni sighed. "No Final Lessons. Always something to unravel."

"Yeah, yeah. Fair enough." Near tears, Aaron embraced Elleni then Ray, who after a second gave in to the gesture.

Achbar bowed to them and pulled Aaron away to the carnival.

Lawanda watched their wine velvet flutter in snowy air. "Folk be real touchy these days, cryin' at every little spit on the wind; even gangstas be bawlin'." She shepherded Elleni and Ray around a gentle rise in the terrain away from Entertainment crews and rowdy carnival crowds. Snow banks muffled the cacophony and worked like a tonic for Elleni's raw nerves.

"Honoré is in a beautiful place," she said to Lawanda as they slogged through waist deep drifts.

"I image him hangin' with Celestina," Lawanda said, a catch in her throat.

"Where else?" Ray said.

"Wish the Captain could've gone in too," Lawanda said.

"You must tell me her story." Elleni had been disappointed not to encounter Celestina, just her voice, but she had no reason to tell Lawanda this. "So many mysteries," she said.

Honoré had slipped away from her and Ray moments after they entered the black crystal corridor. Who could say; perhaps he had found Celestina.

80: Studio City, Los Santos
(April 7, Barrier Year 116)

A black-coffee, starless night. Sidi Xa Aiyé hesitated, uncertain, one foot in a bruised blood Barrier, one foot out. The Wovoka stared at her patiently. His flowing silver face moved at a languid pace. The blue-eyed wild turkey feathers in his war bonnet winked in the breeze. Lawanda rubbed snow at red stains on her coveralls. Her hands were stiff with cold. In the Barrier, Honoré reached a bright red hand back to his ladylove, an almost-smile on his face.

"*Keine Feinde.* No enemies," Sidi said.

Honoré nodded.

Ochre braids swinging, plum lips pulled tight across her teeth, almond eyes shining with Barrier light, Sidi dashed from a white whirlwind into a black crystal opening. Violet disks flashed in and out of focus. Her tall voluptuous figure cloaked in scarlet fake fur was swallowed by the corridor's darkness, but not before Ray Valero's Barrier-dawn eyes registered her presence. He snatched her toward him and Elleni. As the three embraced, the image faded to midnight black.

The sound of ocean lapping against a sand beach surrounded the preview audience. The screen filled with a close shot of Celestina, her face serene. The camera pulled back to a long shot of a magenta ocean at twilight. Celestina walked the sand into the water. A lone dolphin leapt from the waves in an explosion of water. As Celestina disappeared in the dolphin's spume, the image dissolved into a tight shot of the water pulling back from the beach. Celestina's footprints ended abruptly. The tide came in, and they were washed away. Credits for *The Transformers* scrolled across the sand accompanied by kora, cello, and didjeridoo music.

Lights came up in the main screening hall of Mifune Enterprises. The giant Electro-screen went fuzzy. The preview audience stood and applauded for twenty minutes before Aaron had the guards escort them out.

"Now that's a final episode, practically wrote itself." Aaron crunched popcorn from the dispenser in his armrest. "Tadeshi's genius bio-corders put you right between dimensions!" He stuffed in another mouthful. "But I'd like a more upbeat ending. This is too bittersweet."

"It's not the end. You'll do a sequel. I know you," Achbar said from the aisle seat across from Aaron. "When we go into the Wilderness down a ghost-sonata corridor."

"Plenty of colored people in this, Lawanda will be proud, not exotica, but not forced or in white face either." Aaron picked at a corn hull stuck in his tooth.

"Just for Lawanda?" Achbar laughed at him. "Not for you?"

"Yeah, well Stella would have my ass in a sling if——"

"You can't blame multiple personality disorder for aesthetic choices."

Aaron was in too good of a mood to be baited. "Ellington's a perfect location, a Renaissance city. Didn't I tell you? Lose the architecture, focus on the talent in the streets! Audiences eat up throwback culture." He slumped in his comfort chair. "The Celestina/dolphin bit is still not working for me. That's the only thing."

"Celestina wanted you to tell the whole story." Achbar pounded his Healer staff on a floor lamp. "You can't cut that."

"Don't bust the place," Aaron said. "Not over a cheesy sequence."

"Geraldine Kitt sent those images." He stood up and stabbed a chair with the staff.

"Facts don't always work in fiction." Aaron scratched the sparse growth on his chin. "Did you rip open that chair?"

"Celestina said she'd go that way." Achbar marched across the aisle. "I was there."

"Oh, yeah? Been down a Barrier starway, have you? Well, the audience hasn't."

"Before." Achbar snatched popcorn out of Aaron's hand and threw it at nothing. "I was going to blast her."

"Hit Celestina—you?" Aaron sat up in his chair. Achbar never said anything about himself. Nobody had backstory on him. "Go on. I want to hear this."

"She beat me to it."

"Suicide?" Aaron scrambled for his mini-pad to take notes. "Don't stop. I mean, if I'm going to tell the whole story, I gotta know it first."

"Rocks in her pocket, walk in the ocean, the whole bit." Achbar sighed.

"Melodrama. That's what we know how to do."

Achbar paced empty aisles. Black syn-silk burnoose and pants billowed about him. His bald head gleamed as he stopped in front of the giant Electro. The still of water and sand lingered on screen.

"You want to tell it, so just go ahead!" Aaron said.

"Near a seasonal corridor in the Ecuadorian Ocean, Celestina saw the dolphin drowning in an old net. A whole pod of dolphins swam around, anxious, crying, screeching, and whatnot. You could just feel what they were feeling. So in the middle of her suicide, Celestina ripped out of the rock-heavy clothes, swam over, and hacked open the net."

Aaron popped his fingers. *"It's a Wonderful Life."*

"Jimmy Stewart didn't have to deal with a riptide."

"Wait, she saved the dolphin, then the dolphins saved her? Even better."

"She was drowning, the dolphins got her between their bodies somehow and dumped her right at my hideout." Achbar stared at the ground as if Celestina lay in front of him. He was still a damn good actor, holding down a scene with a few words, a couple gestures. "Right under my gun."

"Reforming you is the angle. That'll hook 'em in." Aaron ran down the aisle to Achbar. "Why didn't you tell me before?"

"Green-jelly skin, chest still as a stone. I didn't have to do anything but cash in my fee. The dolphins whistled in my ear, slapped water all over me. These were not friendly flappers. One jumped right in my face, aggressive, like he'd bite my head off. I couldn't stand it. So I put down my long-range piece, and I tried to get her breath to come back, mouth-to-mouth."

"It worked."

"Yeah. The dolphins rose up on their tails, walking on water and hooting. They threw a couple fish at me. The one she rescued blew dolphin spit in my face."

"How much you want to bet that dolphin went down the Barrier starway with Celestina." Aaron spun around. "This is good. This is really good."

"Celestina coughed up brine and stared me in the eye. 'I was an assassin once too,' she said, 'but I'm not sure if a person can recover from that.' Bold, huh?"

"That turned you into a good guy, cured you of killing?" Aaron circled him. "No way."

"She said she had miles to go and promises to keep and every time she tried to run out on the deal, somebody came along and rescued her." Achbar waved his Healer staff in the air. "Death was afraid of Celestina." Achbar nailed the Healer accent, then shook himself. "She guessed she had to do everything first, keep all her promises, and then she could go. Signed me up for the Treaty right there."

"What else? It can't be that simple to make yourself over." Aaron knew how people sanitized their stories.

"I really liked bringing her back to life," Achbar whispered. "I'd never done anything like that, blowing life into someone's body, cheating death. With the dolphins cheering, like some kind of... I can't explain it."

Aaron thought of running up a hill with born-again Sioux at Wounded Knee to face down a madman. "No, I know what you mean."

"Everyday, I'm still working on it. Recovering hit man, a life-time cure." Achbar pointed the staff at Aaron's heart. "We can't cut this bit."

"No, no. Flesh it out with a flash-back to the triple rescue—Ray could play you or you could play yourself." He pushed the head of the staff away from his chest. "Don't point that thing." The crystal was hot and cold, and if he pressed hard enough, his fingers might slip through.

Achbar roared his lion laugh. "Same old Aaron, huh?"

"Hardly. You'd have never told the old Aaron that story."

"You're right. The old Aaron wouldn't have listened."

"Yeah, well, quiet as it's kept, I don't know who I am anymore. Don't know what I'm going to say or what I'll feel." He put his arm around Achbar's shoulder, and they walked toward the back door of the screening room. "Every step I take—surprise!"

81:   Cross Barrier Transmission/Personal
(Cinco de Mayo, Barrier Year 116)

From: Lawanda Kitt in the Badlands

To: Elleni Xa Celest, New Ouagadougou City

Was für ein Wunder ist das Leben! Miracles, that's what we talkin' 'bout here!

I'm sittin' up in these booty boulders gettin' over a bout of that new fire-virus flu. Listenin' to the quiet, watchin' the sun paint this maze of fluted-rock hills. Shadows dance 'round, keepin' me company. Rabbit too big to hang in my pocket, still like to nest in my lap, nibble my belly. I try to mind-doodle some diplomacy every now and then.

Another ghost-sonata broadcast—from Geraldine. Nothin' from Honoré, 'cept that one time, but I'ma copy him on this if you don't mind. Bio-corder say his node ain't nowhere, but the smart-alec machine go ahead and transmit to it anyhow. Go figure.

Geraldine tell me how she and everybody (Tadeshi, Phoolan...) be buzzin' from one Barrier world to the next in that fancy ET ship, in and out of different dimensions and shit, talk about trippin' out! Sis say ain't nobody goin' believe what they seen, what they been thru (she don't half believe it herself), so she throwin' down beaucoup data. Celestina hang in there all the way to Barrier central (where they think the Barrier come from), but Miss Shaman-change-the-world-or-bust won't hear nothin' 'bout comin' back home. They gotta leave her and Aieee!-Aieee! in the middle of fuckin' nowhere. (Dolphin be as ornery as Celestina.) Celestina want folk to see her crossover, so I give 7-Stories the images Geraldine send. He goin' use the ocean sequence for the final episode of his Barrier epic.

Geraldine say she awful sorry, but it be too hard to do a real big info dump, take everythin' she got just to transmit hardly nothin' and then stuff come out all distorted and chopped up. We gotta wait 'til they get back for the resta the story. (ETA forty-eight months.)

I wish I could help you out more, Sister Elleni, but politics got me on the run.

(You could do somethin' with that hair, chill out the freak image…)

Electrosoft Corp think I'ma negotiate some kinda exclusive image-board deal for them with Awa. They can think again. Awa want the board in the public domain. Jocelyn pull the death warrant on me, say I ain't anti-Treaty like she thought. She have the nerve to ask me to be official chronicler of the Treaty Transformation. Shoot, 7-Stories got that covered already, doin' Celestina's whole saga—from the Robin-and-Thandiwe betrayal/murder to redemption and peace. The boy tell so many lies, I don't know what I could add, but Jocelyn put me on the payroll. Bitch ('scuse my French) broadcast that ad-opera one more time of her and Sidi facin' down Duma and Danny to save your booty on Fire Mountain, I'ma whack her myself.

No tellin' 'bout Samanski. Overnight he believe in ET ships, Barrier starways, and powwows with Ghost Dancers and rebel Extras. Whyn't he ever talk to 'em before his ass was up against the wall? Some folk say the scumbag was backin' the Treaty while winkin' at the organ market and gun runnin' to Perez. I don't know, could be lies. Samanski a man who don't like to lose. Watch your back.

Lotta folk headin' off to the Wilderness Zone, but I'ma hang with rebel Extras and born-again Sioux, see what I can do, what I can learn from 'em. Aaron and Achbar like to be checkin' up on me too. So I'm all right. When I first get to this gangsta Zone, couldn't wait to leave, now I'm stuck. Some really wild children be puttin' together a expedition down one of them new corridors to nowhere in this universe… I got a invite, you too. What you think? Let me hear from you.

Lawanda

Forward From: Lawanda Kitt in the Badlands

To: Sweet Honoré, somewhere

I don't wanna hope too much, so I'ma keep it brief. I miss you and the Captain both. Every day, every hour. Look at a leaf, feed the rabbit, smell my food cookin' and just wonder, what would you think of anythin'. Ain't nothin' to take for this kinda ache. At least I got your volcano pendant—I don't have diddly from the Captain. I look up what it mean too. Mokuaweoweo Mauna Loa was a live lava belcher in old Hawaii. That's how I think of both of y'all. (See attached mind doodle. Did you get my other drawing? It's in your pocket.)

I ain't mad at you no more. Along with the punk son of a snake who broke my heart, you had a beautiful person mixed up in there. And I loved all of you cuz of him. Still lovin' you. We had it goin' on, turned some tides, you know what I'm sayin'? Anyhow, I'm there with you, wherever, cuz here and now, this be the Promised Land too.

Love you, Lawanda

82: *Seelenwald*, New Ouagadougou
(Cinco de Mayo, Barrier Year 116)

Elleni and Ray shivered in the chilly moonless night. The wind was wet with ground fog. Alora blossoms hanging from the cathedral tress were balled up against the cold and damp. Elleni had left Sidi's flame red fleece coat in Ray's transport, and he, thinking she was a *Seelenwald* weather expert, had also left his duster behind.

"How much longer?" Ray whispered.

"Don't interrupt, and it will go faster," Elleni said. Sidi's violet disk above the bridge of her nose glowed like a third eye.

"I don't mind how long it takes, I just want to know," Ray said.

"It takes 'til I'm done."

Next to Celestina's tree, they planted saplings for Sidi, Chris, Honoré, and Mokuaweoweo Mauna Loa, for Thandiwe and Robin, and for others who had gone on to dance with the ancestors but whose names they did not know. Every tree in *Seelenwald* had been planted to honor the dead. Elleni insisted on reciting all the praise poems. She usually hated long-winded Healer ceremonies, but not this night. Ray waited for his cue among a multitude of languages, then together they said the last line.

"*Igi kan ki s'igbo*. One tree does not make a forest."

Elleni threw her arms around Ray, as if they played a love scene. Strands of weaver ants dropped from the trees and braided the two lovers into their nest.

"Tell me, Bella, or you'll burst." Ray buried his face in her hissing hair.

"We are the ones the Wovoka raised from the dead!" Elleni said, then she touched his mindscape and they waited to see what visions would come.

83: The Promised Land

There is a Navajo proverb:
I have been to the end of the earth.
I have been to the end of the waters.
I have been to the end of the sky.
I have been to the end of the mountains.
I have found none that are not my friends.
—Celestina Xa Irawo, "Preamble to the Interzonal Peace Treaty"

Thandiwe and Robin stood arm in arm at the edge of an alien beach, farther away from home than they could imagine. Aieee!-Aieee! swam in circles just beyond them, saving her energy for one last leap.

"No enemies," Robin said.

"Not even myself," Thandiwe said.

They walked into the magenta sea.

"*Aboru, Aboye, Aboṣiṣe.*"

May what we offer carry, be accepted, may what we offer bring about change.

Cast of Characters

New Ouagadougou

Celestina Xa Irawo	Diplomat and spiritual leader, architect of the *Interzonal Peace Treaty*
Elleni Xa Celest	Celestina's Geistestochter, spirit daughter, Center of the Healers Council
Femi Xa Olunde	Former Center of the Healers Council
Sidi Xa Aiyé	Member of the Healers Council
Awa Xa Ijala	Oldest member of Healers Council and Celestina's best friend
Duma Xa Babalawo	Femi's protégé and Sidi's consort
Thandiwe Xa Femi	Shaman who disappeared seventy-five years ago (Thandi)
Vera Xa Lalafia	Early Ouagadougian philosopher, author of *The Final Lessons*
Zumbi Xa Dojude	Healer working in Los Santos for the Treaty

Paradigma

Lawanda Kitt	Vice-Ambassador to Los Santos
The Major	Head of Sagan City's Secret Services, advisor to the Prime Minister
Mahalia Selasie	Renegade scientist who defected to Los Santos with her underground choir
The Captain	Head of Lawanda Kitt's security forces, trained by the Major

Armando Jenassi	Ambassador to Los Santos, Lawanda's boss
Jocelyn Williams	Prime Minister of Paradigma
Robin Wolf	Renegade scientist who disappeared seventy-five years ago
Geraldine Kitt	Lawanda's sister, researcher at Sagan Institute, author of *Junk Bonds of the Mind*

Los Santos

Aaron Dunkelbrot	Producer/director, current head of Mifune Enterprises, former Extra
Ray Valero	Entertainment star, Elleni's consort, lead actor in *The Transformers*
Moses Johnson	Aaron's assistant director, former Extra
Achbar Ali	Script doctor and production guru, former gangster
Daniel Ford	Carl Samanski's right hand thug
The Wovoka	Ghost Dancer spiritual leader
Carl Samanski	Big boss and political leader in Los Santos
Jesus Perez	The "soybean king", bad boy ganglord
Stella Jackson	Extra
Chris Valero	Ray's older sister
Piotr Osama	Extra
Tadeshi Mifune	Producer/director, former head of Mifune Enterprises, author of *Surviving The Future, Last Minute Notes*

Glossary

Aboru, Aboye, Aboṣiṣe.
> Yoruba, "May the offerings be carried, may the offerings be accepted, may the offerings bring about change." A salutation to the high priest. A New Ouagadougian prayer.

Aṣe (English transliteration Ashe)
> Yoruba, "So be it," akin to Amen. Also "the power to make things be." The creative principle of the universe.

Babalawo
> Yoruba, "father of mysteries," high priest of the Yoruba religion.

B'ao ku ishe o tan
> Yoruba, "when there is life, there is still hope."

Chi Gong (also *Qi Gong* and *Xiquong*)
> Chinese, Chi (Qi) is vital energy, life force, that which makes a living being alive; acupuncture meridians map the flow of Chi through the body; Chi Gong is the art of manipulating this vital energy in self and others. Celestina is a Chi Gong master.

Deine Seele ist billig (Keine billigen Seelen)
> German, "your soul is cheap" (no cheap souls).

Dide dide lalafia
> Yoruba, "Arise, arise in peace."

Ebo Eje
> Yoruba, "a blood sacrifice."

Egun
> Yoruba, "ancestors, the dead."

Er kann eben aus seiner Haut nicht heraus
> German, "he can't break out of his skin."

Es ist ja noch nicht aller Tage Abend
> German saying, literally, "all the days are not yet evening." Elleni's translation, "all our suns have not yet set." All is not lost.

Eṣu (English transliteration Eshu)
> Yoruba, an orisha, the deity of Ashe. Eshu possesses the power to make things be. He stands at the crossroads, a diviner of truth and falsehood, tempting us with possibilities, challenging us to growth, a messenger of the divine.

Geistesmutter, Geistestochter, Geistesschwester, Geistesvater
> German, literally "spirit mother, spirit daughter, spirit sister, spirit father," etc. Ouagadougian usage: mother (et al.) of my mind and spirit, a relational term.

Igi kan ki s'igbo
> Yoruba saying, "one tree does not make a forest."

Ijala'gun Molu
> Yoruba, "those who are possessed by the Spirit of the Warrior never lose." Ouagadougian usage: If we risk nothing, we gain nothing.

Kali

> Sanskrit feminine form of kala. "She who is black." Major Hindu goddess with death, sexuality, violence—devouring all that exists; she is often depicted dancing on the body of her husband, Shiva, one of the Hindu supreme gods.

Kein Wunder zu vergeuden
> German, "no miracle to waste."

Keine Feinde
> German, "no enemies."

Keine Sorge
> German, "don't worry."

Kora (also *Cora*)

An instrument played in the Gambia, Senegal, Burkino Faso, Guinea, Mali, and Sierra Leone. A traditional Kora is made of half a calabash, cow hide, and twenty-one to twenty-five fishing wire strings. In New Ouagadougou, the Kora is made of goat hide and gut. It has fifty strings—twenty-five are sympathetic resonators, much like a twelve-string guitar.

Kuchen

German, "torte, pie, baked dessert."

Los Santos

From Spanish, "the saints." So-called "Gangster" Zone.

Mo so awon enia mi po

Yoruba, "I tie all my people together," a praise poem for the orisha, Oshun—she unifies the world.

Mako sica

Lakota, "bad land."

Mojubar

Yoruba, "I give homage, I pour libation."

Murahachibu

Japanese, "outcast."

Oberammergau

A village in New Ouagadougou named for a city in twenty-first century Germany.

Ogun

Yoruba, an orisha, the deity of iron, of hunters, blacksmiths, and warriors, also associated with civilizing forces and principles of justice.

Omi tutu, ile tutu, ona tutu, tutu Eṣu, tutu Oriṣa

Yoruba libation, "cool water, cool house, cool road, cool Eshu, cool Orisha."

Ori̩ṣa (English transliteration Orisha)

> The Yoruba deities—manifestations of the divine, of the creative force that permeates the universe.

O̩ṣun (English transliteration Oshun)

> Yoruba, an orisha, the deity of love and fertility, also a warrior orisha who protects her people with "masculine" skill in the use of knives and swords and a knowledge of deadly poisons.

New Ouagadougou

> So-called "Healers" Zone. Ouagadougou was the twenty-first century capital of Burkina Faso in West Africa.

Schnee von Gestern

> German, literally "snow from yesterday," old news.

Seelenwald

> German, "the forest of souls," woods on the outskirts of New Ouagadougou City.

Shade

> German, "too bad" or "oh, no"—a mild expletive.

Sioux

> Ojibwa for enemy.

Shinjuka

> A village in New Ouagadougou named for a section of twenty-first century Tokyo.

Sie haben mich vergessen

> German, "you've forgotten me."

Ṣotito ṣododo ṣoora ma ṣika

> Yoruba prayer, "perform truth, perform righteousness, perform kindness, avoid cruelty."

Der Sternentraum

> German, "the dream of the stars."

Tutu
>Yoruba, "cool."

Vermittler
>German, "go-between, negotiator." Ouagadougian usage: Barrier griot, translator, praisesinger, diplomat.

Vodun
>New World religious practice based on Yoruba and Catholic religions, known pejoratively as voodoo.

Was der Bauer nicht kennt, das frißt er nicht
>German saying, "what the farmer doesn't know, he won't eat."

Was für ein Wunder ist das Leben!
>German, "what a miracle is life!"

Weißbier
>German, a light beer made from wheat.

Wiederaufbauwunder
>German, literally "rebuilding-miracle," related to the Wirtschaftswunder or Germany's economic miracle after the twentieth century's World War II. Celestina refers to the miracle of Treaty reconstruction as Wiederaufbauwunder.

Wokiksuye Cankpe Opi
>Lakota, "Remember Wounded Knee."

Ein Wunder
>German, a "miracle."

Ein echter Zaubertrank
>German, "a real magic drink."

Conversation Pieces

A Small Paperback Series from Aqueduct Press

Subscriptions available: www.aqueductpress.com

Biography

Andrea Hairston was a math/physics major in college until she did special effects for a show and then she ran off to the theatre and became an artist. She is the Artistic Director of Chrysalis Theatre and has created original productions with music, dance, and masks for over twenty-five years. She is also a Professor of Theatre and Afro-American Studies at Smith College. Her plays have been produced at Yale Rep, Rites and Reason, the Kennedy Center, StageWest, and on Public Radio and Television. She has received many awards for her writing and directing including a National Endowment for the Arts Grant to Playwrights, a Ford Foundation Grant to collaborate with Senegalese Master Drummer Massamba Diop, and a Shubert Fellowship for Playwriting.

Mindscape was excerpted in *Dark Matter: Reading The Bones*, a World Fantasy award-winning anthology edited by Sheree R. Thomas. "Griots of the Galaxy," a short story, appears in *So Long Been Dreaming: Postcolonial Visions of the Future*, an anthology edited by Uppinder Mehan and Nalo Hopkinson.

She is currently working on a new novel, Exploding in Slow Motion, for which she received the 2004 Speculative Literature Foundation's Older Writer Grant.

www.andreahairston.com